D0386647

ALSO BY BRAD LEITHAUSER

Hundreds of Fireflies
(POETRY)

This is a Borzoi Book
published in New York
by Alfred A. Knopf.

EQUAL DISTANCE

EQUAL DISTANCE

A Novel by

BRAD LEITHAUSER

*

ALFRED A. KNOPF

NEW YORK 1985

THIS IS A BORZOI BOOK PUBLISHED BY
ALFRED A. KNOPF, INC.

Copyright © 1984 by Brad Leithauser

All rights reserved under International and Pan-American Copyright Conventions. Published in the United States by Alfred A. Knopf, Inc., New York, and simultaneously in Canada by Random House of Canada Limited, Toronto. Distributed by Random House, Inc., New York.

Grateful acknowledgment is made to Macmillan Publishing Company, Inc., and to A. P. Watt Ltd. (London) for permission to reprint six lines from "Brown Penny" by William Butler Yeats in *The Poems of William Butler Yeats*, ed. Richard J. Finneran, copyright 1912 by Macmillan Publishing Company, Inc. Renewed 1940 by Bertha Georgie Yeats.

Library of Congress Cataloging in Publication Data

Leithauser, Brad.
Equal distance.

I. Title.
PS3562.E4623E6 1984 813'.54 84-47859
ISBN 0-394-53971-0

Manufactured in the United States of America
First Edition

Surely for you, Mary Jo

Two loves I have . . .

SHAKESPEARE
Sonnet 144

O love is the crooked thing,
There is nobody wise enough
To find out all that is in it,
For he would be thinking of love
Till the stars had run away
And the shadows eaten the moon . . .

YEATS
"Brown Penny"

CONTENTS

1

WITH MOM IN TOKYO

*

*

He'd been dozing, sleep touching him so lightly that had it not left, like a fingerprint upon a pane of glass, the filmy residue of a dream, he would scarcely have realized he'd slept at all. This dream (already turning colorless, resistant to memory) had taken place at home—not Boston or Cambridge, which over the last two years he'd grown to think of as home, but with Mom and Dad in Michigan. His gaze drifted from his hands, open in his lap, the left palm lopsidedly bunched with the scar of a burn he'd picked up in college, to, miles below, the Pacific, which under its glazed crust seemed to stir and ripple with its own indwelling dream. He'd never seen the Pacific until today. It was so big—he'd read somewhere—that if it were emptied the other three oceans could be poured into the resulting cavity, and still there would be room to spare. His watch told him nearly an hour had passed since he'd last checked—although all measurements of time were tricky and somewhat illusory on a journey of this sort. It was as if time itself had turned a little elastic; he felt himself allied with those select astronauts who return to earth some infinitesimal but nonetheless calculable fraction of a second younger than the rest of us. Noiseless barriers, transparent boundaries, the time zones one after another were dropping away behind him. Soon he would cross, if he hadn't already, the International Dateline, as this aircraft floated effortlessly, the first time he'd ever made such a leap, into tomorrow.

He'd been using, unwisely it now occurred to him, his passport to mark his place in one of the books, *Beginning Japanese*, ranged on the empty seat beside him. He plucked the passport from the textbook and intently read his own name (Daniel Chapman Ott), birthdate (October 1, 1957), and Michigan address (21350 Richhaven Ave., Heather Hills). He would turn twenty-three in a few weeks. He scrutinized again the color photograph, in which his hair had come out redder than in life and he looked either very sleepy or merely stupid. The passport contained a pair of connected dishonesties. He'd boosted, as he regularly did, his height half an inch to six one because "six feet and a half inch," though it had the advantage of truthfulness in an area where so many people fudged the truth, sounded fussy and self-preoccupied. And feeling that anyone who stood over six feet tall should weigh at least a hundred and fifty pounds, Danny had padded his narrow torso with the five or so pounds necessary to get there.

He was comfortable and happy now, and drowsily exhilarated, but from the start this flight to the Orient had threatened to let him down completely. He'd had premonitions of disappointment in the San Francisco airport, watching mixed crowds of Americans and Asians jostling for liquor and cigarettes. He'd warned himself repeatedly not to be naive, yet had gone on thinking that the flight to Japan would initiate him into some sort of Eastern enchantment or mystery. Instead he had found himself seated among American soldiers and American businessmen, both types arrogantly loud, with a reserve of quiet, chain-smoking Japanese men massed behind. He'd been served oily roast beef and a crusty square of cherry pie and then the lights had dimmed for a silent movie (Danny, tired, had declined headphones), edited for flight. Desert images—cacti, tumbleweed, a fat rattlesnake—flickered and dissolved, while mouths stammered soundlessly. A mugging rodeo cowboy kept getting slammed into the dirt, only to rise each time with a brainlessly resolute shake of the head.

Resigned to disappointment, Danny had napped a while and later half-awakened to the emergence of some enchantment after all. The movie was over, the plane had grown sleepy, and the clouds below had scattered to reveal the brimless, abstracted eye of the Pacific. Closing his eyes upon this eye—its lingering glow a kind of interior night-light—and shifting lower in his seat, Danny had felt the steady roar of the engine incorporate his heartbeat and, with a sweet feeling of entitlement, for he'd had very little sleep these last few days, he'd returned to his dozing.

Now more fully awake, though he still felt sleep deposited in the sockets of his bones, he tucked his passport into his shirt pocket and began to review *Beginning Japanese*. He'd meant to study Japanese systematically this summer but had found his life consumed by his job on Wall Street, working far harder than his previous experience as a summer law associate, in Detroit the year before, had led him to expect. By the time he'd ascended from the baking half-hour subway journey from Wall Street to Broadway and Seventy-second, had changed his clothes, maybe jogged in Riverside Park, showered and eaten dinner, he was good for nothing but sleep, his breath a kind of sob in that steamy, fan-whirred apartment that seemed to suck in all the doubtless carcinogenic fumes of the dry cleaners below.

He studied for half an hour by his watch until his fatigued mind rebelled at the labyrinthine absurdity of the Japanese system of counters (different words for the numbers when one was counting people, or animals, or long, thin objects, or flat, squarish objects, or hours, or days of the week). The page swam in the light. It would be good to stretch out in a bed again, but that was still another plane and a train and probably a taxi away—and even then no certainty as to where or on what he would be sleeping. He began another mental postcard home: *Dear Mom and Dad, I'm miles above the Pacific at the moment. I'm a little apprehensive I must admit, but I know everything will work out well! Mom, thanks for the sweater vest, which I'm sure will prove useful. Dad, I can see already why Ford is having so much trouble competing with the Japanese automakers. There's a little Japanese boy sitting nearby, maybe seven years old, who has been playing with a calculator for about an hour. A future captain of Japanese industry . . .* Subsiding again into unconsciousness, one sleep's threshold verging into another's, Danny sighted for the last time that earlier Michigan dream. Things in the dream, it became clear, had not been quite what they'd appeared on waking, no, but then, but now, the dream shivered away. . . .

A few hours later the sea had vanished under another sea, this one composed of dense gray clouds, and they were actually descending into Japan. The plane rocked for a time through an opaque transitional zone where zigzagging flecks of water scarred the other side of the round windows. The dim wing-lights flickered. Then Japan itself unfolded below him in the form of intricate, clogged roads, and, quickly and securely, the plane and runway locked with a passing shudder.

When at last the plane coasted to a halt, after so much waiting and so long a journey, everything began to happen very fast. Danny was thanked repeatedly for flying Pan Am as he shouldered his way—his heart thumping—through a crowd of American businessmen and stepped for the first time onto Japanese soil of a sort, a corridor in

Tokyo's Narita Airport, where to his surprise no one seemed to want to question him, to inspect his passport. When he attempted to formulate a question in Japanese for one of the uniformed women behind the information booth, she simply asked to see his ticket and then directed him, in confident English, down a flight of stairs, where another woman guided him through a light rain and onto an idling bus which, just as though it had been awaiting him, shifted into gear as he boarded. Danny waved at the woman but she, her business done, had turned away. The wheeze of the bus's closing doors was followed by a collapsing sensation in his stomach, as it became at once painfully clear that if he'd made a mistake in deciding to take time off from law school to spend a year in Japan, then he'd made a large mistake indeed.

Danny managed to get off at the proper terminal, to find the correct gate and a plastic chair to rest in. He was tired again, but this was no longer the mostly sweet fatigue he'd known on the plane. How long had he been up? What time was it *really*? He felt irritable and saturated and worn to the bone, and all the Japanese signs, the Japanese voices, continued to grate on him after he'd closed his eyes.

He didn't even try to sleep on the Japan Airlines flight to Osaka, which was supposed to take only an hour but was delayed, perhaps because of the rain. A stewardess in a kimono handed him an English-language paper called the *Mainichi Daily News* and Danny, his thoughts a jumble, spent most of the flight reading a single article, containing nothing he didn't already know, about the American hostages in Iran. In the Osaka Airport, where it turned out he *would* have to go through customs, Danny waited and waited for his luggage to emerge on the rubber-slotted conveyor belt. He knew he wasn't thinking with his usual clarity, his sense of time had been upended, but as the crowd around the conveyor belt thinned away it became deadeningly apparent that he'd been watching the same baggage circulate for a very long while. With disaster crowding in upon him from all sides, he took internal refuge in the compiling of a list, trying to figure out exactly what he would be missing if his baggage were lost. Yet he couldn't seem to concentrate on it.

When the crowd at last had dwindled to four or five an Oriental man in a Japan Airlines uniform sidestepped timidly forward and asked his name.

"Oh yes, Mr. Ott, Mr. Ott," the man said brightly, "so very sorry to tell you, I regret very much, we receive telex here your baggage never arrive Narita Airport. Never arrive Japan at all."

The next moment Danny found himself the Occidental core of a cluster of people in uniforms, five or six or seven, all apologizing and earnestly conveying every few moments, just as if it were a new development, the only information they had: his baggage had never arrived at Narita. The extent of their solicitude, their physical closeness and sheer numbers, was all a little overwhelming, and Danny felt his anger fizzle into a bewildered wish that he simply be placed on the next plane home. And yet in the end he *did* get a little angry, at their happily smug assent when he pointed out how their own airline could not be at fault—clearly it was the American company that had made the error.

Danny was given forms to fill out and a sheet of paper to examine depicting diagrams of various types of suitcases, from which he was to select the model closest to his own. In his fatigue this sheet struck him as an extraordinarily ingenious detective's tool, but it turned out that Danny made a very poor witness. Though he'd been using the two suitcases—a high school graduation gift from his parents—for years now, he couldn't describe either of them with any certainty.

One thing after another: it next appeared that the last bus for Kyoto would be leaving in only a few minutes. Danny was handed a phone number for lost baggage and with the help of a woman from Japan Airlines his shoulder bag was whisked unopened through customs. This woman, who was somewhat pretty, on clacking heels scooted Danny down a corridor and out a door into the dark rain, where huge neon signs bled against the night. He had no umbrella. With a tiny translingual cry she pointed to a bus in the distance, and Danny, forgetting how even to offer thanks in Japanese, cried *Good-bye, good-bye* in forlorn English and reached the bus just as it, too, was pulling away.

Japanese landscapes, the first he'd ever passed through, were whizzing by alongside, but rain had blurred and steamed everything into a realm of white and colored lights. Somehow, though his luggage was apparently in America, he'd felt nearer to it in the airport; by climbing aboard this bus he had severed a link, and it was far clearer now than before that he was thousands of miles from anyone he knew.

In Kyoto, at long last, he went into a fancy hotel and telephoned Professor Umeda, at whose home he was supposed to be spending the night. Twenty times he let the phone ring—a curious, urgent jangle—and as he was hanging up Danny's numbed mind played a vicious trick on him. Just as though his luggage were not thousands of miles away, he glanced wildly throughout the lobby in search of it—desperate, for it was nowhere in sight.

Hoping he was somehow dialing incorrectly, though sensing that he wasn't going to be so lucky, Danny asked a woman behind the hotel desk to help him place the call. She dialed from right there behind the desk, making the call for free it seemed, though this was never established, for again there was no answer. Her apologies were profuse and seemed heartfelt, as if she herself were at fault.

Drawing from his back pocket a last reserve, the rather sketchy handmade map of the Professor's neighborhood he'd received a few weeks ago, Danny said, "This area . . . Is it far from here?"

The map attracted two other desk clerks—men—who studied it for a disconcertingly long while. "This intersection," Danny tried again, "Imadegawa-Dori and Kawaramachi-Dori, is it far from here?"

"Oh no, no, not far," the woman reassured him.

"Is it walking distance?"

"Oh no, no," she corrected again with the same conviction. "You must take taxi."

"Are there any landmarks—any big building there?"

"Many buildings," one of the men said. "Many restaurants."

"Mahkudoenahrudoe, *ne*?" the woman said.

"I beg your pardon?"

"Hahmbahgah," the man explained, and then in response to Danny's continued bafflement stiffened his features the better to approach the stridency of the English tongue and said, "Hahmboogar. Mock-Doe-Nardo."

"McDonald's!" Danny cried, at wit's end, and laughed aloud. The conversation was so absurd!

"And Mistah Donuts!" the woman added triumphantly. "And Kentucky Fry . . . Kentucky Fry," she called as Danny stepped out the lobby's automatic doors. He got into a cab, whose driver asked him an unintelligible grunted question and then, handed the map, studied it even longer than the desk clerks had. "Imadegawa-Dori . . .

Kawaramachi-Dori . . ." Danny repeated a number of times. The driver posed another unintelligible question before pulling away and heading briskly down the wrong side of the street. The Japanese drove on the left side of the road. Danny had never known that. "America?" the driver asked. "America?"

"Yes," Danny said. "American. *Hai.*"

"*Amerika nambaa wan,*" the driver whooped, and for a moment Danny did not understand what he was saying. "*Amerika nambaa wa-a-an.*" Danny felt certain he was heading in the wrong direction—going the wrong way without his luggage and with the meter running. He resolved to stop the cab when the meter hit two thousand yen, but knew, even as he vowed it, that he would probably be afraid to.

The meter read only eight hundred yen when the driver, after further unintelligible questions, braked and the door on Danny's left opened automatically. "Okay," the driver said, "okay." Unsure whether what he'd read about there being no tipping in Japan was correct, Danny passed the driver a thousand-yen note and clambered out into the street. The driver called him back sharply, handed him two silver coins—one hundred yen each—and sped off into the rain.

Lights, cars, people strolling under umbrellas, but no sign of McDonald's, or Mister Donut, or Kentucky Fried Chicken. Danny entered a phone booth and, with an abruptly nauseating suspicion that the entire plan—the nine months in Japan, the existence of Professor Umeda himself—might be a colossal hoax, dialed the number once more, letting the phone ring long after it became evident that no one would answer. Danny stepped out into the drizzle and glanced up and down the street. It was getting late. The McDonald's, the Mister Donut, the Colonel Sanders were probably closed, and open or closed what good was finding them if the Professor was not at home? Yet Danny yearned to know whether he was at least in the general area—yearned to build on what certainties he could.

He walked a ways in one direction and then, fearful of getting lost (which was funny, because he already was), returned to the phone booth and again tried the Professor's. "So this is Japan," he said aloud.

While the phone was ringing, Danny in the edge of his vision noticed someone who might be an American walking by, munching what appeared to be a donut under his umbrella. Danny slammed down the phone and splashed after him. "Excuse me," he called, "but do you speak English?"

The dark-haired figure swung around; it was indeed an American face, and not so many years older than Danny's own. There was a moment's silence as Danny was peered at appraisingly. "Not a single word, I'm afraid." The voice held a trace of an English accent.

"Hey, listen," Danny said, and the words spilled free in a relieved tumble. "I'm wondering whether this is near the intersection of Imadegawa-Dori and Kawaramachi-Dori. I saw you were eating a donut, and I was told there's something called a Mister Donut at that intersection. And a McDonald's, too. And a Kentucky Fried Chicken," Danny went on, feeling it strange the way the other's eyes continued so closely to peer at him. "Weren't you eating a donut?"

The English accent deepened; the tone was one of huge regret. "I wish I knew how to . . . to clear up the misunderstanding we seem to be having. You appear to be under the misapprehension that I speak English."

For a skittery moment Danny sensed there might just be something imbalanced in those dark eyes. Here was the fitting terminus of the whole journey: he'd come thousands and thousands of miles to have a dreamlike conversation with a madman. "I was just looking for a donut shop," Danny mumbled, and turned away.

The other, spookily, caught him by the sleeve. "There's a frightful misunderstanding here. You seem to believe that I speak English."

Danny caught a reassuring hovering whiff of alcohol; perhaps this wasn't lunacy on display but only antic drunkenness. "But you're speaking it *right now*," Danny retorted, pursuing logic to its inescapable, exasperating conclusion.

"*I see light*," this drunk, or madman, or practical joker cried. "I see light at the end of this tunnel. Perhaps now, perhaps we share some common language. Human communi*ca*tion. French, maybe. Or Spanish. Now you see, you see if you were only to address me in one of those tongues . . ."

Danny as though in a dream was being asked to undergo a bizarre trial, a rite of passage, and as in a dream this trial had its own queer and yet queerly appropriate format, for Danny prided himself on his command of languages. "*Je cherche le Mister Donut, s'il vous plaît,*" he said, staring down into those amused dark eyes, four or so inches below his own. His sleeve was still in the other's grip.

"*Mister* . . . *Mister* . . . What is this *Mister* . . . I'm afraid that's an English word . . . Perhaps if I . . ."

"*Monsieur,*" Danny said, yanking his sleeve free. "Monsieur Donut."

"Oh for Christ's sake"—and now an enormous grin emerged—"you mean *Mister Donut*. Why it's right behind you. It's not far at all."

"Thank you, *merci, merci,*" Danny said, and, his curiosity inflamed now that all sense of peril had passed, watched with some regret the other spin away, twirling his umbrella rather than holding it upright to protect himself from the light rain. "Incidentally," the fellow called over his shoulder, "you'd be an utter ass to pass up the toasted coconut. *Bon appétit.*" And he dissolved into the rain.

This encounter was the crowning event, the strangest development yet, and at once Danny knew the night was over. He was not going to try again to reach Professor Umeda, or worry any more about his luggage. There was a hotel nearby and Danny went in, paid what was asked of him from the funny pyramidal stack of bills—polycolored, and diminishing in size as the denominations decreased—and shuffled up to his room, where he sprawled out immediately on the short and narrow bed. He intended to rise soon and wash his face and brush his teeth but it quickly became evident that he was not about to get up, or even to undress. The window was open and for a moment he heard the sibilant traffic on the wet pavement, driving on the wrong side of the road, and also the jumpy rasp of the Japanese phones when he'd called Professor Umeda, and that grinning voice saying "There seems to be a misunderstanding here." Danny settled one of the bed's two pillows under his head and the other over his head and the next moment, like a stone into the sea, he plummeted into fluid caves of opening blackness.

"And now this one. Perhaps I have transcribed incorrectly. *Dose of your own medicine.*"

"No, no. That's right. But that's a difficult one."

A second and more immediate difficulty was presented to Danny by the rash on his right ankle, itching so fiercely it could not be ignored a second longer. With the toe of his left shoe Danny nudged the sock down below the ankle and, his knee bumping the low table from underneath, setting the water in the glasses asway, applied the nippled sole of his running shoe to the rash.

It was Wednesday, so he was having lunch with Professor Umeda. He'd been in Japan only a few weeks now, but already—his baggage returned to him, an apartment obtained—a comforting routine had swung snugly around him, which included a weekly lunch with the Professor. To this lunch, always taken at the same modest restaurant near the university, the Professor would bring a little notebook in which he'd gathered the unfamiliar expressions, most though not all in English, met in his week's wide reading.

Lonely though he was, and though he'd already grown to admire the Professor greatly, Danny did not look forward to these lunches. He was made uneasy in part by having so little to do. He had come all the way from America to serve as assistant to a professor who, at least for the moment, had little use for him. This matter of duties had troubled Danny from the very start, when Professor Wickett had told him how his brilliant colleague in Kyoto, Masahiro Umeda, who was writing a book on warfare and international law, might want an assistant for a year. "But what exactly will my duties be?" Danny had asked, and Wickett, after a pause, had shrugged his shoulders.

And he was made uneasy by the Professor himself, who despite his unflagging kindness was becoming an increasingly intimidating figure. The stiff locutions, the pursed set to his mouth, even the balanced, two-handed way he adjusted his glasses, seemed always to suggest some abeyant form of censure. Over time, conversation grew more rather than less formal, as Danny adapted to what seemed the Professor's unspoken inclinations. On his two visits to the Professor's house Danny had felt too constrained to ask whether his wife, her presence implicitly affirmed by the rice crackers and flowers on the table, was at home.

It was not merely having to deal with an immediate and proximate superior that made things so troubling. No, Danny was used to that—indeed probably felt more comfortable with than without such a figure beside him, for he had a sense of living his whole life reprimanded, praised, directed, and spurred on by a race of men in authority: Dad being paramount, of course; more distantly, now turned ghost, Grandpa Jaynes; and Mr. Coughlin, his tennis coach in high school, and Morris Bramble, under whom he'd written his college history thesis, and Professor Wickett at the law school, and a select fraternity of partners at Horace, Rosen, the Detroit firm he'd worked for the summer after his first year of law school, and at Huck, Meadows, for whom he'd worked this past summer in New York. He had chafed under some of these presences, had quietly battled like hell with Dad over the years, but had never felt the very lineaments of authority and subordination so distasteful as in regard to this civil, diminutive man—no taller probably than five foot three—with the primly dour set to his lips.

"*Dose of one's own medicine*," Danny repeated. "I better start with an example. The Iraqis are now claiming that in their recent bombings they are giving the Iranians a dose of their own medicine. It means doing back to someone else what they did to you."

The Mideast had freshly broken out in war, about which Danny was able to gather only scattered accounts in the four English-language papers sold in Kyoto. It was not yet clear whether America or the U.S.S.R. would be drawn into the conflict, and not certain how Japan, with no domestic oil supplies, would be affected.

"Analogous to a repercussion?" Professor Umeda seized one of his two enormous tempura shrimp in his chopsticks and wedged into his mouth all but the tail, which with an incongruous daintiness of touch he detached with thumb and forefinger and deposited on his plate. In decorous Japan, Danny had discovered, there was surprisingly little etiquette governing what was a proper-sized bite.

"Something like a repercussion. But it usually has moral connotations. Giving someone the punishment they deserve. It's tied up with justice."

At this last word the Professor's orientally folded eyelids underwent a fractional adjustment. "Ah," he said. "Analogous to retribution."

"Yes, very much so," Danny said, "but there's a kind of humor attached to it. Someone who had previously been playing doctor is now being given the same medicine he prescribed for others."

"A medical doctor?" the Professor asked.

"Yes," Danny agreed, hoping to establish a fixed, common outpost in this terrain where opposing languages and cultures kept separating them. "Metaphorically speaking."

At each of these Wednesday lunches the Professor saved for last a portion of plain white rice, which he, with characteristic austerity, seemed to regard as a dessert. At least no other dessert was ever offered

Danny, who had a sweet tooth which he afterwards would satisfy at a bakery.

"It is a familiar phrase? Common?" the Professor asked.

Feeling the pursuit of accuracy guiding him into another bewilderingly nice distinction, Danny said, "Familiar. But not common, you see."

"Yes. Yes, familiar but not common," was the Professor's kind reply.

Danny made no attempt to pay his share of the bill, it having now become established that lunch was exchanged for an "English lesson." Actually, this was a fair arrangement, for while the lessons were brief and tended, like today's, to be unsatisfactory, Danny always left lunch still somewhat hungry.

Mount Daimon, symbol of Kyoto and already a familiar sight to Danny, reclined before them as they walked toward the Professor's class. On its elevated face one of the few Japanese *kanji* Danny knew, the starlike *dai*, 大, meaning big or very much, had been etched. Once each year, on a night in August, Danny had read in his Kyoto guidebook, the limbs of this star were somehow set afire. He'd missed it this year, and would miss it as well next August, when he would again be working at Huck, Meadows in New York.

Danny left the Professor in front of the lecture hall, thanked him once more for lunch, and doubled back the way he'd come, toward the bakery and then to the Professor's office and Minowada-san, the Professor's secretary. Danny had needed only a few weeks to see himself as a natural part of this noisy city. He had already begun to understand and accept as fitting that as a *gaijin*, a Westerner, he was patiently permitted to hold up a bus because he'd neglected to carry the proper change, or to lose his ticket on the train; that as a gaijin he would be everywhere greeted by schoolchildren ("har-row, har-row") who giggled at the foreignness of their own voices; and that he would everywhere be peered at, but especially inside the public bath. (In fact he still wasn't quite accustomed to the bath, where he was stared at not only as the only gaijin but as the tallest and by far the palest naked body in the place.) In his first days in Japan he had been overwhelmed by the ubiquitous vending machines, found even on tiny tucked-away side streets, and peddling everything imaginable—Coca-Cola, ice cream, Hi-C, beer, "health drinks," hot and cold cans of coffee, dried squid, "brandy tea," batteries, sake, condoms, fifths of whiskey, and pornography. He had been struck, too, by the uniforms—in the schoolyards, in the banks and offices—but now on his way to the bakery, waiting for the light to change, he felt instead how natural it was to be standing among nearly a dozen Japanese high school girls in uniform. He was pleased with this sense of his own adaptability, although there were occasions every few days when something would abruptly strike him as impenetrably alien.

He found Minowada-san, as he'd hoped, alone. "*Konnichi wa*," he greeted her, taking the seat across from her desk.

"Good aftanoon."

They had developed between them a limping but pleasurable discourse wherein each mirrored the other's remarks in the other's intractable tongue. Danny's Japanese was clumsy but bold; he would ambitiously hazard all sorts of complexities. Her English was abler but more timid, and she spoke very softly.

"*Ogenki desu ka?*"

"Fine, sank you. And you?"

"*Okage-sama de.*"

With her gold fillings and her lack of any bust, Miss Minowada had not at first seemed pretty to Danny. Yet through some synaesthetic blending of those eyes so dark that iris melted into pupil, her water-soft voice, and the warmth of her tan flesh (Danny had on one pretense or another touched her three or four times), a significant alteration had taken place, and in this land of beautiful women where he knew no women, Miss Minowada, the less than beautiful, reigned as his present queen.

In English Danny said, "I had lunch with the Professor. I ate . . ." The word had vanished—maddeningly, for he'd used it only an hour or so before. "*Yubi.*"

The exaggerated dilation of Minowada-san's eyes informed him he'd made a large error, and her subsequent prolonged giggles that it was a comical one. Her quiet laughter fretted as it charmed him, for while he meant his struggles with Japanese to be amusing, they were not supposed to be ridiculous. "Wait a minute," he cried in Japanese, lifting a dictionary from her desk. "*Ebi*," he announced a moment later. "Shrimp, *ebi*; shrimp, *ebi*; shrimp, *ebi*," he chanted.

"*Yubi*," Minowada-san said, holding up one of her small hands, tan palm outstretched, "means finger. You said, *I ate finger*." She covered her mouth with the same hand and her face shivered into giggles.

"*Ah*," Danny called, "like a cannibal. Do you know the word? Can-ni-bal?" He passed her the dictionary. "C-a-n-n-i-b-a-l. Cannibal."

Minowada-san's drifting forefinger halted on an entry and again she giggled. "*Hitokui*."

"Cannibal. Repeat after me."

"Conniburu."

"*Can*," Danny said in his harshest Midwestern accent. "Like my name. *Danny*. Say: *Dan*ny." To ask her to repeat his name was, it had already been established, an invitation to prolonged, paralyzing giggles; for *dani* in Japanese signified some sort of obnoxious insect like a roach or a bedbug.

"Donny."

"Say: *Dan*ny *Dan*ny *Dan*ny is no *can*nibal."

"Danny is no canniboo."

"Canni*bal*. La la la la la. Lift your tongue behind your teeth. Say: la la la la la."

"Ra ra ra ra ra."

"Open your lips more. Let your tongue tap here." Danny's forefinger rapped against the roof of his mouth. "La la la la la."

Bashful Minowada-san hesitated. Danny watched her tongue behind her gold-edged teeth lift and descend five times, an improved sound, still partly an *r*, partly a *d*, but with something of the light mellow tumble of an English *l*. Danny felt a softening low in his abdomen, and below that a sizable twinge and stiffening, a counterpart attempt at lifting, this one through the binding folds of his undershorts and jeans. It was a confirmation of what he'd already observed while studying Spanish in junior high, Latin and French in high school, German in law school: there was something submergedly erotic in the attempt to master any foreign language, the tongue's attempt to become a more delicate instrument. The two of them were, here in the Professor's sun-washed office two flights above the streets of Kyoto, exchanging vicarious kisses, as he with his English sought to extend the range of her uncertain, experimenting mouth.

"Repeat: I am no cannibal. And: You are no cannibal."

The phone trilled, Minowada-san lifted it to her earring-less ear, and in the first minute repeated the word *hai* at least a dozen times.

How strange the equivalent would sound in English: *yes yes yes yes yes yes yes yes yes yes yes yes* . . . As often seemed the case between two Japanese, this was a conversation that trended along an endless stream of assent. When Minowada-san began to write frantically on a sheet of paper, Danny rose to go, though here, too, he'd not confessed the tremulous information he'd earlier considered imparting to the Professor: today was his birthday. "Bye-bye," he said, adding "la la la la la," but she, who seemed to take her responsibilities a little too seriously, hardly glanced up.

Once on the street, all those last sparking touches of the thrill that moments before had coursed through his body fizzled to nothing in the warm air. It was hard to believe October was already here; the air felt like summer and the leaves had hardly begun to turn. Time seemed to have slowed since his arrival in Japan, and hours loomed large. He had nothing planned for this afternoon, nothing for this evening either.

Danny headed into a little side street he'd never noticed before. The city was easy to negotiate and he had a good sense of direction. He had decided to go downtown, as he did nearly every afternoon. He walked miles every day and had already seen much of the city. Threatening to dead end, this new street veered unexpectedly, funneling him in an uncertain direction before it deposited him beside the river, the Kamogawa, where he jogged nearly every day. An immaculate white heron waded in the shallow water, picking its way with condescending fastidiousness through the rocks and stranded, colorful garbage.

Danny went first to Maruzen Department Store, which had the largest collection of English-language books in Kyoto. He hovered beside the paperbacks and magazines for a long while before deciding to buy nothing, then drifted over to the Royal Hotel, where he picked up the *Japan Times* and the *Mainichi Daily News*, and then to a coffee shop which played classical music where he ate flan and drank coffee and read almost every article in both papers. One of the reasons he'd felt so aimless these last few weeks, he'd recently concluded, had nothing to do with being in Japan: this was the first fall since before kindergarten, since almost before memory, that he'd not been enrolled in school.

He ambled again down to the Kamo River, heading in roundabout fashion toward his room. The same lovely heron, or perhaps another, was mincing through the trash in search of something to eat. Near Imadegawa Street he turned from the river and on sudden impulse began to walk not west toward his room but east toward Daimon-ji, the low sprawling mountain with the star etched on its face, and something extraordinary occurred, just then.

As he turned onto the street he glimpsed through a transection of telephone wires the moon over the mountain and instantaneously, just as if he'd been tapped by some sort of wand, the moon's faded face up there in the faded blue sky struck him with an unprecedented force. His legs actually weakened, as if he were about to tumble to his knees; a warm, charged, rinsing liquid flushed his limbs. Brief as this moment was, it was long enough for him to discern within it that here lay some sort of culmination, a moment other moments had been amassing toward. It seemed the moon through the wires beckoned him, *Danny*, toward some linkage or vantage or insight his mind could not, or would not, quite accomplish. The moment was brief, the wand tapped him a second time, and he was almost his old self again.

Beside him a bus gasped, straining like some wheezing old man for breath. Two children on a small bicycle, one perched precariously on the handlebars, wobbled by. A car honked at the children. The bus, expelling a cloud of gray poison, attained its gear and rumbled off.

The moment was gone. He had felt a pull, a yearning, a tidal suck at the blood within his heart, but what did it mean? where did that leave him? Danny was standing on the pavement at an intersection in Kyoto, Japan, looking up at Mount Daimon and the daylight moon and feeling suddenly the futility of going anywhere. And immensely tired suddenly. So he turned toward home—such as it was, a tiny six-tatami-mat room. Where else was he to go?

Danny napped a while, woke and studied Japanese for half an hour, changed into his running clothes and headed back to the Kamo River. He had gravitated toward it naturally, within days of his arrival, as he had toward the Huron River in college, the Charles in law school. With the sun's going down, the hills that rimmed the city on three sides were shifting from green to blue, their usual color at nightfall and at daybreak. The moon had climbed and brightened in the pinkening sky. The day had cooled, and Danny was able to push himself hard.

He followed the river north along its eastern bank, feet dropping neatly among the stones and shards of glass, the accumulating pain of exertion for a time tenderly balanced against the accumulating pleasure in his own motions. He loved this sense of equilibrium, which never lasted long, for the body always gave out so quickly, and yet which could, while it lasted, make the air taste better and even brighten the floating, fleeting tints on the river's skin.

He continued at a good pace in the fading light, well beyond Kitaōji Street before turning and, without a moment's rest, surging back toward his starting point. He felt the equilibrium dying, pain branching hotly across his chest. With maybe a hundred yards to go, hearing an internal voice announce *Danny pushes into high gear*, he broke into a near-sprint. Sacs filled with bitter acids ripped and spilled inside him and there was no real pleasure left at all—only pride's secondary satisfactions, and the comforting awareness that his run was nearly over.

He was still panting as he walked into McDonald's—the same one he'd been searching for his first night in Kyoto—and ordered a Coke, which he sipped through a straw while sauntering home. To his relief, there turned out to be few people at the public bath. Going to the bath had been worse than usual these last few days as his rash had spread. For years he'd carried some form of this rash on his ankles and wrists—a grown-up variant, sometimes almost invisible, of the eczema that had afflicted him as an infant. Numerous trips to university health services, different dermatologists, various powders and ointments—nothing had wholly eliminated it, and unfortunately he could not even conceal it, as most people could, with a suntan; his fair skin resolutely refused to absorb anything more than a temporary flush or a quick-to-peel burn. As often happened when he traveled, the rash had flared up on his arrival in Japan. Partly to protect himself from stares, partly to protect others (though he'd been assured it wasn't communicable), Danny no longer soaked in the bath's communal tubs, but made do with one of the meager tumbledown showers.

There were many gaijin in Kyoto—hundreds, probably, for Danny saw them wherever he went and frequently offered greetings (which generally were not cordially met, except on the regrettable occasion when he'd run into some Mormons). But what they all did with their time, especially at night, remained a mystery. Along with that recent sensation of time's being expanded had come a marveling that people seemed so easily to fill the hours of their days. Home from the bath, Danny studied German for what seemed an immense amount of time—but only thirty-five minutes by the clock. He'd worked so hard this past year to fit Introductory German into his law school schedule that on deciding to come to Japan he'd vowed at least to maintain the proficiency he'd won. He'd brought with him forty-five language tapes, German and Japanese, pirate copies acquired through a friend who worked in the language lab. He tried to do one hour of German every day, three of Japanese.

His long run had left him hungry. Wary of anything remotely celebratory, which might render too poignant this solitary birthday, Danny went to dinner where he usually did, a Chinese restaurant around the corner where the food was far from good but not awful either. It was cheap and there was always American rock music playing over the stereo and the employees were all young men, so friendly as to actually seem like friends, especially one who had picked up all sorts of American slang—"How's tricks?" and "Take it easy," and "See you around." Danny ate slowly. Having attained real dexterity with chopsticks in the past few weeks, he was now trying to achieve—a lengthier task, for he was far from ambidextrous—an equal facility with his left hand.

The moon had shifted again by the time Danny stepped from the restaurant, a big bottle of beer diffusing inside him. Again tonight there were few stars. Night skies in Kyoto had proved a great disappointment. The city was too bright and its air too sullied; even after a long rain the stars were not plentiful and would look a bit lackluster. On Danny's left a bakery shone with an unexpected orange brilliance. Had it always been that color? Probably—almost certainly. His failure heretofore to observe it properly propelled him down a familiar corridor of thought: would he even have noticed if, while he'd been eating dinner, the bakery had been magically transformed into, say, an auto-parts store? This was a favorite solitary pastime, an old game which he deliberately encouraged himself to play because it seemed to tone his powers of observation. He was forever asking himself whether he would remark the difference if, say, the Hancock Building in Boston were somehow to grow five stories overnight, whether the replacement of maples for sycamores along the banks of the Charles would go undetected. Now if the Kamo River were to widen by five feet a day, and all the bridges widen with it, how many days would need to pass before the opposite bank began to look strangely distant? Danny turned right, away from his room, realizing that despite all the ground he'd already covered today this was going to be a long walk.

Lights and a sound like miniature gunfire drew him toward a kind of pavilion covered over with green netting. Within, four Japanese men—two of them wearing ties, evidently just off work—were swinging baseball bats at balls hurled toward them by powerful machines. *Drawn by the sound of what seemed to be gunfire*, Danny composed as he stood watching the balls being slammed into the bellying nets, *I found a place where Japanese men practice their baseball swings after work* . . .

An elderly man wearing pajamas and wooden clogs came clumping up the street. He scrutinized Danny as an oddity, and Danny with some self-righteousness stared right back, firmed by the conviction that if any objective test of what was odd could be arrived at, it was the old man in his pajamas who would prove the irregular one. Yet the old man's accusatory glance, branding Danny an alien, had stolen the pleasure in watching the batters, and Danny continued on his way.

The way was crowded, whichever way he went. No lawns: the people lived right up against the street, and windows were open. A moment's glance into one of these brought him a plump, bespectacled man in T-shirt and undershorts lying on the floor before an enormous color TV which depicted a teenage girl standing on a snowy mountaintop in a two-piece bathing suit. She was singing into a reverently regarded hand-held microphone. Japanese television seemed to be even more inane than American, though Danny wouldn't have thought this possible.

Everywhere he walked in Kyoto he encountered this same oppressive sense of being made involuntarily a voyeur and an eavesdropper: the bawling children, the smells and sights of someone else's dinner, the radios and televisions, the arguments and naps and calisthenics all lying with dismaying openness before you. Here would be a hunchbacked elderly woman in her nightclothes, a middle-aged man snoring on his tatami mat beside a strew of empty beer bottles, a young woman with head bent in prayer before a household shrine. In Cambridge he used to roam nearly every night along the wide and tranquil streets just north of Radcliffe, big lawns and solid, thick-walled houses exuding an atmosphere of privileged ease and concealed and graceful intimacies.

Nowhere in this new country did he breathe that sense of spaciousness and ease. One house pressed upon another, one narrow street issued only onto another pinched street; crowded houses, crowded baths, crowded clotheslines, and the endless warring of car and bicycle horns, their hectoring, shrill and peremptory, *Let me through, let me through, let me through* . . .

Disappointedly—but with a concessive sense of prepared-for failure, of the existence of a space in the mind already arranged for it—Danny realized that the vague ghost in the air tonight, to whom he'd been mentally transmitting his observations on Kyoto as well as various casual snapshots of himself exploring its streets, was Penny, Penny Cogswell, his girl friend for nearly six years, the last three of high school and the first three of college. For a time after that messy breakup his continued devotion had felt almost noble, a quixotic run against time and change, just as there'd been something appealing, though mixed with buckets of humiliation and shame, in the impotence he'd experienced with the first woman he'd finagled into bed after Penny left him. There had been other women since—though too few—and a couple of bad unrequited crushes, including one this whole past year for a woman in his study group, whose short, homely boyfriend had actually grown up in Hollywood, but all of these other passions had somehow faded with his arrival in Japan. It was strange how that had happened. It seemed he was still hung up on Penny, with a devotion that had long ago become an embarrassment. Time, daily carrying him along more deeply into his twenties, had conspired to transform what remained the largest passion of his life into puppy love (though even in his first year with Penny, when he was just fourteen, the longings and upheavals had been acute, and he'd known that love was never larger), and to be tied to puppy love as one moved into manhood was embarrassing. Oh, the whole notion of manhood was an interesting issue; he had adeptly managed, as demanded of him, to refer to the girls in his classes as *women*, and even to think of them as such, but the guys remained *guys*, not men. *Men* for Danny were still the professors, or, less distantly, the people who came to interview from the law firms (from New York and Los Angeles, from Chicago, Washington, Dallas, Detroit, San Diego, Portland, Honolulu . . . Where did you want to work? If you'd made law review, you had a job in any firm in any city in the country). *Men* were still primarily those dapper figures who had entered the game of buying cars, trying to beat taxes, earning a living.

Danny was tired, and these cramped streets were not what he wanted. None of this was what he wanted for his twenty-third birthday. (And what an enormous satisfaction birthdays had once been for him; on one occasion—what? sixteen, seventeen years ago?—he'd been unable to wait, really *unable to wait*, for the full glacial passage of a year, and Mom threw a party for him at the halfway point, April first. She'd combined it with an April Fool's party, and hadn't allowed—a compromise he'd grudgingly accepted, once having grasped its fundamental justice—the other kids to bring presents.) Still, these streets were to be preferred to the six-mat room awaiting him. Having heard such terrifying stories about prices in Japan, when he'd written to the Professor for help in finding a place he'd stressed the need for something cheap. That had been a huge mistake. For cheap it surely was—under $100 a month at present exchange rates—but he needed more space, and he could have afforded to pay much more. He'd banked a couple thousand dollars this past summer alone. With its ridiculously high salaries to begin with, and its signing bonus and moving and clothing allowances, Huck, Meadows paid as well as any firm in the country. All summer long he'd had this bedazzling sense of being rich—of reaching into his pocket and finding haphazardly wadded there not ones and fives, but tens and twenties.

The room had actually looked promising at first. Umeda had found him a *geishuku*, a room in a private house, with a separate entrance. Living above a Japanese family—it seemed he would have frequent opportunity to practice his Japanese. But the landlord (some kind of mechanic) was never home, and his wife came from the north, Tōhoku, and spoke a dialect Danny couldn't begin to follow. He could understand best the chipmunk-voiced daughter, but he'd quickly grown almost to hate her for the way she played her electone piano, tirelessly wafting through his room wavering renditions of "More" and "Raindrops Keep Fallin' on My Head" and "Days of Wine and Roses" and "My Way," all steeped in a sappiness that had begun to seem little short of pernicious.

A second sidelong glance at what he'd recognized the first time as a vending machine selling pornography brought him a glimpse of a buxom Oriental woman squeezing her breasts into misshapen heaps while sticking out her tongue. It was in part his natural modesty that prohibited his inspecting the pornography sold on the street, but more than this a sense that as a gaijin he was a locus for the neighborhood's multiple hidden eyes. An ambassador from America, he had to behave more decorously than the Japanese themselves might.

Japan had instantly altered him, body and mind. It had made him taller, and tinted his hair a brighter red. And it had somehow lifted him back in time to that mental treadmill where he'd been dumbstruck to learn that his own Penny could be leaving him. He brought refinements to the old arguments, came to them now (and this really was a little funny) with a lawyerly detachment; saw himself in some court of romantic appeals, responding to accusations Penny by now had surely forgotten, correcting for the pure sake of clarity her limp and shoddy reasoning. For this is what had burned him worst, it seemed, during those hideous last protracted weeks of phone calls, and notes, and arguments, and interrogations: how reason had no place here at all. There was simply one unassailable proposition: she didn't love him any more. For Penny, this was somehow a full explanation, a full exculpation.

It was not her fault, she was surely not to blame (time and again she'd explained this) if she didn't love him any more. But one night, late, with snow falling thickly over Ann Arbor, alone in his room, he had felt his mind take an unexampled leap. All the long philosophical speculation about free will and determinism that he'd pursued without progress ever since he'd been able to grasp these concepts now gave way to a glittering certainty. In an instant so quickly traveled that later he'd not been able to recollect the precise path he'd journeyed through the cerebral maze, more crowded and confusing even than the streets of Kyoto, he was debouched before that rare and ancient temple where the answer all along expected him. And so simple and right it was. Penny was pleading helplessness, and hence blamelessness, but her argument was false: *she had a choice.* And if there was a choice, then there was inside the human universe—logically, necessarily—blame. And given blameworthiness, then (up, up above the sadness and the clouds of falling snow) there could be justice as well.

. . .

Danny beside the Kamo River had one foot propped upon a stone bench, stretching his legs before another run, when he heard the omnivorous crunch-crunch-crunch of an approaching jogger on the gravel path. It was a gaijin, and for a moment as the dark, sweating figure pumped by, Danny thought the face looked familiar. He returned to his limbering up, but after a moment the dismissed intuition revived, this time linked to a rain-misted incident, and Danny sprinted after the already distant figure while trying to recall the French word for *directions*.

Danny tapped him on the shoulder and the two of them halted. "*Pardonnez-moi*," Danny panted. "*Je crois que tu es perdu. Est-ce que je peux t'aider?*"

"You better repeat that. *Répétez*. My French is pretty horrible. *Tu parles anglais?*" For a moment there was still a slight chance, though Danny was very good with faces, that this was not the same person. The voice did sound a little different. Then the fellow, peering closely at Danny, grinned, and Danny knew he was correct.

"*Tu es seul dans une très grande ville. Il pleut et tu es perdu*," Danny said, feeling his phlegm-impasted tongue growing grandiloquent. "*Tu me demandes—Où est le Colonel Sanders, où est le Monsieur Donut? Je réponds—Excusez-moi, je ne parle pas français.*"

"I am sorry." In the fellow's dark eyes there was no sign of that craziness Danny had earlier sensed there—only a well-meaning befuddlement. "*Je parle française un peu seulement.*"

Danny grazed the fellow's hairy bare forearm with his fingertips, a counterpart gesture to the clutching at Danny's sleeve that night in the rain, and continued, "*Tu viens de faire un vol de plusieurs milliers de miles*—thousands of miles—*et tu es très fatigué*—very tired—*et tu me demandes: Où est le Monsieur Donut?*"

"Oh you speak some English."

"Not a word I'm afraid."

The cordial, amused, unassimilating look Danny received suggested that here perhaps was a madman after all. "That's what you said to me," Danny explained. "That you didn't speak English. The other night, a couple of weeks ago, at Kawaramachi and Imadegawa. It was raining."

"Oh I *do* remember." The smile broadened to take in little fanning lines of mirth around the corners of the eyes, the whole face being seized by a self-satisfaction completely at odds with the spoken disclaimer: "Oh God, that was terrible of me, wasn't it."

"It was my first night in Kyoto," Danny said. "I'd just flown into Japan that day."

"You're making me feel worse. Just plain abysmal." But the expansive grin remained. "I'm afraid I'd been drinking, I really don't remember all that clearly. If you told me your name, I've forgotten it."

"Danny. Danny Ott." Danny extended his right hand.

"Ott? That's all?" The other backed away in simulated suspicion. "Sounds like a pseudonym to me. Sounds more like an initial than a last name."

"It's Ott, Ott's it," Danny said, drawing on an ancient joke of Dad's. "Still more improbable, my parents are named Alice and Alec."

"Greg Blaising." Their sweaty hands gripped a moment. "You've finished running?"

"Haven't started really."

"I'll run with you then."

They jogged at a quick clip, in silence, northward quite a ways before turning back and heading back toward Imadegawa. With a couple of hundred yards remaining, Danny broke into a near-sprint, thinking he would leave the other, panting so loudly, some distance behind, but Greg stayed with him, step for step, until they halted at the stairs to the street.

"So you've been in Kyoto only a few weeks," Greg said as they climbed the stairs. He turned east, away from the river, away from Danny's room, and Danny followed.

"Mm-hm. What about you?"

"Oh I don't know. Months I guess. I let the immigration authorities keep track. They're very good about that, they do it free of charge." If Danny was right, a second competition was being extended—an attempt to talk with as little panting as possible. Greg was three or four inches shorter than Danny but compensatorily broader, especially through the shoulders. His sweat-drenched brown T-shirt clung to his chest.

"You're American," Danny stated. "I thought you were English maybe."

"I was just talking funny. I often talk funny. What made you come to Japan?"

Their walking had brought them close to the spot where Danny on his birthday had glimpsed the moon over Daimon-ji. The moon was nowhere visible now. "I'm a research assistant to a Japanese law professor. I'm on a year's leave of absence from law school."

"What law school?"

"Harvard."

"Oh that's *good*," Greg said. "That's excellent. You're an achiever. Lord, I'm so weary of all these brainless Americans who come to ancient Kyoto, city of temples, in search of God. It's as bad as India. Worse. The ones coming here are lazier. And more cowardly, they're afraid of dysentery. Spiritual pilgrims too chicken to rub their noses in the dirt. You're not spiritual are you? God I hope not. I went to Harvard undergrad. Class of seventy-five."

"I got into Harvard undergrad," Danny began, ignoring a very faint upwelling of self-distaste. Why, after all these years, and even after enrolling at the Law School, did he still find it necessary to explain to any Harvard College graduate he met that he, too, could have been one of their ivied club? "I went to Michigan instead. Graduated seventy-eight. What are you doing in Kyoto?"

"Oh Lord, you trapped me. Cornered me." Greg's laugh was unexpectedly high and airy, an evenly spaced series of acoustical bumps. "Truth is, I'm looking for God, too. Or a wife. No, seriously, I don't know. I sort of washed up here. Like an oil slick. I thought you might come over now. I live near here."

"I don't know, I godda bathe."

"We'll go to the public bath."

Although he'd spoken no assent, Danny had apparently agreed to this plan; in any case, with this Greg Blaising at his side (who was either a very witty joker or truly something of a crazy man, Danny couldn't decide which), Danny continued walking east on Imadegawa, then north on a street Danny didn't know, always away from Danny's room and the two hours of Japanese study yet scheduled for the day. Greg had said he lived nearby, but they had already covered a fair distance. The shapes of individual trees on the hills of the Higashiyama Range were coming clear, and even Hiei-zan at the northeastern edge of the city—tallest of the immediately surrounding mountains—had swung into new focus.

"My beer store's here. What do you think we need—three of those big bottles, or four?"

"I don't know," Danny said, wary again, for that crazy man's look of amusement had resurfaced. "It's kind of early in the day."

"Good thinking. Four it ought to be, then. Stock up now, huh? Hours of thirstiness ahead."

Greg parted a curtain over the doorway and they stepped into a shadowy interior like a cave's mouth, its dim walls crystalled with brown and green and transparent bottles of beer, sake, whiskey, vodka. "Ma. Tsu. Mo. To. San," Greg called, and a voice from further within answered, "Gurei-go, Gurei-go," and a round bespectacled man emerged, chuckling with anticipatory mirth.

"Ma. Tsu. Mo. To. San," Greg repeated, and the two men laughed raucously and shook hands. "You are very busy today."

"Not so busy."

"I ran very far today, Matsumoto-san."

"Very fah."

"I am very thirsty."

"Very sirsty."

"This is my good friend Danny Ott. Danny, this is Matsumoto-san."

Danny and Matsumoto-san, whose face had instantaneously assumed a look of gravity for this moment of ceremony, shook hands. "Pleased to meet you," Danny said. "*Dōzo yoroshiku.*"

"Danny is student. Very smart," Greg said, tapping the side of his head.

Matsumoto-san's abrupt, squealing laugh suggested that he thought *smart* meant something other than what it did. "Very smart," Matsumoto-san echoed, tapping his own skull.

"Kirin," Greg said. "*Yon hon kudasai.*"

"Kirin. Four bottles," Matsumoto-san said.

As Danny stepped forward to pay his half, Greg edged over, cutting him off. Coins jingled in the cash register. "*Dōmo arigatō gozaimasu,*" Greg said, offering his thanks in what even Danny could recognize as an atrocious accent.

"Bye-bye," called Matsumoto-san, "bye-bye," turning and laughing, carrying his chuckled mirth with him back to the store's interior.

Danny, stooping in the low doorway, pushed head first through the curtain and out into the street. "You're a great favorite of his."

"Ought to be. Profits have doubled since I arrived."

"He seems to find you very amusing."

"I think he thinks I'm crazy," Greg said.

"He called you Gurei-go."

"Grego. El Grego. It's a nickname. Everybody was so unobliging about giving me a nickname, I gave it to myself. I live right down this street."

A young Japanese woman on the corner, tall and spectacularly dressed in a pink and white blouse, pink skirt, pink shoes, glanced at them for a moment in seeming interest before her eyes went dead. For Danny it was a familiar occurrence in this country: that spark of invitation before modesty or fear or something else intervened. "She's very attractive," he said, in part because it was arrestingly true, and in part to forestall, as he stepped into this Greg's apartment, the possibility of any sort of unfortunate misunderstanding.

"Most of them are here. It's terrible."

Grown accustomed to living in a six-mat room, Danny found Greg's apartment—really a small house—absolutely enormous. There were two rooms downstairs (the larger, Greg explained, reserved for his landlady's once-a-month tea ceremonies) and two rooms upstairs, one giving out onto the Higashiyama Range. Greg went downstairs for glasses, providing Danny with a welcome opportunity to play detective in the bedroom. As in his own room, there was a *futon* instead of a bed, but unlike Danny's room, where a plain love of neatness had adapted to the exigencies of cramped quarters and everything was compactly stored in paper bags, here clothes and papers and empty bottles and razor blades and coins and bottles of aspirin were scattered everywhere. Bayer, Excedrin, Tylenol—Danny counted five containers in all. On the base of a reading lamp sat a box of condoms (opened) modeled after an American cigarette pack. "Wherever Particular People Congregate" it said in English. This was even better than the brand dispensed from a vending machine around the corner from Danny's: Swedish Passion Robes. There were surprisingly few books—a *Riverside Shakespeare*, the *Viking Portable Jung*, and a slim book by someone Danny had never heard of, Bashō, called *The Narrow Road to the Deep North*. On the wall hung a poster which just a few weeks ago would have seemed nonsensical to Danny, but which now seemed both queerly logical and unintendedly funny. Two pretty but thick-legged Japanese girls in tennis whites were standing at midcourt, rackets in one hand and something pale to eat in the other. In English the poster said "Sports and Cheese"—and nothing else. Sports and cheese: linked as exotic Western imports.

And taped below the poster Danny found further evidence that Greg's peculiar sense of humor was not unlike his own, a page apparently torn from a Kyoto guidebook with a sentence circled in red ink: "In the northeast, towers the sacred Mt. Hiei, holy to both the Zen Buddhist and Shinto sects, with its amusements park and Skyview Coffeeshop at the apex." So that was actually the Skyview Coffeeshop he'd been glimpsing on the distant summit; Danny had taken it for a temple.

Greg returned with two unmatched glasses, the larger of which (far from clean, Danny noticed) he offered to his guest. Danny resolved simply to drink from the bottle, but was stymied when Greg held up his glass and said, "A toast." Danny splashed into his own glass a couple of inches of beer and clinked it against Greg's. "To the English tongue," Greg said, "which as it turns out we both speak fluently."

"Up and down," Danny said, conscious of having twice within the hour drawn upon one of Dad's expressions. Greg emptied his glass, and Danny did likewise. "You're doing a lot of pain-killing," Danny said, holding up a bottle of Excedrin.

"I get migraines. Sometimes, not often."

"My weak point's my stomach," Danny confessed. He'd read recently that the Japanese traditionally regarded the stomach, rather than the heart or brain, as the seat of the emotions, which certainly seemed the case for him: such a vulnerable zone, which even at the sound of *My weak point's my stomach* had given a testimonial shudder. "Is there a john?" Danny asked.

"Downstairs. Japanese-style. You'll find it."

The phrase "Japanese-style" generally was, Danny had already learned, indicative of discomfort. Carrying his glass, Danny duck-walked down the shadowed flight of stairs, constructed for smaller feet than his, passed through a narrow corridor that doubled as kitchen, turned and found the bathroom sink, which was littered with stray black hairs. Besides the hole in the floor that served as toilet there was a urinal, the first Danny'd seen in someone's house. He washed out the glass with a balled-up washcloth. He did not consider himself overly fastidious regarding food (he'd once flabbergasted and disgusted Penny by fishing a sizable spider from his lemonade before, without a second thought, draining the glass), but certain human traces (a fingernail, or this crust of something unknown at the bottom of his glass) repelled him.

Greg on his return was sitting against the wall, flossing his teeth—which, white and even, would have been fine anywhere, but which here in Japan, where notwithstanding all the affluence most people's teeth seemed to be rotting in their skulls, were exceptional. "Day ol' flaw?" Greg offered.

"No thanks." Danny filled his glass to the brim and stretched out on the tatami. His bare legs were a little stiff with running. The beer was delicious.

There was a silence, not awkward, while Greg cleaned his teeth and Danny drank and listened to the faint, heartening sound of water tumbling into the canal in back of the house and regarded the map of the world on the opposite wall, his own mitten-shaped Michigan leaping out at him: a hand among jewels. Greg set the bloodied string of floss on the *Riverside Shakespeare* and said, "This guy you work for, do you like him?"

"Well I don't suppose it's easy to *like* Professor Umeda. I mean I don't dislike him. He's just very distant. I respect him tremendously. He works like a son-of-a-bitch. He's an international law authority."

"On?"

"On?" Danny repeated.

"An international authority on?"

"Oh. On international law."

"Which is, exactly?"

The intentness of Greg's gaze demanded that Danny present an informed explanation. He lifted himself to a seated position, rising atop the lulling effects of the beer, and said, "There's nothing exact about it. People debate all the time—What is international law? There's the I.C.J., the International Court of Justice, in The Hague, which issues opinions once a decade or so. And there are treaties, and conventions, prohibiting poison gas for example, and established practices of all sorts, sanctioned by time, like embassy members are protected, which was good until Iran seized our embassy. The Professor's also an authority on nuclear weapons. He cuts out articles in both the Japanese and the English-language papers. There is something, something . . ." Danny's mind struggled for the encompassing adjective that would convey all of his ambivalence, the vacillating doubts that shuttled from himself to the Professor and back again; but the unifying impulse failed, bifurcated, trifurcated: "something admirable . . . but cold . . . or dispassionate . . . in the way he cuts out and records these things. 'Soviets Explode Underground N-Blast,' or 'China Constructing Missiles Capable of Striking Moscow or L.A.' That sort of thing. I think he thinks there's going to be a war," Danny concluded and, as the momentousness of this remark seemed to demand, emptied his glass.

Was this what the Professor thought? The very mention of such a war, the destruction of that world on Greg's wall, so hopefully portrayed in all its pastel tints (an image descended from all those classroom maps Danny had yearned toward even as a little boy), seemed somehow especially unthinkable now, ranged as he was in such consummate comfort on this floor. Surrounded by unfamiliarity—a strange Japanese house, a stranger who seemed at times half-crazy—Danny was unexpectedly struck by something familiarly and lovably American, a sprawling ease, a fraternal informality which he hadn't until now realized he'd been missing. Talk faded again; the two of them drank their beer in silence as the light of the room, adjusted by an interceding cloud, turned a subdued blue. The sound of *son-of-a-bitch* reverberated harshly in Danny's ears: it was perhaps the first time he'd sworn aloud since landing in this country. "Come on," Greg said. "You ready to push?" Danny stood, gathered up his glass and two empty bottles (Greg had left his own glass and bottles on the floor), and followed his host downstairs.

Greg's neighborhood public bath turned out to be a place of even greater immodesty than Danny's. The woman cashier sat behind a desk that surveyed both the women's and the men's sides, and another woman, not old, drifted among the undressing and undressed men on a seemingly endless round of tidying up. There was comfort for Danny, however, in not being the only foreigner in the place. Among the sallow, bird-boned Japanese males, Greg undressed was a spectacle, a broad furry bear—there were even faint whorls of hair on his back—but the stares he received didn't seem to bother him. If anything, he enjoyed them. As the two conspicuous gaijin stepped through the sliding doors separating the changing room from the baths, Greg began in an off-key voice to sing, loud enough to mortify Danny, "*The girls on the beach . . . are all within reach . . .*" He stopped singing and then, solemn-eyed, confidingly, "Style," he murmured to Danny. "You'll find I have a great sense of style."

The two of them perched side by side on the bath's little plastic stools, stooping to draw themselves under the low shower heads. At this bath, too, it was the practice that the little boys and the grown men moved relaxedly in their nudity. Only the adolescents, their bewildering bodies having lately propelled them down a breathless and shameful path, kept their genitals concealed behind towels.

Borrowing toiletries, Danny followed one step behind Greg—soap, shaving cream, razor. The mirrors were befogged and he shaved by touch. "You all done?" Greg asked him.

"I'm not going to soak. I've got a rash."

"Where?"

"On my ankles."

"Where? I can't even *see* it. Come on, come on. The whole scrofulous crew in here's got worse rashes than that."

The rash after soap and water *was* barely visible and Danny, his faint drunkenness lifting him loosely, like a swaying load conveyed by crane, perched himself upon the rim of one of the tubs, up to his knees in the jetting flow of burning water.

"They're laughing at you. They're saying gaijins can't take the heat." Greg in one easy horizontal motion slid without flinching into the water, just as the inured Japanese did, until only his head projected.

Inch by inch, a compromise by which the protesting body was willingly made to accept immersion, Danny eased forward until he too was lying up to his neck in the shallow water. For a moment his head orbited toward blackness, then toward a glowing orange, a lulled state of awareness as his body unclenched to the heat. "You're bleeding," he said.

"Mm?"

"A shaving nick."

On the crest of Greg's fine high cheekbone a single teardrop of blood had trailed and frozen. He'd closed his eyes, and his face, which Danny now studied, reddened in the heat. Near the center of his high globed forehead ran a great latitudinal vein from the roots of his apparently thinning hair to the top of his nose. "Heaven," Greg said, eyes still closed, "is surely going to consist of a great many baths. And Japanese pears, served by Japanese women."

"Pairs?"

"Fruit pears. Called *nashi*. We'll get some after dinner. Whatcha thinking about dinner?"

"I should probably go home."

"I was thinking Korean barbecue. And then maybe to Gion, you want to go to Gion?"

Greg took considerable pleasure, Danny had already begun to see, in playing the role of authoritative guide; charmed by this, Danny asked, in the implicitly requested tone of the wide-eyed tourist, "Now what's this Korean barbecue?"

Korean barbecue turned out to be a brightly lit restaurant where customers sat on stools and cooked their dinner themselves on small gas ranges built into the counter before them. Danny's legs had turned to rubber in the bath, giving him the sense, as they'd walked from the bath to Greg's, Greg's to the restaurant, of there being no articulate juncture at his knees but only a general, obliging ductility from calf to mid-thigh. He settled gratefully onto his stool. In Japanese—that same atrocious accent—Greg ordered beef, two salads, two bottles of beer.

"I don't know about the beer," Danny said. "I'm getting sleepy."

"You have to have it with Korean barbecue. It's key. It's part of the ensemble."

Beer, salads, and a plate of raw beef marinating in a brown liquid all appeared within moments and their gas pit was turned on with a hungry *whoosh*. Following Greg's example, Danny with chopsticks nestled the thin slices of beef on the grill and spread them flat. The meat began to hiss and spit and soon needed to be turned over. Plucked from the flames, it was then soaked in a dish of pale broth. It proved spicy—heavily peppered—and altogether delicious. The beer went down, as Greg had foretold, easily. Finding that the little ministering tasks of watching and turning the meat enhanced the flavor, Danny ate gluttonously. Greg ordered more beef and two more bottles of Kirin.

"I don't think," Danny said, "I'll do my Japanese tonight."

"You study every day?"

"Coupla hours anyway. And maybe an hour of German. I took German this year while I was in law school."

"How often do you take a day off?"

"A whole day? Never. Almost never."

"If I had your discipline, I'd surely be a world-famous something by now."

"That sounds vaguely insulting. Makes me sound like one of those dumb plodding types."

"Oh no, not insulting. Just unjustified arrogance on my part," Greg said. "And anyway, I'm older. How old are you?"

"Twenty-three. How old are you?"

"Twenty-*three*? How old were you when you graduated from college?"

"Twenty. I was sixteen when I entered U. of M.," Danny confessed, feeling once more that peculiar blend of embarrassment at his youth and pride in his precocity that had, like some sort of name tag, served to identify him since kindergarten days. "How old are you?"

"Twenty-eight. Two years short of thirty."

"Thirty-two years short of sixty. Look at it that way," Danny said, and laughed. It was, he realized, a faintly drunk thing to say.

"Yuk yuk."

"What do you do all day?" Danny asked.

"I don't know, I teach. I run. I walk around. I eat fruit. I drink too much. I read. I go to bars and try, for the most part with extreme fecklessness, but now and then with heartening success, to pick up Japanese women."

I often talk funny, Greg had told him. Whatever was *funny* in Greg's speech seemed to grow more so with drink. He seemed to love these very long, involuted, clause-trailing sentences; pleasure shone from his fine flushed face. "What do you read?" Danny asked him. "I didn't see many books."

"Gave 'em away. I'm in one of my self-improvement cycles. Nothing but Shakespeare. I'm going to read all of Shakespeare."

"What do you teach?"

"English," Greg answered promptly, as if the question were a little absurd. "You don't teach?"

"Uh uh."

"You're the only American in Kyoto not teaching English."

"Well actually I swap English for Japanese lessons with this guy Nagaoka-san. He's a student of the Professor's."

"You don't get paid?" The tone was skeptical.

"It's an even swap."

Actually Greg had struck a sensitive point, for Danny's feelings toward Nagaoka-san, a graduate student in law who never looked one in the eye, were highly ambivalent. It seemed the Professor had conscripted Nagaoka-san into instructing Danny in Japanese daily life—the public baths, the stores, the buses—a task which the Professor perhaps didn't have time for himself, or felt was too undignified. Or perhaps the Professor, to his credit, simply hoped to find Danny a friend of about his own age. In any case, while glad for the company, Danny had sensed something involuntary and artificial in their encounters.

"You'll have to start teaching," Greg said. "The pay's good."

"I don't know. I'm pretty busy."

"Maybe you'll have to. Nights like this can be very expensive."

"Oh, I don't go out too often," Danny said quickly. "When are you leaving Japan?"

"I don't know. By Christmas maybe. Or as soon as I figure out if the Japanese are right, aesthetically, to peel their fruit. Should I order more beef?"

"I'm fine. What will you do when you leave?"

"Fructify. Vindicate my life. More beer?"

"We've definitely got enough beer." One of the men behind the counter began excitedly to converse with a customer, a tumultuous interchange in which Danny was not only unable to extract individual words but could hardly isolate sounds; it was difficult to believe anyone's ears could decode it. "I wonder if I'll ever be able to speak Japanese."

"I'm in the park the other day," Greg began, drawing pieces of meat from the flames and depositing them on Danny's plate, "and there's this little girl, all got up. You know how they are here."

"The mothers dress them very carefully."

"Anyway she has this little puppy on a leash she's scolding away, a thousand words a minute. Giving the beast a really severe dressing down, mind. And I want to tell her suddenly, 'Honey, listen, I'm a smart guy, and a Harvard graduate, and I've been in Japan six months, and I can't understand a *word* you're saying. Now you don't figure your puppy dog can possibly understand Japanese, do you?' "

The anecdote, to Danny's dispersed wits, carried within it a hint of pathos, an echo of his own isolation; or at least that's what he saw in the first moment. In the next, its humor blossomed and he joined Greg on a beery swing of laughter. "Finish up," Greg said, his own glass drained. "I'm getting restless."

Greg paid the bill. He accepted the five-thousand-yen note Danny handed him, folded it neatly, and slipped it into Danny's shirt pocket. "I'm atoning for the little stunt I pulled your first night in Japan," he said.

"No, look . . ."

"And besides, I never split checks. You can pick up the next one."

Darkness had descended as they'd sat in the restaurant, and blinking panels and swirls of neon had transfigured the essence of the street. They drifted toward the city's night-heart, Gion, the neon signs thickening and growing more colorful, the sidewalks crowding with scurrying men—less leisurely in their pursuit of leisure than Americans—dressed in conservative suits and ties. Greg led him up a flight of stairs to something called the Cowboy Honky Tonk Saloon in whose dark interior, like nothing Danny had ever seen, lassoes hung from the ceiling, the black walls blazed with fluorescent cacti, a Muzak version of the theme from *High Noon* clip-clopped over the loudspeakers, and a diminutive and somber-faced bartender sported a colossal black cowboy hat. In the middle of the room sat a raucous party of twelve business-suited Japanese, all wearing cowboy hats. "What in the world . . ." Danny said.

"They're mad, absolutely bonkers, about cowboys here. I'll have to take you to the True Time Texas. They love me at the True Time."

Danny followed Greg to the rail of the bar, where Greg without consultation ordered sake for each of them.

"I don't like sake."

"You'll have to learn, Danny." It was perhaps the first time either had addressed the other by name, and the sound rang a little peculiarly in Danny's ears. "When in Rome," Greg went on, "drink what the Romans do, huh?"

"I don't know how they drink this stuff."

"You can order something else."

"I know." But this process of lament, of making it known that in his complaisance he was being put upon, offered its own satisfactions, and Danny added, "It tastes like medicine," though actually it seemed to carry little taste at all, only a pleasant heat as it slipped and expanded down his throat. "I still don't know how they drink the stuff," he pronounced, after a while.

"You don't like it heated, you like it cold," Greg said, and ordered a second, chilled pitcher. His face shone with delight, pure delight in overriding opposition.

"I'll tell you what I do like, I like having hills around Kyoto. There aren't any hills around Boston, no hills around Detroit."

"You hiked around in them much?"

"In what?" Danny said.

"In the hills around here."

"No." He revised: "Not yet."

"You're not much for hiking?"

"Oh no, no, I am," Danny said, with a vigor that went beyond any simple desire to correct a false impression; he wished to establish, for all his willingness to be led, that *here* was something—hiking, a passion for nature—at which he was not to be doubted or excelled. "I've spent a lot of time alone in a cabin in Northern Michigan. I once surprised a bear on a trail. A mother and two cubs, and she wasn't much farther away than that guy is now." The bartender met their stares by gravely tipping his hat.

Greg paid for both rounds of sake, calling it unfair that Danny should pay for what he didn't enjoy, and led him outside, where the neon seemed to burn still more brightly. They meandered through a maze of big bright primary colors that called forth from the innermost combs of Danny's mind a memory of primary school—the big glass jars of fingerpaints, the brightest red and blue imaginable, and in a time in your life when color was of such crucial significance, when the question "What's your favorite color?" had naturally been one of the first things you'd ask anybody . . . A memory which was linked—almost miraculously, it seemed, as if their minds were aligned in some fundamental way—with Greg's next remark. "You know, Japan's pretty much a dog's ass of a country, but it's a fabulous place to get drunk in, because they've built themselves a toyland, they really have. All these businessmen, these little boys, these Peter Pans. Look around," Greg was saying, a voice by Danny's ear, as the lights wheeled and flickered and dazzled, red and blue, green and yellow and pink, bursting, vanishing only to blossom, only to burst again in spectacular, harmless detonations. "It's Candyland. Did you ever play that game, a board game, the one with all the colors? It's nothing here but little boys running around in neat blue suits, with a few sweet-faced mamas in kimonos to pat them on the head." The pace around them seemed to have slowed, a loosening to have taken place that eased the eyes to marvel at the lights overhead.

"That's just what I was thinking."

"I'm a mind reader."

"I don't believe in that. E.S.P.," Danny said, though it was true that on numerous occasions, chiefly involving pretty girls in public places, he'd experimented with telepathic commands: *If you like me, brush your hair back behind your ear,* or *Lift your left foot on the count of three.* Meanwhile, barkers for nightclubs and discos with expensive cover charges cajoled them in mixed English and Japanese. In the doorway of one of these clubs—a different sort of barker entirely—stood a pretty girl got-up in a sheer white blouse and upon her narrow hips a puffy, lacy cross between hot pants and underwear. "Come *potty*," she giggled. "Come join the *potty*."

They wandered over to Shijō Street and crossed the bridge over the Kamogawa, where they'd run earlier in the day, its water rippling opulently under the spilled, versicolored oils of the city's lights. "I walk around a lot at night," Danny said, "and you see a lot of gaijin walking around here drunk. People would think we were them."

Greg laughed—that same unexpectedly high sound, that string of small acoustical bumps. "*Odd* they would think that. Appearances are so *misleading*."

"No, I just mean . . ." For there was indeed a distinction to be drawn, though presently an elusive one; Danny wanted to offer his own shrewd observation, something to match what Greg had said about the lights in Gion, which had seemed so perceptive. "I just mean . . ." Danny said, but the distinction was not to be articulated, even though it was perfectly apparent that at least *he* was not the same as all those distasteful red-faced figures. There was some mental unlikeness, some condensed kernel of self-consciousness, some awareness of the distinction that itself created the distinction—*some*thing that made the small difference that was in fact all the difference in the world.

"These Japanese, they take you for a foreigner, Danny, just because your hair is red," Greg said, and laughed again. "But the worst part is, they take *me* for a foreigner, and I was born here."

"Me too. On this very street."

"No. Truly. In Shikoku. My old man was in the service. I left when I was two and hadn't been back since. El Grego, spiritual pilgrim, I mean pigeon, I mean pilgrim, unquestionably I mean pilgrim, returns to the land of his birth."

God, this guy loves himself, a voice in Danny's head pronounced, with no trace of disapproval—indeed, in this expansive humor, with pleasure that it should be so. Off Kiyamachi Street, on the other side of the river, Greg led him up three more flights of stairs to a tiny bar and restaurant called Al Capone, on one wall of which a mural presented a black boxy twenties car, a woman in a flapper outfit, a man in a trench coat snuggling a submachine gun.

"How do you find these places?"

"I work at it."

"I should go home. I haven't been home all day."

Greg ordered for the two of them: whiskeys and water, which went down less easily than the sake had, scraping at Danny's thickened tongue. He knew he was not thinking clearly and for a moment—these absurd stage sets in a sense working—it seemed he was not in Japan but in some trendy place in Cambridge. He found his way to the tiny bathroom, its broken window open, the distant honking and blinking of lights reaching him through a filter of alcohol and fatigue, befuddlement and profound pleasure. He loved elevation like this: not to be pacing the crowded streets at ground level, honked at and stared at, but to be looking down victoriously from above, as from the window of a plane.

Yet upon returning to the table and discovering that Greg had ordered another round, Danny felt a skitter of apprehension, a sense that things were blundering out of reach, and that he would never get home, and that there was definitely something malign or at the very least half-mad in this grinning Harvard compatriot on the other side of the table. Remaining on his feet, Danny downed the drink at a single go and said, "Let's push. I don't like it here."

"Hold on. Have a seat."

"I'm getting restless."

Danny paid the check, perversely satisfied to discover that the drinks were absurdly overpriced. And the simple transaction itself (paying a debt in foreign currency, checking to see that he'd not been cheated, pocketing his change) provided him with an assuaging sense of competence and order. "I need a bus," he said, out on the street again.

"I think they stopped running. Whyntcha come over. We'll take a cab."

"I've got to get home," Danny said, but in the abrupt fluster when a cab pulled up he found himself clambering inside and within moments, it seemed, he was back where the drinking had begun, on the tatami-mat floor of Greg's musty room.

"I've got some lousy scotch downstairs. You want some lousy scotch?"

"No. Nothing."

"So tell me why you decided not to do your undergrad at Harvard."

"Oh I don't know, it's a long story." Danny lifted himself up on one elbow. A welcome cool clarity seemed to be perfusing through him, down from the crown of his head. "Actually, it's an interesting story. This kid named Lenck, Gary Lenck, who went to Greyfield, my high school, and who was two years ahead, he went to Harvard."

"And you disliked him so much," Greg said, laughing appreciatively at his own joke, "you went to Michigan to get away from him."

"No," Danny said, "no," shaking his head, at once resolving to tell the hideous story in complete detail, if only to sweep that amused look from Greg's face. "I went to visit him on my college trip, the fall of my senior year. He was a sophomore. He'd changed his major about five times and now he was majoring in psych and he'd been given a pigeon to study and everything. The day I showed up, he and I go out running. It was raining but he ran me up and down the Charles, miles we ran, I don't know how many miles. And then we went over to Hemenway with some boxing gloves. First we played handball, which he beat me at, and then he took out the boxing gloves and insisted we box right there in the squash court."

"Was he big?"

"Seemed so at the time. I was probably only about five eight then. I grew three inches my first year in college." Another story beckoned—how Danny had entered U. of M. the shortest of the four guys at the end of his dorm corridor and within the span of his vertiginous freshman year had ended up the tallest. Danny hesitated, then went on, "Lenck used to wrestle. My hands were so swollen from the handball I could hardly get the gloves on, but he wouldn't let me quit. Finally he caught me so hard on the ear, I fell down."

Why go into all this? What was the point? Yet that maddening grin was still locked on Greg's face, and Danny continued, "Then he helped me up, and we cleaned up, and he bought me this big steak dinner, and we smoked some dope, and went to this cheesecake place and we ate three pieces each. The following March, I heard . . . Anyway, he went out one night . . ." The bunching muscles in Danny's throat had dwindled his voice to a scratchy whisper. "Anyway, he went up William James Tower with a bowie knife"—the ghastly sound of *bowie knife* ripped open his windpipe, and the rest came with an almost reportorial ease—"and he slit open his stomach, *seppuku* style, they found all sorts of blood up there, and then he jumped through a window."

"Oh my God I dimly remember this! When would this have been?"

"March of seventy-four. You didn't know him?"

"No, no. I read about it in the *Crimson*. I remember they attributed his suicide to the lack of a Croatian Student Center, or the closing of the men's bathroom in the basement of Lamont, or whatever their asinine cause of the moment was." Greg—irritatingly—laughed again.

"Probably. Anyway, a month later I got into Harvard and I said, Hell with it, I'm not going. You got to remember, I'm only sixteen. My Dad hit the roof. I still remember: he called me a chicken shit. The whole thing's kind of a depressing topic. A chicken shit. I don't know why I brought it up."

"You brought it up," Greg proclaimed in an authoritative voice; he was now lying with an arm crooked over the top half of his face, shielding his eyes from all light. What time was it? "You brought it up because today, with its jogging and beef for dinner and drinking, reminded you. I reminded you subconsciously of your friend Link with the bowie knife. Linked to Link you might say."

"Lenck," Danny corrected. "No, no I don't think so," he protested, even as he recognized that the similarities were too striking to be denied. It was an unfortunate association, tying Gary Lenck—who, though terminated forever at nineteen, in Danny's mind continued to age alongside him, to remain a sort of dim older cousin—to this other person, in whose dirty room Danny now lay. Though Danny worked and drove himself hard, and took security in doing so, there were kinds of drive, tinged with desperation, that did not merely depress but frightened him. One or two of the associates at Huck, Meadows had frightened him.

"Your old man," Greg said, arm still crooked over his eyes, "was pissed you didn't go to Harvard. Mine was pissed I did."

"Where did he want you to go?"

"A small, recently-turned-coeducational institution on the banks of the Hudson." Greg's speech was slowing, but that fussiness—with its suggestion of an endless skein of tiny private jokes—was if anything more pronounced. "West Point. Both my old man and my brother, to whom I am related only by blood, are former cadets. Of course Harvard meant communism, defense budget cutters, queers, Kennedys."

"My Dad's a Republican; my Mom's a Democrat."

"You know what my father said the last time I spoke to him, a couple years ago?"

"Where was this?"

"South Carolina. I'd gone home to see my old lady after her lobotomy. Hysterectomy. Excuse me, hysterectomy. Anyway, you know what the old man says? This is a great detail, the really great de*tail*. Now you're thinking he said this as some kind of joke, or at least, at least with some redemptive gleam of irony in his eyes, but no, he was all systems go, he was imparting paternal wisdom." Greg lifted his arm from his eyes to peer at Danny, and his voice plunged into a gassy pomposity. "He said: If right after college, 'stead of all this tramping round the world, you'd gone into the service, son, you'd have two, three years under your belt." Greg's cracking, elongated laugh lifted the vein on his forehead back into prominence. "Oh no, but that's not the best part, the priceless detail is when he appeals to my sound business instincts. 'You like to travel, the service'll let you see the world, and pay you for doing it.' "

"You've been traveling since college?"

The glazing hold of reminiscence was powerful, and it took Greg a moment, eyes swimming back into focus, to answer. "Most of the time."

"What country'd you like best?"

"Oh God, you're going to make me get up, huh? And I'm so comfortable on this floor."

"Why do you need to get up?"

"It's so pissing *rude* of you to make me get up." Groaning theatrically, Greg rose and shuffled over to the world map on the wall. "A geography lesson," he began. "Now here I am, just out of college, still young enough to believe that old age and illiteracy foster wisdom, and I went here"—he pointed to Mexico—"where I ate lots of magic mushrooms and discovered that all my holy men spent their nights cadging cigarettes and watching dubbed American cartoons on TV. All very disillusioning, and I had the runs for two months besides. Mexico was no go; we can cross it off the map." Greg drew an *X* with his index finger across Mexico. "Over to England. Now what I adore about England is the way nobody understands how the empire collapsed decades ago. Com*plete*ly unaware that the phrase *Look at England* is used throughout the modern industrialized world to mean 'Look how a well-educated, powerful and illustrious nation can sink into financial and political decline.' The Americans, the prosperous Dutch and Germans, the ascendant Japanese, all are saying, as a kind of warning to themselves, a talisman, *Look at England*. But the women are deliberately so dumpy and the food's so awful—you know they actually eat french fry sandwiches over there? I've *seen* it. So we can cross them off the map.

"And I went to Germany, where I was attacked by a, really, no kidding, honest to God, a German shepherd, and to Yugoslavia for a while, but for reasons as repugnant as they are vile and obvious we can cross them off the map. And to Crete, where I was cheated so frequently and so clumsily, and where I had to pay a policeman a ten-dollar fine for playing a harmonica, we can cross it off the map. Hell, we can cross old Europe off the map.

"And then our El Grego Figure went to Kenya, where he caught malaria, despite the pills he'd been given, and lay huddled in some mud hut for days waiting for visions of Kilimanjaro, and where they've slaughtered all the animals and are busy putting up pizzerias in the veldt, we can cross Africa off the damn map.

"And now things begin to turn a little grim . . ." Under the glaring lights this recital was occurring in a kind of blur for Danny, who listened in wonderment, for it seemed a virtuosic feat merely to be able to dredge up these distant words—cadge, ascendant, talisman, veldt. "And a sense of expansive angst enters the breast of our fair but dark hero. The world is souring. The realization dawns that what you can't say, what none of the magazines can say, is actually true and most countries really are unspeakable *holes.* I'm speaking strictly mathematically now. Crap, all the crapmakers, are everywhere closing in, you could actually chart it on a graph. So it's off to India, months and months, feeling in all that heat and dust that you've come at last to some taproot of humanity, but the sheer lousiness, the beggars and all the blind people, I'm not speaking metaphorically, if you've never been to India you can't imagine how many blind people there are, with these little flies crawling around their eyes, and you're picking up all kinds of stomach parasites you may never be able to get rid of, oh God no you've got to get out of there, we better cross India off the map. And Nepal, too, beautiful as it is, has got to go. Too many potters."

"Potters?"

"American potters. Insufferable, Jesus. And now our pilgrim, though fully aware that the age is long gone when a young man crossed the sea to make his fortune, returns to the land of his birth, land of the Rising Sun, only to discover it's a humorous mirror, and there really is a country that beats America in a one-on-one Crassness Competition, in mammon chasing, in the pursuit of ugliness. So what the hell, I'm tired, we can cross Japan off the map too." Greg's clumsy erasing swipe grazed the map, ripping one of its top taped corners from the wall. Precariously, the world leaned forward, ripe to fall.

"And what about the United States?" Danny asked, sorry to have this tour come to an end.

"The United States . . ." Greg repeated, his search for the fitting, conclusory phrase almost palpable in the air. "I don't see how anyone who really *loves* America, as I do, could bear to live there, do you?" he asked triumphantly. Exuding satisfaction, Greg returned to his spot on the bedding and—the world all but obliterated behind him—again slotted his arm over his eyes. Danny regarded him enviously. The only foreign country Danny had visited before Japan (except Canada, which hardly counted to a Detroiter) was France, the summer after high school, where he'd spent a homesick six weeks during which he'd written Penny more than thirty letters and received only ten in reply. Drawing on some intuited but unformulated connection to this geography lesson, Danny began to talk about his summer at Huck, Meadows, and about Hayden Corbin, twenty-seven, who truthfully worked eighty hours a week, and who without any redemptive gleam of irony in his eye had explained that his life's ambition was to be able to do "tax by telephone," to know the Code and the Regs so well he could advise a client on the spot.

And with the same sense of lurking analogies, but far too tired to roust them out exactly, Danny moved from Hayden Corbin to Grandpa Jaynes who though dying with emphysema had bought the cabin in Northern Michigan he was too sick to visit himself, and so it had fallen on Danny to bring the old man photos of the place, which Grandpa had taped—that detail, even now, was heartbreaking—into a scrapbook. "He believed in ghosts," Danny added.

An inner uncoiling was what Danny felt himself undergoing as he poured out words to the prone figure on the other side of the room whose occasional grunted assents were the sole proof of wakefulness. He told Greg about Mom's anguished string of miscarriages before he'd at last been born. He told Greg about his parents' long-standing marital problems, and how he'd met his father at a Tigers game hand-in-hand with a dumb-looking woman whom Dad introduced, the need for an outsize lie igniting his imagination, as "my friend Eddie's fiancée," and then how Dad and the girl had both swung round, combing the stands for the missing Eddie. And from there Danny turned to Penny, and the endless fight they'd had senior year in high school, he determined not to graduate a virgin and she equally determined to hold him off, and how he'd won out only to discover from weeping Penny (one of the three or four worst shocks of his life) that while still in junior high she'd been seduced by her twenty-year-old cousin. Oh those tears of hers!—and how in his ignorance he'd misinterpreted them, and tried to console her for his pushiness, his monstrous need to violate, only to have the truth by fits emerge, and the ground give way.

"Junior *high* school?" Greg said. "She was just a kid, she didn't know what she was doing."

"Oh, but she did," Danny cried with some passion. "People do, but say they don't," he added, abruptly wishing he'd had far less to drink, for he yearned to convey, as cogently as was ever possible with something so nebulous and intricate, his conviction that it was the expression of powerlessness that itself created the powerlessness, that this was merely one more means of avoiding one's true freedom. Danny was rambling; the distinction was quietly evading him, elusive as a deer slipping into the woods' perfect camouflage. He told Greg about his vastly ambitious hope to return to law school and write his third-year paper on this very issue, the interlaced relationship of law and punishment and responsibility and free will, and then, distressed to hear himself sounding so vague and perplexed, concluded with an absurd request for Greg's assistance: "You know, any thoughts you might have."

A pause followed. Greg's measured reply was completely unintelligible. "You know, things go in cycles. But I'm thinking better these days. The networks are there. Progress can be made, I never, or almost never, doubt that." Was Danny making this little sense to Greg? It was very late. "I better go home," Danny said.

"You better stay here. We got to get up by seven if we're going hiking tomorrow in the mountains. There's a pillow and a blanket in the corner."

Had they agreed to go hiking tomorrow? Spent, confused, still reeling in that zone wherein every few minutes the mind announces, *Now* I've sobered up, Danny took the pillow and blanket and, curling up around the perfect circle of sleep, dropped into its center.

"It has struck me as ironic that the dead live in much the best neighborhood in Kyoto," Greg called over his shoulder. "Not only the quietest, which admittedly owes a lot to the lifestyle they keep, but also much the best view."

They had come, though not as early as Greg had predicted, to the abrupt edge of the city's eastern hills. Skirting around Eikandō Temple, its pagoda in the grainy morning light an apparition of an earlier age, they'd found beside and behind it a listing, terraced graveyard.

Greg had explained how a backpack was at once indispensable for a trip of this sort and much too embarrassing for himself to wear ("A moustached American wearing a backpack as he wanders off into the Kyoto hills? I'm afraid I just can't . . .") and the duty had fallen on Danny ("At least you don't have a moustache"). In fairness to Greg, he had provided all the supplies, which consisted of bread, cheese, two bottles of Kirin, pears, four donuts, and two books: *Japanese in 6 Weeks* for Danny and the *Portable Jung* for Greg.

Taking stock of his condition, Danny this morning was feeling less hung over than he could reasonably have expected, but heavy-limbed nonetheless, and badly in need of a shower. He sensed, besides, that he'd revealed far too much the night before to a near stranger, and he'd spent much of the morning trying to elicit some equivalently intimate nuggets of information. Danny had not had much luck, though he had discovered that Greg hadn't been quite the vagabond since college he'd suggested last night—he'd at least done a year, or most of a year, of graduate work in English at Virginia. Greg had majored in philosophy at Harvard and had received a *summa* for his thesis on Berkeley. Harsh morning light as they'd sat in a coffee shop had revealed how Greg's hair was graying as well as thinning and how a tracery of wrinkles seamed his forehead and the skin over his high cheekbones. He looked older than twenty-eight. A random question now ("How do you finance all your traveling?") produced what Danny had been seeking: that fussy, syncopated, elliptical style of talk, laced with self-satisfaction, which meant Greg had been launched on one of his narratives.

"My paternal grandfather, whose name I'm not kidding was Theophilus Boyce Blaising, had made a little money, and this is an extremely appropriate place to be talking about it. He was an undertaker in Massachusetts and when he passed away, some of the money left after his incredibly splashy funeral, really a shame the old mule had to miss it, came my way. Fifty or sixty thousand good ones, though they're not actually handed over till I turn thirty. I get the interest now. Four or five grand a year."

"So you travel on inherited money," Danny said. It reassured him to feel that a generous legacy was in large part the reason why Greg had seen so much. When Grandpa Jaynes had died (so stubborn in his poverty, refusing to the end to take money from Dad and Mom), he'd left, free and clear, little more than thirty-seven pairs of trousers.

But Greg said, "Well, that's what I thought at first, that I needed the money. But I don't, I haven't been. If you're clever, you don't. You travel, you meet people manage to go all around the world on no money—tending bar in Sri Lanka, selling their blood in Taiwan."

"Selling blood."

"No, no it's no joke, the Taiwanese have some religious scruple about selling their blood. So the pay's quite good. I sold a couple gallons by the time I left. I can't *tell* you what a joy that was, to discover that I could get by, that the world wasn't going to require me to get a real job job. I mean dicking around, teaching English here, I make more than I spend, and I spend a lot. I think I promised last night to find you a teaching job."

"Actually I'm kind of busy."

"You're going to need it," Greg said, as he had last night.

"Were you close to your grandfather?"

"Hell no, that son-of-a-bitch." Pointing at Danny's face, evidently amused and delighted by the surprise registered there, Greg released again that high bumpy laugh, then said, "I'm convinced he did it just to piss off my old man. They really abominated each other. In any case, it really did piss off the old man, who used to look forward, with what was really ugly glee, to the day I'd graduate and have to face the real world. Instead, I've been traveling all around the world, which apparently, God knows why, is not facing the real world at all."

The two of them were the only ones in the cemetery but everywhere one saw signs of recent ministrations—fresh flowers, raked pathways, swept and washed stone monuments. There were figurines of Buddha, his slitted eyes closing upon an indwelling bliss that outwardly resembled mere sleepiness, and marvelous stone lanterns that were a little like armored helmets, fit for a battle of Goliaths.

"You were talking about some grandfather last night, maybe."

"My Mom's dad," Danny said. "He died just a few years ago." It was perhaps the dimming but still revered ghost of Grandpa Jaynes that had brought to Danny's face the surprised look which Greg had found so funny. For Danny had loved that enfeebled old plodder, a master of stretching a dollar and yet someone forever discovering bargains he didn't need but couldn't bear to pass up—hence the thirty-seven pairs of trousers.

"In the last years of his life he bought a cottage—really no more than a shack—in Northern Michigan. When he was a young man he'd gone up there, from Tennessee, to make his fortune I guess, which he never did make, but later he was really too sick to get up there. I was almost the only one who ever went. It was beautiful, deer everywhere, and that bear I told you about, and fireflies, thousands of them. My parents sold the place after he died. I couldn't believe they would do it, but they did." In fairness, it was true no one ever used the place, once Danny'd headed off to law school, and when a falling branch eventually stove in the roof it was weeks, maybe even months, before the damage was discovered. Still, it was hard to believe they would let the place go. He and Greg had now reached the last tier of graves. Above, unbroken behind an overgrown verdancy, lay the hill.

"There's a path here," Greg said. "Somewhere."

Following, Danny scrambled up through branches, needles, webs, on a path so overgrown at times it seemed no path at all. The ascent was steep and the ground in places wet and friable, willing to uphold their weight only long enough for a new foothold to be planted further up the hillside, and sometimes not even that long as (in a cascade of needles, pebbles, clods) hands would suddenly have to lunge out for an anchored branch or root or stone. The soft smell of earth filled his lungs. Here and there sunlight caught a web glancingly, its strands resembling those scratches on a cleaned pane of glass which alone inform the eye of the existence of an interjacent medium. The steep gradient had canted the trees downhill, and Danny felt himself vaguely pointed at, his heart pointed at, while he felt rising within his chest a pleasure he'd not known since arriving in Japan, since before he'd gone to work in New York. Faint but ubiquitous, unseen insects had set up a clockwork rattling and tapping, all of it somehow pitched at an unfamiliar tempo: an Oriental woods, it seemed, lying enclosed within a variant range of hours, minutes, seconds.

The very sunlight itself seemed to be tumbling where, all of the same height, a colony of gold-tinted ferns streamed down the hillside in a fluid simulacrum of a waterfall. A crow called from further up, beckoning, and another scrambling climb toward a promised ledge brought them, to Danny's surprise, to a second large graveyard. On their left, a wide trail wound down the hill. "We could have come up that way," Danny said, "if we knew where the path begins."

"I do. But I didn't feel like it."

Here there were a good many Christian graves, the crosses thicker-limbed than Danny was used to. There was also—a macabre "great detail" which Greg pointed out—a mailbox into which visitors put business cards as a show of duty done. Danny found the Latin-inscribed gravestone of a nun and he was able to piece together the sketchy endpoints of a life: born in Belgium more than a century before, died here in Japan in 1914, the year of Europe's Great War. Already she'd been dead longer than she'd been alive.

Behind the graveyard lay another path, broad and level, and they set off briskly, the bulk of the hill now shielding them from the sounds of the city. Their path crossed other paths whose termini were indicated by Japanese characters (which neither of them could read) painted or incised on low stone markers. Danny followed along contentedly enough, though Greg didn't seem to know where they were heading.

Their ultimate destination, if any, being left to Greg, Danny could give himself wholly to the task of absorbing his surroundings. The air smelled marvelous—preponderately of pine, but with a hundred other odors tucked in below. It was amazing just what a pure gold—as if flushed completely of any vestige of green—some leaves could assume in the right angle of sun; with others, their green made greener, you'd swear they had to be wet to wear such a gloss. At each of their path's bifurcations Danny, moving on a heady tide, felt himself contrarily tugged, a frustrating but familiar sense that each path not followed meant some rare and irreplaceable loss—some vista missed, some harmonic clump of trees, some rare conjoining trick of bird-flash and -cry. It was an old desire, a yearning to hold in his hands a sort of comprehensive map of lovelinesses (Mother Nature's very own) which would guarantee he missed not a single gemmed toadstool. What had he been thinking, how had he waited this long to get up into these hills?

Greg proved a satisfyingly untalkative companion. With a bamboo rod plucked from some undergrowth he mutely pointed out tiny constructions of interest: a red clump of moss; a vast spiderweb, and the spider itself, yellow and black candy-striped like a hornet, with a garnet daub on its belly; a particolored lichen-spattered rock, reminiscent to Danny of "The Rock" in Ann Arbor, that boulder which the competing fraternities repainted nightly during football season, coat upon warring coat; a blue-black feather. Clouds and the trail's loops and declivities took them by turns from shade to sun in a continuous interplay of brightness and greater brightness. The city, never clearly visible through the trees, now lay well below, its diminished din become the heartening susurration and pebbly clatter of a river.

After a time they turned off what seemed to be the main path, down a rocky trail so steeply pitched it was easier to run in a kind of speeded duckwalk than to walk. Danny's footwork soon accelerated into a headlong pursuit on blurred stone steps and the likelihood that if Greg were to trip Danny would fall with him. Then the ground eased, their footing was their own again, and they came to a spring where three metal cups waited for them on a plastic platter. Greg filled one and passed it to Danny. "Water from the bowels of the earth," he said and laughed. It was the first time either had spoken since leaving the graveyard.

Danny waited, his fingertips cooling against the cup, the water sweetly heavy in his hand. Lifting a second cup, Greg said, reviving Dad's toast, "Up and down." Danny laughed appreciatively: Greg really *did* have style. The water was so cold it hurt—a satisfying momentary ache at the roots of one's throat.

"Whatcha do to the palm of your hand?" Greg asked.

Danny's left hand, lying open on his thigh, at once curled into a fist. Having revealed so many confidences the night before, he was not about to disclose anything further, and offered instead the standard explanation: "I fell into a fire a couple of years ago."

"Injury prone, huh?"

"Not really."

"I've got about fifty stitches in my face alone. Tell me they don't show. This one does, though. Looks like tooth marks, doesn't it?" Greg pointed to a scar over his right eye that Danny had noticed before.

"Yes it does."

"Well that's what it is. When I was in college I spent a Christmas vacation up at this crazy guy's, Freddie Fielder's, in Connecticut, who played on the lacrosse team with me."

"What team?"

"Harvard's."

"The varsity?" Danny asked doubtfully.

"Mm. I was on it four years."

"Did you letter?"

"Mm. Twice."

This information called for a reappraisal, a lifting of several notches of respect from Danny, who had seen Greg run and hadn't thought him especially athletic. Though he'd never seen a lacrosse match, and didn't even understand the rules of the game, Danny knew Harvard's was among the best teams in the country. It occurred to him that Greg might now be lying.

"Anyway, after too much of his old man's whiskey Freddie and I went skating on this pond at night and we decided to play chicken, skate as fast as we could at each other and see who'd stop first. Neither of us quite stopped in time, and his upper teeth hit me right here." Greg tapped his brow.

"His teeth were knocked out?"

"Oh, he lost a lot of teeth. I don't think his, incidentally quite beautiful, mother ever forgave me. She ended up throwing me out on Christmas Eve," Greg said, eyes shining, evidently delighted that she'd felt it necessary to do so.

The hike back up the stone path was slow and effortful, and brought to Danny, whose body never sweated much, a cooling film on the back of his neck. Greg a few steps ahead sweated easily, and his white T-shirt clung translucently to his hairy back. "Tell me about your family," Danny said, and Greg began, a bit breathlessly though less histrionically than usual, to talk about the places where he'd lived (California, Virginia, New Hampshire, South Carolina), about his brother, for whom he indeed seemed to have no use, and his mother, who, notwithstanding his harshness ("she's basically a moron"), seemed to stir some exasperated but profound affection. Her unforgivable offense seemed to be her marrying and staying married to Greg's father, who on at least a couple of occasions had beaten her. "I just abominate that sort of thing, I really do, the physical bullying. The old man used to beat me too, bare-ass with a belt, the son-of-a-bitch, and I never was a kid could take to beatings with resignation, you know how some kids can, as something they deserve. I *knew* even then I didn't. I mean honestly, do I deserve to have some moron with a belt walloping the crap out of me? When I was twelve or thirteen I told him next time he beats me I'm going to get him with a knife while he's asleep. He beat me for *that*, you can believe, but I'd scared him, I'd really scared him, and in the long run I must say it cooled his disciplinary ardor." Greg's long laughter brought tears of pleasure to his eyes.

A little uneasily, Danny joined this laughter; regardless of anger, no one in his family *ever* described another in such terms (Mom had seen to that), not even when he and Dad used to fight so bitterly in high school, or when Dad and Grandpa Jaynes had one of their rare, powerful quarrels. "I'm getting hungry," Danny said.

"Wait. We're almost there."

"I didn't know there was a destination."

"Oh indeed, indeed a destination."

If—and this was an old line of thought for Danny, apt to arise whenever he ventured into unfamiliar terrain—if, somehow, he had been instantly whisked from Cambridge or Detroit to this very trail, with no knowledge of where he was, would he suspect that he'd landed in Japan? Would he know, at least, that he wasn't in America, in South Carolina, say, Greg's home state, where bamboo and kudzu flourished? It seemed he surely would know, but there was no single, isolable tree or plant of which he with his limited botany could say, "This grows only in the East," or "This is Japanese." There was instead only a cumulative impression of foreignness—that sense of the insects' having set up an alternate horology, everything tipped and turned into a queer, convolute Eastern intricacy, different tenors in the bird cries. Or was this merely in his mind? Wonderful, in any case, this luculent weave of sun and leaves, sweat and hunger, ten minutes' wandering spiraling into another ten. "Well yes," Greg said. "Here we are."

Danny for a moment did not know where he stood. They were on a hilltop from which trees had been sheared to expose below, greatly before them, the whole of Kyoto. Danny was installed at the top of Mount Daimon, above the highest tip of that star-shaped character—大 —etched upon its slope.

Kyoto lay outspread like a voluminous harbor, the pantiled roofs of its papery houses lapping to the edges of the hills that embayed it on three sides. The city thrived within a haze of its own making, dust and smoke and dirt, and by means of an enfranchising distance this haze had become a magical veil. Flashes of light—pale silver, like the first stars in a still-blue sky—glinted from beneath this veil and from beneath it, as well, emerged a kind of submusical scraping, a sound of metal planes and glass planes, miles long, rubbing one upon the other.

"Now this doesn't completely suck, does it?"

"It's wonderful," Danny said. "It's really wonderful."

"There's this hopefulness at times—isn't there?—this sense that the world is big, and the people and the forces that ruin everything just can't get to it all."

"Surely you can't object to *this* one," Greg said and Danny answered, "No, this one's okay. I've noticed it before."

When Danny had earlier mentioned his plan to visit a used bike shop, Greg protested with an unexpected urgency. "Hell, you don't need to *buy* a bicycle, you've just got to be resourceful. Resourcefulness is key, it's what makes splurging the rest of the time excusable." So at Greg's suggestion, and armed with tools and a repair kit borrowed from Greg's landlord, the two of them had come down to the river in search of abandoned bicycles.

Though Danny had read in his *Mainichi Daily News* about the problem of abandoned bikes, and had seen them himself every time he'd walked along this river, he accompanied Greg (who was walking a bicycle he claimed to have salvaged from a garbage heap) with little enthusiasm, convinced that in the end the bike shop would be the answer. Most of the bikes along the river were much too small or were stripped and rusted skeletons, and Danny had refused to consider the three or four newer-looking possibilities Greg pointed out, which were not clearly abandoned. Then, "Surely you can't object to *this* one," Greg said, of an old, seatless, red one-speed lying on a gravelly islet in the river and Danny said, "No, this one's okay."

Splashing in over their ankles, the two of them hoisted the bicycle from the river and up the bank to the flat causeway. The back tire was low but sound, while the front, to which a sodden paper bag clung, was completely flat. Greg flipped the bike upside down, resting it jointly on its handlebars and the rod upon which its seat had once sat. He spun the pedal with his hand, which set the rear tire lazily revolving, and pulled back to test the brakes. He gave the front wheel a push and studied its flow. "The front tire's whacked out of shape a bit, but she'll do," he reported and handed Danny a tool that seemed a cross between a wedge and a screwdriver. "Let's get a look at the inner tube."

Danny regarded the tool doubtfully, then placed its tip under the corded rim of the outer tire and tugged. The tire did not pop free, as it was supposed to, from the metal rim.

"Don't you know anything about bicycles?"

"Not much," Danny said.

"I thought you told me you were an Eagle Scout."

"Most of my merit badges were in things like scholarship," Danny said. "And nature. I can identify ten constellations."

"You can teach me some time." Greg took the tool back and within moments, driving it in a brisk circle, had the whole tire detached from the rim on one side. He drew the inner tube out from the other side, set it on the ground and inflated it with a hand pump, then carried the tube down to the river to submerge it in search of punctures.

Apparently there was only one. Greg dried the tube on the thigh of his jeans, which left an ashy smudge, arranged it once more on the ground and applied a bit of sandpaper to the punctured area, so the glue would bite. The patch was self-adhesive and he pressed down hard with the heel of his hand. "Here, I've got something you can do," he said. "Stand on this a while."

So Danny stood on the patch while Greg went to search along the cluttered shore. All sorts of foragers had come down to the river on this cool October day: an old fisherman in red waders, three little yellow-capped children looking earnestly for God-knew-what, a crow, and a couple of wheeling herons—whose name in Japanese, *sagi*, Danny had recently learned and would have no trouble remembering, as it sounded so much like *soggy*. It was a shame the language did not offer more of these natural mnemonic handles, for Danny was disappointed in how slowly his progress came, and disappointed in himself for studying so little these past few days.

Greg returned with a pleased expression on his face, a bicycle seat in one hand and a clump of metal that turned out to be a bell in the other. "Hell, I don't need a *bell*," Danny said.

"All deluxe bicycles have bells. They're instrumental to the ensemble." Greg really was adept with tools and in a matter of minutes there it actually stood: a bicycle. A rusty clinker, to be sure, but one equipped with two solid tires, a seat, a cleaned and oiled chain, a bell, and even a battery-powered light. "Go ahead. Give it a try."

Expecting everything to collapse beneath him, Danny settled his weight charily onto the seat. It seemed secure. His left leg dipped, and then he was riding—riding for the first time in over a year, since the summer before last when he'd worked in Detroit—riding a bicycle salvaged and pieced together out of Kyoto's Kamo River! "I should pay you for it," Danny called over his shoulder.

"You can buy me lunch," Greg called back. He had mounted his own bicycle and they were heading south along the river. The breeze was delicious.

"We already ate lunch."

"A *sunakku* then." Pitifully scant though Greg's Japanese was, he'd picked up quite a few of these crazy loanwords—like *miruku* for *milk*, or *sunakku* for *snack*—which he found endlessly entertaining. "Follow me."

Most bicyclists in Kyoto respected all traffic signals, but a sizable number—and Greg was one of these—did not. Danny on his wobbly but triumphantly serviceable bicycle wound in pursuit through a maze of cars, scooters, poisonous trucks and buses, pedestrians and other bicycles, down Imadegawa to Higashiōji, down Higashiōji to Gion, where they parked at last and Danny followed Greg upstairs into a fruit parlor. The waitress, a pretty though broad-shouldered young woman, appeared to know Greg and she, too, like Matsumoto the beer seller, greeted him with anticipatory mirth. "*Ookii*," Greg said, and held up two fingers.

Danny sat down and picked up the plastic-shielded menu. "What did you order?"

"Bigs. Two bigs."

"I know the Japanese for *big*. Two big whats?"

"Two big fruit salads with extra papaya."

"Where's it on the menu?"

"Beats me. Can't read the menu."

"But the menu's in Katakana," Danny said. "Most of it."

"Can't read it. Can't read any of it."

"You don't read Hiragana either? How do you get around?"

"Handsomely. With grace."

"That's crazy, you could learn in a couple hours," Danny said. "Kanji, now that would take you years to master, but Katakana and Hiragana are phonetic—they're a snap. I'll loan you a book."

"You don't understand, I don't want to learn. I *want* to be illiterate," Greg said. "I regard this as a real opportunity. You know how you're always hearing how millions of Americans can't read and literate people can't imagine what it's like. Well *I* can, I've lived here half a year as an illiterate. Can't read a damn thing."

"It's a dubious honor."

"It doesn't mean I haven't learned scads about the country." Their fruit salads arrived—an enticing, generous arrangement of apple, orange, persimmon, grapes, papaya, and pear. Danny liked this word *scads*, which Mom often used. "You can learn a lot from me. I can save you a lot of trouble. For instance, they blowtorch the tofu in the morning. To brown it. You didn't know that, did you?"

"Do they really? I didn't know that."

"And I can tell you right at the outset that all the 'old Japan' stuff, the talk about Japanese spirituality, is pure crap, is just something they perpetuate to make themselves feel better for what they've done to their country.

"No, I'm not *kidding*," Greg went on, in response to Danny's smile. "Have you been to Ryōan-ji, perhaps the most famous—"

"The one with the stones. Not yet."

"—the most famous temple in Japan? The apotheosis of Zen and all that. Well, you know they've installed a loudspeaker? They've installed a booming loudspeaker that repeats a million times a day, *This is a sacred temple dedicated to silent contemplation*. The reaction of any sane person is to say, This is a tasteless parody, one of those racist fake-sophisticated pieces the Harvard Lampoon, on which I served for a year, specializes in, but it's not. You're actually in the most famous temple in Japan. You don't believe me."

"I believe you about the loudspeaker. I didn't know you were on the Lampoon."

"Quit after a year. But you shouldn't misunderstand me. I don't mean 'old Japan' is any more of a fake than 'old-fashioned America.' They're both equally nonexistent. Vanished with a little click. Just like switching the channel. You want to know my favorite story in the world?"

"Put like that, I can hardly refuse."

"My favorite story in the world is that my mother can actually remember listening to people tap-dance on the radio. It wasn't a joke, *they didn't do it to be camp*. That's the amazing thing. People would sit down, listen to the announcer say, *And now we've got a special treat for all of you, sixteen-year-old Mary Jo Pepper from Tulsa, Oklahoma, dancing to Swanee River*, and then they'd listen: tch tch tch tchew, tch tchew, tch tchew, tch tchew." Greg rendered the tap dancer, as he had the radio announcer, with great gusto. His dark eyes were shining. "Can't you just picture it? My grandpa saying to my Mom, *That Mary Jo Pepper, she's quite the dancer*. Oh God, oh God, and people honestly try to tell you things haven't changed, people haven't changed, Japan's basically the same, America's the same . . . What else can I teach you? I can teach you about the *Bozoku* or whatever they're called."

"The motorcycle guys? The *Bōsōzoku*?" Danny'd frequently watched them thundering up the street in their black outfits, fluttering white headbands wound round their permanented heads and often on their feet, incongruously, a pair of women's shoes. He'd read recently in the *Mainichi Daily News* that the shoes were intended as a sign that they had girl friends—or at least experience with women.

"I call them the *bozos*. Anyway, they are your friends," Greg pronounced sententiously. "Your eye says, *Motorcycle gang*, and your mind replies, *Avoid them*—but in fact you embody everything they would like to stand for: drugs, licentiousness, disrespect for authority, unemployment. They will treat you kindly."

"I'll remember that."

"I've learned a lot here. It was an absolutely immense stroke of good fortune on your part to run into me."

"I think so," Danny said, trying to mirror the other's combined solemnity and facetiousness. "I'm already absolutely immensely grateful for the bicycle."

"Here's another truth. These people are less cynical than we are. It's immensely hard to see that, immensely hard for a cynical people to conceive that other people may be less so. And cynical people, if they also happen to be reasonably polite, think that to call another people uncynical is to call them stupid."

"I like that."

"You want another salad?"

"I'm okay."

"*Ookii*," Greg called to the waitress, holding up a single finger. "But how do we know, across the language gap, that they really are less cynical? We've arrived right at the heart of the matter, haven't we, and surely the first question whenever you're trying to understand anybody is whether it's big gaps or it's little gaps that separate people. Whether, to take the example everyone's apt to seize on as a child, what I call and see as *red* is what you call *blue*, whether we're close together or far apart, you see. And I'm afraid I'm a believer in big gaps."

Danny plucked a grapefruit seed from the tip of his tongue. He had at first taken all of this as another joke, but it seemed the conversation had taken an abrupt turn and he shuffled his wits to follow what Greg was saying.

"I have to, because I spend so much of my time just trying to communicate with myself. Just *that* is hard enough. My sleepy self, or my drunk self, or my stoned self, are forever saying, *Grego, you don't understand this whatever-it-is, it's more complex than you give it credit for.* Then my straight self is saying, *Yes I see what you mean about the whatever-it-is,* and then the other one is saying, *But you don't.* You see what I mean? If it really *is* big gaps between us, you probably don't."

"No, I think I see what you mean."

"It'll all come clearer after a while."

This was another of those remarks of Greg's—encouraging, unsettling—that seemed to lay some claim on Danny's future time. Greg's second fruit salad, no less painstakingly arranged than the first, was placed before him. "Do you think you'll move back to America?" Danny asked.

"*Inevitably, maybe, he said confusedly.* Honestly, I don't know. I mean I can't really go *any*where—can I?—until that map on my wall begins to look enticing again. *Speak to me, O Rand McNally.* But sometimes I do think I've sort of trapped myself. What am I going to do back in the States? I go back, I'm unemployed, I'm just a spoiled bum, whereas here I have a dignified role, I'm an *expatriate.* A sort of Hemingway expatriate seventies-style. Or eighties-style. What year is it?"

"Nineteen-eighty." Again Danny tried to match that playful solemnity.

"An eighties-style Hemingway expatriate, then, which means I still drink too much but I don't box and I don't suffer in silence."

"You could go back to school."

"Oh I've thought about it. Different schools. I even took the LSAT."

"When?"

"When I got back from Mexico."

"How'd you do?"

"Well."

"How well?" Danny, his own reassuring score poised on its high shelf, was looking for a number.

"Well enough to get into Harvard Law if my grades were better. But it does seem to me, to get to the *real* heart of the matter, that there's something valuable in all this—in traveling, in trying to figure things out, in pondering fecklessness. Obviously you think so too, or you wouldn't have risked things by taking a year off."

Greg had said something like this before, converting what was in truth a prudent move (any knowledge of Japan these days was extremely marketable; the people at Huck, Meadows had not only applauded the move but even intimated a willingness, which Danny had not pursued, to subsidize him) into some sort of venturesome spiritual quest. Nonetheless this mistaken view flattered Danny, and he did nothing to correct it.

This was flattery withdrawn somewhat, or transformed into mild ridicule, by Greg's next remark: "I mean I know what you're hoping, you're hoping that after this year off you can go back to law school as a *broadened person*, all set and ready to do a good, solid, bang-up, lawyerly job."

Actually, and perhaps quite insightfully, Greg had struck a vulnerable spot, for Danny *was* hoping this year was somehow going to change him. What precisely he was seeking he could not say (at least not yet), but these past several weeks, perhaps these past several months, he had increasingly come to sense that his life up until now had proceeded too regularly, a linear march from excellent school to excellent school. "I wouldn't have put it that way, but," Danny answered candidly, "I suppose that *is* what I'm hoping. And what about you—what are you hoping to do after you leave here?" Danny pressed again, and added, to cut off an escape route into levity, "I mean except fructify, which is what you told me last time I asked."

"Well of course I belong, you belong, and for the most part it is an advantage I suppose," Greg in his roundabout fashion began. Still, the sardonic look seemed to have left his features; he appeared to be speaking with an answering, if oblique, candor. "We belong to that generation that has resisted growing up more successfully than any in the history of America. I mean *ev*erybody goes to grad school, and then a couple of years to get your head together is almost *de rigueur*, and then there's always the honorable option of a couple more years to deprogram yourself, or to kick a bad drug habit. I mean most of us are still collecting an allowance from the parents at an age when our parents were giving an allowance to their growing kids—which is to say to us, isn't it? That's neat," he added in summation, addressing this to a wedge of pear held upright on his fork. "But you know there is some sense," he went on, still speaking to the pear, "that I'm going to have to do something. That's capitalized—Do Something. And of course the longer I, shall we say, gestate, the larger, the more magnificent, that something's got to be. I mean I hope you can see that I fully understand the piquant absurdity of my position. Eventually I've got to find some sort of lucrative job equal to my brilliance, my sense of humor, my absolute antipathy for work of any sort." Greg held out his fork so that the pear twirled six inches or so before Danny's eyes. "Aren't they extraordinary?"

"Extraordinarily expensive, too. It's a shame fruit costs so much in Japan."

"Oh, but you mustn't let that stop you. Even at twice or three times the price. Pears like this make you reappraise the universe."

"That's quite a pear."

"No, I *mean* that." Greg's gaze was uncomfortably serious and entreating—so much so that Danny's eyes fled upward to fix on the remarkable scar created by Freddie Fielder's lost front teeth. "That a pear as delicious as this would exist, that our palates would evolve over millions of years to appreciate it in all its delicacy—these things have to convince you of some underlying bounty or goodness to the universe. These rare affinities don't have to exist, it has nothing to do with evolutionary survival. It's one of those things like the existence of the clitoris, which of course doesn't *have* to be there, we could procreate quite nicely without it, that tells you the universe is good. Now I'll admit you don't have to feel that way about pears," Greg went on, picking up a segment of orange, "but it does seem to me that everybody, *ev*erybody ought to be enough of an epicure to notice that the blossom end of the orange is sweeter. You owe it to the *orange* to notice. You've eaten thousands of oranges in your life and I can tell by your face you never did notice that."

"Which end is sweeter?" Danny was entranced; he loved this sort of talk—drifting from the comic to the cosmic, wedding a pear to the nature of the universe—and his mind felt receptive and discerning. At the same time he'd been justly rebuked: hundreds, thousands of oranges down the hatch, and he'd never noticed there was a difference.

"The blossom end."

"I've eaten all my orange."

"We'll order some more. *Ookii*," Greg called to the waitress, holding up two fingers.

"I'm not getting off so cheap," Danny said. "This *sunakku* is going to cost me."

"Looks that way."

Danny liked the way Greg offered this, with no trace of apology—

an offhand assent, as though they were discussing something wholly external to themselves. Further, it seemed, in an instant's exchange of glances, that Danny's approval of this small stylistic point was conveyed, as well as Greg's converse appreciation of the way Danny volunteered no reassurances about being happy to pay the check. Again, this sense of an unvoiced understanding between them. And yet when only minutes later Danny mentioned something he'd read in the morning's paper—that a new study suggested Japan's GNP would exceed America's in fifteen years though Japan had but half the population—he misunderstood completely Greg's "That's depressing, isn't it?"

"I found it so." Only by moving outside America, to a prosperous country halfway around the world, had Danny come to understand how much he prized America's economic preeminence. He'd not yet understood this on that first night in Kyoto, when that screwy cabdriver (ironically, the only screwy cabbie he'd encountered in Japan) had whooped, "America number one, America number one." Crass, but rich—the richest country in the world. What else did we have to offer?

"It just means Japan's going to be more polluted," Greg said. "More complacent, even more money-mad than it is now."

"I suppose. But I meant it seems depressing from America's point of view." A pause followed. Greg had bitten a segment of orange in half and was presumably now registering whether it came from the sweet or the bitter end. "You don't think so?"

"I say, let somebody else wear that crown a while."

"It's the poor, you know, the blacks and the Hispanics, it's going to hit worst."

Greg meditatively placed on his tongue the remaining half crescent. "Oh no, no you're right in a way," he said, "and I'm being simplistic. I've certainly taken my share of comfort in this country's opulence. Especially at first. God, it was just like a dream at first, coming here after India and all. Here were all these non-Caucasian faces, and yet the people weren't beggars, they weren't sifting the feces out of their drinking water. They were builders of shopping emporia, importers of designer jeans from France! Christ, it was amazing! It was just as though you'd gone from America to some country inhabited only by blacks, or Hispanics, or some other group you've always had to feel guilty about, and you found they were richer than you were. Were drinking Chivas Regal in front of their big-ass color televisions. No, that was lovely all right. That was real lovely.

"And I started thinking better. About all of these things like big gaps and little gaps. I'd been granted a reprieve. I'm clicking up here." Greg tapped his head and dilated his eyes comically. "The mind is whirring and whirring and whirring."

"It is one of the great beauties of your country, Nagaoka-san," Greg was saying, "one of its durable charms, that there is no meal tax. I order something that costs a thousand yen, and the bill comes. Surprise!" Greg picked up a phantom sheet of paper and lifted his face in mock incredulity, at which Nagaoka-san, who could not be understanding much of this, broke into appreciative laughter. "The bill says one thousand yen. How strange. How inexplicable. One more trick of these inscrutable Japanese."

Although this was technically an exchanged English-Japanese lesson, to which Greg had tagged along (in his own words) as *mere spectator and eater*, Danny contentedly let the conversation turn under Greg's direction. In his muscles and nerves Danny was still feeling the vibrations of the run the two of them had taken today, now harmonizing with the sake's looser-strung hum. Somehow Danny had been under the misapprehension that Nagaoka-san did not drink, and each of their previous classes had been dry. Tonight it had turned out that Nagaoka-san, after initial apologies ("I am easily drunken"), took eagerly to alcohol, uproariously clapping his hands to summon replenishment. His face—as Danny had somewhere read was a common Japanese trait, genetically determinate—had flushed scarlet after the first cup, and exuberance had further disheveled his features. He was someone Danny had never seen before.

"Grego"—it appeared that Nagaoka-san, like Matsumoto the beer seller, thought Greg's true name was Grego—"you will be working also for Professor Umeda?"

"Oh no. Oh no. I am not qualified," Greg said with an almost abject obsequiousness. "Danny is very qualified. Danny worked this summer for the best law firm in New York City. More than two hundred lawyers."

"Two hundred lawyers," Nagaoka-san marveled. The figure had to seem extraordinary to a Japanese. Harvard Law School alone graduated as many lawyers each year as were admitted to the bar in all of Japan. "I don't know about the best," Danny said. "There are many—"

"Danny is very intelligent. He has learned to think like a lawyer. Say something litigious, Danny . . ."

"You talk too much."

"An open and shut case of libel. Or is it slander? Danny knows the difference. I daresay, Nagaoka-san, that Danny is the only person in Japan suitable to be assistant to the internationally famous Professor Umeda."

"Professor Umeda," Nagaoka-san repeated with a gravity that abruptly jolted into a giggle, a promise of merriment.

"Nagaoka-san," Greg said, leaning forward, "tell me what you think of Professor Umeda."

"What I think?"

"Your opinion."

"My opinion?" Nagaoka-san seemed thoroughly puzzled. "He is my Professor."

"What is his reputation?"

"Oh very good reputation. Of course. Very brilliant professor."

"You think he is brilliant?"

"Oh yes, very brilliant. But perhaps."

"Perhaps?" Greg wedged in. "He is perhaps—"

"He is perhaps very—" Nagaoka-san lifted his hands to form two parallel planes. The focus in his bloodied small eyes shifted fretfully from Greg to Danny, who was watching with fascination. "Very solid."

"Solid?" Greg echoed with perceptible disappointment. "What do you mean solid?"

"He has another name, from the students gave him. You say nickname?"

"Yes, nickname, that's right," Greg reassured. "What is the nickname the students gave him?"

"The students?" Nagaoka-san hesitated. Indiscretion had brought to his eyes a charged, childlike apprehension, and to his voice a quavering diminution as he divulged to Greg alone, "The students call him *Wah*."

"War?" Greg asked. "War?"

"*Waru*," Nagaoka-san attempted again, patting in explanation the simulated brick facade behind him "*Wah*."

"*Wall*," Greg cried. "Professor *Wall*. Now that's wonderful, isn't it, Danny?"

The name was funny, and irreverent in a way Danny wouldn't have expected from Japanese students, but more interesting still was the thrill Greg derived in this ferreting out of the nickname of a man he'd never met. There was something disconcerting in this, and it was with deepening dismay, in light of all his own babbling about Penny and Dad and Gary Lenck's suicide a few nights before, that Danny heard Nagaoka-san, under Greg's mellow promptings, explain how on a trip to the Philippines he and his friends had gone to a brothel. More distressing still—for Danny heard this with a presentiment that he could never entirely like Nagaoka-san again—were the comments Greg elicited on the subject of Japan's minority groups: both the Koreans and the aboriginal Ainu, Nagaoka-san claimed, could be identified by their smell. Nagaoka-san had become a pitiable, dismantled figure by the time the three of them stood outside the restaurant, and yet Danny resented the implicitly singular *you* in Nagaoka-san's "You and I must eat again soon" as he bowed toward Greg. In any case, Greg's reply was generous: "Yes, we'll all get together soon. You can arrange with Danny. *Sayonara*."

Sayonara they all called many times and (though it was unclear where anyone was heading) Nagaoka-san went one way and Danny and Greg the other, toward the river.

"You seem to have a knack for getting people to confide in you."

"I'm a good listener."

"I suppose that's part of it," Danny said.

"And?" There was perhaps a tilt of aggression to the question, and to the dark look Greg directed at him.

"I don't know." The sake's wayward effects had crept in a little, rendering less acute Danny's painful sense that of the two people he could remotely call friends in Kyoto, one had been revealed as an ugly racist, and the other—now walking beside him—intermittently seemed menacing. "But maybe there's something a little"—he dismissed serially *inhuman* and *cold*—"a little condescending about it."

"Condescending, Danny?" Once again the sound of his name sounded a little odd in Greg's mouth. "Now old Greg's got his faults, we'll agree, but *condescending*? Impractical? Yes. Demanding? To be sure. Competitive? You betcha. An incipient lush? A lecher? A lay-about? Yes. But *condescending*?"

"Where are we going?"

"I thought we'd go make fools of ourselves, trying to pick up some Japanese women. Of course the main and unanswered question is—Is it worth an extra grand to see bare breasts?"

Danny said, "What are you talking about?"

"Of course it is. Merely to phrase the question is to answer it. A mere additional thousand yen to see not one but two pairs of bosoms. Plus, incidentally, all the drinks you can drink."

Their destination turned out to be a place called Refinement: Premier Disco. The cover charge was ridiculously steep, three grand—nearly fifteen dollars—and Danny protested.

"Come on," Greg said, "you're forgetting my one fundamental life principle, namely, that the money in your pocket is an obstruction, impeding the flow of all the money that's trying to get in. Come on," Greg urged again, and Danny, loosened by drink, by embarrassment at the importunacy of the Japanese woman in the entrance who, lounging against the wall, broke into vociferous pidgin English when the two of them appeared, and by the lifting hope that with Greg beside him he might actually succeed at what he'd never been any good at—picking up a woman at a bar or a disco or a mixer—meekly paid his money and walked upstairs into an enormous room unlike anything he'd ever expected to see in Kyoto. Lights on the ceiling strobe-flashed and circled, scavenging over a dance floor where packed-in black-haired heads bobbed in one drowning collective mass. The music was loud enough to be felt viscerally, as a humming and thudding in the gut. Another wave of unhappy fatigue washed over Danny: he'd always hated places like this where you had to shout to be heard. He followed Greg up to the bar where they ordered screwdrivers, which turned out to be much too sweet, made with some mandarin orange-flavored drink, and which, at Greg's insistence, they guzzled in order to switch immediately to gin and tonics.

"Have you fallen in love yet?"

"Hm?"

"Lots of pretty women here," Greg pronounced.

Song drifted into song without interruption. Most were new to Danny, though all had English lyrics (of a sort—they'd apparently been composed by an illiterate) and were delivered in a familiar style, a kind of dissembled sexual pant:

What's that?
What's that in the mirror there?
Is that . . . my hair?
Or is that . . . your hair?

Greg went for new gin and tonics. A large gaijin woman wearing a blue one-piece bathing suit—an employee, evidently—stepped onto a kind of pedestal at the rim of the dance floor and began to flounce with clumsy energy. Nearer to where Danny stood, a spare young man, also a gaijin, wearing nothing but blue leotards and an open vest, stepped onto a second pedestal. His hairless chest shone in one of the ceiling's sickly blue lights. Standing motionless for a considered while, one hand perched on his jutting hip, regarding with sulky disdain the ordinary bodies below him, he broke suddenly into his own frenzied but deft cat-dance, stabbing with a transfixing finger at an imaginary companion as he sang:

You gave me the moon
And you gave me the sun.
I've got you on my fingers,
I've got you on my tongue.

Meanwhile on the dance floor's third pedestal, most distant from Danny, blossomed a fabulously exotic apparition: the first black he'd seen since arriving in Japan, a big-boned very dark woman in a two-piece lemon yellow bathing suit. She drew Danny's eyes with an almost physical power, as if pulling him from the jaw. Her bare shoulders and belly were besprinkled with sequins that caught the whirling light and flung it back as little glints—stars against her skin's ebony firmament—as she danced with a blend of grace and lassitude. How in the world had this woman ever beached up here, to a job as a dancer at the Refinement? It was an endless frustration for Danny, this hunger he had for the life stories of people he would never meet (a desire akin to that craving for a map of every rarity in the woods), this sense of despair at the absence overhead of any supervisory, celestial body of accountants and bookkeepers. "How about these two?" Greg asked him.

"What's that?"

Greg stepped before two Japanese women as they nudged by, and motioned the first, who was fairly pretty, onto the dance floor. This left Danny stranded before the other—a homely young woman, maybe still a teenager—who gaped at him with what seemed not only impatience but some dislike. Her hair was dyed that hennaed orange-brown so popular among what he'd come to think of as lower-class Japanese women, a color that never seemed to look right. To make things worse, she was wearing cowboy boots, another popular and unappealing fashion, and a miniskirt. Danny drained his drink, set it down inside an ashtray, and led her onto the floor.

The song plunged on endlessly and Danny was able, through a kind of backpedaling pushiness, to maneuver past the male dancer, who pointed suggestively—Danny's red head poking above the crowd—while mouthing the lyrics "Better you than me, better you than me," and over to the pedestal where the black woman, who had just taken off the top of her lemon yellow suit, continued her floating dance. Near-nakedness had not made her any more vulnerable or accessible. Sequined there as well, her breasts were huge, heavily lifting and dropping to a motion that lagged behind the lift and fall of her shoulders. What did they weigh, the breasts alone? he wondered, and uneasily pushed the thought from his mind. He felt nervous about staring at her body (it seemed impolite, though he recognized that such etiquette was ludicrous in a topless disco), and yet underneath such qualms lay a conviction, despite his inability to catch her eye, that they were complementarily allied, he and she, two foreigners, she unquestionably the darkest, he just as certainly the palest, person in the place. It was the mindlessness he always objected to when dancing to such deafening music. And to judge from his partner's face, as she swayed in her cowboy boots and miniskirt, she was equally bored.

You were the mountain I had to get on top.
Love was the motion we didn't want to stop.
The comedown was a letdown I don't want to be mean.
But you weren't even helpful you weren't even clean.

By the time the song had battered to its close Danny was sweating, less from exertion than from the maladroit press of anonymous bodies. He led his partner through a thrashing thicket of arms—for the music had started right up again—and secured new gin and tonics for her and himself. "Do you speak English?" he asked in Japanese.

She shook her head with a vehemence typical of someone expecting resistance. In her own language he said, "I speak Japanese a little," and went on, "The music is good?"

She nodded.

"The music"—he couldn't remember, his head being pounded so, the Japanese for *loud*—"is big, isn't it?"

Again she nodded. A long and it seemed to him uncomfortable pause lengthened. What his own duties were, whether he was free to abandon her, remained problematic. Greg and his partner were apparently still on the dance floor. The black woman had drawn the lemony top back over her starry breasts. The male dancer had taken off his vest. The smell of sweat—emergent animal bodies—fought with perfume. Over the thumping disco music a meaningless team of falsetto voices broke:

> We're criminals we're criminals
> They're pounding at the door.
> Do we make a run for it
> And hope to meet once more?
> Or are we going to let them find us
> Right here on the floor?
> Do me. Do me. Do me. Do me, now.

The drinks were weak and going down effortlessly. He asked her in Japanese whether she lived in Kyoto. Again she nodded. Had he been soberer, had she been prettier, or more intelligent-looking, had the night gone differently so far, had he felt less irritation with Greg for jamming him into this, had he not now felt an old reverberative sadness that places such as this usually inspired, he might have tried harder to entice her into conversation, if only to practice his Japanese; but in any case he needn't feel much guilt, for she certainly wasn't making things any easier.

Greg and his partner at last turned up, holding hands, which seemed to confirm Danny's own responsibilities: there was no abandoning this cowboy-booted woman now. The four of them stood for a while sipping new drinks and carrying on a word-and-hand-signals conversation while in the background the clumsy woman dancer in the blue one-piece covered her breasts again. Greg's partner was beginning to look a little prettier still, even if her laugh revealed deplorable teeth. She knew some English, though, and jabbing Greg in the ribs cried, "You are very funny man."

When the two women stamped off to the ladies' room in their cowboy boots, Greg called over the music, "You don't seem to be partaking of the spirit of the place, Dan."

"I don't know what we're doing here."

"We're drinking. We're making new friends. We're participating in the cross-fertilization of cultures. We're making whoopee."

"Neither one's very pretty. To say nothing of the fact that we can't understand what they're saying."

"But they seem to possess that unique, that peculiar grace—" Greg paused in finicky search for the right word; filtering through Danny's gathering vexation, his tiredness and drunkenness, came the marveling perception that even here, where he had to shout to do it, Greg was *talking funny*.

"You're crazy," Danny called.

"—that loveliness that transcends mere beauty: they're . . ."

But Greg's dramatic diminuendo failed him utterly: the summarizing epithet was lost in the din. "They're what?" Danny cried.

"Accessible," Greg bayed into his ear.

As Danny at last led his partner again to the dance floor he realized he didn't yet know her name, nor she his. Was she really accessible? Greg's observation had released into his thoughts a disheveling curve, and though he didn't find her at all attractive Danny did find alluring the disorderly notion that under the right fallings-out he could somehow (where? and what would it be like to kiss that mouth?) make love to her.

Long receding minutes were ground away under the music's endless thumping, under the tireless grimacing and gesticulating male dancer in his vest and leotards. And how had *he* beached up here? Curiosity was widening . . . "You have a good heart," Greg was telling his girl, tapping his own chest significantly, when Danny and his partner returned to their place at the bar. Danny felt another rise of resentful admiration, and with it a wholly unmixed distaste for the entire place: the watery drinks, the mindless music, the stink, the guy in the vest, the black woman who would not catch his eye. "I can tell you have a very good heart."

To Danny's great relief, his partner indicated that she had to go home. "I'll see her outside," Danny told Greg.

"Come on over tomorrow morning. We'll run all this off."

"Sure, see you tomorrow," Danny replied, while drawing a bit of secret gratification from his intention to avoid Greg for the next few days.

Two redheads (hers artificial), they clattered down the stairs together and out into the street. She began to walk very fast, displaying for the first time all night some lively emotion—anxiety, for apparently she was late. "You need a taxi," Danny said. "Let me pay for your taxi."

He was afraid the offer of money might embarrass her, but she took the notes, first a thousand yen and then a second, with a birdlike dip of the head, as though swallowing them. Five thousand yen—nearly twenty-five bucks—was what Refinement had now cost him. Danny got her into a taxi and she sped off, leaving him with the happy thought that he would never see her again, though with some misgivings that he'd given her too much money for a taxi to any house in Kyoto. He shook his head to clear his thoughts but to his disgust his head would not come completely clear. Self-distaste congealed around a resolve for the morrow: he would return to a soberer and a less expensive existence.

Just as thoroughly as one complex routine had been erected, another, equally comprehensive, now arose to supplant it. For all his firm resolves, Danny the following day found himself at Greg's and each day thereafter. He'd become a sightseer and hiker (trails and temples in the mountains, and Nara's tame deer and enormous Buddha, largest bronze statue in the world, and Kōetsu-ji with its bloodstained wooden ceiling), and an English teacher (his students two doctors, friends of students of Greg's), and a much heavier drinker (especially sake and Japanese whiskey) than ever before. These were welcome changes on the whole, and gave him a chance to indulge a favorite small pride: his chameleonic ability always to adapt, to play the lawyer on Wall Street, the fraternity brother in Ann Arbor, the dutiful son at home, the scraggly unshaven hermit in a cabin on Lake Superior, without endangering something indurate and invaluable at the core of himself.

He'd always followed current events closely—indeed, felt it almost sinful not to do so—but confronted now by Japan's sheer physical distance from any familiar world and the difficulty in obtaining adequate newspapers and magazines, he let this compulsion sleep as well. He would return to that. The world would go on. Meanwhile all the daily unrolling sinister turns—the deepening Mideast war, the increased threat of a Russian crackdown on Lech Walesa and Solidarity in Poland, China's growing nuclear capacities—were left for others, for Professor Umeda, to monitor. And while Danny just a few days before, homesick, had welcomed the sight of other gaijin on the street, he now began (as though he weren't one himself) to resent their presence, to see them as dilutants of his Japan experience, to view them with some of Greg's scorn. Inside this new routine Danny grew certain he'd done the right thing in taking a year off from law school, and felt disturbed—threatened—when from Michigan a letter arrived betokening changes in his new life.

Happy he surely was, though not since the early years of high school had he known any friendship that made so many demands, that pushed and abraded him so frequently. What had surprised him, and it seemed surprised Greg as well, was the tug and pull their minds so soon exerted upon each other. But then Danny, who'd grown so stinting in his appraisal of others' intelligence (finding even on the Law Review—to which he'd been admitted by the lower-caste entrance, not through grades but through the writing competition—that the thinking was limited, a mere mechanical acceleration of mundane processes), had never expected to find himself admitting that crazy Greg, with all his queer locutions, undoubtedly was brilliant. Yet he was. And after two years of law school's drearily meticulous dissections of such notions as justice, free will, responsibility, coercion, Danny was having to concede that he seemed to derive more benefit, move closer to satisfactory answers, in these endless, undisciplined, and often boozy conversations with Greg. Packed though such talks were with unwarranted logical leaps, unchallenged premises, and Greg's idiosyncratic and somewhat ludicrous vocabulary—"big gaps versus little gaps," "non-linked coherencies," "empirically disprovable enlightenments," "accurate hyperbole"—they vibrated with that intimation of a fundamental affinity, a sense that when the two of them employed these largest of undefined or undefinable terms—will, death, time, alienation—they were talking about much the same things. And Greg had read so much more than Danny had. Disorganized as his approach was, Greg the philosophy major had actually read all those people whom Danny knew as mere names—Hegel, Spinoza, Hume, Berkeley, Leibniz.

A tendency toward hero worship was a personality trait that Danny had not only, and not unhappily, long ago recognized in himself, but had formulated a plausible explanation for: his having always gone to school with children older and larger than himself. It was a trait common to the Japanese mentality—one more agreeable custom, like bowing. (That dip-dipping at the waist had from the first felt wholly natural, as if he'd been waiting his whole life to begin showing others respect in this way.) He felt pleased, then, faintly honored, to have Greg saying to him late one night, that jumpy brown gaze steadying under its film of alcohol, "What we share, Danny, and it's an attitude that colors every relationship you'll ever know, is this sense that if two intelligent people will sit down all night and with absolute honesty, with absolute rigor, with a complete abandonment of vanity, try to explore these things, they may actually get somewhere. That progress can be made."

Progress was a favorite term of Greg's. They were making progress as they swung along a mountain path in the morning light, lightly drunk, arguing about capital punishment; progress as they adapted to and further embellished the humor in the roles, chiefly Greg's designations, each had been given. It was Greg's winsome conceit to concoct a world inhabited by pure undiluted prototypes who were forever coming together in absurd and ill-understood collisions. Nothing was qualified; everything was exalted and simple at once. Greg's mythic father was a pure son-of-a-bitch; his mythic mother a pure moron; Professor Umeda, whom he'd not yet met, was a wall—a cinderblock aggregate that housed no human spirit at all. To which was now added that Danny was a naif, a country bumpkin; Greg a cynic and man of the world; Danny somewhat niggardly; Greg prodigal; Danny a prude, Greg a libertine; Danny cool and rational, Greg flash-tempered; Danny a brilliant success-bound lawyer, Greg a brilliant bum . . . characterizations containing their measure of truth, but not so accurate that Danny did not often feel a bit of strain, of non-cool and non-rational anger. Yet Greg had read him right in seeing a devotion to that notion of *progress*—an essential conviction, without which one could never understand how this eager bartering of ideas could be one of the most invigorating activities in the world.

Progress at this juncture was tied to drink, and to the mountains circling the city that seemed to draw Danny palpably, a kind of magnetizing call from his own heart to the stone heart of the mountain. It was one of Greg's pretenses that Danny'd had no real experience with liquor before—hardly the truth, though this sort of drinking, an overlapping and erratic topping up, a deliberate midday insouciance, was something new. This was drink ingeniously laced into the veins and sap of the leaves and branches, spiked into the light of the sun canting through the flaring autumn maples. Danny had temporarily traded in his books, his language tapes, his regimented schedule, to play a sort of game, a charade of dissolution, which was delightful—and now threatened with interruption.

The letter from Michigan was from Mom, two crowded and affectionate handwritten pages which began,

> As you know, I've long intended to visit my friends the Tanizakis in Tokyo. And now with my only child in faraway Japan, across the wide sea, I must delay no longer. You may think this awfully impulsive and flighty of your normally staid mother, but I am thinking of coming *very* soon—in early-mid November. I could get a week or so then. I thought we could rendezvous in Tokyo. I think the Tanizakis may insist on my staying with them (they've always made such a fuss over the way Hisashi inconvenienced us so unforgivably by staying a few days a mere fifteen or so years ago), but I promise to put you up at a handsome hotel at my expense. As you well know, I'm hardly an intrepid flyer, and I dread the transpacific trip, but if my plans meet with your convenience, and if you are able to spare some time from your work with Professor Umeda, I SHALL DO IT! Please call collect. . . .

Apparently Dad would not be coming. Danny had asked them both to come, more than once, but never with much hope, for neither was much of a traveler and both were so busy. Now he'd received the news he'd hoped for—she would come to Japan, he would have nearly a week with Mom in Tokyo and Kyoto—and Danny discovered he wanted only to cancel her visit, which was falling at such a bad time (*progress* was being made) and would require such radical shiftings of role and routine. A network of ramifying burdens opened before him: transpacific phone calls, train schedules and airport rendezvous, a strange enormous city, favors requested of the Professor. . . .

Problems were already upon him, for he had no phone and no idea how to make a collect call. With Mom's letter folded in his shirt pocket, he strolled over to the University to see Minowada-san, whom he'd churlishly avoided since the afternoon nearly a week ago when he'd brought Greg along and she'd acted somewhat smitten, her hand at one point, in coquettish response to Greg's kidding, alighting, or nearly alighting, upon his arm. Thankfully, the Professor was not in. Miss Minowada, standing as she sorted papers on her cluttered desk, seemed very glad to see him. She was wearing a white dress that highlighted the creamy caramel brown of her face. One of her many allurements was this custom of dressing so fastidiously and glamorously for a job which at bottom was tedious and unglamorous and placed her before so few eyes. "How are things going?" he asked her in Japanese.

"Fine," she said in English.

"Fine and dandy? Do you know the word *dandy*? Say: dandy."

"Dondy."

"Say, Danny is dandy." Danny had planted his hands on her desk, mirroring her own stance, and leaned forward so that her eyes, the whites of which contained a little of the yellowing opulence of old ivory, were less than a yard from his own. She laughed uncertainly but held his gaze.

"What is *dondy*?"

"Say: *I* think *Dan*ny is *dan*dy."

"I think Danny is dandy. What is this *dandy*?"

"It means"—Danny began and realized, as so often in attempting definitions, that he had nothing precise and simple to offer—"it means swell." This was apparently no help. "It means I'm a really neat guy. It means . . ." Was he about to step a little too far? To judge from the way she subsequently dropped her eyes he had to suppose so. ". . . that you like me very much. I have a favor to ask," he went on quickly. "I need your help."

It was a laborious process, but he did manage to convey that his mother was coming to visit, that he would be meeting her in Tokyo, that he wanted to telephone his parents collect, and that owing to the time difference it was perhaps best to call at about eight this evening, that he wanted assistance with the call—and that he was, then, asking Miss Minowada to have dinner with him first.

Minowada-san telephoned someone, presumably her mother, for Danny knew she lived at home, and there ensued a not acrimonious but remarkably vehement rush of words, from which Danny could draw little meaning, but which increasingly created the impression—frequent for him in Japan—that he'd somehow erected for someone else huge obstacles which politeness and the language barrier would ensure were never identified. "Yes," Miss Minowada said, when at last she'd hung up, "tonight I can help you."

"And you're sure it's convenient? I can get someone else to help if it's not convenient."

"Very convenient," Minowada-san said.

"Good. Then I'll come back here at five. Five o'clock," he repeated in Japanese. "*Sayonara*," he called over his shoulder.

"Danny is dandy," Danny said aloud, to quiet a variety of nagging qualms as he slipped out the building into a campus courtyard. Mount Daimon hovered in the background, mountainous gray clouds amassing behind it. "Danny is dandy," he said again. Not sure at first where he was heading, he pushed north toward Greg's and broke into a loose trot, Mom's crumpled letter clasped in his hand. Greg wasn't there. Danny let himself in with the spare key he'd recently been given and began to straighten up a little of the mess he'd helped create the night before. They'd been up very late as Greg unfolded what he called the Central Paradox, which involved numerous variations on the principle of infinite regress, and between them they had actually consumed twenty pieces of Kentucky Fried Chicken. Bones and skin and empty beer bottles had been deposited on newspapers, envelopes, the *Riverside Shakespeare*. Danny spent enough time in this apartment, three times larger than his own and with no electone piano underneath waiting to ambush him with "My Way" or "Love Is Blue," that he'd illogically begun to resent Greg's indifference to squalor. These chicken bones could sit for days, begin to grow a second skin of green fuzz, before Greg would get around to removing them.

Danny re-counted his money. Nearly twelve grand—sixty dollars—far more than dinner with Minowada-san would cost. This use of *grand*, which Danny had adopted humorously at first, now seemed natural. Greg's outlandish vocabulary did have a way of infiltrating one's own conversation. In Greg's elevated world, where a person might spend ten grand on dinner, nobody was ever *rejected*; he *got nailed* or *got hosed* or *was given the gate*. Ridiculous old terms from what Danny loosely thought of as his parents' heyday (*hunkydory, hot cha, that would be the chops*) blended with sixties silliness (*groovy, bogue*) and coinages that were surely Greg's own (*wussification* and *wussydom*, *pimpors* and *pimpees*) in straightforward but facetious combinations, for nearly everything Greg said was meant to be if not laughingly funny at least wryly amusing; nothing, it seemed, was ever quite straight on. No one—no one in Danny's whole experience—had ever carried this sense of rich and endless jokes, private and shared, so far into his life. There were routines in which Greg was an Irish horse trainer, some sort of Jamaican con man ("Hey mon, c'mere a second mon, it's a really good prospect, mon"), and an almost wholly hazy figure involved in international espionage.

Danny had assimilated, as well, much of Greg's rather peculiar attitude toward etiquette between friends. Greg seemed actually to resent it when Danny first asked before taking or borrowing something—a week-old magazine, a beer from the refrigerator, some postage stamps. Greg, who'd been given a key to Danny's room, borrowed and pilfered as freely as a looter. Cassette tapes, shirts fresh from the dry cleaners, postcards, shoelaces (plucked from Danny's one pair of dress shoes), guidebooks, combs—they would all disappear mysteriously, or with the briefest and least apologetic of notes, as when Danny returned home from jogging one Sunday afternoon to find twenty thousand yen, nearly a hundred dollars, missing, and in its place a note that said only "Have stolen all your cash, gregO." Greg seemed to relish, on both sides, an effrontery bordering on real rudeness but saved from it by the implicit understanding that the transgressor recognized his transgression and was grateful, really deeply grateful, for being able to behave so outrageously.

Adapting to Greg's schedule was another matter. He was an insomniac, predictably enough, and he'd been waging a constant war to keep Danny up all night—drinking, talking, playing cards. It was a passionate battle, for a balanced schedule was one of the elements in his life dearest to Danny. This hunger for regularity was easily ridiculed by Greg as compulsive, or boring, or *wussyish*, but at bottom wasn't anything of the kind. No, this pleasure was *basic*: Mom and Dad could die, Penny could die, and still there would be this exquisite sense that one was rising with the earth, moving in miniature harmony with its quotidian flowings. In any case, Danny was exhausted now. He drew from his pocket one of his Japanese language tapes and inserted it into Greg's machine and lay down on the tatami, head pillow-propped to show him the map of the world, the mitten of Michigan so prominent, at the bottom of whose thumb Mom and Dad, Alice and Alec Ott of Heather Hills, now presumably lay sleeping. Dawn would still be a few hours off in Michigan.

He woke with a start, fearful without knowing the reason. For one dislocated moment it was still reassuringly possible that his forebodings were substanceless, the mere aftereffects of some bad dream, but when he checked his watch, he remembered: he was supposed to meet Minowada-san at five, and it was already 5:10.

Danny pounded down the narrow stairs to the bathroom sink, jammed an inch-long worm of toothpaste onto his forefinger, swished it around his mouth as he bolted back toward the front of the house, spat the foaming slop into the kitchen sink, snuggled into his shoes, and was outside the house—all within a minute or two. A scattered toss of raindrops had speckled the pavement. He would probably arrive soaked, in addition to being so late, but what did that matter if she'd already gone home? He managed quickly to flag a cab but traffic was dense and it was not much before 5:30 when he bounded up the steps two at a time to the Professor's office. Miss Minowada was still there. "I'm sorry, *suimasen,*" Danny called breathlessly at the door. "I'm sorry I inconvenienced you."

"No, no," she protested, as if the supposition were absurd, "very convenient."

The pressing physical nervousness he'd felt as he'd mounted the stairs shifted into a new sort of exhilarated pressure as Danny led her down the stairs and out the door. The sense of her delicateness beside him made his stomach feel itchy. She paused, there at the edge of the courtyard, a fetching gravity on her face as she studied the sky for rain before deciding it safe to tuck her lavender umbrella under her arm. Her white dress, topped with a pink sweater bound only at the neck, glowed in the last of the gray daylight. She was tall for a Japanese woman, five feet five or six; the lustrous ebony crown of her head reached the jut of his jaw. "What would you like to eat? Do you have any preference?"

"No preference."

Danny had expected this, and he led her without further discussion to a nearby coffee shop called La Chose, which with a typical Japanese blurring of things Western served no food that could be called French. The menu offered pizza and spaghetti, terrible hamburgers, decent curried chicken and fish, and a variety of Japanese food—a wide enough global assortment that Minowada-san presumably would get, despite her assertion of no preference, what she preferred. In addition, the place offered—not at all frequent in this land of fluorescent strip-lit eateries—a gentle gold lighting that promised to soften awkwardnesses and under which Minowada-san, gold teeth and all, looked pretty indeed.

Her prettiness tonight, all the vague yearnings he felt toward her, seemed to impede conversation. Usually their talk circulated around Danny's little jokes, his muggings and double takes, a levity toward which he was feeling disinclined, and yet his attempts to conduct her into serious talk about her family—perhaps she, too, was nervous—were met with monosyllables. Their pizza and salads were slow in coming. She apparently did not drink—initially refused, then accepted but did not sample the cylindrical inch of beer Danny poured for her. After a time, he wound up talking about Mom and Dad, and growing up in Detroit, and Grandpa Jaynes' cottage on Lake Superior. "My parents did not always get along so well," he said. "I think things are better now. When I was growing up, my parents one time separated for three months. Separated—you know? *Wakarimasa ka?* My father did not live at home any more."

"Why did your parents separate?"

The question was a natural one, yet all the same more probing than he would have expected from her, as was the direct whetted inquisitiveness of her ebony eyes; though he'd been talking dispassionately enough, ancient resentments now prodded him. "For many reasons, but I guess mainly because," he said, "because my father was having an affair. *Affair*, you know?" He had read in some newspaper survey (how these people loved surveys!) that something like a quarter of the women Minowada-san's age had not even been kissed, but then again an even larger fraction had had intercourse. Into which of these camps

Miss Minowada fell, or what hot groping niche in the middle, was a total mystery; he was all at sea with this country's women. In any case, whatever her experience, it was indiscreet madness now, impelled by some overriding resentment toward Dad, or some twisted form of flirtatiousness, to add, "He was having sexual relations. With my mother's best friend." Which was not only brutally indiscreet but grossly inaccurate: *an acquaintance of my mother's* would have been more truthful.

Dinner was followed by coffee. Danny's darkening sense of failure in the air—mistake piled upon mistake, lateness followed by clumsiness—was abruptly lightened when they left the restaurant under her umbrella, a steady rain falling, and she hugged his arm in crossing the street, coming near enough for him to catch the whorling scent of her shampoo. The warm impress of her fingertips lingered on his forearm all the way back to the Professor's office, where the call would be made (it was apparently impossible to make an overseas collect call from an ordinary pay phone). Blackness pressed upon the windowpanes and the overhead fluorescent lights bathed the room—an entirely different place now night had fallen—in surrealistic brightness. Minowada-san seemed nervous—to be standing here alone with him, to be playing a small role in the immense undertaking of a transpacific call. She jabbered in Japanese with the operator for a puzzlingly long while, reciting and re-reciting the information Danny had written out for her, then hung up the phone. "Soon, soon," she said. "They will call back."

In a tiny, hugely gratified voice Mom asked, "Can that really be my Danny?" when at last the negotiations had all been made, the thousands of miles traversed.

"Hi, Mom."

"Are you really in Japan? Am I really talking to someone in Japan?" The tiny voice, her own, was blossoming in his ear; Mom's face, her enormous presence, shifted into proximity. Never in his life had he gone this long without hearing that voice.

"You are indeed."

"You sound so *close*."

"I'm as close as the nearest satellite. I'm pretty sure we're talking by satellite. Voices in outer space."

"I've never talked to someone in Japan. This is all so exciting!"

"Maybe I should have prepared something special to say."

"Oh no, Danny, just to hear your voice is special enough."

"You're going to come see me."

"Yes, I am, and *soon*. If it's all right. Can you spare a few days to visit in Tokyo? I thought I'd spend four days in Tokyo with the Tanizakis, and three with you in Kyoto."

"Seven days isn't much time."

"Oh, I know, Danny, but it really is *all* I can take off. You remember I took two weeks in May when Ruth Kornmeister had that nervous breakdown. Oh, why *are* my friends always having such difficulties?" Mom cried, and laughed gaily.

She sounded as though she'd just awakened. While most people tended toward crankiness on first rising, she always verged on heady garrulity—at times almost girlishly silly. *Sleep is her laughing gas*, Dad would often say. Pointedly not listening, Miss Minowada was studying with utmost concentration the opening and closing mechanisms of her lavender umbrella. A Japanese rain was tapping against the windows.

"Now Danny, you must tell me if this is inconvenient for you. Would you really not mind putting up with your mother for a few days?"

"I'd love to see you. Dad, too, if he can come, though I know he's not one for taking vacations."

"No, I'm afraid I'll be alone, if that's all right."

"How *is* Dad? I don't hear him singing, *Danny, Danny, can he, can he*."

"Danny, I'm afraid your Dad's at work."

"I called early specifically to reach him. What time is it there?"

"He's working very hard these days. They're in an absolute stew over the Japanese imports. Did you get the wool shirt I sent you?"

"Momma, honest to God, you shouldn't have. I saw how the postage alone—"

"I saw those colors, and I simply saw you in it."

"A very funny thing. They have clothing stores here in Japan, too."

"I'll try to call Hisashi Tanizaki now. We'll get the times and things all arranged. You still have his number, and address, don't you, Danny? I taped it to your—"

"I've still got it."

"Call me tomorrow, will you, dear boy? There's *so* little time. I'll have all the schedules and things straightened out. And in case there's any mix-up, we'll use Mr. Tanizaki as our home base."

"I'll call you tomorrow, same time or a little earlier. I'm looking forward to seeing you. There's a lot to see here."

"Oh, I'm looking forward to seeing *you*. And if I'd known one could actually speak like this, that they actually have telephones over there, why I would never have let you hide yourself this long from me."

"It's costing you a fortune. I'll talk to you soon."

"Your Dad sends his love."

"Give him mine."

"And pray for Jimmy Carter. He's looking so woebegone these days. I think he's going to lose, poor man."

"Well that will please Dad, anyway. Bye, Mom."

"Bye-bye, Danny. I love you."

Miss Minowada snapped her umbrella closed. "Your mother," she began, reciting with adorable solemnity the question she'd prepared in her textbook English, "is she well?"

"She seems *very* well," Danny said. "But I'm not sure. When you talk with someone over the phone, instead of in person, it's sometimes very hard to say."

"I sense a shift. Enormous forces are at work. A vast change in the cards already's on the way. Young Danny Ott's luck's about to sour."

"It's not a matter of luck. I'm simply better at this game than you are."

"*Hush*. Not a sound. I sense the divine stirring of another prophecy."

It was now perhaps 4:30 in the morning. Ignoring Greg's plea for total silence Danny continued the noisy shuffling of the cards. Greg closed his eyes and fanned his fingers on his tall forehead and in a deep voice began, "I, Grego Blaising, present repository of the transmigrated soul of the great Nostradamus . . . "

"Of who?"

"Oh, God, Danny, how *did* you manage to get so ignorant in just a little over twenty years? It's incredible. Now *hush*." Greg closed his eyes once more. The prophecies—and there had been quite a few—had begun after midnight, little nonsense couplets followed by Greg's elaborate mock-reverent explications. The two of them had begun playing gin rummy at eleven, and had gone through nine bottles of Kirin—six liters—Greg as usual consuming the larger share. They were gambling according to a complicated scoring system of Greg's devising. Danny was presently owed four dinners and three lunches.

"O divine fire, touch me momentarily, worthless pismire though I am, with your blessed panoptic clarity."

Patience thinning, Danny began dealing the cards. This night of gambling and drinking had been intended as a kind of propitiation to Greg, but it had, as such offerings invariably seemed to do, outgrown its intended bounds. Danny had vowed to be in bed by two. In just a little over twelve hours he would be riding the bullet train, the Shinkansen, to Tokyo. As Mom's arrival neared he'd become far too busy to see much of Greg. Professor Umeda had at last given him something substantial to do, two short articles by a noted Belgian jurisprudentialist (who, so far as Danny could see, had many impressive people to quote but nothing to say) to be translated from French into English. Although the Professor wanted simply to scan them, and needed merely a rough abstract and summary, Danny in an upwelling of pent-up scholastic virtuosity had submitted an impeccably typed, footnoted and annotated manuscript, supplemented by his own queries. He'd also, unprompted, begun reading Hobbes' *Leviathan*, so that he might discuss it with the Professor. This project was enormous. Trudging through that multiplex design, the long clause-encumbered sentences and overarching thoughts, Danny had felt new admiration for the way the Professor, working with the original text and a Japanese translation side by side, had managed more than once to traverse the whole. In Professor Umeda, it seemed fair to say, there was something of Hobbes himself—that rigorous intellectual who at the age of eighty-plus commenced to write his autobiography in Latin verse.

The days had been moving quickly, days of transition, with telephone calls to Mom and Dad and Reagan's surprisingly resounding win over Carter and the Republican capture of the Senate all yanking Danny's attention back to his old world; and with a humorously deferential letter from Mr. Tanizaki ("My dear Mr. Daniel Ott"), complete with a bilingual business card (impenetrable Japanese on one side; mysterious English on the obverse: "Hisashi Tanizaki, President, Tanizaki Inc./ Metal and Steel Product"), and a schedule of bullet-train departures and a map of Tokyo all beckoning him toward a new one. On Daimonji and Hiei-zan, on all the hills around Kyoto, the trees were turning.

"Ah yes, here it comes. Here it decidedly comes." Eyes closed, face lifted, his voice descending to a gravelly whisper, Greg intoned,

A frog and a bullfrog go to town.
When one jumps up, the other jumps down.

"Good Lorrrd," he cried, eyes wide in simulated barefaced astonishment. "What do you think that *means*?"

"You got me." Danny began to sort through his hand, which held some promising opportunities but no matches. "You owe me a card."

"Say now, do you suppose it's political? Some kind of comment on postwar American-Japanese relations perhaps?"

"You still owe me a card."

"Or do you suppose it's *religious*. Some puckish comment on the twin secularization of the two principal branches of Christianity. *Go to town*, huh? Huh?"

Danny laughed, despite himself, then said—"C'mon, Grego, I'm tired, give me a card."

Greg lifted his cards at last from the table. "Migh-ty perplexing is what I call it. *When one jumps up, the other jumps down*. Boy, there's hours of thought in that, isn't there? Hours and hours, you'd simply have to say."

"Give me a *card*."

"The thing you don't seem to realize, Daniel, is that I can't just give you any old card. What you and I are taking part in is a vast allegory, we are being carefully observed by outsiders, and everything I do is freighted with awesome implications. But okay, okay, all right, you heartless bastard, take her, press her bosom to your bosom." Greg discarded the queen of hearts.

"Win or lose," Danny said, "this has got to be the last game."

"I think you're right. We want to get there before the crowds arrive."

"There? I have this terrible, this awful sinking feeling," Danny said, with some of Greg's fussed-upon deliberation, "that you're proposing we go somewhere after this."

"To Arashiyama. It's amazingly beautiful, especially right now with the maples turning."

"Greg, it's almost five in the morning. I've got to go to Tokyo tonight."

"Danny, the maples are world famous throughout Kyoto."

Danny laughed, then protested, "Arashiyama, that's way across *town*. It would take us an hour to get there at least."

"How do you know? You've never even *been* there."

"I've seen it on the map."

"What we'll do is this. First, I'll knock for seven"—Greg placed a run of spades and a run of clubs on the tabletop. "You needn't count up, I smeared you I know. That puts us at three dinners and three lunches. Then we'll put on our shoes and catch a cab, which I'll pay for, deducting a mere two lunches from the debt for friendship's sake. Come on."

"Greg, I've got to go to bed."

"Danny, what you've got to do is remember my one fundamental principle: *Nonexcessive excess is worse than moderation*."

"I thought your one fundamental principle was, *Postcoital depression is worth it*."

"That's my other one fundamental principle, along with, *Fecklessness should be pursued feckfully*. Come on, you *have* to come. You've been ignoring me cruelly for months."

"I haven't even known you for months."

"Danny, if you don't go now, you won't see the maples at their peak. You'll go back home next summer, and you'll never have seen them at their *peak*."

Somehow Greg had discovered, and continually deployed to his advantage, the terrible potency which that word *never* carried for Danny, who between partnered feelings of duty and regret could hardly bear the notion of missing things—lovely things within his grasp—for all time. "Grego, I've got to go to *To-ky-o*. Today."

"Come on. Come on. Come on, come on, come *on*. We've got to beat the crowds."

With excessive excess then, full in the feckful pursuit of fecklessness, Danny found himself lacing up his tennis shoes and stepping out, in all his wrinkled and sleepy dishevelment, to meet the freshness of the dawn. As Greg had predicted, they soon found a cab and were speeding up Imadegawa, nearly empty at this hour, though even now in the near-blackness a few shopkeepers were sweeping up yellow fan-shaped gingko leaves and one man was vacuuming the sidewalk in front of a coffee shop. The cab deposited them before the nearly deserted Arashiyama Station. The sun had fully risen but was still more red than yellow. The two of them stood motionless a moment, as Greg peered searchingly to left and right.

A realization struck Danny. "You haven't been here either, *have* you?" he accused.

"Shh. I'm thinking."

"And you were giving me such a hard time."

"This way," Greg announced. They turned left, past closed souvenir shops, and started across a wide bridge. Patchily, in dreamily slow convective motions, mist was lifting over this stretch of river that on one side, downstream, lapped among flat ricefields and upstream wended between maple-papered hills, red and orange and violet. Joy, something as clean as the glassy-edged globe of the sun, climbed inside Danny through the mist of cards and talk and fatigue. These wild suggestions of Greg's tended to be either wonderful or disastrous, Danny had learned, and this walk, the river breeze uplifting on their faces, was no disaster.

"You were talking earlier about your hateful old man," Greg said.

"No, I like the old man very much," Danny said. "By and large."

"Does he look like you?"

"Do I look like him?"

"The child's father to the man," Greg chanted. "And, one might add, it *is* a beauteous morning. Shame you're so illiterate."

"Dad's short."

"How short?"

"Oh I don't know." The remark was perhaps a trifle tactless, for Dad was five feet nine, about the same as Greg. "I mean shorter than me. About your height. He has a moustache."

"Does he look like *me*, then?"

They turned right off the bridge and passed a painted sign dense with inscrutable kanji and pictures of monkeys. Danny recalled from his map of Kyoto something about a wild monkey park. On the right dozens and dozens of rental rowboats, noses to shore, dozed at the edge of the placid gray river. "Dad looks like Dad. I guess he's pretty good looking. You tend to notice his clothes somehow."

"He's a dandy."

"No, no." The word wasn't right for Dad at all. "He's just very careful about his clothes. Even when he's wearing jeans and a T-shirt, everything is just *so*."

"What's your old lady look like?"

"I don't know, Mom looks regular, she looks like somebody's mom. I get my height and red hair from her."

"What does she do again? You told me."

"Now she works for the *Detroit Free Press*, but most of the time I was growing up she—"

"Ssshh," Greg hissed. "Look!"

The bending path opened on an altogether transporting scene. A number of monkeys, maybe a dozen, had come down to the water's edge. Danny stopped dead, knocked breathless, as his assimilating eyes began to prise from the gray surroundings a whole simian community. Monkeys dangled in the trees overhead, peering down at them, monkeys sat along the fence, monkeys had even—as if going out to sea, like creatures in some enchanting fairy story—crept into the rowboats along the shore.

Danny and Greg had impinged on a network that now in response to their presence relayed back and forth a mild, gibbering consultation. Following Greg's lead, Danny began walking smoothly forward, as the network, too, began to shift. Some of them bore pickaback babies, soft fuzzy uncomprehending things, clinging for dear life to their mama's coarser fur. One larger monkey, his threadbare scarlet rump jutted toward them, was fishing in the water with his outsize arm, and brought up, to his patently enormous satisfaction, a long, dripping weed.

These were creatures dwelling inside an agreeable middle zone, neither wild nor domesticated, where a man's presence set off only a chary, quiet alarm. Carefully but calmly they maintained their minimum distance of ten or fifteen feet. But bolder and bigger than the rest, the red-rumped fellow who had rummaged the weed from the river stood his ground at their approach. Simultaneously, by sensed accord, Danny and Greg stopped, no more than five feet from him. He peered at the two humans for a long moment with the poring gaze of a mind hard at work, a scrutiny as profound as he was capable of—before turning, with an agility so accomplished it seemed less quick than it was, and darting up the hill into the forest. His departure was a signal to the others, who drifted off with that same quick and unhurried grace, until within a few moments the accommodating foliage had swallowed their shapes and no trace of them—save a dripping weed on the path—was left behind.

Danny's voice emerged airy with wonder: "That's the first time I ever saw wild monkeys."

Greg's reply brought a slight tarnish to the moment's rare pleasure: "In India, they were all over the place."

Danny instinctively began composing a postcard home, then recollected that Mom at this very moment was inside a plane on her way to see him. "You want to run?" he asked.

"Mm," Greg assented. "But slowly."

They jogged side by side along the path, easily in the cool air, past a lone fisherman wearing a necktie, some splendid maples, a couple of outpost vending machines, and loosely heaped mounds of trash attesting to the crowds present later in the day. On the other side of the river maples in soft-edged enclaves were coming into their true colors—those culminating scarlets and russets and pinks and golds before their leaves lay heaped, too, in loose mounds on the ground. A worried whistle fluttered in the distance, and moments later on the other side of the river a train materialized, not an interloper but somehow a fitting presence, its whirring red cars—radiant as playing cards, leaping hearts and diamonds—blazing behind foliage. Their path brought them to a fork, neither branch of which seemed promising, and they jogged back past the fisherman and the boats where they'd seen the monkeys preparing to go to sea, and crossed the bridge once more, the river's hue having graded from gray to jade as the sun and then the mist rose, and headed down a path on the other bank. Sleeplessness had jumbled all sense of time in Danny's mind and it seemed days ago, not merely yesterday, he'd turned in the articles to Professor Umeda, and he felt an enhancing of that mystical sense, known intermittently since his arrival in Japan, of having landed in a kind of backwater escape from time: it was hard to believe that on the other side of the globe, secured by gravity's traction, classes were being held in the Pound Building and cars were jockeying along the Interstates, that Dad was going off to work and coming back from work and the folded *Detroit Free Press* was landing with a thump on thousands of cement porches, and leaves—there, too—were falling. The river glimmered on his left. The overcast sky had begun to fluoresce in the rising light, gray clouds assuming a silver skin. When the path ended they trotted together up a tumbledown bank of stairs and, panting, settled into a walk on reaching the summit. "Did you notice the fisherman?" Greg said. "He was wearing a tie."

"He's probably heading straight to work."

"Work, work, work," Greg chanted, "all those jobs that other people have exhaust me, literally they do. You know the world's supposed to be so hard, but we're in on the secret of life, aren't we, Danny? The world's a great big pussycat. The world's an initially shy but eventually extremely loose woman, bless her heart, the world's a great big orchard full of windfalls. That's really well put, isn't it? I mean especially given that I've been up all night."

"Is that the secret of life? I always wondered what it was."

Aimlessly they wandered as they caught their breath, making random choices at each branching of the path until reaching by pure serendipity the largest bamboo grove Danny had yet seen. "Oh now this is excellent," Greg pronounced. "This is really *ex*cellent."

Hundreds of elongated bamboo stood in dense enough ranks to eliminate nearly all ground vegetation. The daylight shifted at once, softening, the moment they stepped into the grove; the variable trunks were more gray than green, a ghostly shimmer, in the silver morning light. So abundant were their leaves that in some points the sky was almost lost, as though a roof of moss hung over their heads. Danny rapped on one of the bamboo columns, a hollow knocking. Stroked it, a smooth reptilian skin. "Oh no, this is really *ex*cellent," Greg repeated at Danny's side. Oh, the pleasure Greg seemed able to take in things! Danny had actually seen the skin of his friend's arms nubble with hundreds of goosebumps at the mere playing of a John Coltrane song as they sat in the True Time Texas Saloon. This bamboo had transformed his face: anyone could see the difference. Here was one of his chief appeals, and also a source of some disquiet for Danny: Greg's way of silently suggesting—in his eyes, his flushed skin, an expectant savoring hesitancy in his movements—that the sushi and yakitori he ate tasted better to him than they did to other people, that the pleasures of a dry over a wet towel were more intense for him, the pigments of Gion's neon fanfare somehow brighter. This suspicion always stirred in Danny a vaguely competitive desire—even while he recognized that such impulses were spiritually at odds with the very pleasures, like this bamboo grove, that would compose the competition's subject matter. For the bamboo was magnificent on a scale that belittled such pushy struggles. Danny understood that and yet . . . and yet it rankled ever so slightly to hear Greg saying now, with a gratification that suggested gluttony, "This is fine. Oh, this is very fine."

On the train back to Arashiyama, suddenly exhausted, Danny dropped his head against the glass in a half doze, from which he roused a few stops later at the realization that Greg was up to something. He was standing beside three high school girls in uniform—blue skirts, blue jackets, white blouses, and white anklets. "You do not know the meaning of the word *attractive*?" he was smilingly inquiring, his attention focused on the tallest of the three, a lanky and extremely pretty girl. A serious-eyed creature, she was the least giggly of the trio, although she too was laughing somewhat abashedly, for the conversation—even if its English was little understood—was drawing the attention of people in the train. "And the word *remarkably*?" Greg asked. "Do you know the word *remarkably*?"

The girls tittered, shook their heads to indicate incomprehension, huddled nearer each other in mutual pleasurable nervousness at the untoward adventure they were having on their way to school.

And as Danny watched, incredulous, Greg borrowed pen and notebook from the tall girl, and wrote, reciting quietly as he did so, "You are remarkably attractive." He returned the pen and notebook with a bow, and she, now blushing, bowed in response. She was clumsy, with growth, with a fawn's dawning beauty. "You can look the words up in a dictionary," Greg advised happily, and drawing on his scant Japanese repeated the word for dictionary: "*Jibiki*."

The girls nodded, giggled, peered studiously at the mysterious message this moustached, handsome gaijin had inscribed, giggled again. At the next stop, moving as one collective, beguiling knot of adolescent femininity, they got out. "Bye-bye," "bye-bye," "bye-bye," they called to him.

"Well," Danny said, having risen from his seat to place a hand on Greg's shoulder, "I wouldn't have thought it possible, but you've outdone yourself."

"Charming kids, weren't they?" Greg offered Danny an avuncular grin.

"Grego, those girls were in *high* school. Or *junior* high for all we know."

"They weren't in *junior* high," Greg protested, and added with aplomb, "I thought her a very poised, intelligent young woman."

"I honestly don't know what you think you're doing," Danny said. He went on, "Yes, Officer, I knew the unfortunate suspect. No no no, not well. Hardly *good* friends. I think you could begin to trace his decline as far back as—"

"What I was doing, was helping those kids with their English study. *And* offering a dispassionate tribute to an exceptionally beautiful young woman. *And* looking out for myself in my old age."

"In your old age?"

"Middle age, then. Hell. Now tell me, just tell me you can't see it, Danny, ten years hence? The poor girl's betrothed by arranged marriage to some beastly company man who doesn't even understand she's beautiful. A lifetime of domestic death yawns before her. But just before the ceremony, she takes a last vacation, with her same two high school girl friends, to the Fiji Islands . . ."

This scenario was unrolling with a suspect fluency.

"And here at last," Greg continued, "she sees that romantic man she met one morning on the train, now gray-haired, and pudged out, but the very man she's never forgotten. Their eyes meet, it's love, it's true love, they will never be separated again."

Danny felt certain of it now—certain that he'd been given an important clue to this personality which had begun to fascinate him: for it was true, it was surely true, that in some corner of his quirky mind Greg honestly believed that this morning, with real prudence, he had been looking after himself in his middle age.

This insight triggered for Danny an upwelling of affection and in the cab from Ōmiya Station he began to babble about the dinner he and Mom and Greg would have, the places they would go, and when the cab stopped near Danny's place he stepped out with a flurry of handshakes. "Don't worry," Greg called from within the cab, "I'll pick up the fare, deducting a mere lunch from what I owe you."

"Two!" Danny called as the cab pulled away. "You can deduct two."

"Two," Danny repeated to himself as he turned from the street. He was even more hungry and tired, though it took him a moment to realize this, for he was feeling a little sick; the night's beer was not sitting well inside him. He walked down Horikawa to a coffee shop with a wonderful motto ("world smell in cupful"), and unwilling to decipher the sloppily written menu simply ordered the most expensive "morning service" they had. It turned out to be pizza toast, coffee, Hi-C orange drink, and potato salad. He was just finishing his coffee when, surprisingly, a woman's voice said in native English, "You have a pen or a pencil? Mine just died on me."

It was a gaijin, blonde and somewhat pretty to boot. How had he not noticed her? She was writing an aerogramme just two tables away from his. Much to Danny's delight, he found that he did have a pen. In itself there was little unusual in her approaching him like this; in Kyoto, gaijin turned instinctively to each other for directions, conversation, small favors, advice. Yet the experience of so recently having seen a pen borrowed, Greg roguishly at work among the high school girls, seemed to infuse this simple transfer with a mute fatefulness.

She took the pen and immediately, a crease of concentration between her eyebrows, huddled over her letter and began to write. Danny returned to his seat and, minutely sipping from his nearly depleted coffee cup, studied her face in the shaded periphery of his vision. In profile its angular lines looked harsh, but in that millisecond when they'd linked eyes he'd encountered an inviting, intelligent mildness. Eight fatiguing minutes went by according to the clock on the wall, which was calibrated with romanized letters rather than numbers. DRINKCOFFEE it said, with the *D* beginning at one o'clock and a blank at the twelve. A Japanese-made clock, almost certainly, and one designed (though a person would have to live here a while to believe this) chiefly for the Japanese market. One of the things he'd liked best about working at Huck, Meadows this past summer was how he'd finally begun to appreciate the extremely elementary fact (though one which a student supported by his parents could indefinitely ignore) that nearly everything one ever encountered in a city represented a prototypical cost/benefit business decision; here, for example, someone had concluded that the market for DRINKCOFFEE clocks (mostly restaurants, surely) was large enough to justify the outlay for design and printing and distribution. Danny knew he was not an instinctive businessman, and the originality, the often leaping entrepreneurial ingenuity of others, could be a source of dazzlement. His cup was empty. Did she think he'd given her the pen? He was happy to part with it (a cheap felt-tip), but it chafed him a little that she would just presume he'd done so.

Fuzzily in his tiredness believing it necessary to protect her in any misapprehension, Danny rose fast, paid his bill, and called casually from the doorway, "We'll see you later."

"Hold on. I'm nearly finished."

"That's okay. Keep it."

"Hold on, I'm nearly finished." She did not look up from her letter and, so far as Danny could tell, was not even aware that he'd decided to wait. Three more minutes were ground away by the DRINKCOFFEE clock before she folded up her aerogramme, stood (she was taller than he'd expected), paid her bill, and came to him smiling, those intelligent eyes open to his again. "Sorry to keep you. I've just got to get this in the mail this morning. I've been putting it off and putting it off."

"That's okay."

Danny held the door for her and they stepped out onto wide Horikawa Street. "Which way are you going?" he asked her.

"That way." She pointed south.

"I'm going the other way," he announced—with instant regret. After so long a wait, he should at least have managed to walk some distance with her, whereas now he seemed committed to parting ways right here before the "world smell in cupful" sign. Her appraising stare reminded him that he'd not shaved in days. "My name's Carrie Pingree," she said, and extended her hand.

"Danny Ott." Her hand was large in his own.

"Well thanks again," she said, turning to go. "Sorry if I held you up."

"How long have you been in Kyoto?" Another of Kyoto's hunchbacked old women (permanently canted over from slaving in the ricefields, one had to assume) hobbled between them, momentarily extinguishing all conversation.

"A couple of months."

"Me too. How long you going to be here?"

"I don't know. A couple more months anyway."

"Me too," Danny said with what he realized was pushed emphasis, for this was hardly an amazing coincidence. "I'm a research assistant to a law professor here. I'm on a year's leave from law school."

When the expected questions did not follow, but only another gauging stare, Danny said, "You've got to excuse me. I've been up all night. I just got back from Arashiyama. It was incredible, there were all these wild monkeys running around."

"You went alone?" she asked him. She *was* pretty, though the effect of a pair of light blue eyes, after only a couple of months in Japan, took some getting used to; he had read somewhere, and now could well understand, that Orientals found blue eyes a little scary. God, he was tired.

"With a friend," Danny said, and then, not wanting her to suppose the friend female, added, irrelevantly, "He lives northeast of here, near Kyoto University." She seemed to be losing interest fast, and emboldened by despair he continued, "Listen, I'm going to Tokyo tonight, but when I get back in a week or so, could we maybe have coffee or something?" He appended, pleased with the blend of reason and minuscule plaintiveness in this line, "Most of my friends here are Japanese. I don't know many Americans."

"I don't know. Maybe."

"Do you have an address or something? We could set up a time now."

"Why don't you call me when you get back?"

"Oh, you have a *tel*ephone," Danny exclaimed, in what he perceived was a mimetic approximation of Greg's exaggerated incredulity. But his attempt to readjust his voice resulted in the pompously sententious, "They're very convenient." He was forgetting how to talk.

Carrie borrowed Danny's pen once more and using the back of her hand as a brace scribbled her name and phone number on the flap of an envelope. "Well, I've got to go," she said, breezily tearing off the flap and handing it to him. "Thanks again."

"See you later, *Carrie*," Danny called, and watched her—a tall thin blonde gaijin in ill-fitting corduroy Levi's and sneakers—stride down Horikawa Street. Excitement, pleasure, embarrassment wrung him simultaneously, and Danny broke into a trot that carried him all the way to the door of his room. As he fit his key into his lock he realized that the landlord's unforgivable sixteen-year-old daughter, who even in Japan managed to be egregiously little-girlish, with her Mickey Mouse notebooks and her Snoopy sweat shirt and her pink ribbons and lacy anklets and sailor suits, was playing "I'm in the Mood for Love" on her electone piano. "Danny, you jerk," he said aloud, and stepped contentedly inside.

The room was neat but it had a transient's aura, for he was still living out of his suitcases supplemented by a few paper bags. It was not *home* yet, and perhaps never would be. Mom was going to have a fit when she saw the paper bags, he realized with anticipatory relish. He set his alarm clock for three, when the public bath would open, rechecked his alarm, rechecked it once more, and dropped immediately into sleep. He awoke what seemed only minutes later, the alarm bawling in his ears, went off to the bath, where he shaved and washed his hair, and returned home hurriedly, nervousness beginning to mount. He packed two pairs of pants, three shirts, including the wool one Mom had recently mailed him, four pairs of socks and undershorts, *Beginning Japanese*, toiletries, and a jacket into his smaller, softer suitcase and caught a bus to the station.

He had long looked forward to riding the Shinkansen, which traveled well over a hundred miles an hour, but the train had hardly pulled from the station when a second drowsiness gripped him. He wadded his jacket into a makeshift pillow, with one sleeve trailing as a visor, and dropped into a bumpy and precarious doze. He awoke fully only when they stopped in Nagoya, where all the cars came from—Japan's Detroit, the source of so much of Dad's distress—and again when they began to stream into the enormous outskirts of Tokyo.

The sky had turned the glossless sooty gray that substitutes for blackness in big city skies. As the train hummed along, buildings opening upon buildings, streets upon streets, colossal neon billboards soundlessly proclaiming their advertisements in symbols Danny could hardly understand, a bud of fear unfolded in the core of his stomach. Vaguely, all of this seemed to mock him, to mock the evenings of drinking in Gion, the nighttime wanderings through Kyoto.

And Tokyo Station was a horror. Signs were confusing, voices barked unintelligibly over loudspeakers, vast and misleading corridors radiated off toward limbo. And everywhere there were armies of blue- and gray-suited Japanese *sarariman*—"salary men"—stepping along with that seeming single-mindedness which unwantedly suggested an insect colony—ants or bees. Danny wormed his way out of the station, collapsed into a cab, and passed the driver Mr. Tanizaki's business card.

The driver seemed confused and the ride was longer than Danny had been led to expect. Eventually Danny was brought to a quiet, pretty street and the impression, as the driver sped away, that the pointed-to house wasn't the right one. Danny rang the bell at the sidewalk gate and waited a long while. But the plump man in suit and tie who eventually emerged from the house broke into a welcoming, gold-flecked grin. "Mr. Tanizaki?" Danny inquired. "*Tanizaki-san de irrassyaimasu-ka?*"

"Mr. Danny?" the man cried. He broke excitedly or nervously into laughter as they shook hands.

"Nice to see you again," Danny said.

The man, still chuckling, led Danny into a vestibule, where they traded shoes for slippers, and from there into a living room where, under the harsh fluorescent strip lights which seem to turn Japanese homes and restaurants into offices, Mom was standing. The first momentary glimpsing, as Danny dropped his soft suitcase on the carpet and stepped forward to embrace her, brought for the second time within the last hour a rapid unpetaling of fear at the core of his stomach. She looked awful: pale in the merciless light, haggard, and, simply, old.

Over Mom's shoulder as they embraced Danny saw what must be Mrs. Tanizaki and smiled at her. Japanese husband and wife were both watching this mother-son reunion with tiptoe, rapturous interest. Mom kissed him on the cheek. "Heavens, Danny, you've grown."

"Momma," Danny protested, "I stopped growing years ago."

"No, you *have,* dear," she asserted. "It's a fact."

Mr. Tanizaki introduced his wife. Danny bowed to her, in place of shaking hands, and in response received so deep a bow he felt constrained to dip his head a second and then a third time. "She speaks little English," Mr. Tanizaki apologized.

"And I," Danny offered in her native language, "speak little Japanese"—which absolutely charmed host and hostess.

Mom asked softly, "Is my brilliant son saying things in Japanese?"

"Your brilliant son is explaining that he speaks Japanese very poorly and stupidly," Danny said.

Mr. Tanizaki insisted that Danny take what had apparently been his own seat on the couch, beside Mom, while he moved to a chair opposite. His wife disappeared into the back of the house. "You came to Tokyo by train?" he asked.

"Yes. By Shinkansen."

"Very fast train, don't you agree?"

"Very fast. Very much faster than any train in the United States," Danny said, which again seemed to gratify his host.

"What time did you leave Kyoto by Shinkansen?"

"About four o'clock."

"Four o'clock exactly?"

"Four twenty-two, I believe it was."

Mr. Tanizaki was exhibiting what Danny had grown to think of as a characteristically Japanese fascination with schedules and timetables. The number of hours required to travel from Kyoto to Tokyo was now computed, and the approximate speed in kilometers per hour arrived at. "Now your mother's flight to Tokyo," Mr. Tanizaki said, consulting a sheet of paper on the coffee table, on which he'd evidently recorded her travel log as well, "required a total time of sixteen hours. Approximately. Very long time." He was a small, chunky man with fleshy lips and a thick head of hair scarcely touched with gray.

"And very tiring," Danny said. "Did you sleep at all on the flight?"

"Oh yes, a little," Mom said, but she hadn't. Danny could tell. Mom was terrified of flying. She was bone-tired and she really did look awful.

Mrs. Tanizaki reappeared with a tray containing a pot of green tea and a variety of Japanese crackers. Mom politely accepted a few crackers—her lack of interest apparent to Danny—but eagerly accepted the tea, drawing the cup to her face as though the steam itself was a stimulant. Mrs. Tanizaki mumbled an observation to her husband, and the two of them studied mother and son. "She say to me," Mr. Tanizaki told Mom, "that Mr. Danny look very much like his mother."

"Oh yes, a little like me," Mom said. "But very much like his grandfather, my father. He has the Jaynes family nose"—she touched her own nose—"and mouth. He does have my hair coloring. When I was a girl in Tennessee my hair was red, like Danny's, and very very long, nearly down to my waist."

This flurry of English was obviously beyond Mrs. Tanizaki's capabilities, but not wholly beyond her husband's, in whose Japanese summary to his wife Danny caught the words *face* and *hair* and *grandfather*. Mrs. Tanizaki nodded sagely throughout, mooing *So-o-o, So-o-o* in gently upswinging affirmations, and adding at his conclusion another comment, apparently a strengthened affirmation. "She says," Mr. Tanizaki announced, "Mr. Danny look *extremely* like his mother."

Mrs. Tanizaki returned to her kitchen. Mr. Tanizaki began asking after the acquaintances he'd made during his year at Wayne State, where Mom at the time had been working in the registrar's office. He'd lived alone, in an apartment downtown off Woodward Avenue, while his wife and his two children remained in Tokyo. Though fifteen years had elapsed, he recalled with tenacious intricacy not only the names of everyone he'd met but their families and houses and problems. "And Enzo Caputo, and his two children, how are they?"

"Enzo Ca*pu*to! Heavens, I haven't thought of him in ten years at least. He was only there a few months. I don't remember that he had two children."

"Perhaps I am mistaken."

"No, no you're right. It was very sad. One of them—"

"The daughter. Cerebral palsy. And Emma Vanderpool. Is she well?"

"Emma Vanderpool!"

The disinterment of these names and faces had roused in Mom some of her innate relish in things, which in turn seemed further to kindle Mr. Tanizaki's exceptional powers. The pleasure he was taking in this anomalous role—purveyor of American life to an American—was irresistible; Danny watched, beguiled, as the pudgy little man unearthed the dogwood tree, many seasons dead, that had bloomed in their backyard, and the barbecues Dr. Nebbin down the street used to have, and the name, "Gravy," of Grandpa Jaynes' cocker spaniel.

He asked about Mom's job and seemed perplexed when she explained (something she'd doubtless already reiterated in letters over the years) that she no longer taught high school but worked at the *Detroit Free Press*. "You no longer teach school?" he repeatedly asked, as if each time expecting her to retract her denial; he seemed troubled by the notion of this middle-aged working woman whose career shifted so much over time. "You are *journalist*," he declared at last, with a hungry assertiveness that overrode Mom's "No, not really."

Light-footed Mrs. Tanizaki returned to mumble something to her husband. "I have asked your mother," Mr. Tanizaki explained to Danny, "whether she would prefer to take dinner in a restaurant. She told me she is not so hungry at this time, and we will have here a mere *sunakku* instead. Will you kindly follow me?"

The kitchen also was scoured by overhanging strip lights. Their *sunakku* proved to be an extensive and faintly risible banquet, an incongruous but tastefully set-out mélange of Japanese and Western foods—sushi, onigiri, tofu and Japanese pickles, and cheese slices and lunchmeats, Ritz crackers and McVitie's chocolate-covered grahams, lovely papery sheets of roast beef that must have cost a fortune, tiny plump sausages, chicken and pork, and two large bowls of caviar. Mom, as soon became evident not merely to Danny but to the attentive Tanizakis as well, had very little appetite, while Danny, impelled not so much by simple hunger as a composite urge to make a good showing and to stuff himself with luxuries he couldn't normally afford, engorged vast quantities, especially of the roast beef and, heaped on Ritz crackers, the ebony- and apricot-colored caviar. Much as was already there before them, more kept emerging from Mrs. Tanizaki's microwave oven—something called shumai, which tasted of shrimp, and oden, and meatballs, all of which Mom politely nibbled at and Danny, contentedly eating himself into a surfeit that seemed to occlude his vision, packed away. There was ice cream for dessert, topped with any of various imported liqueurs, and a muskmelon that Mom had no way of knowing could easily have cost, in this country of vertiginous prices, twenty-five dollars. "This is all so . . . so . . ." Mom airily began, and the other three at the table waited. The silence lengthened worrisomely. Her thoughts were scattered, she was not completely here. "So over*whelm*ing," she finished weakly, and giggled in an old woman's girlish way.

"Some coffee indeed?" Mr. Tanizaki asked.

Another short pause. "Coffee sounds nice," Mom said.

"Or maybe you'd just like to go to sleep, Mom. You seem tired."

She smiled with her lips closed. "Well, maybe a little tired."

"To sleep now. You would like to sleep now?" Mr. Tanizaki asked.

"You do seem a little tired," Danny said.

"You are tired? You would like to sleep?"

"Well, actually I guess I would."

Mom's confession triggered an extremely rapid and prolonged Japanese conference. "You are tired. You have flown very far," Mr. Tanizaki said at last.

"Yes, very far indeed," Mom answered with that same unreachable airiness. "*All the way to Japan.*"

"You are very tired," Mr. Tanizaki repeated, offering an unconscious impersonation of a hypnotist. "I will show to you your room. It is very small, I'm afraid."

Danny followed Mr. Tanizaki and Mom, with Mrs. Tanizaki padding behind him, into an unlit back hallway. "This room," Mr. Tanizaki said, "is the bedroom of my son, Koshi, where Mr. Danny will sleep. My son is not here now." A passing glance brought Danny a glimpse of a bed rather than the expected tatami mat and futon. Tonight he would be sleeping in a *bed*, his belly stuffed with caviar and roast beef.

"And this room was of our former daughter," Mr. Tanizaki clumsily continued. "She is married now nearly one year. I sent you photographs perhaps."

"You did. They were lovely."

"Her husband is engineer in Nagoya. You will stay here. I am very sorry the room is so small, and not so nice. Distasteful," he concluded.

"Oh it looks *very* nice."

"You would like coffee now first."

"No, I think actually I'll just go to bed."

Mrs. Tanizaki addressed her husband with an unexpected stubborn forcefulness. It was clear from what ensued that she thought his apologies for the room inadequate, though not clear whether she'd actually understood his English or had judged him solely on the basis of duration. "I am very sorry the room is not so nice," he repeated. "Quite small," he continued, though this was not true. "And not so comfortable. And the bed not so good."

Mom laughed, and placed one hand on his arm, to halt him, one on earnest Mrs. Tanizaki's arm. "Hisashi, it's lovely."

"You would like a shower now. We have new shower."

"Perhaps better in the morning. Thank you both for everything. Everything is *love*ly. Everything is lovely. Your snack was a banquet, an elaborate repast," Mom said to Mrs. Tanizaki, who of course did not understand but, sensing a compliment, replied with multiple bows and muttered Japanese modesties.

"Mom, repeat after me. Go. Chi. So. Sama. Deshta."

"Gochisamadeshta. What did I just say?"

Mr. and Mrs. Tanizaki laughed buoyantly at this.

"You said, or almost said, it was a feast." Danny led her through *thank you* and *good night* and *see you in the morning*, and each of these commonplaces, emerging from this tall befuddled middle-aged gaijin woman who stood in their daughter's door, enchanted Mr. and Mrs. Tanizaki.

"Danny," Mom said, calling over the heads of host and hostess, "it's a thrill to see you, darling."

"It's good to see you, Mom."

"We have much to talk about. But tomorrow. Tomorrow."

"Tomorrow."

"And Danny, I'm so . . ." Again she paused on that word, as if caught, but this time she finished gracefully, if unexpectedly, with a pretty clapping motion of her hands: "I'm so very, very *proud* of you."

"I have this terrible suspicion. Would you like to hear it?"

"Oh very much." Mom's eyes over her upraised coffee cup leaped with pleasure. It was already the fourth day of her visit, but really the first chance they'd had for a leisurely talk. The hospitality of their host and hostess had proved little short of overwhelming. It prodded them gently out of bed in the morning ("I am an early *bird*," Mr. Tanizaki had solemnly announced to the two of them, and looked hurt at the instantaneous laughter this evoked) and pursued them back to the thresholds of their bedrooms at night. They'd gone to Kabuki theater and to various museums, taken the train to Kamakura where they'd seen the vast Buddha and a number of little girls in kimonos and the distressingly squalid seashore, gone to Roppongi for a dinner of Kobe beef and oysters, to the Ginza for a nightclub where kimonoed, bewigged women sang and danced and played Western and Japanese instruments. Twice they'd toured Tanizaki Inc., Mr. Tanizaki's machine shop, which turned out pipe fittings and other small metal parts. They had been with Mr. Tanizaki nearly every waking hour, and when they'd found themselves alone, fatigue, jet lag, and the bedazzlement of the sights all tended to steer conversation toward the immediate and superficial. Here in this coffee shop near Tokyo Station was the first opportunity to speak in their old way, which was conducted (as with only a few other people in his life—with Penny, and now already somewhat with Greg) in a semiprivate language of jokes, allusions, understood obliquities, multiple shifting roles, fragments, and circumlocutions. Danny had many things to say, and still more to ask.

"I suspect we've been misled into thinking Koshi lives in an apartment. I think they kicked him out of his room to give it to me."

The lifting of Mom's eyebrows—bespeaking gratitude, exasperation, and worrisomely deep, accumulating indebtedness—rendered anything more unnecessary. "It wouldn't surprise me," she said. "When he dropped in yesterday, he got stuff out of his closet."

The tabletops in this coffee shop were actually screens for a variety of those electronic games that were even more prevalent in Japan than in America. "Your Mission," the machine typed out in romanized letters etched with an inhumanly cool angularity: "Destroy aliens." It was apparent, among all sorts of perplexities and conjectures, that their accommodations had been a source of controversy. It seemed Mrs. Tanizaki had insisted the foreigners be put up, at her husband's expense, in a hotel. The house was too modest, too cramped, for such illustrious guests. Yet she had been balked somewhat when—in the flurry of calls and telegrams before arrival—Mom had insisted that *she* would pay for any hotel. And evidently Mr. Tanizaki, recalling the few days he'd spent as a houseguest in Heather Hills fifteen years ago, when his apartment had been flooded, wanted to repay kindness in kind: they would invite these guests right into their home.

This was guesswork, as was the question of just *how* rich the Tanizakis were. Though not large by Western standards, the house was hardly as small as the two Tanizakis would have it, and was crammed with every expensive appliance imaginable—three color TVs, a video machine, an enormous stereo, two microwave ovens, magnetized teapots, a sound movie projector. When Mom had met Hisashi Tanizaki fifteen years before, she'd thought him a poor student of electronics and engineering, and it seemed there'd been some truth in that. At the time, he had been preparing to be the self-described "technical man" in his father's small machine shop. But the death (cause unknown) of his elder brother had promoted the technical man into the company's administration, and the father's subsequent death into its presidency, while the small shop (like the Japanese economy which, in its compactness and efficiency, it symbolized) had flourished.

"I don't know what I can possibly send them." Mom increasingly fretted over the thank-you gift she would mail on her return to Michigan. Each new largesse of host and hostess deepened her feeling that any gift would be insufficient.

"You can send them our house. Brick by brick. If you promise to leave my room intact."

"Or something simple like a Lincoln Continental."

"There's no point sending cars to Japan. Theirs are better than ours."

"Don't let your father hear you say it." To Danny's laugh she added, "No, honey, I mean it, he's heartbroken, really heartbroken, about Ford, about the whole auto business. You know it hasn't made it any easier for him to reconcile himself to your year over here."

"No, I suppose it hasn't," Danny said and, despite her plea for sympathy, laughed again. Harsh as it was to admit, one of the boons of living in Japan was its sheer physical distance from Dad, with all his expectations and demands, a distance enhanced because Dad himself never wrote but channeled all messages through Mom's ameliorative hand. What a pleasure it was, to be able to laugh like this!

And yet how strange it was, to be together with Mom again. Although he'd not been away from America all that long, these last months in which he'd neither seen nor talked to Mom somehow had brought on a queer sense of bifurcation. On the one hand, he'd swung at once, naturally, into all their old intimacy, their unique way of talking; yet on the other, he observed himself with great, detached interest, fascinated to study, as if for the first time, these patterns, these things that made him a son.

"You were telling me about your friend Greg."

"Oh I don't know. I see Grego most days. Not every day. We go running. And play basketball, I'm usually the tallest person in the game. He reads a lot of Shakespeare. He's got an astoundingly good memory; he can recite whole long passages."

"Speaking of astonishing memories, isn't our good host the most incredible thing you've ever *seen*? Good heavens, it's un*nerv*ing, I really find it unnerving, Danny."

"He drinks a lot, though. Greg. Actually I've been drinking a lot."

"Well I'm sure you're careful." Amusement was predominant in her response, but a definite mild alarm was displayed as well. Here was a ritual tunneling right back into Danny's childhood, the son's vaguely, exaggeratedly ominous declaration, and the mother's solemn answering show of concern.

"I don't know about Greg. I mean he really is a little crazy, like he has this theory that he's losing his sense of smell, everything used to smell a lot better, and he gets really depressed, honestly, whenever you mention how good something smells."

"Maybe he really is. You know it can happen."

"Anosmia. I think that's the technical word. It comes up sometimes in worker's compensation cases. But the point here is that when Greg and I go into a restaurant he can identify a lot better than I can what's cooking in the kitchen. All this loss-of-smell stuff is just one part of this sense he has of pervasive decline. It's very hard to describe. But he does have this great sense of style, for lack of a better word, this very fussy sort of his-tri-onic way of talking that can be irritating but usually's very funny. He's incredibly bright."

"Well I'm glad you've made such a nice friend."

"Well I don't know how nice he is, but he does manage to develop this kind of devoted coterie around him. There's this Chinese restaurant he goes to where they won't take his money, everything's always free, and this crazy bar we go to, the True Time Texas, where they think he's a Texan and they play John Coltrane records for him whenever he comes in, and his landlady's not only begun refusing to take any rent but is always washing his towels as well."

"She sounds smitten."

"I suppose so, but not in *that* way. I mean she's very ancient, missing a whole bunch of teeth and everything. But she's certainly charmed. It's incredible. But the thing I really admire about him," Danny went on, the topic expanding before him, "is how he doesn't let laziness or habit get in the way too much. He'll decide suddenly he wants to go to Nara just to feed the tame deer, or to Arashiyama at dawn to see the monkeys, and the next thing you know, you're there."

Mom laughed. "Sounds a little like your father."

"Not really. No. Not much like Dad."

"One of the traits that impressed me so, back when your father was courting me, was his ardor for life. Other men simply couldn't keep up with him. Truly, he'd leave them behind. Of course once we were married"—and here her smile fractionally shifted, signaling ruefulness—"that same ardor presented its own difficulties."

The range of permissible topics having broadened, Danny said, "How are things with you and Dad?"

"Well Danny, that's a very long story, and one I should have explained already. Honey, we've separated once more. This time I think for good."

"I thought maybe you had," Danny said, which was almost true. In any case, for her sake he wanted to lessen the weight of her revelation. "The first time I called when he wasn't there. But the next time he was."

"He came that morning to talk to you. Oh now darling, you mustn't look as though some subterfuge had been played on you. Your father simply wanted to talk to his son."

"When did you separate?"

"A little over a month ago. There seemed no point in telling you when I was going to be here so soon."

"But you came partly to tell me that," Danny said, and she, after a slight shrug of her shoulders, as if to say any attempt at concealment from him was useless, nodded.

"In part. Danny, from your point of view all of these endless, convoluted goings-on in people your parents' generation must seem quite incomprehensible. I know that. But I want you to try very hard to understand."

"I understand, Mom."

"Danny, it's so difficult." A painful-looking redness had seeped into the edges of her fluttering eyelids. She seemed about to cry, although her voice held steady and her gray eyes did not evade his. He couldn't bear it if she started to cry. He thought of her carrying the news around for days, waiting for the right moment to break it to him, and this picture impelled him to interrupt her as she was saying, "I don't think you can see how your mother—"

"But I understand," he said. "Now come on. I'm going to take you to the Tokyo Zoo. We'll see a panda. Have you ever seen a panda?"

"A panda?" she said. "Not ever. Have you?"

"Not ever."

"You know, Danny," she said, gathering up her purse, "if Mr. T. finds out we've gone to the zoo without him, he'll be crushed."

"He'll never know," Danny said, partaking of that old pleasure of conspiracy, with all its reverberations of the hundreds of small delinquencies—a dented fender, a lost watch, the true cost of a sheepskin coat—they had snuck past Dad over the years. "For we'll never tell him."

They took a cab to Ueno Station and walked across a park laced with intermittent, tattered sun. The day was cool, and Mom buttoned up her blue sweater. Danny began to talk of Professor Umeda, the Wednesday lunches and the list of troublesome vocabulary words. "He's also an international expert in the legal side to nuclear weapons and the arms race. It's hard to tell exactly what he thinks though. He seems to feel that while the U.S. is merely feckless, the Russians are evil. As you may know, there's a big controversy here about whether Japan should build up its military."

"No, I don't know anything about it."

It was a joy to have Mom again as student, with Japan—a new subject—as today's lesson, for there was always her tacitly conveyed assumption that she could not have been luckier in her teacher, that he was brilliant. She had carried this a little far at times—leaving him faintly incredulous, despite his reasonable forebodings, when he'd not made Law Review on grades—but what a comfort that trick of hers was, really, to any growing child; just as her conviction that Dad was a powerhouse at Ford, a right-hand man to Henry himself (while in fact he was a successful middle-level executive and no more, probably midway between old Henry and some tobacco-chewing illiterate who spent his days screwing bumpers onto Mustangs), may have led to unrealizable expectations now and then, but must have made it easier for Dad to go off daily toward another desk load of drudgery. The only other person to whom Danny'd been able to confide any of his observations about Japan had been Greg, and Greg resisted any reversal by which he became the tutee. Danny went on, "The controversy centers around Article Nine of their Constitution, which we sort of imposed on them after the War. Article Nine renounces militarism, except self-defense, forever. There are a lot of people now, in Japan and also in the States, where people are tired of shouldering all the defense bills for the Pacific, who want to see Japan develop its military again."

"You know it sounds crazy, because everything's so safe and peaceful here, but to the tourist like myself it seems like quite a militaristic country. All the uniforms."

"Definitely it does. All the regimentation. You get this sense here sometimes, of everything just beginning to gear up in some sort of malevolent way."

To locate the panda was not at all difficult. Just beyond the tollbooths a big crowd was pressed against a railing, peering toward a plate glass window some ten feet beyond. Two uniformed men were there to answer questions and to keep the crowd from tapping on the glass. Guiding Mom by the arm, Danny was able to edge near enough to observe, in a far corner of the room behind the glass, that creature emblematic of all the globe's endangered wildlife: a curled black heap that looked like a pile of inner tubes. Watching the heap carefully, Danny could discern, he was pretty sure, the slight slow upsurge and collapse of its respiration.

"Well," he said as they strolled on toward the high bird cages on their right, "now we've seen a panda. And fifty years from now, when all the pandas are long since dead, I can tell my grandchildren about the day my mother and I saw a panda at the Tokyo Zoo."

In one of these wired enclosures—so vast it wasn't so much a cage as an aerial pen—the dark shapes of vultures materialized. Pink-necked, stoop-shouldered, faces a blend of viciousness and small-eyed obtusity, they were more awful than Danny recalled: not merely disgusting but, if you opened yourself to them, horrifying.

"Heavens, they do send a shiver up one's spine, don't they?"

"It's the pink neck," Danny said. "Somehow that's what does it."

"It's the beak. The shape of the beak."

"Raptorial. I think that's the technical word."

The big cats came next, tigers, lions, cheetahs—wonderful loose-limbed creatures, amber-eyed and powerful and admirably indifferent to the flat-footed, gawking passersby. A pacing green-eyed black panther was something else again: a sleek, tightly wound marvel of contained ferocity, his eyes (such rich jade jewels in that ebony body) mesmerizing. They left the panther striding back and forth, back and forth behind them, and bought two cans of soda, which they drank through plastic straws while sitting on a sunny bench. "I heard some news," Mom said, "about your old friend Penny Cogswell."

"Mm?" A tubular column of Pepsi hung suspended an inch from his mouth, then dove down the straw as he lifted his face to look at her.

"She's getting married."

"When?"

"Next month. I have the news from Ann Grayling."

"To anyone I know?"

"I don't think so. His name is Alvin Baron. He's an intern at Beaumont. He grew up in Southfield."

"A doctor, huh?"

"He's supposed to be quite nice-looking, and very sweet, according to Ann."

"When next month? Did she say?"

"I don't recall. I hope the news doesn't upset you. I know you were very attached to her."

"Yes, I was," Danny admitted. Was the news upsetting? Danny, looking inward, was unable to answer the question confidently. As a momentary shock, the news had been unwelcome, just like the announcement that Mom and Dad might be getting divorced, but after the few seconds required for assimilation, how much pain was left really? Danny slurped his Pepsi until it gave a snorting rasp of depletion and tossed the can toward a trash barrel some fifteen feet distant. His shot went in with a subsiding clank-clank. "You're full of news today," he said.

"I suppose I am."

"How old's he?"

"I suppose a year or two older than you. There was a time," Mom went on, "when I thought Penny might someday be my daughter-in-law."

"You wish she were?"

"Not unless you do, Danny."

Again her answer only raised additional questions. *Was* this what he wanted? Would he actually feel better if he were now in the States about to be married next month? Or would he merely be experiencing doubts of a different sort, as one of Greg's fundamental rules—*Whatever path you take, it feels like the wrong one*—came into play? This observation of Greg's linked Danny to a second: "Greg's got this theory," he explained, "that all animals are depressing, and I think he's sort of right. He and I went to the Kyoto Zoo where there's this kind of monkey hill, and where they also have peccaries, you know those South—"

"The ones a little like pigs?"

"More a little like boars. Maybe they were boars, come to think of it. Anyway, the monkeys, mostly out of boredom I guess, or for the sheer pleasure of harassment, chase the peccaries round and round the hill. And you know those crazy peccaries never begin to understand where they are, or why the monkeys are chasing them, or even that they're running in a circle." Wonder and amusement were in Mom's gray eyes, but not that whetted focus that meant his point had been made. "I'm not expressing it well. What is depressing is the notion of living a whole life with even less idea than human beings have of where you are, and what you're doing, and who is manipulating you."

"A little like the breakfast nook," was Mom's puzzling reply. "Or any room with a northern view."

"I don't think I follow . . . "

"You've heard me a million times say there's something depressing about a room with just a northern window. The way direct sunlight never shines in there. I suppose I'm speaking metaphorically."

"So am I, Momma," Danny—quite pleased—exclaimed. "That's it exactly."

"Your Grego sounds like quite the philosopher."

"He is. You'll see. We'll all go out to dinner tomorrow night."

"Actually, Danny, that's another thing I wanted to talk to you about. Would you be terribly hurt if we delayed our trip to Kyoto? Two more days, darling? It's just that Hisashi has made so many plans for us. I had no idea he would put himself out this way. It's as though he's been preparing for the past fifteen years for our arrival. Could you get a couple more days from Professor Umeda? Do you think you could? We'll go to Kyoto on Saturday with Mr. and Mrs. T., if that's all right. He does seem to have his heart set so. Now you must tell me honestly, *would* you be terribly hurt?"

"You mean we'd have just one day in Kyoto?"

"Two really. Two days and a night. Tell me how hurt you'd be."

"I wouldn't be terribly *hurt*. It just seems so kind of *dumb* to come all this way and spend so little—"

"Oh, I know it's *dumb*, but it isn't as if we're not seeing interesting things. You must allow that he's a superb guide."

"Yes he is, and yes I could get a few more days off. The point I'm—"

"You know how Hisashi wants us to see that cottage or whatever it is they're building. And you love mountains. And there's some sort of special puppet exhibition he says we can't miss."

"It just seems a shame not to see more of Kyoto. There's more history in Kyoto than in any other city in Japan."

"Oh, I know it's a shame, Danny—"

"It means we probably won't even get to Nara, where the Buddha's the largest bronze statue in the world. And you don't see the Buddha now, you may never see him."

While well-meant and truthful enough, this was the wrong thing to say, for Mom hated as much as he did pronouncements of this sort. He had summoned to this sun-streaming bench what they'd managed to leave behind them: the huddled vultures, time running out, life's ugly narrowing course. "Come on," Danny said. "We've got lots to see."

They ambled past the bears (Kodiak, brown, polar, and the homely, short-haired but winningly named sun bear), the apes, the lounging hippopotami, the peacocks, the flamingos on their stick-figure legs, but Greg's observation about the depressing quality of animals, or the slowly absorbed effects of all their swapped observations, bled the brightness from everything they saw. They left Ueno Park and went into another coffee shop where Danny said, to cheer Mom up, "Look: gingerbread. I remember the gingerbread Grandma Jaynes used to make."

"Do you? She was such a marvelous cook."

They found seats and ordered two cups of Earl Grey tea and for Danny a wedge of gingerbread that he actually did not want. In truth all his memories of Grandma Jaynes were so remote that he could hardly know whether he was recalling his own experience or the collateral chronicles of Mom and Dad. Grandpa Jaynes, only a few years dead, was still so vivid Danny could occasionally call up the imperious way the old man would clear his throat; but, hardly real, Grandma Jaynes was an illustration for an infant's picture book, a woman whose very limbs were composed of confectionery—pie, gingerbread, cinnamon-dusted custard, brownies. She was also, Danny knew, the largest and most painful loss Mom had ever suffered. *Do you think about her much?* Danny'd once naively asked. And *Every day of my life* Mom had answered—her voice, the look on her face attesting to how sweet it was of him to ask, what profound gratification she could take in being invited at last to reveal her quiet daily homage.

"It's a shame she didn't get to see you go on to law school," Mom said now. "You know when you were just a tiny baby, so solemn you always were, she said, *That boy's going to grow up a judge*. She'd be so very proud of you."

Mom had wanted to name him Daniel Jaynes Ott, but thank goodness Dad had argued that no boy growing up wanted to confess that his middle name was Jaynes. So Mom had compromised with Chapman, which was Grandma Jaynes' maiden name. Danny said, "Well, she had different views of education from Grandpa. You remember the fuss he made about my going to Greyfield."

The place had irritated Grandpa not only because it was a private school, but also (ironically, given the head-shaking horror with which he'd watched the rise of the hippie) because its students wore coats and ties, as though they were "better than the rest." It had irritated him as well—and here the old man had shrewdly fixed on a subtle pretentiousness—that the school had adopted the English spelling for *gray*.

"It wasn't his fault," Mom said. "It was just his background. You know both he and Mama hated the word *hillbilly*, and I can't hear it myself without a little shudder, but his outlook really was formed out in those Tennessee mountains. You couldn't expect him to see the need for educating women. You remember he tried to pull me out of school when I was thirteen."

"Thirteen," Danny marveled, as if this story, which was Mom's very favorite of her growing up, were new to him. Mom was not generally given to repeating herself but here was a tale Danny had heard dozens and dozens of times.

"He was outraged when he found out the authorities wouldn't let him do it. Then when I turned sixteen, he announced I was through with school. Like you, I was the youngest in my class, I'd skipped ahead, and I had the best scholastic record of any junior at Daly. I had a little over a year to go, and he wasn't going to let me finish.

"Well you know what an utter autocrat he was. Mama and I were terrified of him. By the time you knew him well, Danny, emphysema had enfeebled him, emaciated him, but in his prime, as a rigger, he was a strapping, powerful man. And of course Mama hardly weighed a hundred pounds.

"That was the only time I ever saw her really stand up to him," Mom continued, "and she did it for me, not for herself." A washing glimmer, fine as the film which a breath leaves on a pane of glass, had collected on Mom's eyes, but not of the alarming sort that had threatened before. Danny loved this in his mother, the way she was such a strong woman (no one in the world stronger, as had been demonstrated when Grandpa Jaynes had lain so protractedly on his deathbed and she had tended, washed, and shaved him—the last daughterly rites of her life—on so little sleep that finally the nurses, Dad, and probably the demanding dying man himself, had been amazed), and yet was brought so easily to the verge of tears. "They had a long argument, and then he put his foot down and declared he would hear no more about it, and, Danny, that's exactly what she did. She quit talking to him. For days. She continued to cook his meals, and to clean his house, and to darn his clothes, all impeccably, but she wasn't going to speak to him. Or just a monosyllable when he commanded it.

"Oh, Danny, I wish you could have seen it! Of course I was terrified at the time, for I knew I was the ship that had provoked the storm, but in retrospect how funny it was! The man was absolutely discombobulated. Hurling his newspaper, and glowering at Momma and me, and pacing through the house muttering edicts of all sorts. . . . Until finally, at utter wit's end, he says to her, *Eunice, how long are you going to keep this up?* and Momma, absolutely straight-faced, I daresay she was half-serious, looks up from her knitting and replies, *Three or four years maybe.* Oh, he knew he was beaten then. Three or four *years,* don't you just love it?"

And Danny did, he loved this, too; they were linked, mother and son, in a bottomless hunger for these tales of meekness turned plucky, of craftiness outbraving force. Further, this particular story of Mom's had a counterpart which though nearly ten years old he'd somehow in his shaky gratitude never been willing to convey. How he had overheard, long ago, on the night Dad failed to appear at the Court of Honor where his son was made an Eagle Scout, a conversation not meant for him. That was the first time, one of the only times, he ever heard her use really bad language. Danny was in bed by the time Dad got home, but Mom had waited up downstairs. The parental argument, muffled at first, soon lifted sufficiently to enter, the door being open, his dark bedroom. Mom wanted Dad to come up and apologize; Dad was urging her to *let the boy sleep*. It was going to be hideous—terrible, terrible, terrible—if Dad actually were to come up, and yet Danny'd thrilled to the mounting steeliness of her voice: "You're not going to make it up tomorrow. Not going to make it up tomorrow. *Not going to make it up tomorrow*. Listen you son-of-a-bitch, you're going up to ask your son's forgiveness *now* or you're getting the fuck out of this house . . . " What sheer melodrama this would be if Danny didn't retain such an acute sense of lying there, as an adolescent, in his dark bedroom; no, the mortifications of his teenage years remained much too close to be at all amusing. (Indeed, it wasn't clear, even now, that he'd physically passed out of adolescence, for he was still unable to grow any but the scrawniest of moustaches.) Adolescence was still pursuing him: Danny had a dim sense, now and then, of having somehow in the last few years made a narrow, wonderful escape.

"Speaking of getting tough, Danny, if you really want me to, I'll simply tell Mr. T. we've had enough. Or we could tell him you can't get the time off from work."

"I don't mind. Honestly. And I'd like to see the mountains."

"He's absolutely indefatigable."

"They all are here. I can't tell you how dispiriting it is, when you've stopped to rest on your way up to some mountain temple, and along comes some really ancient woman, hundreds of years old, who's much less winded than you are."

"You're sure you're not hurt."

"I'm sure I'm sure."

"Actually, we probably should be going. He's expecting us. He's got some kind of fancy dinner planned."

"And that's just the start," Danny said. "After dinner, we're going to see a troupe of Balinese dancers and then a nighttime tour of an optical glass factory."

Mom laughed gratefully. For one blocked moment Danny feared he'd run out of outlandish possibilities, but then they hopped obediently to his tongue, as he saw himself lifting the two of them free of this grounded conversation, with all its pained revelations and stirred memories, to laughter's elevated and sunny haven. "From the factory, we're going straight to a sumo wrestling tournament, followed by a flower-arranging demonstration at the Tokyo Ward Office, and then to a nighttime kite-flying exhibition, an intriguing and most ancient native custom, and then . . . "

In their remaining days in Tokyo, Mr. and Mrs. Tanizaki took them to a German restaurant and an Indian restaurant and a whiskey factory, to a doll exhibit, and to the mountains near Karuizawa, where to their host's chagrin his family cottage was still some six months short of completion. They were royalty, Mrs. Alice and Mr. Danny, for whose visit edifices should be erected. The finished cottage would share a hillside with bamboo and cherry trees; at this prospect, a Japanese counterpart to Grandpa Jaynes' Lake Superior cabin, Danny for the first time envied his host. They visited a mountain shrine, famous for its spring plum blossoms, in whose autumn-sere gardens Mr. Tanizaki cried out, "You must *return*, a few months, a few months and you will see them." He spoke as if pierced to the heart, and continued with real poignance, his fervor further skewing his English, "You see, the cherry it is not the true flower of Japan, only perhaps this last six hundred years has it been so popular. Always before, the true flower of Japan is the lovely plum blossom."

Either unconscious of the American stereotype of the Japanese as a camera-mad people, or grandly indifferent to it, he took dozens and dozens of photographs of them, until his predictable request for a pose by turns had grown amusing, annoying, and—annoyance evaporating under his beaming goodwill—amusing once more. He captured them with a sound movie camera, with a camera whose film within seconds, as they watched, resurrected their smile-stiffened faces, with a richly appurtenanced Minolta. He was spending, as Mom pointed out, a fortune on film, but what she could not see, and what Danny to spare her continually refrained from mentioning, was the enormous sum of money going out for things that were not great luxuries back in Michigan—the beef, the melons, the imported cheese and wine.

The man had skimped on nothing, and after their last dinner together in Tokyo when Mom, who was only slowly learning not to introduce such topics, spoke of her fondness for sherry, Mr. Tanizaki looked aggrieved. "Yes, you would always drink sherry," he lamented, pained to discover this one box in the vast warehouse of his memory which unaccountably had not opened to him. "You would drink Harvey's Bristol Cream!"

"Oh, sometimes. Anything really," Mom said. "I like wine just as well."

Wines, liqueurs, scotch, bourbon, gin, vodka, cognac, brandy, champagne—all of these his house could boast: but no sherry. "Oh, this is ri*dic*ulous," Mom protested. "This wine is lovely."

A few minutes, he begged them to endure just a few more sherryless minutes—and he was not to be dissuaded. "Danny, you must go with him," Mom insisted, grasping for some measure of concession on the American side. "I insist."

So with Mr. Tanizaki, then, Danny climbed into a Japanese car that carried that pleasant-unpleasant smell of newness, of a machine all of whose accessories—clock, radio, lighter—still worked. At various times these past few days, usually when Mom had briefly stepped out, Danny had been placed beside Mr. Tanizaki, but this was the first time the two had ventured anywhere alone.

When set behind the wheel of a car, Mr. Tanizaki at once became a transfigured man. An unexpected sportiveness showed itself as he swung around buses and slower cars, and when he now stopped for a traffic light he nervously tousled his thick black hair, enhancing the droll impression of raciness. As they sped through the Tokyo night, an inaudible rain between each wiper stroke colorfully blotting the windshield, Mr. Tanizaki said, "When I was in Michigan, fifteen years ago, you told to me you would choose for your profession when you became adult an archaeologist."

This of course had been Mom's and Dad's doing; the seeds of large aspirations had been planted early. "Yes, when I was a little boy, I was very interested in history. I still am. One of the things that makes Japan so extremely interesting to me is how *old* it is, so much *older* than the United States. Its history is everywhere."

"History is everywhere," Mr. Tanizaki repeated, as Danny saw his perhaps somewhat trite observation transformed into a still blander maxim. "And how is your father? Mr. Ott?"

They'd stopped for a traffic signal. A delicacy in Mr. Tanizaki's tone hinted at unforeseen possibilities of confidentiality. Could Mom possibly have said anything? "Well I guess he's fine. I haven't seen Dad in a couple of months, and he doesn't write letters. He is working very hard these days, Mom tells me."

"Oh yes, a very hard worker."

"And of course Ford, Ford Motor Company, is having some trouble. There's all that dispute right now about limiting Japanese imports."

This was a topic Danny had attempted to discuss with various Japanese people. Mr. Tanizaki's response was typical: an abashed laugh, with perhaps a suggestion (or was this merely imagined? For at bottom Danny was deeply protective of Dad in this) of smugness.

"He is very energetic man. You may recall once at your mother's dinner party he broke his rib in wrestling with Gerald Grayling."

Danny laughed. "Yes, he was leg wrestling. Mom has never let him forget it. He not only broke his rib, he knocked over all the party food, too."

"Yes, it was very sorry," Mr. Tanizaki said with no amusement, adding, "Dr. Douglas Nebbin, at whose house I twice took the magnificent barbecue, ministered to him at that time."

"Bump Nebbin," Danny said, and laughed again. "It's a nickname. My father gave it to him."

"That is *bump* like the result of an injury?"

"Sort of."

"Your father, he is still a great painter?"

Accustomed though Danny had become to strange questions issuing from Mr. Tanizaki, so wildly bewildering was this one that it suggested no mere misunderstanding but some elaborate hoax. "Dad a great painter?"

"He was always painting."

"Painting what?" Danny asked, as he simultaneously perceived how this surprisingly idiomatic use of "great" had bent the question awry.

"The walls and the"—the man strained upward for the word—"ceiling."

"He doesn't paint so much any more. He hires professional painters. I guess he doesn't have time."

Mr. Tanizaki, nodding, tendered another aphorism: "Time is short." He resumed, "When I was at Wayne State University, I met your mother in November, the third month in the United States. Your mother, she was very kind to me. I missed my wife and children very much. Your mother, she invited me many times to your home for dinner. I was a guest in your house for three days when the storm flooded my apartment with six inches of flood water. She took me to the concert of the Detroit Symphony Orchestra. She took me to Windsor, Canada, over the Ambassador Bridge, and to Greenfield Village, where I saw the laboratory of Thomas Edison. You understand, I was not her responsibility. She was not my sponsor. Your mother, she did these many actions for kindness purely." Mr. Tanizaki had stopped the car. "You will kindly remain here?" he asked. "I have but one umbrella." It was Mr. T.'s constant preoccupation not to allow his guests anywhere near that sullying point where money was transferred—and he was adept at this.

Danny watched his host scuttle off on his pressing errand while the windshield, the wipers now halted, began to fill with rain. The warmth of the car, the steadily dissolving blur of the glass, the rich dinner inside him, all swelled his delectable sense that clarity had come at last to this whole hectic Tokyo trip. He was only now recognizing what Mom had gleaned from the start, and what had actually kept them from going to Kyoto when planned: that their host loved, idolized her. In a cold and bewildering country across the Pacific Ocean she had entered his solitary life, bringing kindness, and warmth, and that special gift of hers, that irreplaceable flatterer—sincere curiosity. She was interested in his life, his wife, his children, his stumbling, urgent stories of Japan. She had plucked him from the waters of the flood, and he could never repay this. With an unbodied passion that pressed no suit and desired to press none, except to proffer an idealized and always inadequate form of tribute, he would attend her always: she was his angel.

Kyoto in the company of the Tanizakis was as new a city for Danny as the neon-lit one which Greg had introduced him to some weeks before. Danny had never seen so many kimonos or had so many people bow so deeply to him. Here was a small-scale city approaching the Kyoto of guidebooks and tourist brochures, an ancient traditional preserve ingeniously concealed within the noisy racing metropolis Danny had lived in these past few months. He had looked forward to showing Mom the little sidewalk shops selling grilled octopus and cabbage balls, the True Time Texas, the cheap Korean barbecue restaurants, the "world smell in cupful" sign, and was conducted instead into immensely expensive tea parlors and a restaurant where they dined in their own tatami room behind sliding doors tinted with watercolors. Inner recesses of all sorts—back rooms in restaurants, looking out onto miniature gardens, the sanctums of temples, normally closed to the public—seemed to open for unpushy Mr. Tanizaki, of whom Danny was growing increasingly fond.

Mrs. Tanizaki at last had the satisfaction of seeing her guests in suitable lodgings—not the "cramped" and "distasteful" quarters of her own home, but the Nakamura Hotel, Kyoto's finest. There was even an indoor pool reserved for hotel guests on the eighth floor, but Danny, who longed for a swim, who hadn't swum in months, had no bathing suit. They were a happy harmonious foursome, and he found himself reluctant to introduce Greg into it. Not until late after dinner did he take a cab over to Greg's, and on finding no one home Danny felt somewhat relieved. The place was squalid—especially so after the luxury of these last few days. Danny left Greg a note to call him at the hotel in the morning, but they were up and out by eight o'clock ("I am an early *bird*," Mr. Tanizaki declared once more, this time to respectful silence), leaving Greg no way to reach them. They went north to mossy Sanzen-in, which Danny had never seen, and to Kinkakuji, with its fine bamboo and its gold pavilion, a painstaking replica—a loving fake—of the one destroyed by arson thirty years ago, and to lunch at a restaurant whose garden seemed as beautiful as any in the temples, and to a final round of drinks at the rooftop restaurant of a hotel near the station, from which Mom and the Tanizakis would soon be departing. Even abstemious Mrs. Tanizaki ordered a glass of wine on this farewell occasion. In repeated toasts, Danny's brilliance, his personality, his height were commended.

From their perch above the city they could watch the bullet trains heading west, to Osaka, Kobe, Okayama, to Hiroshima . . . "You have such lovely trains," Mom said. "Ours are so lackluster in comparison." Somewhat surprisingly, for she was so adaptable in most things, Mom in her week in Japan had still not weaned herself from lively but perplexing words like *lackluster*. As further illustration of what she meant, Danny added, "Our subways are terrible too. Japan's are supposed to be so good. I'm looking forward to the one opening here in Kyoto."

"You know I never did get to ride the Tokyo subways. You drove us so many places in your *car*," Mom teased, "and treated us to so many *cabs*, that we never did ride the subway."

"You never rode the subway!" Mr. Tanizaki cried, with such passion that both Mom and Danny had to laugh. He was manifestly prepared to ride the subway all day long if that was what it took to please them. "Today," he announced, "we will ride the subway today when we return to Tokyo."

"You've forgotten nothing, Hisashi," Mom reassured, employing again that first name which even Mrs. Tanizaki did not use—an intimacy which ignorance, remoteness, the whole antipodal experiences of their lives, vouchsafed her. "Both of you have forgotten nothing. Your hospitality has been marvelous. Amazing. The whole trip has been splendid, splendid, splendid."

* * *

She woke from a sickening slide, an ugly dream of a tipping airplane (and such a strange flight to begin with, for there had been no stewardesses aboard, only stewards—and all of these were white-haired almost elderly men), to the grounded reassurance that she was lying in bed. This awareness opened onto the further discomfiting recognition that later that very day she would be flying home, across the Pacific, and this (full wakefulness dawning), onto the knowledge that there was still time, technically if not practically, to undo some of her own silliness. She could change her schedule, extend her trip another day . . . Yet in truth there was no time. This too was clear as she lay there, feeling trapped, feeling such a peculiar form of confinement, for it stretched over thousands of miles.

The moment passed, she felt better, she rose from bed and gathered her robe around her. Things were hardly so bad as that, for, whatever her own lapses, the whole trip had been splendid. Magnificent. Indeed, the best trip she'd ever taken. She had experienced so many things . . . To this country she'd never expected to see she had come at last, and found it all waiting for her, as the guidebooks and the TV shows and *The Chrysanthemum Princess,* which she'd read as a girl in the hills of Tennessee almost half a century ago, all had foretold. And found Hisashi Tanizaki waiting for her, affection intact after all these years—so kind, so extraordinarily kind they both were. Dear transparent-faced Hisashi, who himself had altered so little in fifteen years, just a little gray tossed through his marvelously thick head of hair was all, and who had recoiled slightly in surprise at first sighting her.

With that recoiling, and again intermittently throughout the visit, she'd felt—felt such a queer sense of having let him down, and herself down. Her pallid face in the bathroom mirror this morning was distressing, and she would of course be looking a sight worse by the time she landed finally in Detroit. Part of her problem was that she'd never really recovered from the jet lag of her arrival. She had been slightly out of step the whole time. Maybe this was just the newness of Japan, something you got used to, as Danny apparently had. But she hadn't. Despite all the unexpected familiarities (the brand names and slogans, the skyscrapers and game shows on television and *Time* and *Newsweek* on the newsstands), there had been that alien quality, which gave to all the similarities an unreal, pasted-together feel.

Perhaps she should have rested more on her arrival, but her joy had been so great, the sense so strong that she must see *everything*. She'd seen so many things . . . And to ensure that the whole trip did not finally end as one glorious blur, she'd written them down each night, no matter how tired she was. She had also written eight letters and twenty-two postcards and bought gifts for thirteen people (all but two of the names on her list). With luck, she could pick up two more gifts in one of the shops at the airport.

Breakfast on this last morning was, as she'd feared, large and elaborate. She wasn't hungry, and with no Danny there, with his dependable boy's appetite, she felt obliged to eat a portion of everything. Eggs, toast, ham, cheese, milk, coffee, melon. Hisashi played newscaster, as had become the breakfast practice, summarizing the stories in his morning paper (the French and English calling on Japan to further open its markets, Russian troops amassing along the Polish border) while Yasuko bustled in and out. There was no helping Yasuko, so vehement in preferring that guests remain outside the kitchen.

The Tanizakis would be accompanying her to the airport. No use protesting that she could manage by herself. Let indebtedness deepen, then, for in truth she was glad to have them beside her, to place herself and her gift-swollen baggage into their neat, competent hands.

Was glad, too, to settle at last into this train to the airport and partake of its sense of powerful, irreversible motion. Hisashi was reminiscing about a dinner they'd had in Windsor, where apparently a flaming dessert had set a waiter's tie to smoking. Truly, the man's memory was astonishing. That was one of the things that had thrown her off, at the very start. Pleasure though of course it was to have these vanished friends and scenes recalled, it had brought remorse as well, a vague sense of letdown—this realization that someone else had kept the memories intact, while she'd carelessly lost them. They were bright as new coins in Hisashi's mind, that trio she thought no longer existed: Alice and Alec Ott and their eight-year-old boy Danny.

A Japanese landscape was streaming by her train window (the final scenes in her journey, much the longest journey in her life—tiled roofs, dormant neon signs, cars nosing down the wrong side of the road, houses the size of a small garage). The day was cool and yet felt closer to summer than winter; it was closer to winter than summer now in Detroit. A single memory, but as vivid and particular as anything Hisashi could boast, came to mind for her: another train ride, November 24th, 1949, and still hundreds of miles from New Orleans. She'd seen a man wearing a buff-colored hat approaching down the long car, whom by some trick of vision she did not immediately recognize. That trick of the eyes would reoccur now and then over the years, probably happened at some time to every married man or woman, but this occasion was different, for this time the man was and wasn't a stranger: her *husband,* the man she had married just the day before, her own sweet, dear, dashing Alec. And the hat (how funny of him to be wearing that hat inside the train, but he was probably doing it to please her) . . . that hat was one she herself had given him.

A tangled-up mass of misgivings, all the worries and failures of this trip to Japan, now dwindled, left behind, as the train sped along, carrying her and her rich cache of luggage on the first leg homeward. She'd run from things—run all the way over here to Danny, and once here, had run from him as well, but no harm was done and everything would be rectified in the end. Danny, too, had thrown her off at the start. She'd not been prepared for that first sight of him, shying into the Tanizakis' living room, toting his soft bag of clothes in one hand, like some sort of sailor. So tall, so much older than the young man her son she'd come across the sea to see.

2

WITH FRIENDS IN KYOTO

*

*

"Yes. And then?"

Re-borne on a tide of alcohol, Danny's head floated agreeably a couple of feet over his body. His softened voice came slowly. "I don't know why I'm telling you all this stuff."

"You're telling me because you want to unburden yourself. And because you know I'm a discerning listener, and you're hoping I'll give you some needed insight into your knotted psyche. And because you're hoping all this titillating high school sex stuff will give the Grego, to his endless shame and embarrassment, an erection in the public bath. Carry on."

"*I* don't know," Danny countered. "That's really all there is. Penny was the first girl I ever slept with, maybe the only one I ever loved, and it had me feeling very strange, very old somehow, to hear she's getting married."

"So even though she was your first, she'd been screwing her cousin?"

"Once. Singular. *Uno*. When she was in junior high school. She didn't understand what she was doing," Danny said, although he himself could never fully believe that. On the other hand, the millimetric lifting of Greg's eyebrows seemed a nasty show of cynicism. Greg was again failing to see the point—which was the clumsy, burrowing, pained innocence of that whole affair.

After two hours of basketball on a court by the river and a hurried round of drinking, the two of them were propped side by side in the tub of the public bath. Danny had been the tallest person on the court, but Greg, with a light fluttering to his hands, a feinting and a floating poise, had scored the most points. On the wall's other side, where the women bathed, a baby was squalling in sheer desperation, just as if it were being drowned, but its terror was safely remote. The jetting, effacing water held them secure.

"And you say she's marrying this cousin?"

"I say she's marrying someone named Alvin Baron. He's a doctor. Or a doctor-to-be."

"A Jewish doctor?"

"Maybe, I don't know, I suppose so." Of course, of course that was the case—why was he so slow to pick up these details, which everyone else saw as so significant? Hadn't he in effect heard this from Mom, who'd told him that this Alvin Baron grew up in Southfield?

"And you're planning to fly back, sneak into the ceremony, and at the critical moment stand up and admit impediments."

"Well you know it didn't occur to me when Mom mentioned it, but I've been wondering since why Penny didn't invite me. Invitations must have gone out weeks ago. I mean she knew I couldn't come anyway. It would have been a nice gesture, that's all."

"Ahh, but Danny, Danny, you would have showed up. Love calls you to rescue this woman from a life of mere affluence and domestic bliss."

A young girl and her father slipped naked through the bath's sliding doors. Fathers often bathed their daughters on this side, but the girl was bigger than usual, maybe five years old—capable, surely, of washing unassisted on the women's side. The crew-cut father, big-boned and paunchy for a Japanese, hunkered beside the neighboring tub. While his daughter stood waiting, he dipped his plastic dish into the water and rinsed first his own legs and genitals, chest and back.

"Yoriko is hurt at the way you're treating her."

"Who?" Danny said, though he knew who it was.

"Danny, you really must quit breaking hearts and then forgetting all about it. The young woman you picked up at Refinement."

"Oh God, spare me." Greg had a few times since seen Kikuko, the other woman, apparently unimpeded by the enormous language barrier.

"I actually picked up a very nice-looking girl while you were gone and got her into bed, bed here being figurative given the apartment's bedlessness."

"She Japanese too?"

"Mm."

Pricklings of envy itched inside Danny, who had never so much as kissed an Oriental girl. "How'd she look?"

"Black hair. Brown eyes . . . "

"Yuk yuk yuk. You going to see her again?"

"I don't think so. She didn't seem to enjoy things too much. I had the distinct impression she was doing penance for some deep and inscrutable Oriental shame. She'd chosen me as her punishment, which perhaps should be flattering but isn't somehow. Oh God, I've got to get out of this *country,* got to drag myself somewhere where I can get my hands on some good dope."

"Keep your voice down."

"Just a couple lung-expanding hits is all I'm asking," Greg continued at the same volume. "I wouldn't drink so much, honestly, if there was some good dope around. I've been getting worse lately, I really have."

"Where'd you pick her up?"

"That's the really great detail. You're going to love this. At Mister Donut. She was about to make the mistake of ordering one of those butter creams, you know the ones that taste like petroleum, when I helpfully stepped in. Tell me I'm not a hopeless pervert for feeling that all this talk about women isn't ever so slightly more titillating because that little girl's in here."

"You're a hopeless pervert."

"Tell me her presence doesn't alter the vibes, Danny. Tell me that even that old man over there in the corner, *that* one, Christ he's got to be *well* into his second century, tell me he doesn't feel it."

"Greg, she's a toddler. She can't be more than *four years old.*"

"And tell me her big ugly brute of a daddy doesn't feel it. Tell me it isn't oedipal reverberations that are stirring and heating the water in their tub."

"I don't believe in psychology," Danny stated.

"Isn't that a little overbroad? It's like saying you don't believe in astronomy. Or natural history."

"Okay, I don't believe in Freudianism."

"You don't know anything about it. That's one of your great appeals, Danny, though you can't see it yourself. Prep school, college, Harvard Law School—Christ, you even know Latin—and yet you don't know anything about anything."

There was little in Greg's tone to stir contentiousness, and actually the notion of there being something charming to his admittedly shameful ignorance was pleasing to Danny. And the circulating water was so lulling.

"Look at her. Tell me *she* doesn't feel it. Tell me she isn't feeling like the queen of the prom for being the only one in here with a—I'll avoid the word that makes our Danny so squeamish—with a non-male sexual organ? A mound of nothingness?"

"Cunt," Danny pronounced cozily.

"Just *look* Danny."

It was true that while the father seemed sluggishly abstracted, the daughter, her skin the warm brown of a bread loaf's crust, save where (only slightly paler) she sported the humorous phantom of a two-piece bathing suit, was tingling at the touch of the water, or at the peripheral impalpable touch of Western eyes.

"Crew-cut Poppa can pretend the vibes aren't there, but four-year-old *musume-chan*," Greg said, surprisingly culling from his spare Japanese the affectionate informal term for a young girl or daughter, "lacks the imagination, or perhaps has too strong an imagination. *She* knows. From the mouths of babes. You were telling me about your first hard-on."

"I was telling you," Danny declared, with a mock-dignified aggrieved demeanor that was a variation on one of Greg's favorite postures, "about the first, the only real, love of my life. A personal tragedy, really, and I wish you wouldn't joke about it."

"Well go on and tell me. Weep like a fish if you feel like it."

"No no. I'm done. No more."

"Well then, come on. Up, Jack. We got to hurry if we're going to get in a couple of games before dinner." Greg stood; Danny, who had again closed his eyes, felt the water bob and shift at his rising.

"Games," Danny murmured. "You are speaking of course in your characteristically cryptic way. But let me guess. You found us a jai alai court. Or we're going to play bingo at a convention of American Legionnaires." In a high chanting voice the little girl began tremulously to sing; after a moment her deep-voiced father, rousing, joined her. "Or we're going to play strip poker with a group of Iranian—"

"We're going bowling."

"Bowling. Why bowling of course. Silly of me not to see." Grunting, Danny lifted himself from the tub and stepped with Greg out to their lockers. "Bowling, *yes*." Under the indifferent eyes of the middle-aged woman behind the front desk, hardly feeling himself undressed before a woman at all, Danny dried himself and slipped into his underwear and jeans. This country's mix of modesty and casual exhibitionism remained a puzzle. "When I saw Minowada-san this afternoon, after lunch with the Professor—"

"Does she miss me terribly?"

"She told me the Professor's wife had twins last week. I didn't even know she was pregnant. I've been here a couple of months and I've never even met the woman."

"Well you see, Danny, Plumfield's work"—somewhere Greg had discovered that the Professor's last name translated as *plum field*, and he had woven an elaborate network of jokes, somewhat obscure to Danny but of vast delight to Greg himself, in which the Professor was evidently an agent for Scotland Yard—"requires secrecy in all things. He's really much the best man we have out here. The Japs take him for one of their own."

"But doesn't it seem a little strange that he never even mentioned—"

"S.O.P. Standard Operating Procedure. Discretion. Reserve." Greg, always slow to dress, scratched audibly at his bare crotch. "No reason to endanger one's family needlessly . . . "

"And he seems so old to be having kids at all. I'd've thought he was fifty anyway."

"Yes, yes of course," said Greg, who'd not yet met the Professor, "he does manage brilliantly to give that impression."

Bowling, it turned out, unlike so many American activities, had been imported to Japan with little alteration, its tacky quiddity intact. The long tan alleys, the pied shoes, the posters on the walls depicting bowlers in midtoss, arms out and shows of fiercely occluded concentration scored on their faces, the black and maroon and yellow-speckled balls—all of these could have been found on Detroit's Woodward Avenue. The place was enormous—eighty lanes, forty on each floor—but the two of them were the only gaijin, and as representatives of the game's origins and narrow mystique they were scrutinized relentlessly, which made all the more frustrating for Danny (never much of a bowler to begin with) his unusually poor showing. He failed to crack one hundred in his first game. Greg was—predictably, annoyingly—quite good, quite graceful, and hit 171 in the first, followed by a 168 and a 182. In the fourth, Danny bowled his best game ever, a 169, but saw the moment's glory eclipsed as Greg amassed a 207.

They went into the bar at the back of the alley and ordered beer and shots of Japanese whiskey. Greg was always exultant when he won at anything, and his face had flushed and the transecting vein on his forehead that ran from the roots of his receding hair to a little nodule between his eyebrows had, as it also did in laughter or in drunkenness, grown prominent. "If those bastards in Immigration screw me, I may have to leave the country, go to Korea next month to switch my visa, in which case I may want you to go with me."

"There is absolutely no way in the world," Danny announced categorically, "that you're going to get me to Korea in the next month."

"Or I may decide to go alone," Greg said, just as though he'd not heard any refusal. "It seems unconscionable of them to disrupt my studies in this way." In preparation for changing his visa from tourist to culture status, which would allow him a longer stay in Japan, Greg had recently enrolled in, but rarely attended, the cheapest Japanese language school he could find. "So how, overall, was your old lady bearing up to the latest separation?"

"Overall," Danny said, "pretty well I think."

"And it's got you feeling bad?"

"Mm. But more weird than bad I think. It's the combination of things. I leave America and everything starts to fall apart. My old girl friend gets married, my parents separate. The house will never be the same."

They ordered a second round of drinks. When Greg went off to the men's room, Danny found a phone booth and, without giving himself time to make himself nervous or to talk himself into the necessity of delay, dialed the number on the scrap of paper in his shirt pocket. The phone rang three times before a woman said, in English as he'd hoped, "Hello."

"Is that Carrie Pingree?"

"Uh huh."

"This is Danny Ott. I met you a week or so ago one morning. In a coffee shop on Horikawa." Pause. "World smell in cupful." Into the omnivorous silence on the other end Danny tossed additional scraps of detail. "You borrowed my pen. You were writing an aerogramme I think." The flap of the envelope on which Carrie had written her name still bore, in a fainter ink, a zip code which Danny recognized as one from New York City. He hoped she wasn't from New York.

"I remember you."

"You may remember I said I'd call you when I got back from Tokyo."

"Uh huh."

"Sorry if I was babbling that morning. I'd been up all night."

"S'all right."

This matter-of-fact pardon peeved him, and a bit pushily he continued, "Why don't we have lunch tomorrow afternoon?"

"I teach tomorrow. Morning and afternoon."

"How about tomorrow night? Dinner that is, not lunch. Unless you want to have lunch for dinner. Unconventional."

"I've sort of got plans."

"Well are they plans or sort of plans? If they're sort of plans, why don't you sort of break them and sort of go out with me?" Danny ended neatly. In the ensuing pause he resolved immediately to terminate the call if this suggestion, too, were refused.

"Where will I meet you?"

"You'll have dinner tomorrow then?" It was a stupid, reflexive question—for she'd already accepted—and Danny hastily went on, "You know where Maruzen is? Third floor, the English-language books?"

"Uh huh."

"Meet you there at six."

"What's your full name again?"

"My full name's Daniel Chapman Ott. Danny Ott."

"Ott?"

"Ott is exactly it," Danny declared. He decided against adding that his parents' names were Alec and Alice. "See you tomorrow, Carrie."

Greg had returned to his seat at the bar and had ordered still another round of drinks. "I've got a date for tomorrow night," Danny said.

"Come again?"

"I've got a date for tomorrow night."

"Who with? Or, more grammatically but still imperfectly, whom with?"

"A woman I met in a coffee shop that morning we went to Arashiyama." The casual, accomplished sound of this alleviated somewhat the chagrin Danny was still suffering over the phone call's clumsiness. "Her name's Carrie Pingree."

"An American? You're going out with an American?" Greg leaned forward as though to convey something thrillingly lubricious. Eyes popping in sham amazement, he was off again on another of his little jokes and his voice had taken on a breathless huskiness. "A friend of a friend of mine, he once went to bed with an American woman. He says they're exactly the way they are in the movies. Just exactly. It's no exaggeration, Danny. It's no put-on. Like rabbits, like tigresses, like plunging antelopes. *Absolutely wild.*"

Laid upon the river, which tonight seemed to lie as still as a floor, the city's panels of neon created a richly unreal geometric linoleum. On the other side a train—not completely real either, a glowing tube enclosing a crowd of toy people—coasted into the Sanjō Keihan Station, halted, and dispersed its delicate cargo into darkness. "I hate the Keihan line," Carrie said. "It's so damn slow." The date had started badly, with Danny arriving at 6:03, three minutes late, to discover that Maruzen was closed (of course it was closed: he *knew* it closed at 5:45 . . . Why did he do these things to himself?), and for the next sixteen minutes, until Carrie breezed up at 6:19, worrying that she'd shown up exactly on time, had found the store locked for the night, and headed home.

Dinner had been a cordial run of misconstruals. "I know just what you mean," she said on two occasions, and elaborating had gone on to illustrate that she'd skewed or reversed his point, which was hardly her fault, since tonight he seemed even less articulate than usual for a first date. His head felt stuffed with cotton. The food—tempura, soba, soup, and sake—had been lousy. There'd been a maladroit and seemingly emblematic dispute over the bill, with her successful insistence on paying half perhaps an implicit denial that this was any sort of date at all.

Afterwards they'd drunk tequila sunrises at an expensive place called Acapulco while the two singing waiters performed "Esperanza" and "The Girl from Ipanema" and, somewhat jarringly, the Beatles' "Help," and things had gone a little better. He'd let Carrie do nearly all the talking, merely interposing a directional query now and then while beginning to sort out the jumble of her family. Her stepmother and retired father lived in a resort on Fripp Island in South Carolina; her mother and stepfather, whom she called "Fletch," in Princeton. She had a younger brother at Trinity and a stepbrother at Duke and a stepsister at Andover. She'd majored in fine arts at Brown, had worked after graduation first at Yale University Press and then, presumably through her stepfather's connections, though she'd been vague on this and Danny'd not wanted to press her, in the London office of an American investment firm.

"Have you always called your parents by their first names?"

"When they split up it was such a mess for a while, Mom wanted me to call Fletch *Uncle* and Dad wanted me to call Martha, who till then had been Mrs. Philips to me, *Aunt Martha,* and then everybody remarried and I was supposed to call Fletch *Dad* and Martha *Mom,* and I didn't want to call anybody *Mom* or *Dad*. Mom hates being called Helen. She's pretty stuffy. She's very pretty, though. So's Martha, actually."

Across the river, another otherwordly train chugged into Sanjō Station. Danny hesitated and then, bolstered by the lights paving the languid river, he confessed what he'd partially held back from Greg the night before, to whom he'd spoken only of a separation. "When I saw my Mom in Tokyo, she told me she and Dad are getting divorced maybe. I can't decide how upset I am about it, or how upset I ought to be."

"How long have they been married?"

"More than thirty years."

"Well," Carrie replied, with a harsh laugh, "that's as long as you can expect, I guess."

Meant to be engagingly cynical, the remark rankled him instead. There was this slightly discomposing hardness to her: in the lineaments of her face, with its little bony nose and jutting chin, in the faintly nasal voice, so laced with profanity, and the short escaping quack of a laugh. Thankfully, she let the subject drop, for it turned out that having made his admission he felt little impulse to discuss it. Miss Minowada had seemed tall to Danny when she'd stood beside him that first night he'd called Mom, but Carrie was two or three inches taller—five feet eight or nine—and after these months in Japan her height, the crown of her head nearly level with his eyes, felt strange. "I'd be married six months now," she said, "if things had gone as I'd once planned."

"You were engaged?"

"To somebody named Huesing. He's sort of a bastard, but he's all right really."

"What's he do?"

"He's an investment banker for Manufacturers Hanover."

"Manny Hanny," Danny said. Carrie laughed at this, surprised that Danny would know the nickname. "How old's he?" Danny asked.

"Huesing? Thirty."

"Thirty," Danny repeated. His own disadvantageous age—nearly two years younger than Carrie—had not yet been revealed. Actually, that she was older might be propitious: always his close friends, and his girl friends, had been older than he was. "An eligible age. Huesing's his last name?"

"Uh huh. Guy Huesing."

She called her parents by their first names and her ex-fiancé by his last, apparently. "Did you have an engagement ring and everything?" Danny asked.

"And everything," Carrie said.

"You broke the engagement?"

"It was a mutual thing. We were both losing interest fast."

"Had you sent out invitations?"

"Thank God no." She seemed to shudder. "It was messy enough as it was. Look, I hate to say this, but I should be trundling back to the mansion. I've got to teach tomorrow."

"I'll see you home," Danny said.

"No need. You live the other way. I'll catch a cab."

"No, really. You live up near my friend Greg"—whom Danny had mentioned a number of times at dinner—"and I'll drop in on him after I see you home."

"Suit yourself."

It was not clear to Danny as their taxi sped north up Kawaramachi whether he would be saying good-bye in the cab or would be invited inside; nor was it clear, given his ambivalence, how much he preferred the latter to the former. And yet when she offered "You can come in for a drink if you'd like," he said without the slightest tug of hesitancy, "I'd like that very much."

Once they'd emerged from the cab, which Danny didn't even attempt to pay any share of, Carrie said, "See? I told you it was a mansion."

There it was in roman letters on the side of the building: Sunshine Mansion.

Danny laughed. "I'd read they do that, but I'd forgotten how they use mansion"—he pronounced it Japanese style: *mon-shone*—"to mean apartment building."

Her apartment was far nicer than he'd expected. To begin with, it was fairly spacious—a one-bedroom with a decently high ceiling—and there were white, freshly painted walls, and hanging potted plants, and a couch, and a rug on the floor. "I have some vodka," Carrie said. "You want a Bloody Mary or a screwdriver? There's a little rum, you want a rum and Coke?"

"Rum and Coke sounds fine."

"A rum and Coke?" Her whole manner seemed to have altered subtly on entering the apartment, a mellowing hostesslike solicitude emerging, and with it a reassuring hint of nervousness.

"This apartment is palatial." Danny took a seat on the sofa. "What do you pay for this place?"

"Too much."

"How did you find it?"

"Fletch has some client in Osaka who set it up before I arrived." Carrie brought him a drink on whose surface, like a lily pad, a paper-thin circle of lime floated. She'd poured nothing for herself. "That's Fletch there." She nodded toward a photograph on the end table beside the couch. "Last Christmas morning. That's Helen behind him, my Mom, but not so flattering." Carrie released that little barking laugh. "She's actually quite pretty."

A seated silver-haired man in a lime-colored bathrobe was lifting a big bulbous glass to his lips, his crinkled eyes revealing that behind the glass he was smiling broadly. The woman in the background bore the stupefied expression of someone frozen in midblink. Danny swung his own glass toward the man in the photograph, offered a Japanese cheers (*Kampai,* Fletch), which got a laugh from Carrie, who had taken a seat not beside him on the couch but in a chair opposite, and sipped deeply from his fizzing drink. "Do you have any other photographs?"

"Not really," Carrie said.

"You should see my place," Danny said. "It's very small, just six tatami mats, and almost nothing in it. I've got my stuff stored in paper bags."

"Sounds gruesome."

"Well, I like to think I'm partaking in some sort of, I don't know, authentic Japanese experience, but"—Danny warmly confessed—"it can be pretty gruesome. I don't spend much time there."

The confession eased him into a sense of gratitude that would have sounded melodramatic or merely silly had he attempted to express it: a feeling of heady good fortune, a surprised contentment at having landed in this sanctuary of an apartment with its sofa and rug and framed pictures on the walls, across from a blonde woman in a white turtleneck. A silent but comfortable minute went by. Danny drained his drink and set it with a rustling clatter of ice cubes on a copy of *Vogue* on the end table.

"So how do you like Harvard Law School?" Carrie asked him.

"I don't know. It's fashionable to hate it, I guess, but I don't hate it. On the other hand, I don't really *love* it. Some people really are passionate about it, it's amazing." That passion had been one of law school's chief surprises. While in high school, such an ace student and so genuinely catholic in his interests, it had seemed to Danny that his curiosity about *any* field of knowledge was unexcelled by that of his classmates. College had challenged this assumption, and law school had refuted it utterly. For the truth was that in a world populated solely by Danny Otts (a world whose characteristics and implications he endlessly liked to ponder) there would not be a single treatise written on the evolution of the law of debentures or the Rule in Shelley's Case—or, for that matter, about farming methods among the early Northumbrians or the roots of Dixieland Jazz. "On Law Review, most of them are doing it because they're ambitious and that's how you set yourself up for the cushiest and most prestigious jobs and all, but there are a few who honestly do find the Internal Revenue Code fascinating reading."

"So you're going to be a Wall Street lawyer in some cushy office?"

The presence of something snide in her voice seemed—given the spread of this apartment, her admiration for stepfather Fletch, whom (to hear her talk) everyone in London considered an unparalleled financial wizard, and her former engagement to a Manny Hanny investment banker—a little inconsistent, but it was hardly surprising. The richer one was (and Carrie seemed to come from solid wealth), the funnier one tended to be about money . . . a principle Danny'd seen verified again and again at law school. Further, almost every young person Danny met who wasn't a lawyer or a law student seemed a little defensive; even Greg, for all his cynicism, had taken his LSATs. Law school had somehow become an extension of general education, so that not being a lawyer was, in a certain elevated social class, exactly what not being a high school graduate must be in that distant realm of riggers, spot welders, tool and die operators, and bulldozer drivers who erect the workaday world. "Maybe," Danny said. "Though since I came to Japan my main ambition is to become a drunkard."

"You could do both."

"That sounds so am*bi*tious." Using her laughter as a bridge, Danny was able, smiling himself, to cross over to that question whose posing had been troubling him. "Are you free on Sunday?"

"I don't know. Maybe."

What she was doing was likably brazen: saying in effect, *What have you got to offer?* "Well you were saying at dinner you hadn't seen much of the temples around here, and I have spent really a hell of a lot of time walking around the mountains looking at temples and things. I was thinking we could go to this temple I discovered, half an hour south by bus. There's a very famous garden, and there are some temples at the top of the mountain. It's a little strenuous," he went on, voluble not so much from nerves as from a strategic desire to get in as much as possible before she expressed any judgment, "but it's quite pretty and there aren't too many people. There's a fine bamboo grove."

"I guess," Carrie said. "Sure."

"I'll call you and we'll set things up." Having received her freeing assent, Danny lifted himself from the sofa and moved toward the door. Farewells on first dates always tended to be awkward for him and he was determined to exit quickly. Carrie stood four or five feet away, just close enough that had he taken two steps forward he could have kissed her goodnight. As he said cheerfully, "Well, I'll see you Sunday," he was struck by a contrary, familiar sense of futility. Somehow (his failure never properly explained or understood) this angular, pretty woman in the doorway would prove unapproachable.

And yet on Sunday morning, hiking beside her up the long trail, Danny's spirits and body took a transfused strength from the cedars and pines, the jade green bamboo, and the turning, thinning maples. Carrie was again wearing baggy jeans and her white turtleneck. She looked at once less pretty and more desirable than he'd recalled. The air was cool. Danny was buoyantly playing guide, and she seemed to appreciate what he found for her: blood red patches of lichen on stones tumbled in a narrow riverbed, an ancient time-wrung cedar, a spider's web whose strands by some sleight of the light were invisible, leaving for the eye only arrested windfalls (broken segments of pine needle, a downy feather, assorted bits of grit and fluff) magically slung upon a suspended plane of air. Once Carrie nearly slipped on a wet rock and her jerking hand seized his for balance. In that brief moment while her knuckles lay within his clutching fingertips and his eye caught hers, lightly before she wiggled loose from him, Danny discovered an unexpected aptness, the expansion of fair possibility.

He told her about Professor Umeda, whom the students called Wall and Greg called Plumfield, and how the Professor seemed obsessed with the possible Russian invasion of Poland. He told her about Dad's working at Ford and his anger over Japanese car exports, and how he seemed not fully to be joking when portraying the Japanese as a nation of robotlike factory workers and corrupt, book-manipulating managers. He told her about Jack Jacobusse, at the firm this summer, who used to nettle the older partners with the cynicisms he fed the young associates ("While you're here at Huck, don't ever forget that you're really a *high-class* whore; I don't want to hear you're doing any twenty-dollar jobs") but who'd made partner anyway because, as he himself would be first to point out, he knew more about the Ergo antitrust case than any man alive.

Carrie told him about how her mother, Helen, had got her realtor's license and had done absolutely nothing with it except twice require Fletch to move unnecessarily from one house to another in Princeton. Fletch doted expensively on Helen, though no one could see why. Carrie told him how Hugh, her tennis-loving father, had recently decided to move from Fripp Island because he couldn't often enough find a challenging doubles game. She told him how, during her freshman year at Brown, she once went to stay a week at Oxford with a boyfriend everyone in her family hated ("In retrospect, he really was a shit") without anyone's ever finding out.

This was all encouraging enough. They were drawing lines, making claims and fusing alliances, but not in the businesslike manner of the other night. A playfulness, a sweetness linked to the chancy siftings of sunlight through the trees, had entered in. When he was telling her the story of how Dad had engineered him into kindergarten a year early, and she interrupted with "How old *are* you anyway?" the challenge in her voice was a kind of teasing.

"What do you mean—how old *are* you? How old do I look?"

"I don't know, fifteen? You've kind of got a baby face."

"And you look forty. Forty at least. That was one of the things that attracted me from the very start," Danny recklessly continued. "You looked so old. So *wise*."

She stuck out her tongue at him and he, at once no more than fifteen years old, thumbed his nose at her. "I'm twenty-three years of age," he declared. "If you must know. But I'm tall for my age."

The hike was longer and more rigorous than Danny recalled. When he'd climbed with Greg, they had taken to the trail in a hustling, tacitly competitive way that exulted in its steepness. Danny worried now that Carrie might be growing tired, or bored, but she marched sportingly along. And when they reached the indeterminate wooden structures of the sun-pooled lower summit, her face seemed flushed with keen pleasure as well as exertion. "It's pretty, isn't it?" he asked her, at ease now, congratulating himself for bringing her here.

"Mm. Nice."

Further up, they entered a temple wherein low, pillow-shaped clouds of incense floated and, above these clouds, a sleepy-eyed but all-seeing Buddha gleamed goldenly. Danny had grown to love the sumptuosity of these temples, although they still seemed so densely exotic he couldn't imaging how anyone, even a native Japanese, could find them comforting.

Still further up, in a sort of information booth or office, an ancient bespectacled priest in an apricot robe sat hunched over what looked like a ledger. There were few enough pilgrims today that one might have supposed the sounds of their approach would prick his curiosity, but his gaze never lifted from the vertical script. Sufficient stubble had grown upon his shaved head to cap his face in a cool gray shadow.

They left him undisturbed and walked on to a roofed but open wooden structure with benches and vending machines. "The soda machine doesn't do a whole lot for the ambience," Danny said.

"It's a help if you're thirsty, though," Carrie said, and laughed harshly. She seemed to be chiding him. It was true he craved nothing more than a Coca-Cola. "You got a hundred-yen coin?" she asked.

The machine ingested Danny's coin with an ominous silence. Carrie pressed the Fanta Orange button, the coin return, the Coca-Cola button, the coin return once more—with no result. "It's the very worst of both worlds," Danny said. "First they uglify the temples with a soda machine, and then the damn thing doesn't work. You got a coin?"

"Just bills. Shit." Carrie punched the machine with the heel of her hand. "Shit. I'm dying."

"Ask the guy back there for change," Danny teased.

"*You* ask him. You're the one who speaks Japanese."

"You're the one who's taking classes."

"You're the one who said he never hesitates to ask these people for help." Carrie laughed triumphantly.

Danny swung around and, Carrie a few steps behind him, strode back to the old priest, who was still hunched over his book. "Excuse me," Danny whispered in Japanese, and brokenly went on to explain that the soda machine was not working and had swallowed his coin (the only approximating verb he could manage was *taberu*—to eat), and that he would try again if he could only have change for a five-hundred-yen note. The old man removed his glasses and listened with an expression of mild entertainment that verged on but did not coalesce into a grin. He squinted at the money Danny extended but did not touch it, closed his book, and—an unexpected and unwanted move—slowly stood. He stepped through a door at the back of the booth and with tiny steps in his enormously tall wooden clogs ambled over to the soda machine. Danny and Carrie followed.

"I put a hundred yen into the machine," Danny repeated in Japanese, "and nothing happened."

"You want Fanta Orange?" the priest asked in English. The brand name, particularly, sounded incongruous on his lips.

"Coca-Cola," Danny corrected guiltily. "Or anything. Please."

In the next moment—as quietly and beautifully comic as any in Danny's life—this ancient priest in the apricot robe dealt the machine a savage kick with his wooden clog, pressed the Coke button, turned as the can fell with a responsive clang, tranquilly nodded, clopped away. . . .

Carrie appreciated just how funny it was and a moment later the two of them were standing in the cool and brilliant sunshine shaking with near silent mirth. "The wisdom of the East," Danny gasped, "spirituality and a knack for machinery . . . " but to dilate the observation was to dilute it. Laughter graded into a shared well-being, and when he said, "You must come with me to Yawata, okay?, they have a special bamboo garden," it was as much a statement as a question. Already, he had that much of a claim on her.

"Allow me, please, to insert myself briefly here. I will be brief, I will of course be brief," Greg declaimed in another simulation of ritualized deference. Though a Japanese language tape was chirping through the headphones clamped over his ears, Danny was able to hear Greg's every word; was able to discern, indeed, the bulging intonations that probably meant Greg had been drinking. This recognition, for the first time, brought Danny a feeling of weary disappointment—and a tiny hot abdominal squirt of nervousness. He removed the headphones but did not rise from the floor.

"What are you babbling about?"

"*Time*. I won't take much of your time. I know how busy you are. I will be brief." Greg remained in the doorway of Danny's room. "My obligation to you never ends. I am about to commit a rudeness."

These last two statements were part of an elaborate new family of jokes. Having in recent weeks attended a few Japanese classes, Greg had tardily ascertained the literal meaning of a number of extremely common Japanese phrases—*sumimasen, shitsurei shimasu*—and, enchanted by their many-tiered courtesy, he would render them as stiffly as possible into English. "Greg," Danny said, "I've got to start getting things *done*. I have all these tapes I've hardly listened to."

"*Holmes, puffing his pipe, observed, That's an ironed shirt you're wearing.* When do I get to meet this woman you're neglecting all your friends to spend every minute of the day with?"

"I've just seen her a couple of times."

"I'm looking forward to meeting her."

These words seemed somewhat threatening. Carrie, too, was asking to meet Greg, but Danny had put her off.

"You're busy tonight," Greg went on. "I won't even ask. In place of your company I'll settle for a poor second—the loan of eighty grand."

"Eighty grand?" It was nearly four hundred dollars.

"Do you have it?"

"Eighty grand?"

"I would never have disturbed you while you're studying, I'd've come in and got it when you weren't here, but you've developed this horrible new habit of hiding your money so I can't find it."

"Over there in the books. In Mill's *On Liberty*."

"A very nice touch, that. Liberty, indeed." Greg winked at him, wandered over to the books with a slight lurch to his movements (though perhaps this was merely imagined), and drew eight ten-thousand-yen notes from inside the text.

"What's the money for?"

Greg winked again. "I'm going to make us rich," he said from the doorway. "I will liberate us. And I have been brief. My obligation to you never ends. My obligation to you never ends. Carry on."

"You mean to tell me you don't know the Five Warning Signals of Sharkbite? I thought everyone knew the Five Warning Signals?"

"Maybe I did but I've forgotten." Laughter and drink had pinkened Carrie's normally pale complexion. In her powder blue sweater and plaid wool skirt she was more dressed up than Danny had ever seen her, and for the first time that he'd discerned she was wearing makeup. Tonight made the sixth time he'd seen Carrie since the morning, its memory smudged with sleeplessness, they'd met in the coffee shop. "Refresh my memory," Carrie said.

"Let's see . . . " Greg lifted by means of fingers rather than chopsticks one of his tempura shrimp, dipped it into its sauce, and with an exaggerated lifting of his upper lip, a flash of fine white teeth, neatly severed body from tail. The three of them were together at last. Greg had insisted on meeting her before his departure in a few days for Korea.

"The Five Warning Signals of Sharkbite . . . I remember now," he said, crunching on the shrimp. "Yes. Warning Signal One: an abnormal amount of blood in the surrounding water. Warning Signal Two: a strange unwonted sense that one of one's limbs is missing." Greg refilled to the brim Carrie's tiny sake cup. "Three: a sense . . . Now how did they phrase it in the pamphlet? Oh yes . . . A sense that you're swimming and swimming, but somehow not getting anywhere. Four: now let's see . . . "

Danny excused himself and went into the men's room where, needing to justify his presence to the Japanese man with permanented hair who stood before the washbasin mirror, he pretended to urinate. Once the man had departed Danny stooped for the mirror (he was always having to stoop in Japan) and confronted the sulky glare of a slow-witted kid. Through what retrospectively looked like Greg's subtle promptings, he'd had far too much to drink. By the time he'd begun to sense a malevolent motive it was already too late: his mind had thickened, his tongue grown slow. Yet it wasn't just the drink. At the outset he'd found himself subsiding into silence, into a gathering rage, mixed sensations of betrayal and helplessness, as Greg so openly came on as the charmer, and Carrie just as openly as the deeply charmed. For the first time in weeks, since his arrival in Japan, Danny had found himself wishing he were back in Cambridge, back at law school. How damned stupid, how unlikeable that face in the mirror! Shameful, his tendency to sink into a sullen, capitulative silence when things didn't go his own way. But there he was.

He washed his face with cold water, realized there were no paper towels, and dried face and hands on the sleeve of his wool shirt. He'd been jittery all day long—a feeling compounded when he'd gone to pick up Carrie and discovered her in a skirt and makeup. As she sat on the sofa brushing her hair he had approached from behind and—heeding some garbled inner imperative—had kissed her lightly but audibly on the cheekbone. It was the first time he'd kissed her and there had been no discernible response. No comment, no slight adjusting acknowledgment of her body. He was left with the befuddling impression that somehow she'd not noticed.

"I wanted to tell that little girl," Greg was saying as Danny returned to his seat, "that if she wanted her puppy dog to understand her, she shouldn't speak to it in *Japanese*. I've been here nearly six months, I wanted to tell her, and *I* can't understand a word you're saying, honey. Danny, surely you must have an okra." Greg held out on chopsticks an oblong object that glowed a dull green under its lacy tempura skin.

"No thank you," Danny said.

"I'd eat it myself, but they're rigidly prohibited on my diet. Don't laugh," Greg said to Carrie, who in laughing had extended her hand on the tabletop to touch his arm. "It's true."

"You don't seem to be on any diet."

"I'm on the Blaising—that's with an *s*, as in my family name—the Blaising Delicious Diet, and it's no joke, young lady. You honestly haven't heard of it? All foods, everything, fruits, meats, dairy products, are strictly scrutinized in terms of their deliciosity level. I dutifully try to eat as many delicious things as possible every single day. People say to me, with admiration and real respect, *Don't you ever break your diet?* And I tell them, quite honestly, *No, I stick to it religiously*. The diet's more self-denying than it sounds. Now you take the Brussels sprout. A dandy little vegetable, really, packed with all sorts of marvelous nutrients, economical, versatile, easy to cook, and yet simply because of their somewhat repugnant flavor I am forever barred from eating them. To say nothing of the noble lima bean. But I interrupted you, Carrie. You were talking about your ex-fiancé, the noble bank teller."

"He's an investment banker."

"I'm a terrible listener. Danny'll tell you. Isn't that right Danny?"

"Sometimes. Sometimes that's right."

"Now why *is* that?" Greg asked Danny earnestly. "Why do you think that is?"

"You get a little self-preoccupied maybe sometimes," Danny said. The conversation's abrupt pivoting seemed a trifle odd but Danny moved with it eagerly, for here lay observations he'd been longing to deliver. He went on, "You get caught up in your, in these . . . mental constructs, which you maybe a little arrogantly think other people can't understand, and then you want to expatiate. You're contrarily pulled between an optimistic—"

"But don't you see," Greg interrupted, his face radiating triumph, "don't you see how terribly grave and pitiful the problem has become? *I'm not listening to you right now*. A tragedy is what it is, a tragic, tragic handicap. But Carrie, I interrupted you about your fiancé, the bank security guard."

"Investment banker. In Manhattan. And I didn't bring him up, *you* did."

"But we were talking about diets. Do you know what the guiding principle, the motto, of the health food fanatic is? *Flavor is Nature's way of telling you something isn't good for you*. I mean you *know* how bland their food is. Now just tell me his *real* name and I'll drop the subject, Carrie. Surely you weren't actually contemplating sacred matrimony to anyone with an astoundingly prepped-out name like Guy Huesing."

This amused her greatly. "His name is Guy Huesing."

Greg refilled her sake cup. "Just tell me this. When he was at Princeton, did he belong to an eating club?"

"Now that's not *fair,*" she, again giggling, protested. "Many people at Princeton—"

"The case is closed," Greg proclaimed. "Everybody go home to bed, the case is closed."

Danny for all his gathering resentment was watching in fascination these volleys at Carrie's fiancé. Whereas Danny had instinctively approached the subject with delicacy, Greg at once had intuited through Carrie's giggled expostulations that she enjoyed hearing the wedding plans belittled. "But surely," Greg said, "surely anyone named Guy Huesing who would willingly go to Princeton, and then to Wharton, and then to a Manhattan bank, cannot possibly understand that his life is too stereotypical to be real. He doesn't exist. And marriage to a nonexistent person is still illegal in most states. Danny knows the law.

"Now when I was a Harvard freshman, I was going with a South Carolina girl whose father believed that overeducation was the greatest problem in America today. Just my luck, huh? But what you had to love about that cantankerous prick, he could deliver these platitudes—Outlaw guns and only outlaws will have guns; We've taken prayers out and put sex in the schools—as if he'd just coined 'em. He had absolutely no idea that like this guy, like this guy Guy, this guy Guy guy, someone shut me up, he was living inside a joke, and was being ridiculed every night on the tube he watched so religiously. Now listen, for I am about to impart a great truth." Huge satisfaction had ruddied Greg's face. "In this world there are three types of people. There's that vast group who honestly don't see they're everywhere being parodied and their lives have been appropriated by someone else's jokes. And then there are those few who see and manufacture the parodies."

"What's the third group?" Carrie asked him.

"The third group is people to whom this generalization in no way applies. At least I'm honest."

Greg had managed to get the bill while Danny was in the men's room and now drew from his pocket a ten-grand note, doubtless one of those plucked from within *On Liberty*. Greg said, "No, uh-uh," as Carrie scrabbled in her purse, and she abandoned her search with a docility never displayed when Danny'd sought to pick up a check. "You can be in charge of buying donuts. We may need dozens of them. Donuts are very big on my diet. On account of their high deliciosity level, you see."

"Maybe we'll run into your friend," Danny said thickly. "At the donut store." The words emerged as a childish taunt. What target was he aiming at anyway?

"You have a friend at Mister Donut?" Carrie asked Greg.

"Danny is alluding to a woman, an extremely nice woman, I once befriended at a Mister Donut. Danny meets *his* women in coffee shops." Satisfaction—again—was pasted all over Greg's face, belying the self-deprecation with which he now gracefully deflected Danny's stroke. "And I must say, given the present company, that his seems much the wiser practice."

Out in the street at last, a damp but refreshing November breeze shuffling the fallen yellow gingko leaves, Danny settled a sulky pace behind Carrie and Greg. The drink was turning sour inside him as he sobered. "Do you want to hear my favorite story in the world?" Greg asked Carrie, and commenced the tale of his friend at Harvard who, needing an illness to spring himself from an exam he must otherwise flunk, ran six miles in a cold rain wearing nothing but gym shorts and tennis shoes and then lay down for ten minutes in a puddle. "He woke up the next day feeling absolutely *bully*, and having little time to spare he began hitting himself over the head with a beer bottle until he'd raised a lump he could take to health services." "No." "*Yes*. He went into health services and said he'd been wrestling with his roommate and now was seeing double. He was excused from the exam, took it three months later, and flunked it anyway." "Not really." "Very really." Then Greg told the story, again familiar to Danny, of the psych professor at Harvard, a nationally known figure, who chose to study flirtation patterns among undergraduates and wound up impregnating a homely Catholic sophomore in Mather House.

Under the bathing light of Mister Donut the three of them were visibly drunk—if Danny translated aright the bemused, swapped glances of the two overweight girls behind the counter. Greg selected eleven donuts ("Twelve would be piggish") and they wandered back into the street's tolerant darkness. When Greg offered him the box of donuts Danny was tempted, in a reflex of balky anger, to refuse, but this would only be again to meet superficial kindness with petulance. In silence the three of them drifted along, committing a breach of etiquette that Professor Umeda, who delighted in recounting the indecencies committed by gaijin in Kyoto, had once remarked upon: walking and eating at the same time. The thought of the Professor—whom Danny hadn't seen in four, no five, days—tossed a splash of guilt into the murky, acidic wash of Danny's anger, confusion, fatigue, and constricting frustration. What was the Professor doing now, while Danny was walking drunk and donut-stuffed in the dark Kyoto streets? Rereading Hobbes? (Danny, after a racing start, had not yet finished the third part of *Leviathan*.) Puzzling over a curious antinomy in the theory of John Locke? Awful as Danny now felt, he sensed that the evening's consequences were far worse than he'd yet appreciated and, further, that he wasn't helping matters by walking a step behind while Carrie (matching seduction with seduction) told the story of the affair one of the London investment bankers had had with a Pakistani cleaning lady. It turned out that Greg and Carrie were both teaching in Osaka the next morning, and they arranged to ride in on the train together.

At the corner of Imadegawa, where Danny's path naturally forked from theirs, Greg stopped. "How about a run tomorrow afternoon?"

"Sure," Danny said, edging northward to indicate that he did not plan to leave them.

"You going to try for a bus?" Greg asked, though he surely understood the buses had quit running hours ago.

An impulse toward recalcitrancy for its own sake, as much as any chaperoning desire not to leave them alone at the tag end of a drunken night, prompted Danny to say in a voice of faultless conviviality, "I'm sure the buses have stopped. I thought I'd crash at your place."

Greg's fractional hesitancy gave way to a gracious, "Good, great," and the three of them continued north to Carrie's. She invited them in and stirred up a new round of Bloody Marys. Danny sat on the sofa, listening with annoyance to Greg dilate, just as he himself fatuously had done his first time here, on the luxury of this apartment, which in fact, by any decent American standard, was a pretty sorry and tacky place. "Danny," Greg exclaimed incredulously, "did you see she actually has a *shower*? We got to start coming over after our runs."

"Feel free to use the shower," Carrie said; and seemed only retroactively, by a wave of her hand, to include Danny in the offer.

"And American toothpaste! I saw what definitely appeared to be a very large tube of American toothpaste."

"Hugh, my Dad, sent it over. I told him I couldn't stand the Japanese stuff."

Greg took a seat beside Danny on the couch and Carrie dropped into the chair opposite, crooking her thin nyloned legs—bony, muscular, desirable—over its arm. Greg now, in a process Danny well knew, turned from raconteur into interrogator, and Carrie talked about her family, her job in London, her broken engagement, her sister and brother and stepbrother. It turned out that her mother, whom Danny had come to picture as someone like the surprising wife of Jack Jacobusse (who for all his salty talk about being a high-class whore had married a fair-spoken blueblood from Bryn Mawr), was a violent-tempered woman, subject to nervous disorders, who one afternoon, employing a manicure set, had destroyed over seven thousand dollars worth of her own clothing, including a fur wrap Fletch had given her for Christmas. It turned out that Carrie's stepbrother at Duke, once seemingly Harvard-bound, had been thrown out of Choate for dealing drugs.

"I'm afraid your friend Carrie and I have been setting you a bad example," Greg said to Danny when at last they stood outside the Sunshine Mansion. Danny turned these words over in his mind. The phrasing was skillful, the "your friend" balanced by the implicit pact between the two older, the two example-setting members of the trio. Danny had somehow expected Greg, who couldn't help being aware of the hostility in the air, to be at a loss for words. "One should never bitch about one's family after the age of twenty-five."

It was a pleasure to correct him. "Carrie's twenty-four."

"Actually, it shouldn't be permitted after freshman year in high school."

Danny would have much preferred to take a taxi home now, but by his earlier decision to tag along he'd committed himself to crashing at Greg's. If there was going to be, as now appeared, a kind of submerged battle between the two of them, Danny must not lapse into any more sulky caprices.

"I like your friend," Greg went on. "There's something appealingly romantic in a young woman's going halfway round the world to nurse her broken heart. Or her broken pride anyway."

"What in hell are you talking about?"

"About her broken engagement. This guy Guy. This Huesing character."

"Their breakup was a mutual thing," Danny said, correcting Greg a second time.

"Mutual?" Greg grinned and lifted his eyebrows, his face in the slanted silver of the streetlights taking on that familiar expression of ugly knowingness. This cynicism of his always said *I'm nobody's fool*, and yet in its very desire not to be duped it misconceived, Danny steadfastly held, that sunny half of the world which was innocent and naive, bumbling and truthful and guileless. "Danny, Guy Huesing dumped her flat. Make no mistake on that score."

Danny the next day began telephoning Carrie's a little after one. From the first, he didn't permit himself to call as often as he wanted, partly to rein in the panic inside him, partly because in one vivid scenario Carrie was actually home and knew who was calling, and each jangling attempt to reach her only made him a larger chump. Vivid, wild scenarios abounded this morning. In another, Carrie and Greg had decided on the train to Osaka to forgo their teaching jobs, and at the moment. . . . This moment, here in the phone booth, propelled the same unlucky ten-yen coin into the slot and pushed the same alarming dial tone into his ear. He dialed again the same losing combination of numbers—and again no answer.

While it was true that neither Greg nor Carrie owed him anything; and true that any claim based on *having met her first* not only sounded childish but was logically absurd; still the sense of an injustice being committed against him accumulated with increasing power as he bicycled over to Greg's. Admittedly, nothing was established yet. But the soft core of his stomach was steeping in acidic premonitions, all leading him now, once he'd knocked at Greg's apartment and received no answer, to let himself in with his loaned key and heavily ascend the stairs to peer into the bedroom.

Sprawling on the floor, the humorous box of condoms ("Wherever Particular People Congregate") on one side, his eyes nesting in the other direction, on the world map, Danny waited a while for Greg; then, insupportably restless, he went over to the True Time Texas, from which he telephoned Carrie. No answer. How silly was he being? He was doubtless overreacting—sensed that in some dim way his mind had linked up Carrie's arrival in his life to Penny's getting married, and to his parents' separating. But what he knew with certainty was that he simply couldn't endure the prospect of finding himself again (without ever knowing how or why, and that was always the worst part: that he so little understood where he'd fallen short) outmaneuvered in this ticklish, numinous business of securing a woman's affection. In just five days Greg would be leaving for Korea, and then Danny would perhaps be able to straighten out things with Carrie, and straighten out his own feelings, and he would be himself again.

Just five days . . . and yet long enough, it turned out, for an inner rotation to take place whereby Greg went from being merely irritating and manipulative to being infuriating and insidious (Danny feeling real hatred beginning to center on that stocky body and dark-eyed face with the tooth marks implanted in its brow), and Carrie went from tantalizingly capricious and pretty to flighty and beautiful. Danny took Carrie to dinner at the Chinese restaurant in the basement of the Royal Hotel and despite spending over eight grand and going through three bottles of sake never managed quite to exorcise Greg's ghost from the conversation. The three of them went to the Kyoto National Museum, where Danny's artistic evaluations were met with an embarrassed silence. Carrie spoke with the authority of her fine arts major, Greg with the authority, presumably, of being the Grego Figure. It was true that Danny'd never had much interest in visual arts, other than a skeptic's pleasure—reaffirmed each time one read about a museum's unwittingly hanging a painting upside down or about shoddy counterfeits foisted off as priceless originals—in believing the whole thing a multimillion-dollar scam, but he knew more about the Japanese culture and history which lay behind these artifacts than did either Greg or Carrie, and their failure to see the magnitude of their blindness seemed pure arrogance.

In his resentment, watching as they drifted huddled in quiet observation from faded painting to chipped pot to tarnished brass figurine, he felt that merely to have nothing further to do with either one was to place them at an insufficient distance. No, if these two were indeed to become a couple, Danny must not simply sever all ties but eradicate their every trace and memory. The vision he could not bear, the one that steeped his stomach in corrosives, was that of these two from the high altar of her bed solicitously discussing how well he was adjusting to their romance . . . No, he would not only cut himself off from them, but from all other Americans in Japan (those scruffy-faced parasites), and would begin working hard (as he should have all along) under Professor Umeda, and begin sleeping with (though even in fantasy this last seemed to present impracticable problems) Miss Minowada.

The next day, in a better mood, he took Carrie to the Kyoto Zoo. They giggled over the alligators, stacked like logs in their watery tank, immobile as death although their malicious unblinking eyes stood open. Entrancing, too, were those animals like the raccoon and porcupine, the everyday denizens of Danny's own Michigan woods, masquerading in this Japanese zoo as exotics. Over a late lunch of tempura Danny (with some misgivings, for behind an ostensibly laudable effort to deepen intimacy through candor he recognized a supine attempt to win her through pity) told Carrie all about Penny Cogswell, who would be a married woman before Christmas.

Five days proved time enough to establish its own sort of routine: a period of vacillation and paradox, wherein Danny felt furious with Greg and yet reluctant to let him out of sight, and unreasonably resentful when Greg at last hinted he'd rather be left alone. Danny couldn't seem to resist mentioning Carrie to Greg and yet would shift the subject, clumsily, when the conversation threatened to turn serious. Greg made things worse by so often acting privately amused. The clear implication was that he savored watching Danny make such an ass of himself—which, Danny supposed, was justified. A need to delay, to temporize and monitor, all went into this routine, which, like an earlier one, was broken by a letter from Mom—the first he'd received from her in the weeks since her visit.

The night before the letter arrived, enjoying a renewal of cordiality on the eve of Greg's departure, Danny had been cajoled into playing cards until almost dawn, then while listening through a haze of red-and-black fatigue to Greg ranting about a persimmon he'd just peeled ("Fruit like this conclusively proves the universe is basically good! It makes you change your fundamental assumptions! Inhumanity, greed, squalor are mere aberrations!"), Danny had fallen asleep on the floor.

It was noon by the time he reached home and found the letter. "My dearest boy," it began in Mom's even, precise handwriting.

> I'm afraid I wasn't completely honest with you during my lovely sojourn in Japan, and I must now beg your forgiveness. I believe I have misled you (not deliberately, Danny, but perhaps from a somewhat selfish desire to spend as carefree a holiday as possible with you in Tokyo)—may have misled you as to why I've decided to file for a divorce.

Danny lifted himself from the floor and crossed over to the wall where the bags that held his clothing looked on in a neat row. Dread had turned to a certainty of disaster, as if within the penumbra of his vision he'd already caught the explosion lying further down the page. In the street below a loudspeaker was bawling incomprehensible Japanese as Danny read:

> The truth is that I have fallen in love with another man. Darling boy, this is so very difficult for me to write. I've always wanted to shield you from your parents' various problems and indiscretions, but surely full candor is required now. I want you to know that, despite your father's infidelities, until last February I had always respected my marriage vows—and still have, in the strictest sense. And I believed I always would. I'm not sure how much I can ask you at your age to understand about the passions of people of your parents' age, but you must try to believe me when I tell you my life has changed for the better. I am in love with Douglas Nebbin, and I'm happy to say that Douglas is in love with me.

All of the dark and aggregating menace catapulted into bright absurdity—sunny weightlessness—as for one spacy moment it seemed Danny had never heard of Douglas Nebbin. Then with a grunted "Uhh" of weighty recognition, Danny stuffed the letter into his back pocket and, not stopping to put on a jacket, raced over to Horikawa, where he caught a cab for Greg's.

In the back of the cab, Danny read the two-page letter straight through four times. It was dated almost three weeks before. "Bump," he said aloud. "Bump Bump. Bump Nebbin."

Greg's door was unlocked. "Grego," Danny bawled, "Grego," as he pounded upstairs. Greg was lying on the floor, his *Riverside Shakespeare* and a bottle of Kirin both open before him. "Grego," Danny announced, collecting himself as he stooped in the room's low doorway. "My mother has decided to marry a clown."

"Come again." Greg's upper lip lifted in anticipatory relish.

Borrowing some of Greg's aplomb, though his remark concluded with an unintended, snorted laugh, Danny repeated, "It's my mother, she's decided to marry a clown."

"A clown by profession?"

"Worse. A clown by nature. The man's a complete and utter fool."

"Well, that's much less interesting, isn't it?"

"It's terrible is what it is. It's absolutely, completely fucking terrible. My mother's going to marry a fucking clown named Bump Nebbin. The man is a complete laughingstock. A fucking jerk. A buffoon."

"I like the name. Bump."

"Dad nicknamed him, Dad's been playing poker with Bump for years and has taken him for literally thousands of dollars. Literally." Danny's speech was clogging in his throat, which happened only when he was about to cry or when, as now, he was so choked with anger or frustration that he could not expel the words fast or vehemently enough to relieve the mounting passion inside. He paced over to the world map and swung around to face Greg, still stretched out on the floor. "Bump is so stupid he thinks his nickname stands for a bump in poker, when you raise the bet, but actually it's short for bump on a log."

"Your old man's got a good sense of humor."

"Grego," Danny pleaded, "Grego, the man's a fool. My mother is about to marry a *fool*. A laughingstock. A complete and utter buffoon." Danny had sought from the start to make the confession somewhat comical, but finding that this role now radically obstructed all attempts to convey the moment's gravity, he veered into an uncharacteristic outburst: he turned and with one scratching downstroke ripped Greg's map from the wall.

For a moment they stared at each other, Danny still panting audibly. "You know you're wearing shoes on the tatami mat," Greg said mildly.

"I forgot. I'm sorry. Grego, I'm telling you the guy's a laughingstock."

"Let's go out for a drink."

"I don't want a drink," Danny said.

"Something to eat then."

"I'm not hungry."

"Well I'm both. Come on. Come on," Greg urged. "You've got to talk fast, I'm off to the airport soon."

Obediently, Danny followed him down the stairs and into the street. "We've got to call Carrie," Greg said. "She's supposed to meet us."

"Carrie? When was this arranged?"

"Earlier. You two are saying good-bye to me."

"How were you going to get in touch with me?"

"I had a feeling you'd get in touch with one of us, which given the pattern of these last few days wasn't all that unreasonable. Now come *on*, Danny, you're whining. You got to relax."

Danny relaxed, or at least gave a show of it until seated in the True Time Texas, at which point in a flood of words he brought forth everything he could recall of Bump Nebbin, who lived just down the street and whom Danny had known his whole life. Bump in his gardener's gloves and ridiculous straw hat pottering among his backyard roses. Big-bottomed Bump in his always impeccable tennis whites lurching and slipping over the court. Bump at the Tuesday night neighborhood poker table, putty in Dad's hands, beguiled into folding winners and calling with losers, yet genially. showing up week after week for another fleecing. And Bump forking out over two hundred dollars for an ugly thoroughbred dachshund, a yapping sausage of a dog, which he named Pumpernickel but soon began to call Sandy, which was short for Sandwich. "He's clumsy, really clumsy, not just playing tennis, where it makes you want to laugh, but just simple things, like when he's barbecuing a steak. He's always having these backyard barbecues, he wears this big apron and everything, and half the time he manages to drop the steak on the grass."

Beer and egg salad sandwiches appeared magically, for Danny hadn't realized they'd been ordered. He uncovered still more remote memories. Of Mrs. Nebbin, dead of breast cancer maybe ten years now (or more than ten, for it was in regard to her that, always acquisitive of new vocabulary, Danny'd asked what a *mastectomy* was; oh, the answer had horrified him), and how she and Bump used to ride along on a tandem bicycle in the summer. She used to bake fancy Christmas cookies. Danny'd liked silvery Mrs. Nebbin. And how he'd once seen the two of them on the tandem, Bump pumping along energetically in front and Mrs. Nebbin glancing from side to side with a dazed smile on her sweet face and, it seemed, tears splashing down her cheeks. Danny felt himself losing the thread of his invective, memories dovetailing into other memories, scorn into pity, into softness, into the elmed streets and angling dulcified morning and dusk light of his boyhood.

"You got your Mom's letter with you?" Greg asked him.

"Uh huh."

"Let me see."

With some reluctance, although he now wanted Greg to know the full story, Danny handed over the crumpled letter. Greg's globed forehead immediately creased latitudinally in deep reflection. "It's dated nearly three weeks ago," Danny said. "I guess she sat on it a while."

Greg didn't answer. In the considerable amount of time he was taking, Danny felt unspecified hopes begin to burgeon; somehow, Greg was going to assist him.

"She writes very well," Greg delivered at last, folding the letter and placing it beside his plate. He picked up a triangle of sandwich. "I liked that phrase, *My strong and doubtless outdated views of decorum*. Quite alliterative, without being—"

Disappointment sharpened Danny's voice into a near-whine. "That's not really the point."

"Oh no, that's very much the point," Greg mumbled with his mouth full. "She doesn't write like any fool."

"*She's* not the fool. Bump is."

"She doesn't write like anyone who's in love with a fool." Greg unfolded the letter once more. "Now what about this. Here. 'As you know, your father has always treated Douglas shabbily, and I have great admiration for the dignified and good-natured way Douglas has endured your father's gibes over the years.' Now what about that?"

"*What* about that?"

"You gave me to understand Bump never realized he was being made a fool of."

"He doesn't."

"*She* says he does."

Yes, *she* said he did. Was it actually possible that that big-bottomed man in the straw hat knew himself to be a figure of fun? Could there actually lie underneath those bland features the redemptive insights of someone who, as the most observant party, savors the last laugh? It would be wonderful to be able to think so . . .

"I'm a little puzzled by this 'in the strictest sense' stuff."

"It seems quite clear," Danny said stiffly.

Carrie showed up, suddenly an unwelcome interloper in his eyes, though she looked pretty in a suede jacket he'd never seen before. "You have to be good to our red-haired boy," Greg told her. "He's having a bad time." Carrie took the chair beside Danny's and Greg explained briefly what had happened.

"What does Bump do?" Carrie asked.

Her matter-of-fact use of the nickname, which on Greg's lips had carried a solacing sense of shared irony, irked Danny while also bringing home anew the monstrousness of this proposed alliance. "He's a professional clown. I don't know," Danny said. "He's a doctor."

"What does he look like?"

"Like a bump on a log."

"How tall is he?"

"He's tall. Maybe six two."

"What color hair does he have?"

"I don't know. Gray. White."

"I'll bet he's quite good-looking," Carrie said. "Sounds like a real catch."

Was Bump good-looking? Danny could hardly remember how he looked. The critical fact, the one which rendered irrelevant all questions of appearance or occupation, and the one which Danny was having the most difficult time conveying, was that Bump was *Bump*. Therein lay the horror.

More sandwiches and beer were ordered. Conversation shifted, Greg began talking about his plans for Korea, jokingly making arrangements for the dispensation of his belongings if he was not allowed back into Japan. Danny let the chatter pass unheard. Then, abruptly, it was time for Greg to leave, and Danny, this palpable touch of ceremony making the departure real, was shaking Greg's hand and feeling an unexpected and anxious regret. "We'll go with you to the airport."

"No need," Greg said. "And remember, you can stay the whole time at my place. Escape from the electone piano."

"We'll walk you there now."

"Don't. I can't stand good-byes like that." Greg slung his coat over his arm and shuffled away, calling over his shoulder to Carrie, "Take good care of our red-haired boy."

"Wellll," Carrie said, "are you looking for a baby-sitter?"

The joke seemed to carry—spoiling any humor—the suggestion that Danny had been whining. Across the table Mom's crumpled letter still lay beside Greg's plate. Danny jammed it deep into his back pants pocket. "I don't understand, I don't speak English," he said in Japanese; then in English, "What are you doing today?"

"Shopping. You wanna come?"

"Sure."

They went to Takashimaya, where Carrie bought an extension cord and a bottle of wine, and to Maruzen, where she bought an expensive scarf and a book of crossword puzzles, and to Meidi-ya, where she bought Cheddar cheese and Twining's Earl Grey Tea and McVitie's Digestives. Danny played the role of porter, consolidating bags into larger bags as the purchases mounted. Carrie's thanks over cocoa in a coffee shop on Kawaramachi suggested she'd seen enough of him for the day, but he managed to get himself invited back to her place, and from there to some kind of party at some American friends of hers. All afternoon, walking through the crowds, his chilly hands gripped around her parcels, Danny composed letters home, and one also to Dr. Nebbin, which forthrightly began, "Dear Bump, I've always considered you an egregious ass."

Carrie changed into a skirt for the party, which turned out to be a dismal gathering—nothing but Americans, eight in all, and all of them teachers of English. Gaijin. There were simply too many of them, Danny's homeless compatriots: floating people, lazy pilgrims who lived off the generosity and curiosity of this bustling, prosperous people. The party's hosts were an older married couple, Frank and Angela, who looked so much alike (wan, fair-haired, with identical small-bridged noses that bulbed into a hemisphere at the tip) they seemed siblings rather than spouses. They'd lived in Japan for eight years and spoke Japanese even less well than Danny. Pervasive, remarkable ignorance in no way impeded conversation, however, which centered around the soullessness of the Japanese, their materialism and automatonlike capacity for work. Beer was served, and the wine Carrie had contributed, while a frizzy-haired man, Peter Haas, maybe thirty, discoursed with wild imprecision about Japanese trade regulations. He called Carrie "Care" and turned out to be a potter. Another man, named Aaron, who was in the lengthy process of divorcing his Japanese wife, confidently and with equal ignorance spoke on crime in Japan and the American criminal justice system.

"I don't think that's quite right," Danny said.

"Aaron, you better be careful," Carrie said. "We've got a Harvard lawyer in the room."

"A Harvard lawyer?" Peter said.

"Japan *has* capital punishment," Danny corrected, "and the rising American crime wave seems to bear no clear statistical relation to the presence or absence of capital punishment, although there's some evidence that in rare cases capital punishment may actually serve as an inducement rather than a deterrent." Ignoring the gaze of patent boredom with which Aaron was watching himself disabused—that clogged resistance to learning anything—Danny concluded, "Some studies suggest that the death penalty may provide an allure for certain criminals bent on destroying themselves," and sipped from his beer. His knees were tucked against his chest, for the night was cold and the room unheated. Suddenly, in another of those rapid turnabouts he'd known these past few days, he wished Greg were here: Grego, who'd left Nepal because it was too full of American potters.

"All I know," Aaron said, "is that when I leave my house in Japan I don't lock the door."

"Surely you know more than that," Danny said, which was snotty but he couldn't resist it. "But in any case, your facts weren't quite right."

"The *fact* is that Japan is a much safer country."

"Maybe, but that isn't the fact you quoted." Danny delivered this with some passion; he felt himself a standard-bearer again, as he had so often as a history major in college. Everywhere, at every moment, people were bending the facts of history, sometimes out of mere sloppiness, but mostly out of partisanship . . . The liberals, the conservatives, the politicians, the women, the rich, the blacks, management, labor, the abhorrent professional liars at *Pravda* and Tass—ideologues who for all their dissimilarities harbored a mutual conviction that theirs was a cause to which the truth was rightly subordinated. "You said something else, you said something else entirely." And in a pique of righteousness he returned to earlier inaccuracies, correcting Peter on the unemployment rate in England and a woman whose name he hadn't caught on her assertion that the Apollo moon landing occurred in the same year as Bobby Kennedy's assassination. And when, later in the evening, Angela, his hostess, erred hugely on the number of people immediately killed when the bomb was dropped on Hiroshima, he set her straight, too.

"I was just there," she replied. "Only a month ago."

"No one disputes your itinerary," Danny said, varying an endlessly successful line employed by Professor Zutto in Secured Transactions. "It's your statistic that's in question." Poor Zutto: the man was dying, his intestines doubly eaten by ulcers and cancers, and yet he used to have them laughing out loud, big rolls of hilarity, while steadily inculcating the most boring subject Danny had ever encountered.

"You must be a great *reader*," Peter the potter said, and everyone laughed, just as though some witty, devastating anathema had been delivered.

No one, certainly not Carrie, who did not even walk him to the door, was sorry to see Danny leave early. The night was cold enough that his breath emerged in gray wisps under the silver panel streetlights, and Danny said aloud, "The truth must be protected," and, delighted by the unintended funny plumminess of the remark, added, "It will liberate us all." From a vending machine he bought two large bottles of Kirin and went over to Greg's where some time after midnight, having finished both bottles, he sat at the table Greg used as a desk and began typing a letter to his father.

Because he'd never in his life received a letter from Dad, to write him was to drop words into a void—much like stammering one's message, after the beep of a tape recorder at the other end, into a telephone. Danny worked steadily, though, and finished the letter at a quarter to three, not once having risen from his chair. It was four pages long, single-spaced. He had tried to work thoughtfully, tempering his bewilderment and rage.

Danny began to reread the letter, set it down neatly on the table, and borrowing a hooded turquoise sweat shirt from the floor rambled out into the dozing street. Even now, with most of the city lights extinguished, there were few stars visible. It was always this way in Kyoto, even after a scouring wind all day had blown straight and cool and clean from the mountains. Since moving to Japan he'd not had a night, not a single night, when the stars blazed in all their opulent, chunky solidity.

He wandered first to the murmuring river, its puckering surface catching streetlights and occasional headlights and stray bobbing glints that were quickly folded back into the current. Then he walked past Carrie's apartment, all lights out, then south to Imadegawa-Kawaramachi, dead, too, except for the temporary sweep of a taxi. The McDonald's had been closed for hours. Standing beside it, indeed almost directly beneath the golden arch, and catching from there a glimpse of Hiei-zan ("sacred Mount Hiei" as described on the guidebook page taped to Greg's wall), with its "skyview restaurant and coffeeshop" just barely visible as a black silhouette at the summit, he was visited unexpectedly by a memory of New York. Thoughts of New York had all but vanished since his arrival in Japan, as one exotic environment expunged another. What he now recalled, with such vividness, was just how he'd felt the week in July he'd worked late every night on the Shiomee case. On June 30, 1978, a cofferdam had collapsed in a rural stretch of Texas, drowning thirteen workers. The tragedy of their deaths (Danny had read some of the local newspaper accounts, had glanced at the rows of victims' faces) perforce soon lay buried beneath a deluge of legal complexities—issues of jurisdiction, comparative negligence and contribution, indemnity clauses, disclaimer provisions, worker's compensation allowances, contractors' and subcontractors' responsibilities, expert witnesses, shifting burdens of proof, preservation of evidence, OSHA regulations. The litigation paperwork was bottomless. Danny would leave the office after midnight to find Wall Street still dimly restive in the warm night, not just the watchmen and cleaning men and the lights in offices where problems pressed even more heavily than the cofferdam's collapse, but a few couples strolling arm in arm in this mysterious unresidential neighborhood, and solitary figures hustling toward clandestine errands, and a sudden upwelling of unanswerable questions—What were these people up to? Where, collectively, were all of these expensive, sleepless offices heading? What was he doing here?

He would have to write Huck, Meadows soon—very soon—to say whether he would be back next summer. He'd been avoiding the question. The work this past summer had been exciting, far more enjoyable than hard work was supposed to be, and yet Danny now found, though not sure why, he didn't want to return next summer. Greg had mentioned going "island hopping" across the Pacific, which was one possibility, or Danny could spend the summer alone in cool New Zealand, in steamy Sri Lanka . . . Settled once more into the musty, comfortingly familiar stink of Greg's room, he began in a dispassionate mood to proofread the letter. When he came to the phrase, "I don't mean to blame you for what's happened," he picked up a pen and printed firmly in the margin, "That isn't true. I blame you for everything." Yet this, too, was a lie, a melodramatic one, and after a moment's reflection he squeezed in a "nearly" before "everything." With a gratifying sense that he'd said something true at last, or at least not untrue, at least not falsely dramatic or cerebral or magnanimous, he crumpled the four sheets into a ball and tossed them toward the Mister Donut box that served Greg as a wastebasket. They landed short. He lay down on the futon and, the hood of Greg's sweat shirt still over his head, he fell asleep.

Early the next morning, after he'd uncrumpled the letter to his father, reread it, and decided it was not wholly contemptible, and if not mailed should at least be saved, Danny rode Greg's bicycle over to Carrie's. After a long delay she came to the door wearing some pink furry slippers and a yellow and green floral bathrobe, a blanched film of sleep still papering her face. "Top of the morning," Danny said with exaggerated heartiness. "Uhn," she grunted, playing her own exaggerated role, and gestured him inside. She shuffled over to the couch in her slippers and plopped down with her long legs folded over the arm.

"Sorry to get you up," Danny said. "Can I make you some coffee?"

"Hnn. Tea. Please."

Relieved to find she intended her gruffness to be appealing, and hence wasn't truly angry about the party, Danny took happily to the role of ministering servant. Carrie had tins of all sorts of expensive English tea, a taste she'd developed in London. He made for her a cup of Vintage

Darjeeling with milk, for himself a cup with milk and sugar. Carrie opened her eyes as he passed her the mug and said, "We drank too much last night."

"Shame on you. I'm sorry if I was rude to all those jerks."

"They're not jerks," she said, but forcelessly; there ensued a comfortable silence as they sipped their tea.

"You want some toast?" Carrie asked. "Or Cheezu Toasto, as they say in the Japanese coffee shops."

"I'll make it."

"No, that's all right."

So now it was Danny's turn to lie on the couch and watch food being prepared. When Carrie's hair was dirty (the case more often than one might expect of someone who had the luxury of a shower), she would wear it pulled back, as now, in a ponytail. Danny watched her cut bread and cheese, and when she'd set them in the toaster oven he rose from the couch and (her eyes tracking him, her hands frozen on the knife and loaf of bread) wordlessly approached her. It was apparent to her at about the same time as to him, for he'd had no conscious design as he rose from the couch, what it was he was about to do: taking the nubbly upper arms of her bathrobe into his hands, he kissed her, once on the cheek and once snappingly on the mouth. She laughed and said, "Danny, what are you doing?" but also, fetchingly, her pale face flushed. She set the knife and bread aside. Finding in silence a stronghold, Danny stared into her blue eyes, stepped forward and, though she swung her face at the last instant, managed once more to kiss her near the mouth. She laughed again and said, "Danny, I haven't even brushed my teeth yet," and flushed still more deeply.

"I thought," Danny said, returning to the couch, "we could go to Kobe today. I remember you said you'd heard there was a good Indian restaurant. And there's that art exhibit you wanted to see."

"I don't know where either of them are. I've never been to Kobe."

"Either of them *is*. Me neither, that's all part of the fun. Carrie, how 'bout it?"

"It would take me forever to get ready. I've got to shower and everything."

"I'll wait," Danny said.

She brought him his cheese toast and disappeared into the bathroom. "Is it okay if I bring a blanket out here? It's kind of cold," Danny called.

"Or go in and lie down if you want. I'm going to be a while."

Danny finished his toast, cleaned the crumbs from his shirt with a licked fingertip, and shuffled into her bedroom and lay down on the unmade bed and closed his eyes. He seemed, lately, to be resting everywhere but in his own apartment. There was a smell here, too, much fainter than at Greg's and a kind of inverse odor—a soapy, powdery, flowery scent, more vegetal than animal. The words *I haven't even brushed my teeth yet* echoed with enriching promise. They seemed to imply that what was lacking was not volition but mere timeliness; clocks everywhere, the precise wheels meshing, were revolving toward the opportune instant.

Danny had nearly dozed off by the time Carrie at last returned from the bathroom. "Out," she said. "I ga change."

"I won't peek. I'll cover my head with a pillow."

"Come on. Out." The look on her hard-boned face was one of indulgent, feigned impatience. She liked him, she really did, he was nearly sure of that.

So why, then, was the scenario in his head so inconceivable—that she would now demonstrate that easy carnal eagerness one found in the movies and the correspondence columns of men's magazines? Why impossible that she should flutter over here in her bathrobe to join him on this bed? On his way past her, ticklingly aware of her clotheslessness under the robe, her skin still warm with the shower, he flicked a swiping hand toward her bottom. He balked his swing at the final moment and his fingertips grazed only the robe's nubble. Yet as he stood waiting in the living room, his fingertips actually warmed and tingled at this oblique and unremarked contact.

Danny carried this sense of oblique pursuit throughout the long trip to Kobe. For they were constantly touching as lightly as though by chance—his leg against hers as they sat in the crowded train, hand brushing hers as they drifted through the tiny art show. She'd worn a skirt and makeup and she looked quite pretty, a prize anywhere, but especially so in this country where her height and her blondeness and her Occidental angularity caught eyes wherever she went. The exhibit, too, an assemblage of old German art from a private collection, was an unforeseen pleasure. Many of the paintings and etchings excelled at very sharp natural detail. He knew it was unsophisticated, but always he reveled in detail for its own sake—favored a keenly etched tree, each ruck in the bark offered up to the eye, over a muzzy one; loved the yapping dog whose every alerted hair stood individually erect, or the street scene in which the mullioned windows and accumulated bricks evidenced a degree of care commensurate with the actual composition of a medieval town. Partly what such detail conveyed was reassurance: the knowledge that it was not merely sensibility, but a solid and cool craftsmanship, that forever debarred him from being able to duplicate what the artist had done. And it brought him a longed-for sense that painting might be truly noble, as it was supposed to be. One of the things he loved best about Nature was its unlimited warranty that every detail would be seen to, that one could plunge headlong into a cypress swamp, where no one had walked in years, hoist a fallen log and find every silky white-haired root, every decomposing scrap of duff, every writhing slug, done to a consummate finish. Nature cut no corners, and Danny was grateful for this, grateful for everything and, oh, so full of love this morning!—for the distant Michigan woods, for the dear dead German artist who had gone to all the trouble of painting what must in his own day have been a dirty and nondescript street, for dear Carrie who bore herself in the gallery with an unconscious stiffness, a jerky stateliness, as if she felt herself about to be challenged. "I'm no dummy," Danny abruptly said aloud—and recoiled, at once mortified at the unbidden sound of his voice and mystified as to what exactly he'd meant by this.

Dense with gaijin businessmen, who were speaking not only English but German and French, and with panels and panels and tubes and tubes of abeyant neon lights that owlishly waited for nightfall, the streets of Kobe evoked Tokyo and the days when Mom's nearest pursuer was the idealized Mr. Tanizaki. Danny recalled, for no reason, something wonderful that Penny had once done. This was way out in Lansing, an hour-and-a-half's drive from Detroit. He'd gone out there with the Greyfield tennis team, and midway through his match he'd looked over and there she was on the sidelines—so unexpected a face it honestly seemed his eyes were playing tricks.

The Indian restaurant was actually quite good, and he and Carrie ate themselves into a slow-moving contentment; on the train home, she leaned her head on his shoulder and for ten minutes or so, while Danny tried to hold himself quite still, she closed her eyes.

Yet things began somehow to sour once back in Kyoto. The weather was turning raw with sleet or snow. Carrie seemed restless, tired of his company, and it would be a couple of hours, at least, before they could consider dinner. When Danny remarked (seemingly an unexceptionable observation) that the common practice among Japanese mothers of dressing their little boys in very short shorts on such a cold day was pretty peculiar, Carrie replied that she saw nothing odd about it. This was merely a different culture. Yet their little legs, Danny could not help pointing out, had turned bluish with cold!

On Carrie's suggestion they entered the charged din of an electronic games parlor. They played Space Invaders twice, and she won both times, once narrowly and once handily, and Astral Defenders ("We are the Defenders—Mission: Destroy Aliens"), which she won twice and Danny once. She was actually quite good at these games, which Danny had never much cared for. He changed a thousand-yen note into hundred-yen coins and they moved from game to game in the pulsing darkness, to the sound of electronically roiled horns and bugles and buzzers and bells and maddeningly repetitive (the more so as they evoked his landlord's daughter on her electone piano) organ runs. They played Big Boy Basketball, which Danny won once and tied once, and Asteroids, which Danny lost three times in a row. Danny felt a towering headache being erected, girder by girder, at the base of his skull. At Carrie's urging, and she was not to be dissuaded, Danny changed another two grand into coins, and eventually another, as they moved into games unfamiliar to them both, where their coins bought them very little time, a few thrashing moments was all. Yet unskillful though they both were, she was beating him steadily, and, laughing, she said so: "This is so good for my ego. I'm *trouncing* you at nearly everything." Feckless Danny saw his little forces exploded by floating missiles, chased down mazy corridors into deadly cul-de-sacs, nuzzled off the road by outsize trucks, blasted by pirate galleons, gunned down by silhouette cowboys, decapitated, eviscerated, immolated, cannibalized, atomized, even seized in a roc's talons and carried off beyond the screen's edge, from which no one ever returned. "We've gone back to the caves. It's a new race of troglodytes," Danny called as they stepped into the comparative quiet of Kawaramachi Street.

"What?"

The sky had grown dark and the wind's bitter sting felt bracing. When Danny asked her to have dinner with him, indifferent to her response, she paused a moment before, with equal indifference, assenting. "Wait here," she told him, "I got to make a phone call." Yet at the sight of her clopping across the street in her skirt and heels, the muscles in her lean calves hopping, his indifference collapsed into a sense of hopeless, self-castigating desire.

They went to an overpriced Italian restaurant on Kiyamachi, where two waiters collided with an enormous shocking din of shattered glass, and where after dinner Danny badly unnerved himself with a little game. Carrie had gone to make another phone call and Danny was playing with the plastic straw from his glass of Coke (his failure to order wine had drawn an actual grimace from the waiter), speculating what it would be like to have to breathe through a windpipe of so small a diameter. He breathed in and out through the straw. One would never be able to jog or play tennis, but one could live all right, one could still get by. While sucking in, he narrowed the aperture further by partially blocking the other end with the ball of his thumb. One could still live, even with so small a windpipe, but this was approaching real hellishness. His breath rasped in the plastic straw. He narrowed the aperture still further and sucked in desperately, and then in his mind's eye he beheld a colossal seated ghost, emphysematic Grandpa Jaynes, whose once powerful rigger's hands clenched the edge of the wooden dining room table, knuckles and veins raised as he struggled and struggled just to get a little of the earth's free air into and out of his lungs. Carrie returned and Danny, sweating a little, paid the bill (Carrie today seemed as set on his paying everything as she usually was rigid about going halves), and they took a bus to Carrie's, where she made Bloody Marys and at her prompting they played Scrabble. The game was interminable, and Danny slipped behind by steady increments. His mind wasn't on it. They'd placed the board on the floor, rather than at the kitchen table, and Danny was continually having to fidget as his back tired or the forearm he'd propped himself upon fell asleep. When he stretched his leg over her leg, she slid out from underneath with a kind of absent automaticity, as though his advance was a chance oversight. This day, begun so promisingly, was falling apart. *I haven't even brushed my teeth yet.* That she could concentrate so intently on this game was both discouraging and insulting. Covertly he studied the jut of her ankles beneath her nylons and the shallow bulge of her sweater at the breast. Desire had taken him as badly as it ever did: an expansive uncoiling that threaded down his legs to knot behind his knees, and climbed in nausea-inducing filaments up through his stomach to touch, physiologically, his heart.

At last all available tiles were fitted into their mosaic of defeat and Carrie tabulated the irrelevant final deductions for the precise total: he'd lost by 44 points. She suggested a second game and Danny, taking a supine, perverse pleasure in thwarting his own inclinations, agreed. He lost the second game by 51 points. It was 11:30.

"Come on," Danny said, "we've got to hurry if we're going to make last call at the Texas."

"I don't want to. It's freezing out there."

"Come on," Danny insisted, for he'd surely won some measure of pliancy. "Come on. Come on."

"It's co-old," Carrie whined, but she was laughing as she did so.

Yet on reaching the True Time Texas over Carrie's grumbling Danny found it wasn't the sanctuary he sought and he wanted no part of the two half-liters of beer they'd ordered. Restlessness again began to nibble at him. He sensed that things—already botched—were steadily becoming worse; he should have left Carrie hours ago.

Instead he now led her, again over protestations, from the True Time Texas to Greg's. What was the point of going to Greg's, she wanted to know, where it was going to be cold and there was nothing to do?—and because Danny had available no clear answer, either for her or himself, he said only, "Come on, come on, come *on*." In Greg's room it was cold enough to see your breath. Danny turned on the slow-to-activate panel heater. Carrie propped her head against the wall and wrapped a blanket about herself, from which emerged only her mocking eyes.

Why *had* he been so insistent, when they could have gone back to her place, where heat, among other luxuries, was plentiful? With every shivering moment working to make him look that much more ridiculous, Danny lay beside her on the mat, outside the blanket, and kissed her briefly, then dipped for a longer second kiss. Carrie kept her eyes open, he discovered, opening his own midway. She said, "I'm freezing."

"You're the one under the blanket."

She lifted the blanket's edge and he slid in beside her and drew his arms tightly around her. She was skinny, like him. Even with their many layers of clothing he could feel that kindred spareness, the protuberant ribs and hipbones. He kissed her again, her mouth loosening a little to his, although he glimpsed through the filmy thatch of his long half-closed eyelashes her open, observant eyes. He lifted his face and planted on each of her eyes a kiss, which closed them. She opened them once more. Again he kissed them shut, and she laughed, pleased at this. He kissed her thin bony nose, while on guard against her eyes opening, and kissed her jutting chin. He kissed her whorled earring, his tongue tracing along to where, a conjunction not of taste but of texture and temperature—flesh and metal—it pierced the lobe. The air was cold on their faces, and the earring left the momentary chill print of its inorganic hardness on his tongue.

"It's late," Carrie said. "I ga teach tomorrow."

As he had this morning, when he'd kissed her beside the toaster oven, he took refuge in silence. Her mouth opened to his kiss, tongue-tip touching tip. She eased back for him, sighing. Three times he licked her neck in long swipes that dried his tongue while his hands reached under the back of her sweater. When his fingers over her shirt found the clasp of her brassiere, she jerked as if about to protest, but thankfully it came undone at a single pinch. Its silent release offered him a gift of time, liberation from the moment's constriction, while behind him the panel heater ticked as its electric nerve system began to kindle.

"I've been an awful bitch, haven't I?"

"Not so awful," Danny said.

They looked into each other's eyes a moment and then Carrie hugged him, fiercely, for a long time, maybe a minute, as immobile Danny grew increasingly aware of the dark damp plunging of his own heart-beat. Her grip loosened, accompanied by a grunted "Uhn," and when his mouth found her mouth again the tightness in her jaw had eased and her tongue swiped across his upper lip. For some reason he thought of a wet sponge passing over a pane of glass, a cleaned windshield at a filling station. Ahead, blue sky. His hands slid easily up the front of her sweater, under her blouse, to her small breasts, and her breath turned loftly in his ear. Penny used to whisper his name: "Da-*nee*, Da-*nee*." Carrie began to stroke his back, under his sweater vest but over his shirt, her long nails snagging a little on the cloth. Danny killed the light and dropped his head beneath the blanket, and then beneath her bulky sweater, his mouth homing on those same breasts she'd refused to show him just this morning. Standing there in her furry pink slippers and bathrobe, ordering him out of the bedroom. Even then he had felt the gears turning, clocks and minutes conspiring to move them here—a few hours later, a few blocks distant—where everything was altered.

She began to stroke his hip, the proximate heel of her hand turning him sidewisedly erect in the swaddle of pants and underwear as her own hips began to pitch. Yet when his hand settled below her waist, she tugged it away.

Her skirt had floated over her knees and he deposited his hand on the somewhat abrasive mesh, like a windowscreen, of her stockinged thigh, but when his hand began to ascend she again pulled it away. "This isn't a good time," she whispered.

Danny broke his silence to say, over the yammering at his temples, "Oh no this a very good time." His voice emerged in a kind of childish singsong. "This a very good time," he repeated, and dropped his hand again on her nearly naked leg.

"This isn't a good time," Carrie repeated, enclosing his hand in hers. She kissed the palm of his hand. "Maybe . . . something else," she seemed to say, but he wasn't sure. Nor was he sure what she might be offering. Yet it was clear this wasn't what he wanted.

"This is an exceptionally good time," Danny chanted. "I don't know if you, there are . . . " He paused. With their hands they had crossed a barrier not yet traversed in their speech and he feared making some mistake. She knew the condoms were there (she'd laughed over them when Greg had given her a tour of the place), and yet actually to mention them was perhaps to suggest a design that Danny himself, at least consciously, had been unaware of. "You know those condoms over there."

"I mean this isn't a good time for me. I've just started my period."

Why was he always so slow about grasping such things? "That's all right," he told her hurriedly, to suggest that he'd understood all along. "I'd still want to, if it's all right."

"You don't mind using a condom?" A dispassion had entered her voice; it was as though this were a purely hypothetical question. Clearly someone else, her Huesing, her guy Guy, had minded.

"I don't mind them," Danny said, although most of his few encounters with them had proved mortifying. He'd always had such trouble getting the damn things on. Was one even necessary if Carrie was in her period? This disclosure of bleeding between her legs had subtly transformed the bundle of her body in his arms. With Penny, they'd usually abstained—moved to other activities—those days of the month.

"Why don't you wait here," Carrie said, and slid out from under the blanket.

The moment she'd left the room Danny turned on the light, a sense of momentous incredulity adding a tremble to his hands. Unbelievable as it was, it now appeared commitments had gone far enough that not even Carrie could evade him. His fumbling hands hurrying, he opened the pack of condoms and found that one of the two inner boxes was missing. How many had been used, then? From the second inner box he drew forth a string of four in green aluminum foil. The mature thing to do, probably, was to accept their presence in an almost businesslike fashion, as a necessary tool, but he'd always been drawn toward romantic attempts to make them wholly unobtrusive (and then disastrously would have to halt everything as he fought to get the thing on). Better not to risk that now—though she might think it irregular to find him already ready. He tore open the foil, lowered his pants, and in the fluorescent light, discovering that what he continued to think of as his *dick* (though the word had a somewhat childish ring, and he'd conscientiously been trying to switch himself mentally over to *prick*) had begun to slacken, he momentarily took upon himself—aware of all the excruciating irony—the task he'd been hoping to pass to another for months now. The sound of footsteps slapped his hand away with a guilty jerk. But in an instant he had managed to slip the thing on, to turn off the light, and to draw the blanket over himself. Outside, in the street, an old woman, perhaps two old women, or an old woman and an old man, were talking. In the cold, and at this late hour. Their voices were dim, not a single word or even syllable intelligible, and yet merely by the intonation, a high-pitched streaming that lifted again and again toward a plea for corroboration, it was borne in upon Danny that they were speaking Japanese and he was thousands of miles from everything he knew.

The ground beneath his feet gives generously. However lightly he steps he is plunged in over the ankle. Frigid snowmelt oozes up to slosh almost to the tops of his pliant new waterproof boots and the humic ground releases his foot with a luscious, reluctant kiss. There is nowhere to step that does not disturb this marvelous murmurous inbred bed of organic laminae—brown leaves and the ribs of ferns, stems and husks and follicles, needles and fur, all in the April sun sleeping, steeping toward spring's multiplex explosion.

The light in this dream congregates in agitated pools, batting frenziedly here and there like golden tadpoles. The environs are familiar, for this is a little like Waugoshance Point on Lake Michigan, or the flats around the mouth of the Two Hearted on Lake Superior. It is the genius of this place to engender in an enchanted union of coolness and sumptuosity a joy that brings to all things whetted edges: the lacy, crystalline bloom of hoarfrost, the chlorophyll-filled pluckiness of each autonomous pine needle, the distant cedars, the scabrous rock-faces, the pellucid stepping-stones of pond water.

And Danny is tracking. He has glimpsed through the window of this dream, and may soon again glimpse, a cleanlimbed family of deer. Almost *heartbreaking*, that moment, as they pored over him with eyes of such consummate gentleness as to seem almost otherwordly—nomads on the chartless flatlands of another planet. Nothing in creation pulls at the heart like distance. Equal to this domain's demands, the tawny sun had clung idolatrously to the slope of their like-tawny flanks and lit from below their tipped, enviably expressive ears. Then their collective glance had dropped from his and the family—twenty, thirty or so—quickly and without a sound had flown. But this was the zone wherein they lived, those warm tawny beasts with candles in their eyes: here where nails of ice had hammered winter into the ground and the frost's velvet geometry perfected the sun.

Carrie in trying to wake him was finding him, he apperceived, resistant. She was leaving; she had to go teach. She was fretting and offering apologies. He lifted his head from the pillow and caught a kiss on his upper lip, dropped his head back and plunged at once into another sort of sleep, opaque rather than radiant, deep and dreamless. This was unusual, sleeping like this—so heavily, so late into the morning.

Nearly noon when Danny came to abruptly, wide-awake. He padded downstairs to the freezing bathroom where he discovered a muddy smear, like a coffee stain, at the base of his undershirt. Mystified for a moment, in the next he realized, with squeamishness and exultation, that this was Carrie's own blood. Blood was on his underwear as well, and at the roots of his pubic hair, and along his belly like some kind of war paint, and—it was everywhere!—caked into the nails and cuticles and seams of three fingers of his right hand. A strong shiver grabbed him by the shoulders and shook him. Racing along, Danny washed his hands and face in the tap's gelid water, brushed his teeth, and urinated. Upstairs, he scavenged among the litter of Greg's floor until he located some not too unclean underclothes, which he traded for his bloody ones. Carrie would not be back from Osaka until later this afternoon at least. Danny rode Greg's bicycle downtown to Maruzen where he looked at American magazines, most of them boasting photos of Reagan grinning that infuriating elastic grin (the thought of Mom in distant Michigan seeing the same magazines, and feeling a similar disappointment and faint revulsion, somehow cheered Danny a little), and browsed among the books. Turned so that its cover faced outward, the better to stare from the shelf, Hobbes' *Leviathan* brought on an influx of guilt, and Danny in propitiation bought Locke's *Second Treatise on Government*, another of Umeda's favorite texts. With the book and some tuna sushi and two pieces of chocolate cake under one arm, he rode back over to Greg's. The long sleep had done him good. Locke before him, Danny's mind engorged the paragraphs in whole blocks, as happened only when he was at his best.

At four he wandered on foot toward Carrie's. He found a flower shop and bought half a dozen roses from a rather spectral old woman who seemed to be losing her hair. Carrie wasn't home. Outside her door, he wrote a little note to insert among the flowers. "How about another round of Space Invaders?," but on realizing the words contained a bawdy double entendre he hastily tore the note in half. He waited, pen poised, for a new message, but nothing came. He wrote once more "How about another round of Space Invaders?" and then, quite suddenly extraordinarily pleased with himself, pleased and complicitous, he started walking back toward Greg's. Sheer exhilaration propelled "Boodlededoo!," a pure nonsense word, from his chest, and then he was off, at a quick jog, running in the fine Kyoto sunshine.

Danny located some soap, shampoo, and a dry towel (there were always clean dry towels at Greg's—his landlady saw to that) and headed over to the public bath. Perched on one of the low stools, no one close by, Danny scoured the remaining evidence of blood from his hands and body. So much blood: it was as though (something he'd never done, once it was revealed that Penny had first slept with her cousin) he'd gone to bed with a virgin. As he lowered himself into the tub, its intense heat seemed to fill and swell within him like a breath, a beneficent insufflation that emerged from his mouth in a grunted cry of contentment: "Omm." He submerged himself to the neck, dropped his head against the tile, gazed at the ceiling a moment, closed his eyes, and gave himself over wholly to the water's fire.

"What's the matter with Carrie?" Greg asked a second time.

The first time, in a fruit parlor in Kyoto over mangoes and whipped cream, Danny had managed to elude the question. Now, again seated, this time in a sushi bar in Osaka with shrimp and tuna and bonito and sake warmly bulked inside him, an answer seemed more manageable, though Danny remained apprehensive. For hours now—in the fruit parlor, in the train to Osaka, here in the sushi bar—they'd both been moving warily. "Tell me again. What did she say?" Danny asked.

"I don't know, we just talked a couple minutes. She just sounded sort of weird. Distracted. She was talking about going home in February."

Actually it was Greg, back today from Korea, his face covered with the thick roots of a beard, who seemed altered—*weird*—to Danny, who was feeling a resumption of that unease Greg had inspired in their first encounters: intimations that the mind behind those keen brown eyes truly might be a bit unbalanced. Weird. *Weird* was the catchall term for the day. Asked how he liked Korea, and why he'd stayed longer than planned, Greg had said little more than that it was weird. "Korea seemed so *weird.* The people were very nice, I took an instant shine, liked them better than the Japanese, but I don't know, maybe it was just me, I felt so *weird* there." Greg looked changed—looked older with the beard.

Any change in Greg was regrettable, for what Danny wanted (though sensing this would prove impossible) was to carry on as before, to continue that pursuit of *progress*. Toward this end, he had agreed to come tonight to Osaka for the sort of evening, sodden and expensive, Greg loved best.

"It's just for a friend's wedding," Danny said. "She'll be coming back."

"Did you see a lot of her?"

"Pretty lot. In fact . . . " Danny halted; then, discovering that this *in fact* had at last committed him, continued, "we started sleeping together."

Had Greg earlier in the day played detective, a role he liked to play at playing, he might have discovered this on his own; Greg's sheets, which Danny had washed twice, still bore stubborn bloodstains. It was hard to picture Greg, though, ever noticing the relative cleanliness or filthiness of the sheets he slept on. Greg peered at him with what seemed to be only light, characteristic amusement. All uneasiness appeared to be Danny's alone, who dropped his glance to the filleted eels stacked in the glass counter before them.

"I thought that had begun *long* ago," Greg said matter-of-factly . . . but surely this wasn't true.

In any case, to Danny's relief there seemed to be no resentment in the air. Greg talked for a time about a crazy American he'd met in Korea—actually remet, for they'd first crossed paths in India—who had smuggled five thousand pens ("Pens?" Danny asked delightedly) from Japan to Korea. "But the great detail," Greg went on, "the really great detail, is how he tells me he'd have brought more but didn't know how he'd explain having any more than five thousand pens if he got caught." The phrase *great detail* was so frequently on Greg's lips that Danny jokingly had begun to refer to *Greg details*. This endless search for the colorful and ridiculous, the compressed, absurd quintessence of anything, was one of Greg's most likeable traits, and it had turned out that the two of them appreciated the same sorts of Japanese idiosyncrasies: the young schoolboy wearing a regular watch on one wrist, a digital on the other; the porn magazine whose cover promised "How to Sex"; the man who, according to the *Mainichi Daily News*, was apprehended for jaywalking and, right there on the street, confessed to being a bank robber—these were *great details*. More shrimp was ordered, and two more pitchers of sake. Danny drank and refilled Greg's cup with a kind of hurried gratitude, a mute show of pleasure in meeting no resentment. Greg ordered *toro*, the richest part of the tuna, and two more pitchers of sake, and these two were followed by another and—though Danny was losing track, containers seemed to appear by themselves—another.

When at last they swung from their stools Danny felt himself drifting on a smooth, fluent glide that threatened intermittently to topple. The charged street was like no street he'd ever found in his own country—a chemical bath of neon, beetling blocks and lines and circles of lights, rhomboids and cones and pentagons, blinking and scampering and dilating and exploding, layering beneath and overtopping each other, and multiplying and multiplying interminably. The tuxedoed men and miniskirted women who served as barkers and as lures called out to them enthusiastically, reading in the Americans' visible drunkenness an easy compliance. Greg had begun—earnestly, rapidly, and obscurely—philosophizing, and the flow of words themselves, like the lights, was washing over Danny, who nevertheless marveled at how his friend could remain so steadfast in his obsessions. "You see that it is," Greg was saying, "the fundamental problem of my life. I burrow in so deep—I really do—I send out all sorts of scouts that make all these connections, set up all these networks, extending things, truly extending things . . . "

Whatever the point Greg was attempting, it was clearly not worth the effort of its formulation; yet the almost palpable sense of internal tumult drew from Danny a sympathetic quelling arm which he placed—just as if they were two drunks linked merely to support themselves—on Greg's shoulder. But Greg, plunged in too deep for this, shrugged himself loose and began again: "I work at that, I honestly work very hard at that, and connections are made, they really do seem to be made, but Danny I can't verbalize them. They come up changed, just like those fish that live way down and when you bring them to the surface—"

"Blowfish," Danny interjected, but this wasn't quite right. . .

"By a kind of crazy, mocking twist, they emerge in the form of platitudes."

A man wearing a clown outfit was trying to entice them into a building where, if the advertising photos were to be trusted, big half-naked gaijin women wrestled each other in vats of mud. Danny had read about that. Another successful American import. Redressing the trade imbalance with mud wrestling. Lord knew he hated the way he'd always related to women—his clumsiness and jealousy and old-fashioned squeamishness and all his mooning helplessness at a mixer or singles bar—but he had to be grateful that the spectacle of women wrestling in vats of mud didn't deeply excite him. Or bondage—which the Japanese male seemed so keen on. At every porn vending machine there it was, the ropes and ropes and ropes. You had to be grateful, you really did, profoundly *grateful*, if you didn't feel any desire to tie a woman to your kitchen table. This realization cheered, heartened Danny. He thought of that hypothetical world that was populated only by Danny Otts (rather, that world in which all the males were Danny Otts, while the women were left unchanged) and felt cleansed on perceiving that it would be a planet without rape. He was not paying enough attention to poor Greg, struggling so hard, but was instead letting the words and the clear lights and the muddy photographs slide by, with the hum and honk of the open electronic games parlors. *I'm trouncing you at nearly everything*, Carrie had said. The night they first went to bed. Still, he was listening enough to realize that Greg's attempting this discussion at all was evidence of ongoing friendship, and enough to understand that they knew a common frustration with the ineffable.

"You forgo all kinds of ease, you honestly work hard while knowing that most people aren't, that they think *you're* slacking, and what do you come up with? You come up with *Life is strange* or *You only live once* or *Death is larger than anything*. You come up sounding just like some dumb-ass fool, which is to say just like everybody else.

"And you get the feeling that when the truth comes it will come not to some desperate solitary thinker, but to some technician, some plodding computer programmer. You know that's how they solved the four-color theorem. You know what the four-color theorem is, Danny?"

Amid all the flashing brightnesses Danny's mind coalesced, regimented itself toward mathematical expression. "For any two-dimensional object, like a map, you only need four colors to ensure that no two colors ever overlap."

"Bless you. Bless you, Ott-head, for knowing that. But you know that's how they solved it. No apple falling on Newton's head. They beat it to death with computers. They clubbed the damn thing to death."

NO PAN, NO BURRA said the signboard held aloft by a shabby old man whose look of soured patience and resignation suggested a striker. But he wasn't a striker, Danny realized, he was a pitchman for a restaurant or coffee shop. NO PAN, NO BURRA seemed some sort of garbled attempt at a French or Spanish rendering of No Bread, No Butter, but (a second realization) that wasn't what was intended. As the voluptuous little red-haired cartoon nude below the words made clear, this was Japanese-English for no panties, no bra.

This clarification was followed by a surreally harsh sharpening of focus—Greg's face in the particolored light, the scruffy barbarian's beard, the crazy fix in the eyes—and, next, a coldness at the numbed core of Danny's stomach. What time was it? Was it too late to make the train?

They made the last express train with only four minutes to spare, Danny responsible, despite his swimming head, for buying the tickets and finding seats, while Greg continued his endless rambling discourse. An achingly beautiful young woman in a simple blue frock—looking like an "office lady" from a company or bank, but why hadn't she changed out of her uniform?—lowered herself into the seat ahead of theirs, directly before Greg. Though Danny's glimpse had been brief, he'd caught an impression of a minutely grained perfection—that sense that even her eyelashes were perfectly spaced—and he watched her reflection in the vibrating window with genuine longing. Greg, too, had noticed her, and at last had fallen silent.

"Pretty women make me so sad," he announced after a while. "Don't they make you sad? Danny, don't they make you so *sad*?"

The lights in the train were inhospitably bright, establishing a cold tube of metal and glass and infected humanity, into which a lovely pliant plantlike curlicue of perfume had entered. "Sad?" Danny said. "No, not sad. Hardly sad." The word he wanted lay deep inside him, coiled at the base of his overworked stomach. But what was it?

"Yes, sad. Surely *sad*. It makes me sound terrible, it comes out all wrong, like most things, but in fact it's one of the really decent things I can boast about. Because I can honestly feel that, all that poignance, the opportunity lost day after day. Pretty women—" Greg cleared his throat in a way Danny knew well; the aphorist was about to emerge. " . . . are a reminder, a reminder of all the fine places you'll never wake to in the morning.

"It's so *sad*, Danny, I was in Peru, in this old inn where everything was white, walls, chairs, floors, you woke up and it was just like being inside an egg."

"Ab ovo," Danny said.

"And I got up really early and I went out on this balcony and there's the sun and the mountains, and a gold dog trotting purposefully along, dup dup dup *dup* dup dup, dup dup dup *dup* dup dup, as if he knows just exactly where he's going, and this flowering bush with enormous pink blossoms below me. And I say to myself, *This* is the scene I want to etch permanently in the mind. Kid, *this* is the one, years hence, you want to be able to re-create exactly, down to the petals on the blossoms. And I remember my legs were stiff and I was wearing cutoffs and a T-shirt, barefoot, and my hair was long then, almost down to my shoulders, and thicker of course.

"So why isn't that scene etched, Danny?" An enormous fatigue, spreading far beyond the hum and clatter and coursing of this train, had engulfed Danny, and he closed his eyes on the girl's ghost-reflection. "Why can't I see those mountains as they were?" Greg asked accusingly. "Why has the smell of those flowers vanished? One could simply answer, Because you can't remember, but hell, that's no answer . . . Why *can't* I? Why out of all the billions on billions of moments in my life can't I, using all my will, pluck out one, just a single damn one, and keep it intact? Now is the betrayal merely organic, just some shifting in the brain's chemistry? Is it just because we're incompletely evolved, we're all just dumb apes that happen to ride inside of trains? Or Danny does the failure lie in some complex battle of the will against something else? Something perverse, some fucked-up, slimy twisted little ugly bastard with a toy shovel inside you that fucks up everything?"

Greg, too, was beginning to tire. Lifting one eyelid, Danny watched him knuckling his eye sockets, canting forward enough that had he possessed the keen sense of smell he said he'd lost he might have caught, under the perfume, the secondary scent of the girl's shampoo. Danny closed his eyes once more, reminding himself to remind himself to drink lots of water and toss down some aspirins before going to bed. He'd probably crash at Greg's.

At Ōmiya Station the girl, as Danny noticed through slitted eyes, got up to leave, and when she stood one of her lustrous hairs, which had entwined itself around the metal handclasp at the top of the seat, snapped. Danny watched her go, sweet ghost, shuddering as the train once more shuddered onwards. And then Greg, whom Danny had thought asleep, plucked the hair from the metal clasp and thoughtfully began flossing his front teeth with it.

"Oh God that's terrible," Danny mumbled. "That's absolutely, terribly *terrible*."

"I thought you were asleep," Greg said. "And it is hardly terrible," he added, with that dignity he assumed with such relish. "Danny, it's an act of love."

On the day after the strange day on which he first learned that John Lennon had been murdered by one of his fans, Danny was wandering around Kyoto's downtown with Carrie and Greg when he actually bumped right into Professor Umeda. It was the Professor's secretary, Miss Minowada, who had broken the news to Danny early the day before. Haltingly, she had first told him only that John Lennon, Danny's favorite of the Beatles, was dead. There had been a moment for Danny fervently to hope (and on later reflection it seemed only one more symptom of how insanely violent his country had become that these would be his first thoughts) that Lennon had not been murdered, or if murdered that the killer was not an American. But of course he had been murdered, by an American, and in New York to boot! (And eerily, by a sinister coincidence, the killer was named Chapman—Danny's own middle name.)

Now, on the other side of the world, Greg was getting his first peek at Professor Wall, at Agent Umeda. Bent on some mischief, surely, he invited the Professor to join them for a bowl of noodles and to Danny's surprise and alarm the Professor consented. Neat from head to toe, hair sharply parted and shoes shined, the Professor was wearing another conservative three-piece suit. Although he had a four days' growth of beard, Danny was the least scruffy-looking of the three Americans. Carrie—who seemed either to dress fashionably and carefully or casually and sloppily, with little variation between—was wearing a pair of blue jeans much too big for her narrow waist, bunchily held up by a stringy Indian bead belt, and her dirty dirty-blonde hair was pulled back in a rubberband-held ponytail. Greg had on a sweat shirt that, Danny now noticed, managed at once to be wrinkled, stained, and torn.

Over cups of tea, the Professor inquired of Greg and then Carrie where they'd gone to college, offering a deep nod when Greg said Harvard, a shallower one when Carrie mentioned Brown. He asked Greg what had brought him to Japan. This was the first opportunity Danny'd had to watch Greg explain himself to someone who might be considered an authority figure, and though handling it with assurance Greg didn't show quite the aplomb Danny would have expected. "I'm teaching English. And I study. I used to be a graduate student of English literature, but now I'm studying on my own."

For ten minutes or so, until the food arrived, "The Wall" lived up to his nickname. Greg's roving, probing questions about Japanese politics, the rising movement toward greater militarism, the decline of student radicalism, were all met by a hedging recourse to notions of consensus—"Many people believe so" and "That is one common belief" and "Perhaps it is the growing attitude." Greg's broiled salmon, however, inspired the Professor to recount an anecdote. "It is said, I do not know if this is true, it may simply be unfounded rumor," he began, with that stickler's cautiousness that could make his conversation so laborious, "that the Soviets, who are very fond of salmon I am told, decided to stock their eastern rivers with salmon from their western rivers. But when the fish were moved, they swam out into the ocean and came to settle in the rivers of Japan." The Professor laughed aloud—a sound Danny had never heard—and for one brief astonishing moment a consuming, shattering mirth overran the man's saturnine features.

Greg temporarily confounded the Professor by paying the whole check and refusing—resolutely—the five-hundred-yen note the Professor brandished. Yet as they were parting in front of the shop the Professor seemed to find a comforting inspiration. "At my house, as I have mentioned the possibility to Danny, on the twenty-seventh of this month there is to be a small gathering. I hope you will come," he said to Greg, "you both will come," he said, motioning to Carrie, and with a look of righted equipoise he waved to them and marched briskly off.

This broadened invitation was an unfortunate turn. Danny instinctively sought to keep all dealings with the Professor separate from his

American friends, just as earlier he'd sought to keep his relationships with Greg and Carrie separate. Blend them together and you immediately had problems. As a threesome, he and Carrie and Greg had all sorts of problems. If the three of them had only formed some sort of stable unit before Greg's trip to Korea, things would be far easier now; yet their few previous encounters had been so jumbled and veiledly hostile that no pattern existed which might adapt itself to a situation where Greg was inevitably offered the role of outsider—Danny now reasoned. He himself had been prepared, if placed in such a role, to sever ties with both of them. He could feel sympathy, then, for Greg—who, predictably, didn't seem to ask for any.

A new pattern of jokes had briefly flowered in which, almost as though they were his parents, Danny was pressed into the role of ingenue—the innocent, the wet-behind-the-ears. Taunts were made about his youth (though Carrie was not much older), about his sheltered private school education (though Carrie's schooling had been posh enough), about his freckles and skinniness (though Carrie certainly was skinny), about his shyness and gullibility. For a time Danny played along gladly, aware that the jokes were not slights so much as a makeshift means of moving them toward some trilateral accord, and feeling, further, an obscure guilt, a desire to expiate that unspecified transgression that resided at the core of all their problems. Yet their joking soon began to rile him, especially Carrie's. For it seemed she *was* hostile, even though she, of any of them, had the least grounds for hostility.

And it was Greg, significantly, who after a time dropped this line. Sensing Danny's vexation, or simply growing bored, Greg redrew the routine to group Carrie with Danny. He began addressing them as "you kids" and calling himself "Uncle Gregory," a name which seemed oddly to fit him in those early chilly weeks of December. Strands of gray became visible as his beard grew in, not just at the temples but sewn here and there along the jawline. He had gained weight, or perhaps it was merely the heavier clothes; he was looking thick around the middle.

Danny had also worried that for one reason or another Carrie might stop sleeping with him on Greg's return. This hadn't happened, quite—but she did withhold herself capriciously, as a tactic or perhaps merely through simple lack of interest. Early on, Carrie had told him

I don't want a roommate. While encouraging insofar as it was a tacit affirmation of their ongoing future, the remark jarred against Danny's conviction that between men and women things so intimate should never require open expression. Rather—hints and gestures, divination, the unvoiced yet understood. Here was a great danger, one of the things that constantly put him off with Carrie: he could never be certain she wasn't about to say something awful, something crushing and unforgivable, and how could he ever actually love someone under these circumstances?

Yet if not the first skittery stirrings of love, what were these impulses that sought always to lead him, down so many gray streets packed with shoppers and blinking lights and Santa Clauses and aluminum Christmas trees, toward the Sunshine Mansion? Why was he always willing to surmount so many vague and on Carrie's part steadfastly unacknowledged obstacles just to get her into bed—or better yet, more privileged still, to be allowed to spend the night? Waking in Carrie's bed to darkness and the promise of hours of further darkness, Danny would be forced to question his motivations. Her apartment was warmer than his, it was true, and he preferred a bed to the mat floor, but a night in this room was hardly comforting. For in sleep (just as in everything else it seemed) Carrie was hotly erratic; she tossed and bounced, and sometimes clung fiercely to him, not snuggling so much as grimly affixing herself. The endless tugging, this sense of a soul not at peace, would drag him in the night backward toward menacing dream-regions, dim cliffs and fires and rope bridges, skew but seemingly inescapable chains of logic that led almost syllogistically to some crushing end. And morning light did not always soothe his disquiet. Carrie would wake heavily, dazed like a fighter rousing from a knockout; and while she never made this so damningly clear as to call Danny by the wrong name, there did appear to be instants on waking when she didn't know who he was and he lay as a ghost in her arms.

Yet to this same bed she brought an unspoken sense of experience greater than his own, and these were ghosts of another sort. Danny had to admit that in some way this charged and excited him, these vague, deliberately vague presences: though on those first couple of dates she'd gone on about her broken engagement and he about Penny and his parents, by one of intimacy's paradoxes it now became far harder to discuss past personal matters. For one thing, Carrie had grown formidable; he had more at stake, more to fear from what might issue from those thin, much-kissed lips of hers.

At the same time she began to seem an increasingly vulnerable and uncertain figure to him. Often she'd told him how all throughout junior high and high school she'd been "uncool and unpopular"—which initially Danny had taken as a joke, but now he began to understand how this might have been true. He was given intimations of what she might really have been like: a tall skinny nervous girl with braces on her teeth and an uncontrolled barking laugh. This uncool and unpopular, but extremely endearing, girl would emerge in little unreflective moments, as in the way Carrie, completing a crossword puzzle, would call out a self-congratulatory "*Ta-daa.*"

There was something childish, too, in Carrie's always having her parents and stepparents send her things for which she surely could have found acceptable Japanese substitutes—or the American goods themselves, if only she'd bothered to shop around. Toothpaste, shampoo, magazines, pens, underwear, cough drops . . . Punning on her name, she called these frequent brown parcels Care packages, and the truth was she often wouldn't get around to opening them for a day or two. It was as though she wanted parents and stepparents vying with each other—or at the very least was constantly testing and retesting their allegiance. Yet Danny, facing the prospect of stepparents himself, couldn't bring himself wholly to disapprove of this game—felt too keenly that contrary pull which sent one halfway round the world but kept one forever looking nostalgically over one's shoulder.

It was a confusing time, and for all his conviction that most intimacies needn't be vocalized, Danny sought spoken reassurances from her. On two occasions, both Sundays, they lay in bed and made love all day, Carrie only getting up now and then to renew her diaphragm cream or to bring him something—mostly imported chocolates—to eat. Desire that was an ache inside him became as the day lapsed another sort of ache, itself perhaps merely another facet of desire. All the muscles in the wall of his stomach seemed frayed and he held himself in by wrapping his hands around his thin belly. This was an ache which continually instructed him, falsely, that only one more act of love was required to erase it altogether. Intermittently on those two Sundays he'd wanted to talk about *this*, their being in bed together, but Carrie had proved evasive. She'd joked, and called him *darling*, which she sometimes did, and stuffed his earnest mouth with chocolates. He'd wanted to ask her how many men she'd slept with or whether she'd ever done it in the back seat of a car. His hunger for reassurance seemed to extend beyond a need, which he recognized as immature, for an explicit admission that she loved going to bed with him. What chiefly disturbed him was how these long timeless Sundays seemed to have so little bearing on anything else. A mere hour after they'd gone to bed, the two of them having joined Greg at the Texas, Carrie would be teasing him, Carrie and Greg would be teasing him (while Danny's semen was still manfully thrashing against the spermicidal jelly inside her) about his "boyishness."

It was true that Carrie had begun teasing Greg too—mostly when he began one of his crazy philosophical monologues. She could be quite harsh about it. She who had listened to him so raptly those first few times now seemed to find his speculations irritating. "What the hell are you talking about?" she would say. Or simply, "Oh bullshit." Greg himself seemed to enjoy these challenges from her; his eyes would light up as he rambled unflappably along ("Now if you assume, if you assume, there's some man in your brain who's in charge of closing doors, who does this without your even asking him to, indeed who's hardly aware of you, just as you're hardly aware of him—" "What the hell are you talking about?" "—the question is, Is there some way of countermanding his orders, I mean can Carrie open Carrie's mind?" "Oh bullshit"). But Carrie's comments angered Danny. She seemed to *want* Greg's talk all to be nonsense. She wasn't rooting for him—as Danny was. And this seemed almost cruel of her.

Meanwhile the problem of Christmas gifts daily mounted. Danny had a vacillating fear of embarrassing himself by spending too little or too much on Carrie. He asked her if she'd like to go in with him on a gift for Greg, for whom shopping would be easy. Danny had already settled on the gifts: a new map of the world, to replace the one he'd ripped from the wall, and an enormous basket of fruit, which in this season was going to be expensive, so Carrie's help would be welcome. But Carrie didn't want to help, for she'd already settled on her own something for Greg: a pair of gloves.

A pair of gloves . . . What did that mean Danny himself might expect from her? And what did that mean he should plan to spend? Bewildered, though happily so at first, Danny wandered up and down crowded Kawaramachi, Teramachi, and tiny shopping streets that seemed to have no name. One cold night powdered the city's surrounding mountaintops with snow, and Danny would emerge from a shop to be pleasantly re-surprised at how the slopes had grown nearer and more delicate. Clothing of any sort, he'd decided, was out. Women's clothing stores were always a foreign land, in which he was an unregistered alien, and with his broken Japanese he could expect little real assistance from any of the rattled Japanese shop girls. Jewelry was too intimate. He thought about perfume, and even went so far as to inhale, assisted by a deeply beautiful and grave young Japanese woman, a bouquet of scents that dizzied and prickled him as he looked down into her guileless, inquiring black eyes. He considered what seemed to him a lovely Japanese watercolor print of horses (Carrie loved horses), but any sort of artwork was too risky. He settled on a little box of absurdly overpriced Godiva chocolates, a handsome two-volume paperback of *The Tale of Genji*, which Carrie had often though perhaps not quite seriously vowed to read before leaving Japan, and—with a Detroiter's lingering loyalty to Motown Records, though the company on making it big had sashayed out to L.A.—a new Stevie Wonder tape, "Hotter than July."

Christmas was in Danny's mind a season of vaguely imperiled joy. Each year, for as long as he could remember, he had listened to gloomy reports on the dangers of commercialization. This had been a wistful refrain of Mom's, and an aggressive lamentation in the Sunday schools—first the Unitarian and then the Methodist—she'd dragged him to during his boyhood. Here in Japan he'd met the real thing at last: a Christmas that had no religious content whatsoever, a shopowner's creation compounded of tinsel, cardboard reindeer, high-piled toys, and jazzy carols piped in over loudspeakers. The effect was at once depressing, humorous, giddy, and reassuring. These people were crazy. He tried to describe his feelings in the Christmas card he sent home—a card to both Mom and Dad, at the Heather Hills address. He wasn't about to send anything yet to Dad at his new address in Troy. To do so was to acknowledge, almost to approve of, the separation. Whereas to send a letter addressed to them both in Heather Hills was to work in some small way toward a reunification—or at least to reassure oneself that things in Michigan were basically unchanged and needn't be worried about too much. He found, a little to his surprise, that he *could* put the matter out of his mind for days at a time—something that was possible because, from this distance, the whole prospect of a divorce (or a marriage, as well—Penny's marriage) was unreal. His parents, like Japan, like law school and Wall Street, like these blinking reindeer, weren't quite real.

On Christmas Eve he and Carrie and Greg went out for Chinese food at the Royal Hotel, thence to the True Time Texas for sake, thence to Greg's where among the strewn dirty plates and clothes, the empty bottles and bloodied strings of dental floss, Greg was given his map, his fruit, and his gloves. "Oh Jesus I'm so mortified," he said, though he looked mostly pleased, flexing his hands in his new leather gloves. "I'm afraid I don't have anything for either of you."

"That's all right," Carrie said.

"Merry Christmas, Greg," said Danny, again feeling sorry for him. Then, "You got a cake, someone sent you a cake," Danny cried happily.

A one-layer chocolate cake with white frosting sat in a box on the floor. Irregular pieces had been removed evidently by hand rather than with a knife.

"The old lady. It's pretty horrible I'm afraid. Rock hard. I think she must've sent it sea mail. Have some."

Danny broke off a large wedge for himself and a smaller wedge for Carrie. The hardened frosting had cracked like dried mud. The cake *was* pretty dry and horrible. "It's not bad," Danny said. "And you've got to admit it was nice of her."

"Very nice. I was touched."

"I've got something for Danny at my place," Carrie said. This was reassuring news to Danny, who'd been wondering what to do with the gifts for Carrie still in the plastic bag he'd been lugging around for hours; it seemed to guarantee that he'd be spending the night there. He would wake up with a woman on Christmas morning. "You can come too, Greg, and watch him open them."

"Well, I'd love to, but I can't bear not to be alone at Christmastime. Besides, I've got to go to the baths. I always bathe this time of year."

Greg did not see them downstairs. Leaving him among the litter seemed a little depressing to Danny, who called up another "Merry Christmas, Greg," as he opened the front door. He heard no answering farewell, only the contented slap of leather fist in leather palm. Carrie tossed the remainder of her cake into a trash bin but Danny with a sense of awakened duty to Mrs. Blaising finished his piece. Carrie's place was cold, too, but comfortingly neat. Danny slipped his coat over a hanger in the closet. Carrie turned on the larger of the two portable gas heaters and they sat on the couch, hands dropped in each other's laps, legs outstretched toward the heat. "When I was a little kid," Carrie said, "I used to ask Hugh"—her father—"what he wanted for Christmas, and he always said, For you to be a good girl all year long. One year when I was about eight I even wrote out this note, promising to be good for a whole year. I don't think I held to it." She laughed. "Hugh's still got the damn thing. He threatens me with it now and then."

Danny, pleased, laughed with her; Carrie rarely spoke of her childhood, and rarely spoke of her father with any real daughterly affection. She would grant him fondness at a distance—but loyal, daughterly affection seemed reserved for Fletch, her stepfather. Toward these two strangers Danny had developed a partiality for her true father and a resentment of her stepdad. "When I was in high school," he said, "I had this teacher I kind of idolized, Mr. Mann, who was later thrown out for drugs. Anyway, he seemed to think we were all a bunch of snotty little materialistic brats, and he made us draw up a list of our life ambitions. It was all anonymous but he read mine to the class; I guess I was the only one who'd passed his test. I still remember mine. There were three. To be an environmental lawyer. To be a good father. And to be so fluent in some foreign language, any language, that I could be mistaken for a native over the telephone."

"You're lucky." Carrie drew her stockinged feet back a little from the heater. She was wearing new wool slacks and the heel of his hand in her lap could trace the elastic edge of her panties. "You may get all three."

"I don't have any at the moment. And Huck, Meadows is hardly an environmental law firm." Ironic and ridiculous as it was, when Danny had been weighing his various summer job possibilities a little over a year ago (and he'd had offers from most of the best firms in New York, including a vertiginous one from Cravath, Swaine and Moore, perhaps the most prestigious firm in America), he had leaned toward Huck, Meadows in part because he liked the name—with all its pastoral, Midwestern overtones, Huckleberry Finn and rolling, cow-dotted slopes. In fact the firm represented Preserve Mining, responsible for discharging asbestos and taconite fibers, as well as tons of other less notorious poisons and carcinogens, into lakes and streams around the country. He again recalled Jacobusse, whom, too, Danny had idolized a little, him for his slyness and corrosive humor and his impeccable but flashy suits: *Remember that you're a high-class whore.*

"You'll be a good father."

Carrie's remark freed him from the moment's moral culpabilities—his betrayal of that high school junior whose ambitions had been read aloud to the class. Gratitude, love for her, pressed upon his voice and turned it thin—"Yes. Yes, I think maybe I really will be."

"This drunk guy on the train today, who'd spilled ink or something all over his shirt, put his hand on my leg." Carrie nudged Danny's hand. "The bastard."

Usually these complaints (which were frequent) about the advances made on her by Japanese men annoyed Danny, who sensed that except when, as today, the man was thoroughly forward and obnoxious Carrie more or less felt flattered. He wished she didn't, but it seemed that she did. This wasn't mere jealousy on his part (though he could be quite jealous, especially of the three Osaka dentists she taught English to; they were forever taking her out to unreachably expensive places). Increasingly he'd grown to see that she felt uncertain about her looks. She certainly mentioned looks (her mother's, her stepdad's, her friends', Danny's own—one of the first things she'd asked him was, "Do you think you're good-looking?") often enough to make him uncomfortable. If his hunch was accurate, this partly explained the enigmatic appeal of Japan for her: in this country she was clearly a prize. And Danny had felt absolutely brilliant when he'd realized that it was perhaps no coincidence that in that snapshot of Fletch which Carrie had chosen for her end table Carrie's mother wore the moronic look of someone captured in midblink. Now, feeling no annoyance, but still swollen with love, he said in jokey praise, "Carrie, you're his fantasy. He dreams of you. All of these Japanese businessmen are dreaming about tall blondes riding commuter trains."

"It's true the other way, too. For you," Carrie said.

"What's true for me?"

"All the women here. They think you're cute. I can see that." Flattery, merely . . . or had Carrie actually seen some evidence? Danny hadn't, or hadn't in any unequivocal way. In any case, this was exactly what he wanted to hear. There were few suspicions he yearned more heartfully to authenticate than his occasional sense that these dark, almond-eyed women whose glances he daily met felt some attraction, some answer to that desire which in his few months here had grown so profound. He had read that gaijins in Japan—like blacks in America—were commonly regarded as super-sexed and this image of Carrie and himself now excited him. Oh, to believe that in the eyes of Carrie's neighbors (who watched his comings and goings with politely downcast glances of enormous curiosity) the acts soon to take place here tonight were elevated and extraordinary.

"Speaking of fantasies, do you have elaborate fantasies?" Carrie asked him.

"How do you mean?"

"The men who write into *Playboy* and things always have such elaborate fantasies. And some guys have told me theirs."

"I don't know." Danny wanted to ask who, and what, but didn't. Instead he cleared his throat and said, "I guess not. The fantasies always seem to break down over logistics somehow. Like maybe in the fantasy I'll be making love outside, in a park say, but then I start worrying that the ground's too cold."

Carrie's high, bubbling, unexpected laughter was adorable. "Oh, Danny, that's just like you, so literal. So *cu-ute*," she drawled and riffled his hair. Apparently he, too, had said just the right thing. "You are so *lawyerly*," she said, offering the last word in a playful, puffy baritone.

"Or we'll be making love in some really cramped place, and I'll start worrying that I'm hurting them."

"Them. Plural?" The outlandishness seemed to please her.

"*Them* in the ungrammatical singular," Danny said. "Her. You."

"Do you fantasize about black women?"

"No," Danny said after a moment—guilty that this would be so. "Not usually." He recalled the black woman dancer at Refinement. Was she still baring her breasts for a living? He'd wanted—absurdly—to rescue her.

"How about Japanese women?"

Another pause. "Yes," he confessed, again guiltily; racial guilt in this matter was inescapable. "I didn't before. I guess it's being here. If I went to Africa, I'd probably start fantasizing about blacks." He recalled the Stevie Wonder tape. "I have something for you."

"Wait," she said. "Don't move, I'm too comfortable." She had dropped her head on his shoulder and he inhaled the scent of her shampoo (after going around dirty-haired and ponytailed for days, she'd washed her hair this afternoon). With his eyes closed, the steady whir of gas in the heater was a little like rainfall.

The logistical problems in his fantasies had amused her—painting him as an unimaginative plodder—but there was another side to this sensitive topic which he needed to feel she understood. He opened his left hand palm up in her lap and said, "You know this little scar here I told you when we first met I got by falling in a fire? That isn't what happened."

"What happened?"

"It's kind of a long and crazy story. You really want to hear it?"

"Sure."

"Well, when I was in college living in the Crater, you remember that's what we called the frat house; my bed was right beside this hot water pipe that used to get incredibly hot. Anyway, this was right after Penny left me, and it's kind of embarrassing," Danny said, although pride was what the story mostly stirred in him, for it vindicated a conviction—perhaps the dearest conviction about himself he held—that he was, though no one would guess it to look at him, a young man of extraordinary ardor. "Anyway, I was having this dream about Penny, we were in bed together, going at it. And in this dream my hand started to get really hot, but I didn't care, I overrode it, because I was so glad to be with her again, and I so much wanted to finish." Carrie giggled. "Which I did," Danny resumed, "and then you can imagine I woke up with a bang. I'd had my hand wrapped right around that pipe. I had second degree burns, and the devil of a time explaining to the doctor how it happened . . . "

Carrie lifted his open scarred hand to her face, kissed it, and (more winsome still, as lovable a thing as she'd ever done) giggled happily and guiltily. Danny laughed guiltily; then they both were laughing, lightly, happily, and scampering around the room like children, gathering their Christmas gifts together. Carrie opened the tape first, which seemed genuinely to please her. She kissed him on the mouth and on the ear, bounced over and inserted it into her machine, returned and embraced him. As, simultaneously, Carrie said "Merry Christmas, darling," and with a rumpling bass line the music commenced and

Danny bowed his head into her neck, he experienced another powerful sense of good fortune. How much better to be here than to be outside walking the streets, to be sitting over at Greg's philosophizing among the squalor, to be lying alone in one's six-tatami-mat room, an electone piano quavering below.

The gift-wrapped box Carrie handed him was of a lightness that suggested a shirt but it turned out to contain, somewhat alarmingly, a sweater, a green Pringle sweater from Scotland. In all his shopping these past few weeks Danny had learned just how absurdly marked up in price these imported sweaters tended to be.

"It's supposed to match the color of your eyes, baby. Hold it up. Let me see. It's supposed to match your eyes."

In an instant his own gifts were revealed not only as meager but mean-spirited. Wasn't the tape something he himself wanted to hear, and the chocolates something he himself would help to eat, and the book actually a mild reproach of Carrie's habit of forever hanging on the brink of initiative? Danny held the sweater to his chin and said, "There's a couple of other little—"

"Wait," Carrie ordered. "Hold on a sec." She drew from the floor beside her another rectangular box, this one much smaller and thinner. "Here. Open this, it goes with the sweater."

Danny's guess this time was correct: a scarf. He hugged her penitently, overcome, but she in her excitement would not be held. She pulled away and said, "See, the green in the scarf's supposed to match the green in the sweater and your eyes, and the brownish red's supposed to match your hair. Let me see. Try them on and let me see."

"First I want you to open something."

"No, try them on first. I have to *see*."

The sweater fit perfectly and the soft scarf fondled his neck. Carrie's dabbling hands patted and tucked, adjusting the sweater's fit and the scarf's loop of achieved casualness. She turned on another lamp for a closer examination. "Stand up again," she said. "Let me see . . . Turn into the light a little more. You know you have such beautiful coloring."

This was a compliment various women, a few his own age and a larger number drawn from among his mother's friends, had paid Danny, and one which he never met comfortably. Yet now it pleased him, just as it secretly thrilled him to have her gaze wrapped so tightly upon him as he stood in the room's center, moving his body according to her directives.

"Turn a little this way," Carrie commanded. "More. Let me see," she commanded. "Move a step closer."

No worse than merely boring—after the first hour this was how it appeared Professor Umeda's party would turn out. For Danny, having anticipated some disaster, mere boredom was comparatively welcome.

He'd done everything possible to see that things went to the Professor's satisfaction. He'd worn his newly laundered gray suit, had made sure that Carrie wore a skirt, and had loaned Greg—whose one sportscoat, a brown corduroy, nearly matched his brown corduroy Levi's, creating a sort of informal suit—an appropriate tie. Danny had warned them both, repetitively, lest they fail to appreciate his seriousness, to be on best behavior.

Impossible as it was to foresee what any sort of party at the Professor's might look like, Danny couldn't begin to prepare for all the evening's pitfalls. He had expected little or no alcohol, perhaps only some sake, and had encountered instead—perhaps another of the Professor's intermittent assertions of cosmopolitanism—imported scotch, Campari, Grand Marnier, and cognac, as well as domestic beer and whiskey.

The guests, too, were something of a puzzle. All were young. There was an extremely dark-skinned polyglot Indian from Bombay in a three-piece suit, and a tall Korean whose brother had apparently been a student of the Professor's, and three Japanese law students, including Nagaoka-san, whom Danny had not met for their weekly exchange of language lessons in nearly two months. Danny'd never been quite able to like him after the night Greg had elicited from him the claim that he could identify Koreans by their smell. Did *this* room smell strange to him?

Kneeling on the floor, the nine of them for a time conducted a single English conversation, warmhearted and platitudinous, but soon the group divided along linguistic lines—English spoken among the three Americans, Japanese among the others, with the ambi-verbal Indian, the only one wholly adept in either medium, straddling both conversations before settling in with the Japanese. Mrs. Umeda, who'd been bustling in and out on hostesslike errands, and who evidently at no point would actually be sitting down to join her guests, now entered with a bowl of mandarin oranges. Greg took one and began, one-handedly, to peel it. "You know, today's the twenty-seventh," he said to Danny, and nodded meaningfully.

Carrie cleared her throat twice. It was a mannerism she had. "What's so special about the twenty-seventh?"

"Greg thinks it's a lucky number."

"No, no, it isn't that Greg *thinks*." Greg's enunciation had taken on a familiar, fussy exaggeration; evidently he'd been dipping deeply into the Professor's imported scotch. "It is a very special number."

"When Greg goes to the baths, he always puts his clothes in locker twenty-seven."

"And his shoes in shoe-locker twenty-seven," Greg added, speaking of himself in the third person.

"And if it's already taken?"

"Then he knows I'll have a, a bad day tomorrow. It's Uncle Gregory's horoscope."

"That's crazy."

"No, far from crazy. It keeps the evil spirits away. One must placate the evil spirits. Evil evil. Tell me, how do you keep the evil spirits away, Carrie?"

That insinuative way in which Greg could pronounce one's name caused Carrie to stiffen. "I don't," she declared.

"Some little daily rite?" Greg hinted. She shook her head. He went on, "Some propitiatory ritual? Some imprecation? Some chant? Some . . . " His drunken wits rummaged for a synonym and came up doubly rewarded. "Some charm? Some talisman?"

"No, nothing like that."

"Nothing?" Danny said. A little annoyed at her claim of living by pure rationality, he divulged a closely guarded kernel of information. "I used to go around without leaving fingerprints."

Greg's face swung slowly toward Danny, who beheld a gradual, familiar alteration on those dark features: a relishing grin, a sharpening in Greg's eyes toward discerning sobriety. "Actually, I just thought of something I *do* do—" Carrie began, but Greg was no longer interested. As Danny had so often seen, Greg was exhilarated, seized, hot on the trail of another *great detail*.

"No fingerprints? Really? You mean you wouldn't touch anything?"

"Not really," Danny said. "Sort of." He never should have mentioned this. Secrecy longed to restore itself, but it was already too late.

"How could you get anywhere?"

"I'd go anywhere. I just wouldn't leave fingerprints. I was a kid, this was years ago."

"How would you open a door?"

"Push it open with my shoulder. Or something. It's not too hard, it's no big deal." Danny upended his glass of scotch and found he'd already emptied it.

"What about a key?" Greg was grinning broadly now. Carrie, too, while spitting the seeds of an orange into her palm, was looking on with an undesirable closeness. "How would you handle a key?"

Although often capable of forgetting this, Danny at bottom was scared of Greg in a way which, so far as he could tell, Greg was not scared of him. Greg with all his probing seemed forever to be positing the existence of something vile at the pit of Danny's soul. Danny, looking inward, had long ago concluded that while numerous shames and uglinesses abounded there, no such evil existed—and yet these diggings of Greg's always made him jumpy. "It's not so hard," Danny said. "I mean it's no big deal. You just hold it between your knuckles."

"What about a glass? If you're having a drink?"

"Oh I don't know . . . You pick the damn thing up. I mean I wasn't compulsive or anything. I was just a crazy high school kid. Everybody's crazy in high school."

"You did this all the way through high school?"

"Good God no. Just part of senior year. And when I first arrived at college." Danny again reflexively lifted his glass. Recalling in midmotion its emptiness, he placed the round edge thoughtfully against his lips a moment before setting it down, a gesture that falsely suggested he wished a refill. Greg dangled the bottle of Dewar's invitingly; Danny, chagrined at how much of the Professor's expensive scotch had already been consumed, said—"I think I'd like some of that Nikka whiskey. Just a little."

Greg nodded obligingly and filled Danny's glass fuller than Danny'd wished with the domestic whiskey, topped his own even higher with scotch. "Now this thing with the fingerprints, did it start up all at once, or did it sort of creep up on you?"

Rescue came in the form of the Professor's wife, who appeared wordlessly in the doorway, waiting for her husband to notice her. The room's several chatter receded; Professor Umeda glanced up, nodded, and his wife came forward, gentling her advance with a high but edgeless flow of Japanese. She conferred a moment with the Professor, then padded from the room in her slippers and returned moments later with what was perhaps the actual cause, or half the cause, of this party: a tiny, blinking, myopic, extremely red-faced baby wrapped in a blue blanket. Only the child's name, with its feminine *ko* ending—Naohiko—seemed to indicate its swaddled and presently minute sexuality.

The three Americans were the first to be honored with an inspection. Danny's memory obediently retrieved the word for "baby" in Japanese—*akambo*—which he'd probably retained because its roots were so appealing: literally, *red child*. He said to the Professor's wife in Japanese, "Very pretty baby, isn't it?" and to the Professor, in English, he called, "She is a very beautiful girl."

The Professor blinked a few times behind his thick spectacles. "It is a boy," he pronounced, and added with typical superfluous precision, "a male child."

"Oh . . . I thought . . . " Danny began embarrassedly. "Isn't the baby's name Naohi*ko*, I thought . . . " He smiled at the Professor, hoping to convert his mistake into a foreigner's appealing befuddlement. "I thought *ko* was strictly a feminine ending."

Awkwardly the Professor attempted an answering smile—a kind of flinch at the mouth, more like a grimace of pain than any show of pleasure—and said, "Ninety percent, ninety-five percent of the time, that is true."

"Well, a very nice-looking boy then," Danny said, leaning once more over the child, near enough to catch the rising warmth, as from a just-baked loaf of bread.

Carrie was the only one of the three Americans—the only one in the room, it turned out—to touch the child. The mother's face reddened with pleasure, just as though *she* felt the stroke of Carrie's long index finger along the bunched puffy ridge over the infant's eyes.

Mrs. Umeda seemed about to carry her bundle back to its room when Greg rose shakily, in his hand a refilled drink, and declared: "A toast to the child."

Danny wondered—Was this socially acceptable? This country's notions of propriety were so rigid and peculiar . . . In any case Greg's motion set the room in rapid motion, a Japanese readiness for ceremony swinging into play. A toast was drunk, and then, after an uncertain pause, Nagaoka-san offered in Japanese a second toast, another lifting of glasses, and the Professor's wife scooted from the room.

She returned a few minutes later with the second baby, wide-eyed and wan in comparison with her brother. She wore white pajamas and was wrapped in a matching white blanket. To determine this one's sex Danny would have needed no clue; some softening modification of her brother's already soft bones and features attested to the child's bewrapped femininity.

"She changed its pajamas," Greg said to Danny, in a voice somewhat too loud to be a whisper.

Danny stepped nearer and hissed—"It's twins, you idiot. I told you that."

Again the child was inspected and praised, though less extensively—either because the guests had already seen enough babies, or because this one was a girl (Danny was not sure which). Whether or not a toast had been appropriate for the baby boy, one certainly seemed required now—but Greg, who had sunk back to the floor, beamed vacantly when Danny bobbed his glass up and down by way of prompting. So it fell on Danny to say, first in Japanese and then in English, "To the lovely baby girl."

While the men drank toasts the Professor's wife held the lulled baby and Carrie stroked its wide forehead. Carrie leaned closer, smiling, and then the child—who had perhaps glimpsed something she'd never seen and could not compass, a pair of blue eyes that opened right into the back of the skull—began to howl. The Professor's wife shushed and patted and rocked the blanketed bundle but the baby girl, her face now as flushed as her brother's, would not stop screaming, and shamefacedly, reddening herself, the mother hustled the child from the room.

Carrie, too, was looking tightly shamefaced, and Danny felt sorry for her. There was an awkward pause during which the child's muffled wailing could be heard. Fresh drinks were poured, and conversation sprang up in new little groups, Danny with the Korean, Greg with the polyglot Indian, and, somewhat surprisingly, Carrie with the Professor. Nagaoka-san meanwhile (if eavesdropping Danny was correctly interpreting the rapid Japanese) was telling his countrymen how Danny was extremely brilliant and had worked for the best law firm in New York—exactly the story Greg had told Nagaoka-san that disillusioning night last fall. The tall Korean was telling Danny about a friend, also Korean, who'd been robbed his very first day in America. Nodding condolences, Danny meanwhile was trying to eavesdrop in the other direction on Carrie's conversation with the Professor. It was apparently about London. Danny caught the Professor's elaborately enunciated "Queen Elizabeth Festival Hall." Carrie was talking earnestly and, as was her way, in reinforcement at one point she brushed the Professor's olive-hued hand. The Professor, like the baby girl, seemed to recoil from her, fractionally, although his intent gaze remained on hers and—could this be?—seemed if anything to warm with pleasure.

Greg's voice lifted into full intelligibility. He was speaking in that all too familiar style of discrete phrases, word clusters that served as dry stepping-stones for a sodden mind. For he was now really drunk, having reached that stage of dogged truth-pursuit in which Danny had once seen him ask a waiter in a German restaurant whether his clothes—suede shorts, knee socks, suspenders—were intended as a joke. "But don't you find India *depressing*?" he was preposterously inquiring of that solemn sable face before him. "That was the thing about India . . . I couldn't see how the poor people . . . endured it. Of course amazing people are amazing, but I couldn't see how the rich like you did either."

Danny slipped away from the Korean in midsentence and while crawling across the tatami floor called out to the Indian, "How long have you been in Japan?"

"All those people with flies . . . " Greg continued, "around their eyes. Did you ever look *closely* . . . closely at the flies crawling around their eyes?"

Danny turned to Greg with what he hoped was publicly a cordial grin and, employing an idiom he hoped no one but an American would understand, said quietly, "Can it, Greg. Can it right now."

Greg halted a moment. "Another thing . . . I've been wondering," he said, turning from face to face to draw everyone in, although he did not look at Danny, "is why when you Japanese decide to have a good time . . . do you never invite any women? Doesn't it seem a little . . . dull? I'm not talking about prostitutes, I'm—"

"Grego."

"I know there's a valued tradition here of prostitution. I just mean some nice, sweet, intelligent, good-smelling—"

"Grego, you s.o.b., can it. I mean it."

Their glances linked at last. Within the glaze of Greg's eyes a pinpoint of spite seemed to glimmer and then dissolve into amusement. He smiled beneficently. "When I first went to Europe," he began, pausing to down the remains of his drink, "I went with someone named Rob Mohney . . . very much like our good friend Danny. And Rob used to study maps . . . and guidebooks and languages . . . And I told him if you want to get along well . . . well you're better off learning how to juggle. Now you're thinking that I'm speaking metaphorically. . . . " Greg drew a mandarin orange from the bowl, prodded it with his fingertips, selected another and another and another. "And everywhere we went . . . " He tossed an orange into the air.

For a splendid cluster of seconds some dormant playfulness in their seeded cores awoke and the four oranges bobbed weightlessly. Greg continued his narration. The Professor looked on intently. "Everywhere we went, I made friends faster than Rob . . . with all his guidebooks and his studying. Because I went to their hearts, my friends, *I went to their hearts*. I'd toss some—"

An orange bumped to the floor, and a second one, both rolling across the tatami. "Shit. Double shit," Greg muttered. Clearly it was time to leave.

Carrie assisted in the departure. She gathered the oranges from the floor and, helping to flank Greg, offered hurried thanks to all. The dark night was soberingly cold. Greg was wobbling and Danny took one arm, Carrie the other. "Beautiful children," Greg pronounced in summation, slurring his words so that both emerged as disyllabic, the first rhyming with *rueful*. "Exceptionally intelligent-looking, too."

Something extremely unwelcome, a tide of hatred, swelled inside Danny. Yes, he *hated* Greg sometimes when he reached that point where his words were slurred. It seemed a tacit compact was being broken, one in which they'd pledged to each other that while dissolution was to be pursued, the two of them weren't going to descend those final steps where they were pissing their pants, or falling down, or unable to talk. "Do you think the Professor was appalled?" Danny asked Carrie, speaking across Greg as though he were not there. "He looked pretty appalled."

"He did look a little taken aback."

"Plumfield is a very clever agent," Greg offered thickly. "But I don't think he got much out of *us* tonight. After all, you gotta get up pretty—"

"I just hope he's not pissed off."

"Piss off," Greg said. "Pissss."

"I don't think so," Carrie said. "I think he just thinks we're crazy."

"I think he thinks we think," Greg said. "But do we?"

"I think maybe he had the party so we could see the twins," Danny said.

"No, *listen*," Greg urged. "This is very neat. I think he thinks we think—but do we?"

"Grego, why don't you just shut up for a while?"

"I believe he believes we believe. But do we?"

"Jesus," Carrie said, "how much did you *drink*?"

"*I* believe. Ah buh-lieve," Greg said in the tones of a black preacher. "Ah believe in the sanctity . . . of the physically graceful." He lifted his voice, which now had taken on hints of a fine English accent. "I believe in the juggler, and the cat, and the pole vaulter . . . "

"We better just get him home."

" . . . and the wind, and the sipping hummingbird . . . "

"Grego, I'm really losing patience. We're going to get ourselves arrested."

"Fuck it," Greg in his loud voice answered, the *it* emerging muddily. From the darkened houses Japanese eyes were training upon them. "I merely say fuck it."

"Okay," Danny said.

"You know I've decided recently that it's truly fair to say I've got a drinking problem. You know I hesitated to say so. I mean it always sounded so damn arrogant. You know, you think of all those great minds, *those truly troubled truly great minds,* that have had drinking problems. I mean it sounds so boastful. But there it is."

"There it is," said Danny.

"You know I'm leaving soon. Japan. I am. No, *really*."

"No one's disagreeing with you."

"I'm going island-hopping. You can catch up with me, you two, if you want. All the way across the Pacific. That's precisely what I'm going to do. Leaping like a blindfolded cat in a circus. I really *am*, Danny."

Greg's needless assertiveness spoke again of something unaccountable—an encircling sense of fear. And with this recognition came to Danny an emotion that was the opposite twin of his hatred, one that touched his own soul with a painful, loving, panicky helplessness. Sometimes he would sense that for all their shared comradely talk about truth and women and travel and the nature of time, for all the pleasures and similarities, Greg really *was* screwed up at the core, twisted or banged up enough that he must ineluctably meet some ugly, disastrous finish.

"I'm going to become an expert scuba diver," Greg said.

"You can if you want to. You're a remarkable athlete."

"I wish I hadn't dropped those oranges. That was the one unforgivably *gauche* thing I did. Or one of two. One of two."

"It doesn't matter. I didn't even know you could juggle."

"I had one priceless insight tonight. I saw straight into the essence of the Japanese character. Forget all those books you're always reading, Dan-dan, they can't compare with my insight. Here it is." Greg deepened his voice: "The reason the Japanese have to be so serious, so ceremonial, is because . . . " But Greg's priceless insight had momentarily fled and a horrible silence ensued while he racked his wits. Then victoriously he announced, "It's because they don't have anything sacred. Senility," he added. "Drink gives you valuable insights into what it's like when your mind starts to go. You must take advantage of *ev*ery opportunity."

"There may be something to that," Danny said.

"To what? You're not even *listening*. Don't you see that there's nothing profane in this country? That this is the only country in the world where money and television aren't even the least bit crass? And that's why they don't object to turning their temples into supermarkets?"

"You may be right."

"You're not even *listening*. Your devotion to the pursuit of truth is halfhearted. You know that, don't you, Danny? I'm speaking now as your darker but better angel."

"I suppose it is."

"That's a terrible really vicious insult, what I just said to you. That's the worst fucking thing you can say about anybody."

"I suppose it is."

"The Japanese," Greg said, "are much too straitlaced, *qua* people. It's terrible."

"It is terrible."

"That's why I pissed . . , or that is the principal reason, I suppose, why I pissed, into Plumfield's wastebasket. A small gesture, but one does what one can."

So wild was all of this, and emerging in so quietly philosophical a tone, that it carried only a little menace. "You did what?" Danny asked.

"Pissed into the wastebasket. In the bathroom."

"Oh no you didn't." Fear seized Danny's throat as palpably as any hand.

"Oh yes I did. Pissss off, as Carrie'd say."

"Grego, you better be kidding." Danny stopped and pulled Greg to a halt as well. Those wild drunk's eyes peered up at him in the streetlight's silver glow.

"Copiously, I'm afraid. Whoooosh. Like a cataract."

"Greg, this isn't funny. Tell me you're kidding. *Please* tell me you're kidding."

"I'm not kidding, Danny."

"You're not kidding, are you?"

"I'm not kidding. Whoooosh."

"You know, I'll never forgive you if you're kidding," Danny said. "And you know, I'll never forgive you if you're not."

"Well, well that seems only reasonable," Greg concluded. "Listen, listen, not to worry, Danny, he'll never know who did it. Short of some sort of urinalysis, and even then—"

"Oh you stupid, stupid bastard," Danny cried. "He'll know who did it. Of course he'll know who did it. *Can you see one of those Japanese guys pissing into the Professor's wastebasket?*"

"It's conceivable."

"Or that Indian in the three-piece suit?"

"The very man to pin it on."

"Oh God, I've got to go back there. I've got to find it before they do. Carrie, I'll—" It had not yet been settled whether Danny would be going home with her. "I'll see you tomorrow. Get him home in a cab, huh? Oh, you stupid, stupid bastard."

Danny turned and sprinted off in his heavy dress shoes. "I was only trying to help," Greg called after him.

A hard thudding sprang up in Danny's head, behind his ear. If the wastebasket had already been discovered, things were going to be worse, much worse, for his going back at all. Danny still wanted to believe that Greg had been joking, but the flatness of that *I'm not kidding* all but ruled this out.

Danny paused to gather his breath before ringing the Professor's bell. Everything hung in the balance of these next few moments. There was a long delay before Professor Umeda, dressed in a blue robe—the first time Danny had seen him in anything but a suit—swung open the door. He peered at Danny through his glasses. "Yes?" he said.

Danny stepped into the house without being invited and panted, "Professor, I'm so sorry but I left my keys here, I'm pretty sure I left my keys in the bathroom. Can I go look for them?"

The Professor stared once more with disconcerting evenness, then said, "Yes, of course."

Danny slipped out of his shoes and skimmed over the tatami mats, the Professor padding along behind. Fortunately, the bathroom door had a working lock, a wooden bolt which Danny slid into place. For a panicky moment Danny saw no wastebasket. It was tucked well beneath the sink, as if exhibitionist Greg had been motivated by some primitive contrary impulse toward concealment. The basket sloshed heavily in Danny's yanking hands. Wadded up papers floated in the still-frothy urine. As Danny tipped the basket into the toilet, his hands were shaking more violently than ever in his life. With cruel sharpness in the harsh light he glimpsed himself as from above: bent over the toilet, he was a hysterical child, a spastic, a monster, his hands shook so in his terror and rage.

Four days, most of them spent with Carrie at Carrie's, elapsed before Danny next saw Greg. Danny was lying under a blanket in his own small refrigerated room, studying Japanese, when he heard what might or might not have been a knock at the door. The house rattled so in winter, the flimsy wood-framed windows shuddering, that Danny was forever hearing the knocking of visitors who turned out to be ghosts.

The door opened and this particular pale ghost turned out to be Greg, who asked deferentially, "You busy?"

"No, no," Danny said. "Come on in."

Greg took only a single step into the room and closed the door behind him. Danny remained outstretched on the futon, head propped on a pillow. "I just wanted to say, God I'm sorry about the other night."

Apologies from Greg were extremely common; he was always *mortified* or *chagrined* or *overcome by embarrassment* about something, but these were confessions accompanied by that gloating grin which always obviated the need for any answering pardon. Today's apology was something else, something unprecedented—Greg seemed truly sheepish—and it offered an opportunity which Danny, though his anger over the Professor's party had subsided into a pleasurable sense of having played the hero's role in what was a good story, couldn't resist exploiting just a little. From his languid, regal prostration on the pillows and mats Danny held the prospect of power, and the reassurance he now tossed to Greg contained its deliberate scrap of qualification. "I wouldn't worry about it too much."

"Oh God, I'm awful," Greg said, with a trace of humorous exaggeration in his voice, but sufficient gravity that Danny in an equalizing impulse of sympathy lifted himself enough to lean his back against the wall and said, "It's really cold, isn't it?"

"Mm. My hands are freezing."

"What happened to the gloves?"

"Oh God, don't tell Carrie. I lost the damn things."

Danny laughed. "That didn't take long."

"No, it didn't." Huddled in the doorway, Greg really did look quite miserable.

"So what you been up to?" Danny asked him.

"Oh God, I don't know. Actually, actually now, I spent a couple incredible days, drunk and sober, asking myself . . . " Greg knelt on the floor. His eyes had sharpened, his face had lit. No one, no one Danny had ever met so visibly enjoyed telling a story. " . . . asking myself, *How am I going to make it up to my good friend Dan-dan*?"

"No big deal. You pissed into a wastebasket."

"Oh it isn't really the wastebasket. Anyway, after a couple days I got off my butt, hustled, turned productive, and managing to outwit the sharp-eyed authorities, came up with a belated Christmas present for you." He tapped the pocket of his sweat shirt.

"What is it?" It was *trouble*, surely; uneasiness had already put its squeeze on Danny's stomach.

"It's unadulterated magic. It's sun, earth, water and, finally, fire. It's some of the best, the choicest, the most cerebrally uplifting marijuana I have ever encountered."

"Grego, I don't even like the stuff."

"Danny." A pained look tautened Greg's face, and his tone was that of a teacher dealing with a willfully slow student. "Stuff this good is unobtainable in Japan. And if you *can* find it, it's amazingly expensive. I thought I had a couple ounces, not this stuff, that's why I borrowed the eighty grand a while ago, but the deal fell through. I was only able to get two joints. What a sacrifice—hey?—for me to give one of them up." He fished from his pocket a paperback called *Under the Volcano* and drew from its pages a thick joint which he held out to Danny. Greg's eyes, so steadily on Danny, were at once peremptory and imploring. "I'm giving you the most valuable thing I own," Greg said; and Danny, with a sense that disaster was being invited into his life, accompanied a moment later by a distinct internal thud, took the fat little paper wand between his fingers.

"Where shall I hide it?"

"Anywhere. It's no big deal."

"They'll throw me out of the country if they catch me. And never let me back in."

"They're not going to catch you." Greg sniffled; he seemed to be coming down with a cold. "It's wastefully thick. You're better off rerolling it into two or even three joints. I mean, hey mon, it's really fantastic stuff, mon," he added in his Jamaican drug-dealer's voice.

"Where do I get papers?"

"At the tobacconist's."

"He'll know why I'm buying them."

"You're a paranoid."

"You're no longer reading just Shakespeare."

Greg slipped the book back into his pocket. "We seem to be touching on all my failings this morning."

"How come you're not?"

"Oh God, I don't know. Why is it, Dan-Dan, that we flee from the very best things in life? It's a question I'm going to ponder deeply, after I've smoked my brains out." Greg rose and turned toward the door. "I'm going to smoke my brains out, and then try to figure out why I drink too much."

"Let's have lunch first."

"Some other time."

"Greg," Danny called.

The moment suddenly felt symbolic, as though this departure might be larger than it appeared. "Listen, Greg, don't worry about the other night. I've forgotten all about it."

"I haven't," Greg answered, and snapped the door quietly behind him.

"You haven't," Danny said aloud, to himself, as he listened to Greg's slow feet on the stairs. While he'd forgiven Greg everything about the party, Danny was hardly sorry to have him out of his room; nor was he sorry, as the first days of January shivered along, to have Greg's role dwindle in his life. One component of the exorbitant ease Danny experienced while lying, as he so often did these days, upon Carrie's couch was the knowledge that he could justifiably absent himself from all of Greg's wildly-timed sessions of alcohol and cards and circuitous maddening introspection. Danny'd done enough of that. He was righting a balance now, as he lay for long hours studying Japanese and eating toast topped with one of the expensive English jellies and marmalades that had arrived as a Christmas present from Helen and Fletch, Carrie's mother and stepfather. He was broadening his circle of acquaintances, going out to a few parties with Carrie's other gaijin friends, some of whom weren't really such bad sorts, and out to a few dinners with Dr. Kobayashi and Dr. Miyazaki, his two English students.

Notwithstanding Carrie's earlier remark about not wanting a roommate, Danny was spending most of his nights at the Sunshine Mansion. At times she complained, hintingly, about this, and in proud response to these or to some other annoyance—for the truth was they squabbled a good deal—Danny sometimes stayed away at night. But into the darkness of his own cold room would come desolating thoughts of that apartment, of its gold lamps and its shower and its jars of Tiptree jelly and of Carrie herself shedding her clothes for a nightgown. Her appeal was dense and polychromatic, and, for the most part happily, he conceded that she'd ensnared him. Oh, he was half in love with her—adored the way she kept exposing tenderness behind gruffness, agreeableness behind a need to be cajoled, the way she would suck her thin lower lip while doing a crossword puzzle, or would lift his hand in bed (as though it were something inorganic, a mere implement) to attend to an itch that her own gnawed nails couldn't scratch satisfactorily. He adored her tentative aggressiveness, as epitomized in that repeated light clearing of her throat when she sought your full attention. Were he really to fall in love with her, it would be only his second time (it now had become clear). Oh, he'd waited, for so long, for so much longer than he'd admitted to himself, for Penny to return to him. But she was no longer Penny Cogswell at all. She was Penny Baron now, she was a married woman on the other side of the world. *Good luck.*

Why he and Carrie squabbled so much—and *squabbled* was the word she always used to describe it—was something Danny did not fully understand, although it worrisomely seemed they both depended on these struggles to maneuver themselves into a deeper intimacy. At least that was often the result—lovemaking after arguing, with what ostensibly was a show of having made up in fact serving as a purifying extension of grudges and frustrations. There was some tainted, lurking ugliness in all of this, Danny dodgingly sensed, but the pull was profound, the eventual moments of joy wholly satisfying, and the relationship's overall effect seemed recuperative. This sense of shared, endearing clumsiness pervaded these days; in the best way each of them could, they were linking up, twining their highly divergent temperaments. These mental linkages were never quite smooth—corners bumped and pinched, shapes met and recoiled—just as physically (the two of them so fidgety and skinny) their embraces so often turned painful. Danny was always finding himself ground underneath a sharp elbow or hipbone. It was as though all paths to that culmination which was as softly delicate as *ikura,* those globed orange fish eggs in the sashimi bars, as soft as moss after rain, lay strewn with teeth and bones.

While what ultimately lay at the nub of their squabbles remained a mystery, as the days rolled on Danny (in what he recognized was a characteristic lawyerly penchant for lists) began to isolate traits of hers that irritated him; for increasingly as his claims on her grew greater it was irritation rather than disapproval he felt. Chief of these irritations was that *she* was so easily irritated. Slow service in a restaurant would make her *mad*, a stranger's taking her picture simply because she was a blonde gaijin would make her *mad*, a snapped shoelace would make her *mad*; an envelope whose glue wouldn't hold, a cassette tape that unraveled inside the player, an omelette that stuck to the pan, a woman bank clerk who counted the withdrawal five times before finally handing over the money, a jammed door, a loud siren, a long wait for a bus would make her *mad.* And when the bus arrived at last and they stood wedged among a swaying crowd of bodies, "Damn, this thing is hot," she'd say accusatively, as if *he* were at fault. While so much of his own upbringing had consisted of attempts to harmonize Mom and Dad's contrary lessons, on this one point they were in full agreement—you mustn't let small annoyances trouble you overmuch. Dad's rationale seemed to be that there was something unhandsomely small in a man's complaining; while Mom, the nearer in temperament, with that wisdom of the partially subjugated, seemed to feel that only sweetness of temper kept one unsullied day after day. So even while Danny recognized something paradoxical in becoming angry because another person had become angry, Carrie's short temper irked him all the same.

But most irritating, most hurtful, was Carrie's relishing so little his stories about Mom and Dad and growing up in Michigan. For his part, Danny sat enchanted whenever Carrie unfolded the complex, peripatetic tales of her Mom and Fletch, her Dad and Martha, Princeton and New York and London and Fripp Island. Hers was a family not only richer than his but of a lavishness with its money alien to everything he'd known. Mom and Dad had always been so prudent: the fine house in Heather Hills that had proved over the years such a solid investment; the cars Dad leased so cheaply from Ford; the life insurance policies, the mounting bank balances and Ford stock. Carrie had grown up rich in what was for Danny at once a stereotypical and a faintly mythical way. The Pingrees had gone on Caribbean cruises, belonged to more than one country club, owned a summer place on Block Island. That he could see the appeal in these stories of hers, but that she seemed to regard his own as scant and provincial, hurt him and worried him. She could never truly love him without loving these things. Yet he couldn't manage to convey his conviction that his tales about Mom in all her diffidence and strength, about Dad returning from the War (with two Purple Hearts) to join the ranks at Ford, about Penny Cogswell, seduced by her cousin, and about Grandpa Jaynes, that embittered old man dying of emphysema in a shadowy house on a rundown street in Detroit, who nevertheless harbored a fresh dream of a cabin on Lake Superior, held an illimitable richness. Deep within Danny, where Carrie as if deliberately would not peer, lay something surprisingly indurate and adaptable and resolute and marvelous, something which had fabricated from all of these elements the improbable accomplishment of himself.

Which of his traits angered Carrie was less evident. She called him "overanalytical" once, which he couldn't quite deny but also couldn't quite consider a fault; indeed, it often worried him that, compared with Greg, he didn't analyze often or profoundly enough. She called him "hangdog" a couple of times, which was less clear and more troublesome. She called him "childishly possessive" when he blew up after she canceled a date at the last minute to go out to dinner with one of her Osaka dentists, but Danny had to believe that deep down *she* recognized he had all the principles of basic etiquette on his side. And he irritated her (but this hardly counted, as it was deliberate) by taking her at her word and often using Japanese terms for English ones. Carrie had one day decided that to improve their Japanese they should speak it as much as possible with each other, but his greater vocabulary seemed to annoy her and she soon tired of this game. He went on playing it anyway—partly in exasperation with himself for having learned so little of the language, but mostly in irritation at her laxity and her resistance to learning anything from him.

And she told him once he had no "tact." This seemed somewhat absurd, for surely if *she* had tact she would never have made such a remark directly. Yet it was possible he didn't really have a sophisticated sense of proper psychological boundaries in an affair (a word which, with all its adult overtones of illicit assignations and guilt, he had trouble applying to himself and Carrie). It was not his place to complain that she wasted so much money on imported luxuries like Brie cheese, which, when you decoded the Japanese wrapper, turned out to cost over ten dollars a pound. "It's none of your business, damn it," she said, and added crisply, relishing this chance to blast him while remaining wholly in the right, "and I notice you go on eating whatever I buy."

Yet Danny couldn't completely override the feeling that her money *was* his business. When one cold January afternoon he went with her to her bank and discovered that her account held over a million yen, almost six thousand dollars, he felt betrayed. This seemed treachery, duplicity—for didn't it make a mockery of their long conversation one night recently about the best countries to visit if one could only afford the trip? And she, to judge by her abruptly sidelong manner, knew herself in the wrong.

"Where did you get all that money?"

"Brought it over. My parents, and Fletch, wanted me to have it."

"Wanted you to have it for what?"

They were squabbling on the street but it didn't appear that anyone was noticing. The only person clearly within earshot was a boy about seven or eight who stood beside a dripping gutter swinging his umbrella like a baseball bat at falling water drops. The lovable fervor he brought to this game seemed to make a joke—as so often happened at such times—of their inept and petty combat.

"For an emergency," Carrie said.

"What sort?"

"I don't know." She shrugged. "You always jump on me. An *emergency*."

"What sort of an *emergency* . . . " Danny began, his mimicry mocking her unreflecting retreat into an emergency no one could hope to gauge or prepare for. "What sort of *emergency*, Carrie, would require nearly seven thousand dollars?"

Her departure was nearing. Evident in all their tangle of feelings was the knowledge that they were developing powerful claims upon each other. Slowly, clumsily, the bonds were being forged—as he fixed her tea in the morning (in their little London enclave tucked within an apartment building in northern Kyoto), or as they drifted off (after poorly planned but thrilling acts) into complementary sleep, she with the taste of semen in her mouth and he with the taste of spermicidal jelly. One morning, as from her bed he watched her crossing naked toward the bathroom, those hungry-looking cavities behind her skinny hipbones suddenly evoked a mental declaration: "Carrie, darling, you know I'm going to miss you when you're gone." The words hung unspoken, ready for delivery despite all their foreign overtones (for unlike Carrie, he'd never been comfortable with these terms of endearment—"darling," "honey," "sweetness"—that seemed at once too heavily adult and too lightly the language of the movies), while he listened to the faint plumbing of her urinating. Yet her matter-of-fact face as she reemerged silenced him, and the words burrowed inward.

Her leaving compelled him to think of her operating in that other, non-Japanese world out there. This notion made him nervous, and when one afternoon his eye chanced upon a letter she was writing to a girl friend in New York and he read the phrase, "inevitably calls 'downside risk' (Oh God) is so big. *You* know.", it deeply depressed him. The tone hardly seemed to be Carrie's, and the world to which it was sent was one in which it was not clear that he had much to offer her. She would be gone a month (or so she said—Danny worried she might never return), with a couple of weeks in Princeton and a couple in South Carolina. At night he liked to rub her back—the shoulders a knot of muscle and tendon and protuberant bone—and talk about spring in Japan, which because neither of them had ever experienced it could loom in his imagination as an imparadised tapestry of cherry and plum blossoms. And they would take a trip, as had once been arranged: he, Carrie and Greg, heading north through the Japanese Alps to the east coast of Tōhoku, reputed to be the wildest shoreline in Japan, and on to Hokkaidō. The talk served as an inducement, to draw her back over the Pacific Ocean.

Meanwhile another trip, once casually bandied about, melted away. With varying seriousness Greg a few times had suggested heading across the Pacific—Yap, Ponape, Truk, where the Japanese fleet had been sunk and one found the best wreck-diving in the world. The trip would have to be made in the summer, after Danny's commitment to the Professor ended, and this would mean not going back to New York and Huck, Meadows. Of course this could have been arranged, the firm would be willing in any case to offer him a job after graduation, and Danny toyed with the idea, and with other summer plans, before sending off to New York, nearly a month late (he'd promised to let the firm know by December 15), a letter saying they should expect him in June and asking their help in finding an apartment.

The decision left him simultaneously relieved and downcast; he felt a former world, with all its interwoven demands and competitions and affections, returning to claim him. On the couch with Carrie, morosely he confessed, "Maybe I should have taken the summer off. Just to travel. It'll be harder to get three months off, later on in my life." In truth, Danny had been daydreaming about taking off far more than three months. . . . He would drift around the world, as Greg had—would see Bhutan and the Seychelles. This vision was somewhat embarrassing, for he recognized it as an only-slightly-grown-up variant of the child's fantasy of *running away from home*. Yet in a child's idealized way there was a beautiful, simple logic to it: if the parents were going to abandon their roles—if Mom and Dad were really going to get divorced, as all of Mom's letters attested, and she truly would be marrying Bump Nebbin—then the son would too. He would disappear.

Danny had finished rubbing Carrie's shoulders and had begun massaging her ankles. When she was a little girl she'd studied ballet, and her mother used to knead her feet after class. So little inclined to reminisce over her childhood, Carrie nonetheless liked to recall this, and still savored the feel of fingers probing her toes and her fine high arches.

"You mean all that island-hopping? With Greg?" Her tone was caustic. She was lying on her stomach and her voice, pressed against her chest, kept emerging with a teasing, erotic resonance.

"Mm. Why not?"

"I don't know, it just seems kind of crazy. With all that endless crazy talk of his."

"I think he makes a lot of sense."

"I know you do, but it's all talk. Greg's a loser, Danny."

Danny wished she wouldn't say things like that. "And how about me?"

"You're a winner," she said quickly, but again her tone sounded disparaging.

"And what about you?"

"I'm a winner, too," she replied, but after a pause.

Danny planted one hand on her bottom, affectionately, for he didn't want to jeopardize his chance of soon making love with her, and said, "Then why when you say that about me, do you make it sound like an accusation?"

They squabbled endlessly, but Danny was devoted to her; he and Greg were getting along quite amiably, but Danny was feeling guilty toward him, guilty and sympathetic, and he experienced no envy at all when Greg with huge satisfaction confided one afternoon in their fruit parlor near Yasaka Shrine that he'd started going out with a Japanese woman. None of envy's contracting chill—rather, its opposite: Danny warmed with a hope that this woman might somehow induce Greg, who was looking terrible, to take better care of himself. His beard, though now grown to a reasonable length, still somehow managed to suggest not deliberate growth so much as a simple neglect, for a very long time, to shave; his knuckles were chapped with the cold; and there was an ugly, bloodied split in his chapped lower lip, at which he dabbed now and then with a wadded napkin. Here was a familiar pattern, an endearing one lately turned a little disquieting: that conflicting behavior whereby Greg would take so little pains for his own comfort and yet would, as in now ordering a second five-dollar fruit salad, pamper himself as well.

"Her name is Noriko." Greg's dark eyes shone with pleasure. "And she really is excellent. I don't mean to portray her as any sort of iconoclast, but she's not your typical, beaten down, depressingly deferential Japanese woman. She said her parents were always trying to set up an arranged marriage for her, but she refused to marry a jerk. Quite unreasonable of her, huh? She said her parents have sort of given up now that she's an old woman. She's twenty-eight." The little joke pleased Greg, with a mirth that seemed to turn inward rather than—the usual practice—seeking an acknowledging laugh from Danny. This was an extremely subtle shift, the sort of thing Danny would never have noticed in anyone he knew less well or cared less deeply about. As it was, he couldn't be certain whether he was justified in this feeling that the two of them had grown even more distant in the past few weeks than heretofore understood.

"What does she do?"

"She's a sort of go-fer, lower-rung English teacher at my school, and she hates it. I'm trying to come up with another job for her."

"I didn't know you'd been going to classes."

"I haven't. Or hadn't. I met her at Refinement. She recognized me."

"How's her English?"

"Better than my Japanese." Greg laughed again. "And another thing about her . . . " Greg leaned forward confidingly. His charged tone and the clandestine cant of his shoulders were those of a man who might be about to announce *She's got a nice ass* or *She's great in bed.* "She's a Christian. And you know there are very few in Japan."

"About one percent of the population," Danny said.

"Still researching everything, huh?" Greg said, with that same inward amusement that left Danny feeling peculiarly distanced. "It's so winsome of you."

Her name turned out to be Noriko Yamaguchi, and though Greg introduced her informally as Noriko, when the four of them met for dinner just a few days before Carrie's departure, Danny pointedly called her Yamaguchi-san. Carrie, compromising, called her Noriko-san, though this soon became plain Noriko. They made an awkward foursome, for which Greg was chiefly to blame. With that unhelpfulness typical of him in social situations, he had chosen to play the role of observer rather than participant in the conversation. Yamaguchi-san's English was fair but stiff, and common colloquialisms left her bewildered. Danny and Carrie were soon exchanging familiar stories in monosyllables, ostensibly speaking to each other but conducting the whole conversation for Yamaguchi-san's benefit. Greg and Carrie began to drink a fair amount, Danny very little, and Yamaguchi-san, though she allowed her glass to be filled, almost nothing. All of these abstemious Japanese women. She was less pretty than Danny had envisioned but was, as he soon began to appreciate, extraordinarily enticing. Listening, talking, she did not drop her eyes in the usual Japanese woman's fashion. She was entrancingly direct, curious, frontal. In a country in which both women and men tended to look younger than their age, she seemed a few years older. Appraisive lines were tucked underneath her intelligent-looking eyes and at the edges of her mouth. To her credit, she asked questions when perplexed by a word or phrase, and when she spoke English her discomposure revealed less embarrassment at her shortcomings than simple frustration: she wanted, earnestly, to get her point across. When after about an hour she went off to the bathroom and Carrie, who by now had drunk a good deal, topped a hand on Greg's and announced, "Gregory, she's adorable," this seemed to Danny an unfair or an undiscerning dismissal. Many Japanese women were adorable; this Yamaguchi-san was something rarer and finer.

It pleased Danny to find himself walking beside her on the quiet street outside the restaurant. Greg and Carrie were some distance behind. The night air moved mildly for February and the sky was clear. The lights along the top of Hiei-zan leading to the ski slope and the sky-view coffee shop were bright and firm and particulate. Yamaguchi-san seemed tiny beside him. She was also, he'd noticed at once, buxom for a Japanese. In the faint light she watched him intently as he talked.

"So you don't like your job," Danny said. The four of them had discussed this at dinner. "What sort of job are you looking for?"

"It is very difficult," Miss Yamaguchi said. "You see, I am a woman." The word came out *woo-mon* and Danny felt somewhat smitten at this pronunciation. "In Japan there is not so many good job for woo-mon. They do not pay so much mah-nay."

This pronunciation, too, beguiled him. Whereas *money* was always somewhat crass, this *mah-nay* was something rich with pure loveliness.

"Would you like to visit America?"

"I am afraid," Yamaguchi-san said.

Was she expressing a general fear or (something Danny was sensitive about) was she responding to bizarre, barbarous America's most recent spectacular bloodletting—this attempt on President (and former movie star) Ronald Reagan's life by a young man in love with a teenage movie starlet? Lunacy. By chance it had again been the Professor's secretary, Miss Minowada, who had broken the news. What a bizarre thing this was if you only considered it: to have to feel apologetic for the way your country's most famous politicians and celebrities kept getting gunned down by strangers. "Greg found me two very good teaching jobs," Danny said. "Teaching very rich doctors." These jobs had recently turned even more lucrative. Danny had been asked to edit some medical papers written by academic friends of Dr. Kobayashi. So technical were these papers—written for scientific journals—that Danny often could not even understand what was being tested or proven, although he had read with great interest an article about some laboratory rats that were given a choice of water bottles laced with various concentrations of alcohol.

"Often he talks about you," Yamaguchi-san said.

"For me it was very lonely in Japan at first. Especially before I met Greg. He has been a very good friend to me."

"He tells you are the best friend."

Given all the anger Danny'd felt, and the relief these past weeks as Greg had grown more distant, it was all a bit ludicrous to be feeling this way: but the words thrilled Danny. For Greg had that knack, still there, of drawing one into a competition—with liquor-store owners and Chinese restaurant proprietors, launderers and bartenders and bums—for his affections. "What did he say?" Danny asked. "That I am his best friend, or that I am his best friend in Japan?"

"Oh *yes*," Miss Yamaguchi said firmly but ambiguously.

"He is very charming," Danny said. "He is very funny."

"Yes," she said, and laughed softly—a captivating sound. "You know, he will call to the person on bicycle when it is very loud, '*Bureeki o naoshite kudasai.*'"

Bureeki o naoshite kudasai: Fix your brakes. It was a lovable image, for here was nutty Uncle Gregory in a nutshell: a bedraggled, bearded foreigner advising the polite and doubtless flabbergasted natives to behave with a little more consideration. And the way Miss Yamaguchi told the story, with that little laugh of hers, was appealing because it settled a question Danny had been pondering all evening—whether Greg's allure for her simply lay in his being an outrageous gaijin, or whether she had somehow detected, across the vast linguistic and cultural chasms, his rare charm. It seemed she had vaulted those chasms, and at this realization Danny's envy woke at last and he felt for her a solicitous foreboding as well. Both emotions coalesced around a joined observation and inquiry: lovable though he was, Greg was trouble, and wouldn't it have been better for her, for everyone, if the gaijin she'd attached herself to had been not Greg but himself?

"Do you think he is hoppy?"

"Happy? Greg?"

Miss Yamaguchi with admirable directness was probing him. She had wanted this conversation as much as he had. She was hoping for answers, but how was he going to begin to explain what was, even if she had a perfect command of English, a labyrinthine undertaking? Still, her own fair effort demanded at least an attempt to convey his conviction that, screwy as Greg was, there was something not just likeable but noble about him. Truly, noble. "No, I don't think so happy," Danny began. "You know, Greg is very serious about things. I don't think he has any choice. I think that is just the way it is."

"Yes," she said with enthusiasm, as if what he was attempting to express had not become faintly ridiculous in his effort to render it into monosyllabic English.

Danny went on, "He believes, and I guess I also believe, that if you think very hard you may come up with answers that you need. In that sense, though he is often very gloomy, he is an optimist. Optimist—do you know that word?" asked Danny with a pleased sense that in formulating these thoughts so starkly he had perhaps illuminated something for himself. She nodded *yes*. "But it *is* very hard, and often he drinks too much, beer or sake. Do you find sometimes he drinks too much?" Danny was getting in some probing of his own.

"Yes," she conceded—nervously. "Too much."

"Actually, I don't understand it very well myself. I think he has troubles. I think he has troubles here, you know," Danny said, tapping his own skull in illustration.

Yamaguchi-san's eyes bulged queerly, as with fright. Madness—she seemed to think Danny was hinting at madness.

"He has troubles *here*," Danny amended, tapping below his collarbone, but again alarm flashed in her eyes, as though Danny were suggesting a physical ailment. Greg and Carrie, their voices uncapped by drink, were closing upon them; the conversation with Miss Yamaguchi was coming to an end. "He has," Danny attempted a final time, "trouble in his *soul*."

"In his *soul,* yes," cried Miss Yamaguchi, as if Danny had offered with *soul* something not evasive or vague, but direct and concrete and helpful at last.

It was a term which Greg, somewhat surprisingly, given all his talk of *inward forays* and *mental progress being made,* never employed, but one which Danny in the past few months, though it continued to carry no religious connotations, found increasingly useful. For what better term to describe the sensation when you're standing drunk at the window of a high building giving onto downtown Kyoto and discover that every word of Japanese which you'd amassed over the past few months has slipped off you like snow from a slate roof and yet instead of feeling unnerved or destitute you sense some vast interior richness independent of all knowledge?

Or, again, what better term, though imprecise, to approximate the troutlike leaping within and the quick, scintillant snap when words you'd not before dared utter suddenly and marvelously break from your tongue? The day before Carrie left for America she realized that she'd not taken, as she'd promised she would, any photographs of Japan with the camera her stepfather had given her. In a nervous and affectionate rush the two of them shimmied into clothes and burst outdoors snapping pictures everywhere.

Misty, gray, winter-withered, this was not a morning auspicious for color film. Holding hands the entire half-hour journey, they took a train to Uji, to which somehow neither had ever gone, although, through photographs, the celebrated temple of Byōdō-in was familiar to them both. In the gray light the temple looked unexpectedly austere and was, though neither mentioned this, a disappointment. Carrie took pictures anyway—nearly half a roll—before they bustled off in search of lunch.

Half an hour later they emerged from a noodle shop to discover that the clouds were breaking. "Hey. It's clearing. Honey," Carrie said, again taking his hand, "let's go back."

"Back where?"

"To Byōdō-in. The light's different now. It'll be prettier."

"It's not much different."

"But it is. It's going to be. Please. Please, Danny."

So Danny paid their admission a second time, and the two of them strolled again around the pond, through sere gardens where—soon—profusion would reign. Wanting things to go well for her, Danny was happy to be proven wrong. The light had shifted. Prising sun had rooted into the mist, divulging a topical shimmer in pond and rockface, wood and frond. "Look how much better it is," Carrie said. "Danny. Danny, look at the way the sunlight's caught the top there! Oh, this is going to be good. This is going to be good."

She was excited—was jittery—even girlishly thrilled—as she fumbled with her camera. These lights and colors enlivened her, just as on Christmas Eve she'd yearned so keenly to see how the colors of sweater and scarf would match his face and hair. He was wearing the scarf now.

Carrie took her share of pleasure in things, but to see her girlishly, bubblingly thrilled was so rare a sight it elated Danny. Something leapt within, just like a fish, and the words issued unbidden from his throat: "Carrie, darling, you know I'm going to miss you terribly when you're gone."

"This terrible, sinking feeling"—Greg was calling over his shoulder, his words emerging in short-breathed packs as the two of them clambered up the hillside. He was a few strides ahead of Danny. They were on the way to the summit cemetery they'd visited the first time they went climbing, back in October. This hike had been Danny's idea; he was feeling miffed at the way Greg had maintained his abstracted distance in the week since Carrie's departure. "This terrible feeling that she thinks I could save her . . . from drudgery. That she wants to marry me. Obviously, if she'd consider such a possibility . . . she hasn't a clue what real drudgery is all about."

Danny accelerated his pace to draw even with Greg, who still did not look at him. "What makes you think Noriko wants to marry you?"

"Oh she just *does*. I don't blame her, I mean her job's so sucky and all, and I naturally look like a ticket to freedom. But the thing is, if I just thought she was trying to use me, it would be much easier. The thing is," Greg said, and glanced at Danny, his tone taking on a diffidence and faint wonder all the more endearing for his usual arrogance and bluster, "you know I think she really sort of loves me."

"Why's that so hard to believe?"

"You know it makes me very nervous. I say to myself, *Grego, if the realization that someone you really like really likes you makes you nervous you're in bad shape*. And I answer myself, *You're in bad shape*. Because you know I really can't rescue anybody. Not now, anyway."

"What do you mean, *Not now*?"

Greg seemed to resent the question; his reply, though a kind of joke, delivered in a rumbling bass voice, seemed to contain an uncharacteristic petulance: "Lea' me 'lone, lea' me 'lone, lea' me 'lone."

And in the cemetery, where enormous crows called to each other above the maze of memorial stones, Greg did another peculiar thing. Danny'd gone ahead, wandering contentedly among the bizarre blend of familiar and exotic—Christian crosses and Roman numerals on the one hand, stone lanterns and kanji on the other. He turned to find Greg crouching as if to read an inscription, but his eyes were closed, his fingers interlaced: Greg was praying.

Greg rose and coming over placed a hand on Danny's shoulder, his squinting eyes and hushed voice establishing an atmosphere of parodic conspiracy. "You know you mustn't tell anyone," he advised Danny. "You may recall, that's how they knew old Tricky Dick Nixon had finally lost his marbles. It was a huge Watergate scoop, Woodward and Bernstein, and all over *Newsweek,* with even an artist's watercolor conception of the startling event. He actually prayed in front of Henry Kissinger, *and asked Henry to join him*. Can you imagine—asking Henry Kissinger to pray?"

By the time the two of them finally descended, nightfall was moving in, as Kyoto's second quiddity, a constellated grid of gold and silver lights, began to emerge. At Danny's insistence, overriding Greg's vague objection that he had "things to do," they went to a tempura restaurant on narrow Ponto-chō for dinner. With Greg so taciturn, customary rules had to be reversed—Danny serving as the impetus for more food, more drink. After splitting five or six pitchers of sake and four orders of tempura they wandered across the river, its lights swaying, everything swaying, and Greg seemed to be feeling better, declaring, "You know as many times as I've drunk I still get this fresh feeling that the change is not inside my head, but *out* there. It's as if the city has, quite obligingly, or maybe just a little drunk itself, begun to wobble."

Brighter than any colors in a dream, the illuminated city shuddered and broke and re-erected itself in the river. "Walking across this bridge, like this," Danny began, formulating one of those overwhelmingly vast assertions Greg loved so much, "is my favorite thing in the world."

"Now I've been thinking about free will—you remember, you asked me long ago to think about it. You were going to write some paper about it."

"My third-year paper." The words seemed a kind of electric alarm, bawling in another room, attempting to call Danny back over a great distance; for it was, momentarily, not quite believable that he would ever again be sitting, as within a few months he surely would, in the stacks at Langdell, organizing a third-year paper. And he'd been planning to make such progress on it this year. . . .

"Anyway, I came up with this aphorism for you. God, I love aphorisms. If I could have been born anything, what I would have been born is one of those old men who live in the mountains, huddled in a goatskin, with one of those long *long* beards, who pilgrims come to for advice. The pilgrims battle dragons and avalanches and floods to reach you, and all you do is lay some crazy aphorism on them."

"'Two frogs go to town,'" Danny recited. "How did it go? Your prophecy?"

"Anyway, are you set and ready? Here it is. Most people don't mind being rats in a maze, provided they can beat the next rat to the cheese. You like it? You see, it's really not *freedom* we're looking for."

"I *do* like it," Danny said. He placed a hand, lightly, on Greg's shoulder.

"Does it make too much sense? Is it not cryptic enough?"

"It's perfect."

Enticed by a woman in black fishnet stockings, they went into a place called Captain Rico's where they ordered two bottles of Kirin. There were a number of gaijin within, including two men sitting nearby who were, to judge from their haircuts and builds, American soldiers. One was wearing over his cropped head a cowboy hat. Greg's observation that there were two types of clean-cut gaijin in Kyoto, and the way to distinguish the Mormons from the soldiers is that the former wore ties, actually was somewhat accurate. "I'm talking a full-scale operation," the one without the cowboy hat was saying, ostensibly to his companion, though at a volume sufficient to reach all surrounding tables. His very short blond hair was combed back in what Danny thought of as "greaser style."

"You ever wore a cowboy hat?" Greg asked Danny. "I mean since you were a little kid?"

"I don't think so."

"I've done so many asinine things in my adult life, but I can truthfully say I've never worn a cowboy hat. It's really the one thing I can be truly proud of."

Danny laughed but Greg did not; he seemed to be receding again into glumness, and the two of them sat for a while in silence. Such unnecessary heavy glumness, and Greg sometimes would live with it for days at a stretch. "You got it ass-backwards," the loud man in the cowboy hat was insisting. "Everybody's got the technological *muscle*, it's a question of expertise."

"I had an idea," Greg abruptly began. "It's a new kind of restaurant. You take some very famous, swanky restaurant, in Manhattan or Georgetown, say, prestigious as hell, the kind of place where they set out all sorts of fancy bread and stuff nobody touches, and down below, in the basement, you open a restaurant where you peddle the leftovers. How do you like the idea?"

"I like it a lot."

"Can't you see it? You sit down, you ask the waitress, *What are tonight's specials?* and she says, *There's a guy up there's hardly touched his Trout Amandine, with any luck you'll get most of it.*" Greg had begun to laugh softly, but deeply enough to spring tears. That he always found his own jokes more amusing than anyone else's was somehow a lovable trait.

"What about the board of health?"

"Lord, Danny, you're so literal-minded. Let go, let go."

Carrie, too, had called him literal-minded; and it was true that the great obstacles in his loosest daydreams, in which he might be winning Wimbledon or sleeping with movie actresses or being appointed to the Supreme Court, were always bureaucratic mundanities like regulations or schedules. "Besides," Greg went on, "Reagan's going to abolish all boards of health as antibusiness. Now tell me, can't you see it, Dan? The clientele made up of street-people gourmets, some college kid and his date waiting to see what will emerge from the gods dining above? Part of a melon? Three-quarters of a fried oyster? The ham removed from a Veal Cordon Bleu? And the ripple of excitement in the place as word goes around that somebody upstairs just ordered Chateaubriand for two? Danny, you ask the waitress what there is to drink, she sniffs a glass and says, *Smells like a martini. You want it?*"

Somberly, pragmatically, they explored the ramifications of Greg's restaurant scheme—the need for certain minimum regulations, such as, *No food served in which cigarette butts have been extinguished*, and for a lottery priority system to settle cases when two customers claimed the same leftover, and they agreed on the restaurant's name and slogan: Greg's Good Used Food—Serving Only What's Still Basically Fit to Eat. On a tide of entrepreneurial fraternity, Greg cheered at last, they returned to the cool night air. They bought sweet potatoes from a pushcart vendor, and crossed the river once more, peeling the foil from the potatoes and eating as they went. Down Ponto-chō, more tunnel than street, past the tempura shop where they'd had dinner, they wandered, until the collective ringed uproar of a crowd drew them onto a playground above the river. Even as the two of them edged toward the center, the grunted cries of the spectators (though Danny could make out nothing of their Japanese) told him in a language all men understand that it was a fight this crowd had congregated for. One of the fighters was standing, the other lying on the ground. To Danny's surprise, they were not Japanese, but gaijin, and for a moment Danny could not absorb what was happening. Then his mind took in the greased blond hair and a tumbled cowboy hat.

The man on the ground was the one who'd been wearing the cowboy hat. The other, the blond man, was kicking him—hard, very hard. The man on the ground was releasing faint cries while trying to keep his face and stomach protected with his hands, and the blond man was methodically moving here and there, trying to plant a completely unobstructed kick.

What happened in the next few moments seemed to happen very fast. Greg lunged out of the crowd and his body hit the blond man's at the hips, both of them landing atop a teeter-totter which plunged beneath their mingled weight to the ground. They rose separately, Greg took a swing at the blond man, connecting, the blond man turned and swung, apparently missing, and Greg stepped forward and sank his fist into the blond man's face. The blond man collapsed backward, his flailing hand catching the chain of a child's swing, his trunk twisting as the hand failed to uphold him. His body dropped, seated, to the ground. He looked up dazed, smeared runnels of blood obscuring his mouth and chin. "Get up, get up you motherfucker before I *kick* you," Greg cried, but the man said and did nothing. Then he shook his head, rolled and crawled a few feet along the muddy ground, stood, and trotted off into the night. Next the police arrived, four short shrill gesticulating men with billyclubs who, minatory for all their comic overtones, apparently mistook Greg for the original assailant. His arms were seized from behind and a billyclub brandished at his tousled head. A crowd of what seemed dozens of people, Danny among them, each screaming an explanation, Danny's the only one in English, descended upon the police, from which cacophony it was apparently made clear what Greg's role had been. He was released. A whistle was blown, a command shouted, and the crowd fell silent. Danny stepped forward and in broken Japanese supplemented by hand gestures tried to indicate his willingness to give his name and address as a witness. He was rebuffed and then, his meaning perhaps come clear, crisply ordered to produce his alien registration card, which by a lucky break he was carrying. Greg did not have his, and he was seized again. At this point the kicked man, who had been helped to his feet, wincing, clutching at his chest as though ribs were broken, displayed remarkable self-possession.

"Unida Stay Military," he announced, drawing from his pocket some form of identification. While one of the policemen examined this by tiny, pen-sized flashlight, the soldier said, "Unida Stay Military here. Everything's okay. *Zenbu* okay *desu,* everybody. Military here. Military here." He waved the policemen back with one hand, and they deferentially retreated a few paces. His other hand was still wrapped around his chest. "Strictly an internal matter," he declared, and to Danny, wits doubly dazed with drink and the fight, for a moment it seemed the man was speaking of his injuries. "Unida States Military matter. Strictly internal matter. Everybody back home."

The police consulted each other, nervously, in clipped questions and pauses in the semidarkness, and then it became evident no one would be arrested. "That's right, everybody go back *home*," the soldier advised, as though he had become the sole peace-keeping force. "*Zenbu* okay *desu nee*."

The crowd began to disperse. Danny retrieved the man's cowboy hat for him. "You okay?" Danny asked him. "You all right?"

The soldier leaned forward; Danny for all his own drinking caught a ferocious stink of liquor. "No problem, cowboy," the soldier said. "No problem."

Greg was still theoretically subject to arrest for not having his alien registration card, but the police had drifted away from him. The four police—two and two, a neat square—followed after the soldier (who again waved them off) at a respectful distance. It was unclear whether their function now was peace-keeping or merely solicitous. Greg and Danny turned in the other direction. "Hey!" Danny called, catching a glimpse of Greg's face in the white light of a coffee shop, "you're all banged up."

Greg grinned ecstatically. "Ought to be. The bastard put some power behind it."

"I thought he missed." And at once Danny found he could not stop talking. The fight played itself over and over in his mind and his tongue buzzed with repetitive chatter. He was elated, he was envious, he was angry at himself for his instinctive hesitancy, he was proud of himself for what somehow felt like a shared triumph. They drifted into a noodle shop, where Danny inspected Greg's face, already swollen and red under the left eye. Greg was saying very little, only repeating now and then, "I don't think so but I maya broke his nose, I thought I heard something crunch the second time I hit him," while holding an *oshibori*—the hot washcloth that preceded the food—to his cheek. His left eye was narrowed, and would continue to narrow, but the right one positively shone: Greg was exultant.

"You are a hero," Danny cried.

Embarrassed, Greg shook his head, flexed his fist on the counter, smiled.

"You have struck a blow for the man who's down. You have fought for freedom," Danny pronounced, discovering that through grandiloquent cliché he was able to express both his envy and, much the preponderant emotion, his admiration. "Greg Blaising, you have struck a blow for peace. A blow for justice. You have freed a man from the oppressor's boot."

Professor Umeda had reached that stage of his meal where only white rice remained. Across the room a beautiful young Japanese woman, dressed in what the ads called "Trad Style"—topsiders, a preppie pink sweater, wool skirt, blazer—was slurping her bowl of noodles so loudly that everyone in the restaurant could hear. Acceptable etiquette though this was in Japan, Danny after all these months still found it unsettling.

For the first time in any of their lunches, seeking to subvert the Professor's complacent habits, Danny had ordered dessert. An ice cream parfait. Ice cream was never very good in Japan, but he'd gone ahead anyway.

Lunches with the Professor were still to be dreaded—sometimes only slightly, when Danny felt he'd been helpful, sometimes greatly. Last week an embarrassing thing had occurred. Danny had had a friend mail him a book on international law which he'd intended as a gift for the Professor. But the Professor had insisted—absolutely insisted—on paying for the book, the upshot being that the Professor had incurred an expense for a text of dubious worth to him. Danny had offered to scout through it in search of information useful to the Professor, but he'd not been able to come up with much.

It was hard to tell exactly what would be useful to the Professor, whose manuscript, so far as Danny could see, attempted to combine two discrete fields. The first was legal theory, jurisprudence, as spun chiefly through the contract theorists—Hobbes, Locke, Rousseau—and here Danny felt he could be of genuine service. There had been some profitable talks and Danny a few times had corrected misapprehensions of the Professor's (though the abashing truth was that the Professor, despite his limited English, had just as often corrected

Danny). The second field was international law, about which the Professor seemed to have convictions Danny not only could not share but could hardly envision. The Professor would speak of "well-established canons of international law" or of "developments in international law" as though this law had some concrete, unquestionable existence; whereas Danny at law school had quickly come round to the prevailing view among both students and faculty that the term was something of a joke. From Hobbes and Locke to whatever branch you like—Austin or Kelsen or the legal positivists, Holmes, Frank, the legal realists—it was clear that law originated with a sovereign authority. Law was *power* first: that was the *sine qua non* of any legal system. But where was the sovereign in the Professor's system? In the UN? In The Hague's impotent International Court of Justice? In the pieties of international conventions that were respected only until greed or war made it expedient to shatter them? In an international symposium of quirky law professors?

Nonetheless, over the past half year Danny had begun rooting for the Professor in this quixotic struggle. This short, humorless, lipless, olive-skinned man stood up in solitary opposition (it almost seemed) to all the ugly facts of international rape—as Russia maintained its invasion of Afghanistan and threatened to reswallow Poland, as Libya engorged Chad, and Vietnam Cambodia—and to all the cynicism of all the lawyers and professors Danny knew. As he slogged through Machiavelli, Hobbes, Locke, Rousseau, through bewildering, contrarily pulled U.S. Supreme Court cases, through contemporary articles of fellow theorists working in English, Japanese, French, or German, the Professor was doing what Danny with his nebulous plans for a third-year paper had vowed to do: he was applying rigorous scholarship to an abstract legal notion. Justice. While these lunches were to be dreaded, the man was a true exemplar, Danny had little doubt of that. His was a nobility akin to that displayed by the Japanese courts in those cases (read at the Professor's recent instigation) dealing with the legal implications of Hiroshima and Nagasaki. With a rationality that was almost heartrending, these judges had attempted to assimilate what surely were the most horrifying events in all history into the tenuous, wobbly constructs of human law. The temptation must have been strong simply to shrug one's shoulders and say, "This is too horrific an event to compass within our legal system." But they had not done that. The courts had carried their familiar legal terms and concepts—just compensation, eminent domain, jurisdictional immunity—into the rubbled epicenter of the blast. The cases had crystallized in Danny's mind a resolve, steeping for months, to visit Hiroshima in the spring.

"Your friends," the Professor said, "are they well?"

Although delivered in the form of a polite inquiry, such a question from the Professor seemed almost unreasonably prying. . . . Of course Danny was still sensitive about Greg's performance at the party in December. "Yes. I don't know, I guess so. Greg is thinking about leaving Japan. And Carrie's gone right now, gone back to Princeton for a wedding. A friend of hers's wedding."

"Miss Pingree, her study of art, it is progressing well?"

The Professor, either because he could not comprehend a single woman's just "hanging out" in Japan for months, or because he politely sought to lend her visit an industry it didn't possess, had seized on the notion, drawn from a lateral remark of Carrie's, that she was pursuing an avid study of Japanese art. The subject of Carrie now seemed to be directing Danny, as was so often the case in his discussions with Japanese people, into hopelessly complex explanations. He said instead—"Yes, I guess pretty well."

"And when will Miss Pingree return to Japan?"

"Carrie?" Danny's question was in part an offer; the Professor needn't call her *Miss Pingree*. Umeda nodded, a tautening of his mouth suggesting a slight distaste—as if to say, *Who was Danny*, neither husband nor relative to this young woman, *to be attempting to eliminate distance between Carrie and Professor Masahiro Umeda?* "Soon, I hope," Danny said. "Two weeks supposedly."

Danny's parfait had come with a wedge of apple whose skin, severed most of the way up but not detached, hung as a sort of flap. The Japanese generally did not eat apple skins and this one had presumably been left as a decorative stripe of color, to be removed before eating. Danny placed the entire wedge, skin and all, in his mouth and crunched down upon it.

"You eat the apple skin," the Professor observed.

"Mm." Danny swallowed. "Also peaches and pears. Generally, we don't peel fruit in America. You know, nutritionally, a lot of the nutrients are in the skin. The same's true with rice. Unpolished brown rice is better for you." Danny concluded this heresy by peering at the Professor's emptied rice bowl.

"And grapes?"

"Oh I like grape skins. Their tartness." Danny scooted the parfait dish into the middle of the table. "That was good. Mmm. I was very hungry. How is your family? Your wife?"

The Professor's expression remained severe. "Quite well."

"And your children?"

"Well also thank you very much. When I was visiting Professor Horne at Harvard, you recall he may be visiting Japan this spring, he kindly took me as guest to a restaurant in Newton, Massachusetts. At this restaurant, for a—an unchanging amount—"

"A fixed price?" Danny offered.

"A *prix fixe*," the Professor replied in a proud cosmopolite's French. "For a *prix fixe* one could eat as many beefsteaks as one wished. The table beside our table, there were two very large young men, and one of them ate seventeen beefsteaks. And many large pitchers of beer, also. The waitress told us this was the record number."

"Seventeen steaks," Danny marveled. The story was a humorous one, but it had not flushed any grin from the Professor, who added, imparting his own nutritional lesson, "So much meat is not healthy. It is more steak, I think, than most Japanese eat in several years."

As if this anecdote of overindulgence itself had brought on dyspepsia, Danny's intestines emitted an audible whine followed by an abrupt, unignorable crumpling sensation. He excused himself and retreated into the cramped bathroom, where it occurred to him that Horne, who had a reputation at the law school as a brilliant eccentric, and who had once delivered a complete lecture wearing a Groucho Marx mask, had obviously chosen that restaurant as a kind of joke. He'd wanted to see how the straitlaced Japanese professor would respond to exuberant American gluttony.

And stepping from the men's room, pants zipped, hands washed and hair neatly combed, Danny experienced a second abrupt sensation—this one quite irregular. Light hopped to the lenses of the Professor's glasses as he glanced up from the table, his eyes disappearing behind a whitely opaque flash, and for an instant Danny viewed an image that seemed to be what the Professor himself was seeing: a tall, thin, red-haired young man stepping from the malodorous bathroom.

And with this image came a realization that the Professor had placed him, racially, among the earth's coarsely calibrated—the hairy and unshaven, the hasty swallowers of vegetable husks and fruit peelings and unchewed steaks. In Danny's mind a note of protest immediately sounded: surely the Professor was cosmopolitan enough to appreciate that these variations in diet and dress went no deeper than custom? Or that to an American there was something humorous but also a little disgusting in any pretty and demure young Japanese woman who slurped her noodles so loudly one could hear her across the room? But these were questions and rebuttals that could never be presented, eventual accords they would never attain. The distance was simply too vast. Like an insect under a microscope, Danny was caught, held in the seizing glance of the Professor's spectacles, and never in a whole lifetime could he present himself justly to this man.

3

ALONE IN HIROSHIMA

*

*

Danny in Maruzen Department Store drew from the shelf a huge Japanese dictionary of the only type he could comfortably use, one in which the Japanese words were written in roman letters, and having taken a preliminary look to see whether anyone was peering over his shoulder, rummaged the pages for a word not listed in his own dictionary. Here it was. *Seibyo*. Glancing once more over his shoulder, he carefully copied it onto a scrap of paper. He found the second word he was looking for—*rinbyo*—and added this to his scrap of paper, placing beside it the letter *G*. And so with a third word, *baidoku*, beside which he scribbled an *S*. He fit the dictionary into the waiting gap on the shelf, folded the paper and tucked it into his wallet, scooted down the stairs and out to where his bicycle stood chained to a tree.

The air was flush with spring growth, one of those mornings that tug at your chest, urge you to sprint, to hurl stones a great distance, but Danny was on his way to the clinic of a Dr. Wako, friend of Danny's student, Dr. Kobayashi, the pediatrician. Dr. Wako was some sort of internist. Danny was not at all certain he was heading to the right sort of doctor, for he'd been unwilling to confide with any specificity in Dr. Kobayashi, who had met Carrie a couple of times. Indeed, Danny'd been unwilling himself to admit his fears, which opened ugly vistas all along the horizon.

Carrie, back for nearly three weeks now, had returned to him bewilderingly changed. The physical alterations were most immediately felt, for she'd cut her straight blonde hair and had had a permanent, and she'd got a deep tan in South Carolina and in Trinidad, to which she'd unexpectedly gone with her father and stepmother. It was probably true, as Greg insisted, that she was looking far prettier now, and there had been for Danny a profound momentary lift in enfolding in his arms, beneath him, this unfamiliar woman with blonde curls wreathing her face and a body whose new color teasingly accentuated the retained fragile paleness of its erogenous zones, but ultimately these alterations unsettled and grieved him. It was not merely their way of attesting to the existence of another sort of life endlessly going on—beaches and sailboats and an urbane and natty leisure—toward which Danny felt disdain softened a little by an outsider's envy, but which for Carrie seemed to hold an enormous, undiluted attraction. For she had changed toward *him*, too, though this was less clear, and was perhaps only a reflection of, a response to, his own unease. In any case, gone was the time in which he had spent nearly every night at the Sunshine Mansion. She had reasserted her need for privacy, and he'd slept with her only four times since her return.

A crowd (Danny had so hoped there would be no crowd) was gathered in Dr. Wako's waiting room. As he'd expected, he was the only gaijin, and all eyes—adults and children—fastened on him as he stepped forward to give the receptionist his name. He then retreated to a corner where, standing behind the *Japan Times*, he reviewed the words copied from the dictionary.

Less than a minute later, in a discomforting display of favoritism, a nurse called his name—which came out, as so often in Japan, *Ought*. Strange red-haired Mr. Ought hastily followed her, ignoring the mild eyes of all the waiting room's slighted, inquisitive occupants, into a large room where Dr. Wako, a gray-haired tiny man—no more than five feet tall, very short even in Japan—awaited him.

"Good morning," Danny said in Japanese. The doctor seemed excited and his broad grin nervous. Gaijin patients were doubtless a rarity.

"You are not well," the doctor said in English, with that leveled Japanese inflection which makes it difficult to tell whether a question or a statement is intended.

"Perhaps I should go to another clinic," Danny said in Japanese, as he'd prepared. He lowered his voice to keep this from the two nurses in the room, and continued in prepared Japanese, "I think perhaps I have venereal disease." The doctor nodded deeply. His grin was unfazed.

Danny was not quite prepared for the doctor's next request, in stiff but unambiguous English, that he remove his pants. There was a sort of screen, affording some privacy from the nurses but not much.

Danny stepped behind it, removed his jeans and, at the doctor's deep confirming nod, his undershorts. Danny's genitals, generally unprepossessing enough to be a source of some worry, now seemed to hang with a perverse, satisfied corpulence. This doctor was so small! When Dr. Wako began slipping a crisp green elastic glove over his right hand Danny was horribly reminded of the condom he'd worn that first night with Carrie. The doctor's touch was soft, yet when he nudged the dwindled chancre which Danny's fingers had parted the russet crotch hair to reveal, a thud of distaste hammered the base of Danny's spine. His glance shot to the wall, where a framed photograph depicted what must be Mrs. Wako, though half a head taller than her husband, and, half a head taller again than she—Danny's height it would seem—their two sons.

"Last year," Dr. Wako said, with the same gleeful grin, "I went ten days to New York City. It is very *wild* city."

What in the world, what in the world could he mean by that?

"My friend, my girl friend, just came back from New York," Danny said, his pants still down, nurses fulfilling their duties just a few feet away. One shuffled past the edge of the screen. He dropped his eyes; presumably she dropped hers. "She grew up there," Danny continued, which wasn't accurate but perhaps did manage to convey the one thing he burned to clarify: that if he'd contracted some disease, he'd not done so through any depredations of Japanese womanhood—all those demure dark creatures so ticklingly exemplified by the voices on the other side of the screen.

Danny's blood pressure and temperature were taken, the thermometer placed not in his mouth but in his armpit, a blood sample was siphoned from the crook of his arm, and his tugging heart was prodded at by a cold stethoscope. If the two assisting nurses understood the purpose of these tests they gave no sign. Danny was told to come back in two days, when the results would be in. "I went also to Las Vegas," Dr. Wako confided in parting. "A wild city. Very wild. But"—the grin on that tiny head was devilishly large—"not so wild as New York City."

"Pardon me for . . . disturbing you like this," Danny huffed as he pedaled furiously down Imadegawa. After these last few days of sunny spring weather, the air had turned close and cool, the swollen gray sky now beginning to spill a few drops of rain. Danny had no umbrella, no raincoat. He began to pedal even faster. His head was pounding.

Danny ran a red light and was tinnily honked at by an old woman on a blue motor scooter. "I'll just take . . . a minute of your time," he rehearsed, with the same arch formality. "I come on what . . . I guess you could call . . . business."

His anger climbed with him as he mounted the stairs of the Sunshine Mansion and it crashed inside his head when Carrie came to the door in a bathrobe. Endless idleness—she hadn't even gotten dressed yet.

He pushed past her into the room. *"Hey,"* she called, a little testily herself, then shrugged her shoulders at him as he stood collecting his breath in the middle of the room. She turned to the sink and began to fill a kettle for coffee.

All of the arch obliquities dropped away and what issued without any preamble from his mouth was, "I was just notified that I've got syphilis."

Carrie jerked around, recoiling from him. Her eyes widened and her hand shot protectively to her abdomen. "That means," she said, "that means I've probably got it too."

He could say nothing for a moment, he could only stare at her. Not even his blinding anger could prevent him from seeing that this hushed, this going-bug-eyed-by-degrees display of hers was genuine, as was her revulsion: she just didn't understand at all.

"Of course you've got it," he cried, his voice leaping shrilly. "You're the only one I could have gotten it from." He recalled Dr. Wako's knowing, roguish grin, that lubricious precise grin as he'd explained that if Danny happened to know the woman who had infected him, he should urge her to seek treatment. "The sad truth is," Danny said, his voice under better control, "you're the only one I could have gotten it from. Now I don't know whether you picked it up from some Trinidadian gigolo, or the Princeton football team, or whether you got it from Greg, and I don't really care—"

"Greg?" Carrie looked befuddled. Then she moaned and her face crumpled in an augury of tears. "Oh, it was Guy."

Now it was Danny's turn for a spell of confusion; his memory simply locked, perhaps because she always referred to her ex-fiancé simply as "Huesing," and Danny had no idea whom she meant.

"That son-of-a-bitch," Carrie said. She'd begun to cry. "That son-of-a-bitch. I went to bed with him . . . when I went back. The night of the wedding. God, I'm such a fool. I'm such a pathetic *fool*." And to Danny's dumb bewilderment she came forward, crying, her bathrobe having fallen open, her chest exposed, and she laced her arms around him. He had come for a fight but now was mutely offering solace. Sniffling, she began to explain all about the wedding, a huge fancy affair on Long Island, and about Guy, who had led her out of the reception to show her his new Corvette. Her weeping grew wilder and at times she had to repeat herself. Guy had offered to show her his fish. He'd developed a new interest in tropical fish and had bought a colossal *seventy-five-gallon tank* (another fit of weeping). And the two of them had driven that night, she knowing just what was happening, and furious with herself all the way, to Manhattan, where Carrie had spent the night. "In the morning, two of the fish had died, which *serves him right*," Carrie said, and Danny almost had to laugh. Yet when Carrie in her open bathrobe began to tug Danny toward the bedroom, although her design did not seem sexual, anger exploded again and he broke from her arms. "I have to think," he cried out. "Carrie, you have to give me time to *think*. Just give me some *time*, will you." He was heading for the door. Now *he* talked in a rush, while she did the nodding. "You should go to a doctor. It's no joke, people used to die from it. You have to go to a doctor, Carrie," he cried.

When he reached Greg's, though breathless from pedaling, he was collected enough not to blurt out any crashing confessions. He followed Greg—dressed in sweats—up to the bedroom, which was musty and squalid even when gauged against the usual standard. Today there wasn't, as Danny usually felt there was, anything appealing about the disarray. "I've just come from the post office, where I came up with a little paradox," Greg said. He was limbering up on the floor, sitting with one leg outstretched before him, one tucked behind. Danny remained standing. "I think you'll like it. I wrote it down, it's over there on the table, but I think I can recite it. Here it is. 'It's not merely prohibitively expensive but actually impossible to mail a letter in Japan—at least in the customary way.' You see," he went on, "you give the man your envelope, he says, *That will cost 120 yen*. You say, *Okay* and buy a 120 yen stamp, affix it, hand the envelope back to the man. Now he weighs it again, and with the additional weight of that stamp it now costs 200 yen. *Okay*, you say, and you buy an additional 80 yen stamp, affix it, and hand the envelope back to the man. But now the thing weighs a little more, not much, it can be sent for just 280 yen. . . . What do you think?"

"And I've just come from the doctor's, where I was told I have syphilis."

"No kidding?" Greg's face manifested happy interest; his grin provided a horrible link to Dr. Wako. Everyone seemed to find this topic so thoroughly amusing. "Your first time?"

Danny nodded. "I just told Carrie. I should probably also mention that I told her I thought you might have given it to her."

"Me?" Again, there could be no doubting the surprise. "Danny, I've never touched her. Or she me, for that matter. Honestly, you know I wouldn't do that to you, you know that, don't you? But I'll bet," he said, brightening, "I can figure out who it was!"

"She told me. It was Huesing. Guy Huesing. Her ex-fiancé."

"I *knew* it." Greg sat up straight, gloating jubilation written all over his face. "I told you that long ago. Remember? That first night I met her, I told you she was still stuck on him."

Danny felt a commanding need to make another sudden, melodramatic exit. He placed a hand on the sliding door and said, "You're awful, Greg. And you think everything's awful. And when things turn out awfully, you're just so God damn happy to be proven right."

All sorts of prerogatives, Danny discovered, had suddenly become his. For the most part he was welcome now to stay overnight at Carrie's whenever he wished. This meant little at first, so long as Danny believed them both to be diseased, but even after receiving what Dr. Wako, in proud English, called a "clean bill of health," Danny found that his previous ardor had withdrawn. The act with Carrie was tainted; the infection remained, lodged in the mind. The mind is a swamp, Danny envisioned, while around him every foot of Kyoto ground not blanketed by cement began to stir to spring's sweet, fetid summons. Feeding on its own decay. It was not logical, but one psychological result of the infection was an abiding, ineradicable suspicion that tiny industrious spirochetes were working night and day with antlike tirelessness to undermine his brain. And every quirk and momentary lapse in his thinking—a minor stutter, a failure to salvage from the swamp a name or a date or a Japanese verb, and the queer, serried dreams he'd begun to have almost every night—only fed his multiplying suspicions. Just as it made no difference that Dr. Wako had declared him purified, so Danny was not reassured by the knowledge that it would take years before that monstrous microscopic army could actually begin to alter his brain. For the fear had been planted and sown right in his very bloodstream and no drug devised could expunge it.

Whatever the cause, his thinking had turned a little peculiar—there was no doubt about that. All of these crazy dreams, many of them set in Heather Hills, and he'd grown so short-tempered with Carrie, even though she was trying, it was clear, to be more agreeable. Gone was that habit of hers of busily erecting qualifications, challenges, exceptions as he talked, that reflex which said, *I don't know yet which side of this issue you're on, Danny, but I'm sure I'm on the other.* And yet agreeableness wasn't, or was no longer, what he wanted from her—indeed seemed only one more depressing symptom of spiritual lassitude. Danny was struck anew by how little she accomplished in her days, while always on the verge of taking up photography, or a serious study of Japanese, or daily jogging. Hours on end she lay on her couch doing her crossword puzzles, or writing a letter, or simply listening to music, while her camera, her Japanese tapes, her jogging suit went unutilized. And *The Tale of Genji* sat on the shelf.

Danny vowed to spend less time with her, with Greg (who also, to be fair in distributing disapproval, was extraordinarily unproductive), and to devote himself to his language study, his Hobbes and Locke, his readings about Hiroshima and Nagasaki—and yet, succumbing to his own curious lassitude, he would find himself time and again seeking out the two of them. If solace was his hidden motivation, to have his wounded pride assuaged and the fears about the spirochetes quieted, he was surely looking in the wrong place. Merely to lie beside Carrie, to feel the bony stab of her hips against his, was to experience waves of disquiet and anger which mocked all of their exchanged declarations of forgiveness. In Greg's company Danny, uncharacteristically, seemed always to be complaining, and about anything—the weather, the Japanese love of business cards, the mindlessly identical Western food in the coffee shops. Greg had turned quieter these days, listening with a heavy patience that on a couple of occasions (his eyes dilated and blurred) made Danny wonder whether he had again "done the impossible" and replenished his marijuana. In any case, Greg was still drinking a good deal, but with little of that seductive camaraderie which had so often nudged Danny along into later hours and further bottles and wilder talk. What had they talked about? For there had been times when the thoughts between them had leapt far faster than any straggling words could accommodate, with implications and analyses tripping over each other in a breathless volley of interruptions and apologies and fresh interruptions; times when these conversations had been the most exhilarating thing in Danny's life and had promised a greater likelihood of answers to which he might still want to turn in ten years time than any book, or any Thoreau-ish solitude on Lake Superior, seemed to offer. It was strange, this sense of depletion, of having so little to talk about. For it was the same face, with those cutting dark eyes and thinning, graying hair and that globed forehead with its permanent tooth marks—the same face that would now be peering at Danny in an expensive bar off Kiyamachi Street, a cheap sleazy bar near Kyoto Station where some *Bōsōzoku* drank their beer without first removing their motorcycle helmets, a "true English-style pub" where a number of young "office ladies," fresh out of their uniforms, sat waiting each in turn to sing into a relayed microphone. It was Danny now who pushed to go out, pushed for another bottle, with the hope always that unexpectedly the two of them would surface from these sewerish nights upon that shore where no one discoursed more brilliantly than they, where progress might be made in the crucial question of time's true nature, or the conundrum of memory, or the riddle of free will.

Greg was apparently no longer seeing Noriko, though this was not something he wanted to discuss. Nor did he want to hear—though Danny often could not check himself—complaints about Carrie. Nor did he want to talk about when he was going to leave Japan, or what he planned to do next. He had made things difficult, Danny sometimes felt with resentment; he had deliberately grown distant. Yet at other times it seemed Greg was hardly to blame. He had no choice. *Things go in cycles* he was always saying, and now he was deeply down and suffering again (badly, it seemed) from migraines.

Danny really had no one to confide in, then, when he received a letter in its own way as upsetting as the one from Mom some months before that had sent him—too anguished to bicycle over, too much in need of immediate counsel—by taxi to Greg's. The envelope bore a Michigan return address but no name. Danny did not immediately recognize the handwriting. The letter itself was also handwritten, and a frightened Danny—for this was the first letter he'd ever received from his father—leapt first to the unexpected form of signature: "Your old Dad." He scanned the page for disasters before reading it straight through. Not merely the contents, but the tone itself was wholly surprising:

Danny

Greetings, my son, from humble Detroit. It's been hard times around here for your Dad, I'm afraid. Your mother and I were divorced on Tuesday last. Amiably, to say the least. She wanted to give me everything. Well I daresay you have some idea of what she's like. I had to fight tooth and nail in order to take a bit of a screwing on the settlement. Some 31 years of wedlock. Nearly a third of a century.

She says she's going to marry Douglas Nebbin. Sounds to me a little like jumping from the frying pan into the deep-freeze.

Actually Bump's all right, and obviously kind as Christ. So forgive the little joke of a man whose pride has been hurt and who feels himself somewhat at sea.

It's hard times these days at Ford, too. Your fellow Japanese are giving us a real drubbing. Newest contingency plan is to re-open the war and bomb Nagoya.

Anyway, you recall how your old Dad for years and years has vowed to go once around the world before reaching his dotage. Well, at last I'm actually going to do it. Beginning with Las Vegas, then on to California, Hawaii, Saipan (where I took a bit of shrapnel in the leg, you recall), Hong Kong, India, Egypt, Kenya, etc. etc. Quite an itinerary. I'll be in Saipan end of May/early June. Can you meet me there for a couple of days? Will reimburse airfare, pay hotel, everything, etc. Let me know soonest.

Your old Dad

The tone was a surprise, but with successive rereadings Danny began to hear his father speaking in every word. That flat, man-to-man, comma-less opening ("Danny"). All the familial references ("my son," "your Dad") appropriated with such ease just as though they'd been cozily corresponding for years. The shift from *Douglas* to *Bump* that undercut the sincerity of his defense of Dr. Nebbin. The failure to explain why an itinerary that included Hawaii and Saipan and Hong Kong didn't include Japan. The little joke (at bottom probably affectionate, a reminder that Danny had been away from home long enough) about "fellow Japanese," and the little joke (at bottom quite ugly) about bombing Japan.

Meeting Dad in Saipan! The prospect immediately loomed vast enough to reshape every aspect of Danny's last few months in Japan. A remote Pacific island was materializing for the conclusion of this strange year . . . Danny could go island-hopping after all! Dad's offer meant adventure, and also an old hopefulness, the sense that some mutual understanding might now be imminent; and also dread. Standing in his six-tatami-mat room beside the fragile paper bags that enclosed his few belongings, Danny felt the letter as an incursion, a rupturing wave. Everywhere, patterns that had lasted Danny's whole lifetime were being dismantled. Now came divorce, letters from Dad, Mom to be married to Bump Nebbin, moving vans, and Dad a bachelor, acting out his so-long-talked-of dream of "making the big circle."

The letter, folded neatly inside his shirt pocket, created a faint but perceptible pressure upon Danny's chest as he sat that evening at dinner with Carrie and Greg. Habit alone seemed to bring the three of them joylessly together night after night. There seemed so little choice in what to do. Night after night the same boring options: go out for good overpriced Japanese food you tired of after a while?—or out for lousy overpriced Western food that only muddily recalled the things you'd once so enjoyed eating? To drink a little?—or to drink a lot? After an hour's eating and drinking, the unmentioned letter still pressed against Danny's chest.

Carrie, who had chosen the restaurant on the humorous but as it turned out gastronomically unsound basis that it specialized, according to its sidewalk billboard, in "Itarian Cuisine," was the loudest grumbler about the food. She had ordered veal which wasn't to be cut with the dull knife she'd been given. She was drinking white wine, Danny a little beer, Greg—with a sullenness that irked Danny—beer and whiskey. "You know, you were the one who chose this place," Danny said finally, to shut her up.

"I didn't hear you raising any objection," Carrie said. She hated being reproached like this.

"And you don't hear me complaining now, either," Danny said mildly, not looking at her. He shouldn't have said anything. It seemed a good time to change the subject. "Greg, I got a letter today from my father. You remember, I'd never gotten a letter from him before."

So vacant was Greg's stare that Danny wondered whether he should repeat the remark. "What'd he want?" Greg asked at last.

Danny handed the letter to Greg, who studied it a long while, and said, "He writes well, but not so well as your Mom," and passed the letter, despite Danny's beckoning open palm, to Carrie. She read it quickly and said, "Saipan. That sounds exciting."

Danny placed the folded letter back in his shirt pocket. "So my parents are divorced."

"So are mine," Carrie said.

"A pity mine aren't," Greg added.

"You guys are no fun," Carrie said later, over cups of cappuccino that had arrived topped with one of the maraschino cherries the Japanese were forever placing on any remotely Western food. Danny never ate them, having somewhere read that they were carcinogenic. No one had spoken in a few minutes. "Let's go to the movies," Carrie said.

"It's too late," Danny said.

"Not Gion Kaikan. They're all night tonight."

"What are they showing?"

"I don't remember. They're in English, though. I remember that much."

"Was it something good?" Danny said. "You remember that much, Carrie?"

"I don't remember."

This pleasure she was displaying in being so ignorant was actually an implicit reproach. Of course she was suggesting that he was deficient in flexibility, in spontaneity—as though there was something picayune in wanting to know what film one was going across town to see. "Do you know what time the shows are?" Danny asked.

"Nope."

"Are you even sure they're in English?"

"Couldn't swear by it."

"Are you fairly confident they're in some Indo-European tongue?"

"Danny," Greg said. He was rubbing his eyelids with his fingertips, like someone who has been reading too long. "Danny, do you realize just how tiresome you've lately become?"

Greg's brown eyes languidly opened. Their abstracted look was gone.

Danny felt a cold, clenching sensation in the muscles of his arms and thighs. Excitement, nervousness, eagerness . . . The two of them had had their moments of anger, of bickering, but this was the first time either had been so openly hostile.

"And I suppose you're not?"

"And I suppose you're not?" Greg parroted, lifting his voice to make of Danny's a ridiculous schoolboy's taunt. "You see, we're tired of it, Danny. Exhausted. It's your *hu*morlessness that makes it all so insufferable. Can't you see how ludicrous it is, the way you've been somberly dragging your syphilitic penis around like some sort of Byronic clubfoot? What's the matter, has little Danny's pride been hurt? Has he begun tardily to realize that his girl friend's had the hots all along for her ex-fiancé and took young Danny on because she knew he'd be manageable?"

"*Greg* . . ." It was Carrie, her face flushed, who interrupted him. She was angry, really angry, and she crouched over the table as if about to depart. "I don't have to listen to this. I don't have to listen to this crap."

"Of course not, Carrie-kins. But still you do. Because you want to. Just the way our Danny, suddenly struck dumb, wants to, too. Because I'm saying what you both have been aching to say, or aching to hear said. So you can just sit down, you can just drop all that stagey indignation.

"Danny won't admit his pride's been hurt. Danny, who blanches at the mere sound of *fuck,* has suddenly caught the smell of another man on his girl friend's genitals, and Christ, he doesn't know what to do. So he goes around sulking and making a royal pain of himself. And you, Carrie, you can't talk because you're feeling guilty for having been a liar from the start and jerking him around for your own convenience, and because maybe now that you've gotten caught you realize he's actually a decenter, nicer sort than the bastards you usually choose to go out with. The truth is that in our friendly little threesome everybody's pissed as hell under all this grown-up slimy-assed cordiality, but I'm the only one who'll admit it. You're not leaving, Carrie. I'm leaving." Greg drained his whiskey. "I only wish I'd run up a bigger bill to stick you both with," he said and, bowing to the two of them—a mockery of Japanese etiquette—he left the restaurant.

A stunned silence ensued; Greg had fully achieved the dramatic effect he'd so obviously striven for. "God, he can be a pain," Carrie said. "He's so goddamned—" But the summarizing, dismissive epithet died weakly on her lips: "I don't know." Routed, the two of them rose from the table, split the check, and stepped out into the street. As they walked around two of those young motorcyclists whom Greg called *bozos*—permanents, track suits, women's pink shoes—Carrie's fingers brushed Danny's arm, inadvertently or perhaps as an invitation to take her hand. Danny burrowed his own hands deeper into his pockets. The two of them clumped along in silence. How much of what Greg had said was actually valid could not at once be determined, Danny would have to mull it over, but it was indisputable that he and Carrie had done a poor job of understanding each other. Of course he'd not wanted to understand Carrie—or at least Carrie's other relationships. Until recently he had resisted the obvious deduction which that scrap of paper where she'd first written her name and phone number should have corroborated. That paper (still sentimentally lodged in his wallet) had been torn from an envelope that bore a New York City return address. She'd been writing Huesing in the coffee shop on that very first morning—and had borrowed Danny's pen to do so. She had, surely, been writing him all along; had talked with him on the phone; had probably sent him a Christmas gift.

This sense of exposed failure between them, which compelled them now to go out for coffee when they probably both wanted just to go home, offered the opportunity—Danny perceived tiredly—for their relationship's replenishment and perhaps even expansion. Things could be built anew. But glancing across the coffee-shop table at Carrie—that slight, bony-bridged nose, the small blue button eyes, the permanented hair, the tan on her cheeks fading under a scruff of peeling skin—he recoiled at that opportunity's multiple demands. He felt relieved when, on their bicycles at the corner of Kawaramachi and Imadegawa, where a decision about the night would have to be made, she smiled sweetly at him, with true affection, and asked him to call her tomorrow. He'd already decided that if she invited him over he would accept, but he preferred to go back to his room.

To go back to his room, which, though he'd spent the vast majority of his nights here, still did not feel like home and which, spring now arrived, Saipan only months away, doubtless never would. Something in Kyoto had lately come into bloom or some combination of scents had commingled to bring strongly to his nostrils the smell of semen. It was so strange, time and again throughout the day, to be inhaling that smell. He'd wondered whether Carrie or Greg noticed it, whether the whole racing city—the gold-toothed old women carrying their bags of fruit home from the market and the men in their blue suits, the mothers with their decked-out toddlers, the clustering bunches of girls in their school uniforms—smelled it, too.

Danny lay on his bedding in his shirt and pants. Before long, but in different surroundings, he heard the clop-clopping of a horse's hoofs. Rising, though still flat on his back, he fixed the horse to a pebbly pink dirt road, beheld a sunny crumbled stone battlement, overlaced with vines and papery purple flowers, and knew himself to be in Saipan. The vision faded as his mind rose further to grasp the realization that he was in Japan and was hearing the wooden clogs of some old man wending home from the bath, but there was time enough, before this ascendant knowledge blurred all else, to link the battlement to Peru, where the horse better belonged, and a landscape Greg had once described as glimpsed from a sunny white, a wholly white room. *Ab ovo*. To be reborn. But the horse, mournfully, was passing, and then the wooden clogs were gone.

Rain which since morning had darkened the sky to a gray like dusk's had now, just past noon, eased up a little and the sky was lightening as if with the approach of morning. While Danny was standing at the corner of Imadegawa and Higashiōji, scratching at a small patch of rash on his left cheekbone (his eczema usually confined itself to his wrists and ankles and this escalation to his face was quite alarming), he was accosted by a young woman in a gray rain poncho. "Excuse me, this way's the way to Ginkakuji Temple?"

"You're an American?" The wet, wide, flat-featured face, with stray black hairs slipping out from below the hood of the poncho, was Asian. Danny stepped forward solicitously, to gather her face beneath his umbrella, but diffidently approached only near enough to dribble a string of water-beads from the umbrella's rim onto her cheekbone. He moved a step closer.

"From Oregon," she said.

"You look Japanese."

"My father's Japanese. My mother's Chinese."

"This is funny," Danny said. "All year long, I've been asking the Japanese for directions, and now I'm giving *you* directions. Ginkakuji's that way." He pointed down Imadegawa toward a range of hills that, enfolded in mist, were present only to him. The traffic signal had just freed the wet slither of cars on Higashiōji; she would have to wait a moment. "You've been to Japan before?"

"First time," she said.

"You came by yourself?"

She nodded. "Just a week ago."

"You like Japan?"

"Huh."

Her grunt was more abdominal than usual for an American—what Danny had come to think of as an Oriental affirmation—and in conjunction with something faintly skew in her pronunciation of English, as if in childhood she'd been weaned from some other mother tongue, prompted him now to say less as question than observation, "You speak Japanese."

She laughed. "Oh a few words . . . sayonara, ari*ga*too, ohio." He'd been wrong: her accent was ghastly.

"If it's okay, if you want, I'll walk you to Ginkakuji. It's pretty there and maybe it won't be so crowded now. What with the rain."

"Swell." The casualness with which she accepted this offer was perhaps, or perhaps not, a discouraging sign. The signal changed and under the cozying circle of Danny's umbrella they swung into the street.

"My name's Danny Ott."

"Judy Ishida."

Pronunciation of the last name had been Americanized, with a heavy stress placed on the middle syllable. Fumblingly, in the suspended middle of the street as they walked, they shook hands. Hers was wet and cold, enhancing his pleasurable sense of providing shelter, and as his foot touched the opposite curb he experienced a small feeling of radiating joy—the first pure joy he'd felt these past few weeks. It was far too early to say where, if anywhere, this encounter was going, but he had just now—with uncharacteristic ease—met all the initial requirements of picking up a woman on the street.

He was playing guide, a favorite role of his anyway, and Judy proved an exceptionally satisfying audience. For one thing, every detail he pointed out seemed to astound her: the woman glimpsed at work behind a tofu shop, baby hung on her back; the clothing store that advertised its blue suits in English as "success outfits"; the withered old woman carrying a James Dean (". . . atmosphere of young beast . . .") shopping bag. And she laughed generously at all of his little jokes. But perhaps most important was the simple, immense gratification in (that slant-eyed face upon him) explaining Japan to a Japanese, or half-Japanese.

Not even a daylong rain had driven the sightseers from Ginkakuji. Under their particolored umbrellas clusters of high-heeled women—middle-aged, probably part of a bus tour—clicked past the carp-filled ponds and the climbing slopes of moss. The garden was not all the worse for their presence: the umbrellas were pretty, and the rain seemed to shrink and soften their voices. "Wow," Judy said, an open-voweled exclamation, as he pointed out things he liked: a lemony carp, a luminous patch of gold-threaded moss, a stand of bamboo. It was a word she relied on, as American as her grunted "huh" was Japanese. In fact her vocabulary, laced with "you knows" and "wows" and "terrifics" and "okays" and "swells," seemed almost designedly inarticulate. He was relieved to discover that she, though now on a semester off from the University of Oregon, hoped to become a veterinarian; she had to be fairly bright, he reasoned, and Danny liked bright women. She was in her junior year, which meant she couldn't be much older than twenty.

He led her to a nearby coffee shop. Everything in Japan, she said, was so *terrifically expensive*. They ordered pizza toast. She took off her gray poncho to reveal a bulky gray sweater. He'd guessed right: in answer to one of his questions she told him she was twenty, though as she sat spooning up a chocolate ice cream sundae she looked even younger. Danny reminded himself that the gap in their ages was not so much larger than the one between himself and Carrie, though here the difference, as Judy chattered away about her dormitory and the weekend drinking parties and her problems in settling on a major, felt enormous. And while there were not many cases from which to generalize—only four, to be precise—it was perhaps an unfavorable sign that he'd never succeeded in sleeping with a woman younger than himself. When Judy got up to go to the bathroom Danny was given the first glimpse of her at any distance. Her shoulders in the gray sweater, her hips in the blue jeans, offered a not wholly expected, and not unappealing, breadth. She was proportionately wide, as her face was wide.

"There's a temple not so far from here, with a very famous garden," Danny said on her return. "You want to go, Judy?"

"Swell."

Outside, a northbound bus wheezed up as they reached the corner and they climbed aboard. Though Judy seemed content blindly to let him serve as guide, he had her unfold her map and showed her where they'd met, where they'd walked, where they were now heading. Her hands, which lay for a moment on that side of the map propped upon his thigh, were small.

There were no sightseers at Shisendō—not a strolling soul. The bamboo *shishiodōshi*—a word Danny had learned the last time here, had since forgotten, and now tried by forceful mental recitation to lodge permanently in his memory—clapped again and again against its stone. It was to scare away *boars*, he said—to which Judy replied, "Wow." He showed her how it worked: the stream in time filling the hollow bamboo column, which tipped on its axis when critical weight had been reached, decanted all of its water, and lightly slapped back against the stone. *Clack!* Wait. Soon now. A clean lovely sound of wood on stone. *Clack!*

Again Judy seemed appreciative of everything he pointed out, and truly this was one of Kyoto's most beautiful temples. Yet Danny's sense of relish had faded. Perhaps it was only the growing lateness of the day, but this garden seemed less awakened by spring than had Ginkakuji, with something obdurate and lifeless about its rain-swept asymmetries. His stomach had turned nervous—a familiar sensation lately—and he led Judy out of the temple, passing once more through the room of the thirty-six plump Chinese poets (all but two of whom were bearded, she pointed out; Danny liked her for noticing this little oddity). Surmounting her vague protestation that she should perhaps be getting back to her hotel, he was able by luck to get them quickly onto a bus that would stop very near the True Time Texas. The thought of running into either Carrie or Greg while escorting this new-found woman was delicious.

Neither Greg nor Carrie was seated inside but Danny, showing up with a strange woman, was treated to gratifying, collusive grins from the employees. He ordered hot sake. At the first touch of it on his tongue, blossoming against the roof of his mouth, he felt better. "Half-Japanese and half-Chinese, that's a strange mixture. I didn't realize until I came to Japan how much they can hate each other."

"My father's strange." Judy laughed almost boastfully at this. "He was born into this terrifically good family. Real prestigious. But his mother was just a housemaid in the house, so my father's illegitimate. He left Japan when he was fifteen, and never came back again."

"And married his own sort of housemaid: a Chinese," Danny said. Greg was often psychologizing in farfetched and intrusive ways which Danny resented—but this analogy seemed so obvious he felt Judy could hardly dispute it. Yet her nod seemed grudging. If she'd simply missed the point—a slap at Japanese racism—his remark might seem rude, though she didn't look offended either. "I come here a lot," he said, "but not so much lately. There were some American friends I used to see all the time, they really like it here."

This somewhat misleading use of the past tense beckoned him toward voluminous amplification: toward the whole bewilderingly complex tale of his relations with Carrie and Greg, further complicated by the distant counterpart tangle of dissolution and remarriage in Michigan. More than a week had passed since the night Greg had strode from the restaurant, and Danny had seen him but once, Carrie but twice, since then. Greg had been friendly enough, as had Carrie; both had spoken excitedly of that long-proposed trip through the Japan Alps to Tōhoku and Hokkaidō, to which a new twist had been added. A friend of Carrie's, Peter Haas, whom Danny had met at that lookalike couple's party in the fall (the night before the night he first slept with Carrie), and whom Danny still resented for the way he'd said, with the self-congratulation of a master wit, "You must *read* a lot," owned a van and was perhaps willing to make the trip. The advantages of a van were numerous. The disadvantages—chiefly, having to go anywhere with a jerk like Peter the Potter—somehow seemed less obvious and enormous to Greg and Carrie than to Danny. In any event, Danny in his own mind had already withdrawn from this trip and settled on a substitute—a solitary journey to Hiroshima. And from Hiroshima he would head to Miyajima, one of Japan's "Scenic Trio," and from there to the Oki Islands in the Japan Sea, about which he knew only two things, both hugely encouraging: they were mountainous, and they were deemed so remote that the government's official guide to Japan granted them only a paragraph. Danny was at last achieving a desirable distance from Carrie and Greg, but he also had to concede he wasn't doing particularly well. Intermittent bouts of jitteriness, similar to what he'd experienced so often that first year in college, afflicted him throughout the day, and he'd awoken one night this week from a dream, not in itself so upsetting, that had left a tightness in his chest and some difficulty breathing. And on another recent, and worse, occasion he'd been eating an egg salad sandwich when he'd realized that his hands were shaking noticeably. Worse even than the shakiness (which passed as soon as he concentrated upon it) was the knowledge that they'd been shaking for a while without his perceiving it. And he'd begun that old game, though now somewhat as a joke, an ironic comment on his edginess, of being careful where he left his fingerprints.

Judy was waiting for him to continue. Danny closed the door on Carrie and Greg, and asked Judy instead about her family (two older sisters—one a banker, one a housewife), her previous travels (California and the Southwest, and many family trips to her mother's relatives in Chicago, which was as far east as she'd ever gone; she'd never stepped within the quadrants of Danny's everyday world, delimited west and east by Detroit and Boston, north and south by Lake Superior and Tennessee). He refilled her glass, and his, and ordered a second and eventually a third round of sake. "Why do you want to be a veterinarian?" he asked her.

"Because I love animals," Judy answered simply.

"So do I," Danny said, hoping to match her simplicity. "I always wanted to be an environmental lawyer." And again Danny was struck, this time sadly, by an unconsidered use of the past tense. He went on quickly, "We could go to the zoo tomorrow. Would you like that?"

"Swell, great," Judy said. "But Danny, don't you have to work?"

The sound of his name—always that thrill when a woman first uses your name—prickled the hair on his arms. He explained for her briefly the odd nature of his duties, drawing a picture even more singular and less arduous than was the case. In fact, at the moment he'd been given a number of articles, fortunately in English, on which to prepare memos.

"Japan is so expensive!" she said. "I'm already running out of money."

"How much is your hotel?"

"I don't know. Maybe twenty-five dollars?"

He'd not consciously intended the previous question to steer into his next, but the awareness that to Judy it probably would seem so induced a slight stutter. "You can c-crash at my place if you want, save money, hm? You know, no"—he dismissed the clumsy, nerdlike sound of *hanky-panky* but what arose instead was scarcely better—"no funny business." His motives were a tangle but he lifted to her face an expression that felt as though it displayed only a beneficent hospitality.

"I don't know if I can. I already checked in."

"Have you paid yet, Judy? If you haven't paid yet, there's not much they can do."

"They have my backpack."

"That shouldn't be any problem."

She went along agreeably enough as he found a bus heading for the station. Despite what he'd told her about the ease of retrieving her pack, he felt tinged with criminality on entering the somewhat dilapidated hotel. Yet after an exchange more ludicrous than acrimonious—the old proprietor speaking in her bad English, Danny in his bad Japanese—Judy was allowed her backpack, a large tatterdemalion object which Danny swung victoriously onto his shoulders. Judy opened the door for him and he stepped out into the rain. Inside, he had left no fingerprints.

The rain had at last diminished to a faint drizzle, accessible to the senses more by vision than by touch: slashes of light in the streetlamps' glow. The timing of Judy's arrival, the smoothness with which the two of them had passed from a request for directions earlier in the day to this street, the heft of her pack beneath his arm—these things were altogether remarkable. Whatever bond the two of them shared, it was surely growing more intimate as they walked beneath this shared umbrella they scarcely needed. The encounter in the hotel had left Danny exhilarated, a feeling which again, abruptly, swung toward jitteriness. Unwilling to undergo the sickly lights of a bus, he hailed a cab.

"Are you hungry?" he asked her.

"Huh. I could eat something."

He had the driver let them out at a restaurant near his apartment—not terribly good, but better than anything else he'd found in the neighborhood, and quicker. Within minutes, tofu and tempura and sake had materialized before them. She had said she could eat *some*thing, but she ate everything. She was voracious—like a stray dog, like a street urchin—and again Danny was able to savor the sense of having performed a rescue. She asked whether the students at Harvard Law School were intense, and he told her the story of pimply Karl Teeters, looked on as unlikeably fanatic even among the fanatics on the Law Review, who before enrolling had audited classes for a year in order to get a jump on his classmates. The story, often funny, now struck Danny as enormously dispiriting, and moved by the impetus of gloom he told her how he'd been reading a great deal about Hiroshima and was planning a trip there in a few weeks. Then to lighten things he began explaining to her—as a tie-in to her complaints about the expensiveness of Japan—Greg's theory about the impossibility of mailing a letter when she, with no show of concealment, yawned cavernously. Her glance caught his and she said, with a somehow endearing lack of embarrassment, "I'm so tired."

And *I'm so tired* she said again when they were at last settled in his room, but this time, because it seemed an attempt to ward him off, it was not endearing at all. Should he be trying anything? he wondered. Was he being a chump, or merely decent, in lying now on the thinner of his two futon on one side of the room, having given her the thicker one and the better pillow?

From downstairs came a maddeningly jaunty version of "Raindrops Keep Fallin' on My Head."

"That's the landlord's daughter. I *despise* her," Danny declared with grating vehemence.

Judy at the other end of the dark room giggled at this, as though he'd gotten off another witticism. And this giggle, a failure to take his hostility at face value, had a purifying effect; Danny felt his rancor dissolve into vexed amusement. A few moments later, just after the bouncing song ended, he heard a change in Judy's breathing, a descent into a seashore rhythm. She'd already been carried off. Heartened by this sound, at once relieved to have all opportunity to make advances on her withdrawn, and hearing in it an engine against loneliness, Danny was content to lie on his back, head propped upon the inferior pillow, and to stare for a long while at the gray ceiling.

Sometimes it takes a long rain, washing all the crud out of the air, to make evident what a magnificent city this once must have been, Danny standing by the window wrote mentally to no one in particular. Above the street of cracked asphalt, flowerpots, low tiled roofs, the sky was a glorious blue, its cumulus banks a rich mass seemingly as solid as masonry. Behind Danny, her face open to the light, Judy lay sleeping. Turning to study the planar, simple beauty of her face, Danny was felicitously struck by an identicality which—though it must be a hackneyed commonplace, a cliché, to the Japanese themselves—conveyed for him the very freshness of the world, of spring itself: the word for flower in Japanese, *hana,* was the same as for nose. A *flower*—abloom there in the pacific lineaments of Judy's face. "Hey," Danny called softly. "Up. It's beautiful out. Up."

The extravagant loveliness of the morning demanded revised and more ambitious plans for Judy's last full day in Kyoto, and in less than an hour's time they were settled together on the train to Byōdō-in, their linked hands resting on his thigh. She was wearing the same blue jeans as yesterday, which (Danny more solicitously than distastefully had noticed) needed washing, and the same bulky gray sweater, which might prove too hot, for the day was already warm. He had looked around nervously for Carrie in the station, this morning's situation wholly different from yesterday afternoon's, when he'd actually hoped to run into her at the True Time Texas. Though he and Judy had scarcely touched, her spending the night had rendered him faintly, excitingly complicitous.

Danny asked about Judy's father—a fascinating figure. Despite his having left Japan when only fifteen, Judy told him, he still spoke an accented, broken English. He watched hours of television every night. He didn't understand the situation comedies, didn't think they were funny, but loved the police shows with their violent and unambiguous conclusions. He'd owned a variety of small but apparently quite successful businesses. Beginning with a secondhand store, he'd managed, despite his poor English, to buy a liquor store and an apartment building. This story of an immigrant's entrepreneurial ascent proudly filled Danny, touched with homesickness this lovely morning for his freewheeling native land, with the conviction that America comprehended a more generous vision of democracy than Japan could ever know—a sweetness of feeling that radiated around him to enclose within it this hybrid and faintly grimy Judy in her gray sweater and jeans. "He's just *strange,*" she said, of her father, laughing, but the sweetness had touched her, too, and she was happy to be recounting these stories, which she did all the way to Uji.

On that raw rainy February day when Danny had come here before, with Carrie and her camera just before she left for America, the famous street where tea was roasted and sold had huddled behind shutters. Now the air was clogged with tea's deep, enlivening smell as he and Judy bobbed, linked hands swaying, past the numerous identical tiny shops with their bags and vats and tins of tea on street-side shelves and boxes and tables. It looked a bit like marijuana; Danny remembered, with a shudder, the joint hidden in his room.

Changed utterly from that last time, the gleaming temple of Byōdō-in reposed within a serene and hardly real beauty. Against the morning's flawless blue, it was almost, though not really, too perfect, looking like a postcard of itself—chemically retouched, pigments enhanced at the instance of a busybody Chamber of Commerce. "It's beautiful, isn't it?" Danny said. *"Huh,"* Judy assented; and Danny, whose mind this morning felt very keen, large and clear as the open firmament itself, realized, as surely Judy did not, that these two favorite terms of hers, "huh" and "wow," were palindromes, and this coincidence, though it signified nothing, so pleased him that he had to take her hand once more. "It's terrific," she said. "Real beautiful."

It turned out that Judy had never eaten *okonomiyaki*, which Danny now bought from a sidewalk vendor outside the temple. They ate with their fingers, in a little deserted park by a river. "The Japanese call this Japanese pizza," Danny said, "though what something made up of cabbage, octopus, and eggs has to do with pizza I've never discovered."

Judy laughed at this. Danny loved the way she had of making him feel so witty. She then asked in an abruptly serious tone, "Do you think I'm crazy?"

She picked up a large wedge of *okonomiyaki*, blew on it, and placed the whole thing in her mouth. Mumbling, her mouth full, she explained, "I mean to have stayed the night at your place, when I hardly know you."

"I don't know."

He was feeling contrarily pulled, very glad that she'd stayed and yet conscious of a duty to advise her against such behavior. "You know it's probably a very bad idea. Really. I could be dangerous. I could be a *fiend*," he said, dilating his eyes and baring his teeth.

Judy laughed. "I wouldn't have normally, but I *knew* I could trust you. I could just tell. I could tell by your *face*."

"I guess so." The notion that he was so transparently trustworthy was somewhat worrisome.

"Did you like working in New York, Danny?"

"Yes," he said. "Yeah. I guess so. It was very strange, and the firm's very competitive. And all the buildings, you know, the tops so high above you, like mountains." Knowing that he'd hardly conveyed the impression made upon his level Midwestern mind by that strange, unearthly terrain which people apparently got used to, vast glass towers mirroring other glass towers, those sheer escarpments of steel and brick, at the bottom of which taxicabs and trucks and motorcycles hurtled, he limply repeated, this time accompanied by an elevating of his hands, "Like mountains."

What he wished to express to Judy was not only some sense of New York, that city she'd never seen, but some picture of the world of Huck, Meadows, that rarefied zone of decencies and intrigues, of drudgery and cleanliness and rapacity, of the realization, for the most part reassuring in this world in which so many people founder, that everyone you worked with was extremely bright and successful. Her inability to perceive that world, even had he been able to describe it, was a shortcoming—but, conversely, that world's failure to assimilate a moment like this, Danny Ott seated with a Japanese-Chinese-

American college girl in a park near Byōdō-in, where a temple far older than America flourished in the sun, was also a shortcoming. At this inkling of reciprocal blindness, Danny felt that familiar wormy jitteriness stir in his abdomen. He hurried Judy up from her seat, tossed the *okonomiyaki* papers into a trash bin, and hustled her onto the train.

Back in Kyoto, faced again with the unlikely but dangerous possibility of running into Carrie, they went to the zoo where in great rising amusement they watched an emu—uglier cousin to the ugly ostrich—peck and peck spitefully at, and eventually, in an all-consuming dudgeon, swallow, a page from a magazine, and where Judy tipped over a can of Pepsi, splashing the front of Danny's shirt. From there they went to Nanzen-ji, to see the tiger paintings Danny was so fond of. Trips to various art museums this past year with Carrie and Greg had left Danny even less confident than before of his ability to distinguish a good from a bad painting, but toward these tigers in their emerald bamboo groves he felt quite certain that the painter, someone named Kano Tanyu, dead three hundred years, had known a love purely beyond all art for the magical flowings and promptings of animals. And Judy liked them, too.

Then—feeling very jittery again—it was back to his apartment, where Danny changed out of his stained shirt. He put on one of the pressed shirts from the dry cleaners that he kept around for formal occasions that never seemed to arise.

"This is a funny country," Judy said. "There aren't any laundromats."

"There aren't many. But actually there's one pretty close. You want to wash your stuff?"

"Sure. I don't know. I don't have soap or anything."

"I do. I need to run a wash myself."

"Really I should wash *every*thing, it's *all* dirty. But I have to wear *some*thing." She laughed.

"You can wear my sweat suit if you want. That way you can wash everything."

"Don't you think I'll look a little crazy?"

"It's crazy not to wash everything," Danny told her.

He waited outside the room while she changed into his maroon sweat pants and sweat shirt. She giggled when she emerged. "Do I look athletic?"

"Extremely."

Carrying their laundry down the street in the dusk light, the two of them presented a picture of coed domesticity far more fitting for Ann Arbor or Cambridge than Kyoto. The tiny laundromat was crowded but, jumbling their clothes together (more Judy's than his, for in truth he hadn't needed to run a wash), they managed to fit everything into two of the tiny Japanese washers. These were the sort with porthole windows, and Danny watched a moment as the water streamed down and their mingled clothes began to churn and thrash in an impassioned sudsy tangle. "Do you mind going out to eat in those sweats?" he asked her.

"Just as long as it's a really crummy place."

"Oh, it's nice and crummy."

Danny took her around the corner to the Chinese restaurant where he'd eaten alone on his birthday. They ordered fried chicken and egg foo yung and fried rice and beer. In an interim moment while the beer stood before them but the food had not yet arrived, the waiters in the kitchen and the only other customers just having left, Judy said, "You know, you've been so *nice*," and Danny said, "Don't sound so sur*prised*," and Judy laughed at this, and then he leaned over and kissed her—briefly, for the kitchen door swung open, but long enough that, her mouth instantly opening to his, their darting tongues touched.

Midway through the meal, Danny got up to shift the clothes into a dryer. Outside the laundromat, his eyes again fell on that comical condom vending machine—Swedish Passion Robes. The coins in his pocket, gathered for the laundromat, jingled encouragingly, and on impulse, with but a single shamed glance up and down the street, Danny—though this seemed wildly ambitious—made his purchase.

Yet back at last in his room, dinner and beer inside them, their dry clothes folded, it rapidly became apparent that his ambitions had not been so wild after all. They were soon on her bedding, the thicker futon, their mouths linked in passionate adhesion, and his hands under her/his maroon sweat shirt, tracking exploratorily across the broad field of her back. Danny's head began to float. Her breasts, when he'd removed the sweat shirt, tasted faintly of copper, recalling from boyhood, so heartbreakingly vast a link, that old forbidden flavor ("Never put money in your mouth—it's filthy") of brown pennies on the tongue, just as that boyhood flavor of pennies—another enormous arching and aching link, piloting him far behind conscious memory—perhaps recalled the taste of breasts. The drawstring of the sweat pants seemed to have come untied on its own and his hand slid effortlessly within. His left hand slipped up along the inside of her thigh until his fingertips sensed, though they did not quite touch, a darkly radiating warmth. His hand fluttered to her side, the brawn behind her hipbone, and, anticipating some show of resistance, began gently to tug at the tops of her panties.

She did not resist, but this tugging nonetheless did produce, inside him, a second tugging, a resistant pull of nerves, a premonition that he was going to make a botch of things. He'd never in his life been to bed with an Asian woman, never before today so much as kissed one, and all of the looking and longing he'd done these past few months while living among these people accumulated to press so forcibly upon him he felt shaky; of course, he'd felt shaky for weeks now. Tentatively, prepared to retreat, his fingertips tracked down along the deep drum of her belly, fearful of finding her Oriental body all but bald there—a wispy brushstroke of hair like that of some of the men and boys in the public bath—but came instead upon a surprising and deep luxuriance. The glorious incredulity he always felt on discovering that a new woman was apparently prepared to let him enter her body dazzled and dizzied him. "I have a . . ." he muttered, tapping at his pocket, and though *condom* was not yet spoken her nod seemed to mean this would be necessary.

"You're so *thin*," she whispered when he'd shucked his clothes and settled himself gingerly on top of her. The light in the room, random-bounced street glare, was such that her darker skin blended into the floor, the walls, the bedding, while his own glimmered wanly like a ghost's. "You're *shaking*." He nuzzled his face against hers, the hair at her temples scratching delectably at the eczematous patch on his left cheekbone. His shoulders were still trembling as, with her own fingers, she guided the key part of him—sheathed in reptilian plastic skin—across the thudding threshold of her body. "Mmoomm," Judy murmured, deep in her throat.

And then he felt instantly so much better than he could ever have hoped that he almost wanted to cry. This was all *in*, and what he seemed to be feeling, and what moved him toward weeping, was not so much desire (though his body showed every aching, rigidified sign of that), but a sense of her own good-heartedness. "You're so *nice*," she'd said in the restaurant and it seemed she felt this, too: the matchless surprise one experiences at meeting a stranger's kindness. In the cradling plunge of her hips resided all of the world's kindness, its mercy and goodwill and absolution. The friction along his left cheekbone created a second localized vortex of sheer rapture, while below, the ample warmth of her bottom, rising out of and dropping into his cupped left hand, was a richness beyond measure. His thoughts tipped, tipped and spilled.

This was like riding on a river the way a wind rides atop a river. The image was remarkably apposite, for here was the smoothest fall imaginable, cushioned curve and twist and flow. And the trees along this river, which he knew so well, were pine and popple and elm, sisterly clumps of birch, dressed in their clean rags, and here one did not find birds fashioned in the extravagant beauty of the East, but the clean and functional beauty of the red-winged blackbird, the robin, the hummingbird, the phoebe; here along the banks of this river Grandpa Jaynes had dreamed of, a superior headwater. *Here*. He'd come home.

Alarming thunder drifted, neared, and solidified to become a knock on the door. "Who the hell . . ." Danny said, lifting himself up on one elbow. His first thought was that it was Greg; his second, that his landlady had come to complain about his having a Japanese woman in his room. "Wait a moment," he called out in polite Japanese. He was wearing only an undershirt and undershorts. In the dark, he stepped quickly into a pair of coin-jangling pants and found the door. He'd never dreamed it would be Carrie.

"You're a hard man to reach."

"Carrie. Wow. Hi. Yeah, I guess so."

"You were sleeping?"

"Pretty much. What time is it?"

"Fully ten o'clock. Or not much after. You're such a *night* owl, Danny," she joked, and intruded one arm into the room's dark interior to tap him affectionately on his bare forearm. In her other hand was a paper bag.

"It's Courvoisier," she said. "One of my students gave it to me. I thought we might have a drink. Or we could go out if you'd rather. In for a drink, out for a drink." She gave that little barking laugh.

He saw that she was nervous and, despite his own anguished nervousness, saw that she was finally doing just what he'd requested all year long; always *he* had had to be the one who, after a spat, called *her*, came to see *her*. Even at this hideous moment (And what in the world was he going to tell her? How was he going to ease her safely out of here?) he was touched by the picture of her bicycling over in the dark, not knowing whether or not she would find him home. "It's very nice of you," Danny said.

"You going to keep me out here all night?"

She said this teasingly, as though Danny were playing a coquettish game. A paralyzed pause ensued; he didn't know where to begin. This was followed, from behind him, by an indistinct murmur (Judy seemed to be calling, or talking in her sleep), which though it made Danny wince wasn't completely unwelcome. For he'd been waiting for something from above, from outside himself, to initiate the explanation. "You see, I can't invite you in," Danny said. "It's really a long story, but I've got company, Carrie."

Danny beheld on her face exactly what he'd dreaded: that slow familiar hardening, masked by a brittle cordiality. "Sorry to get you up," she said lightly.

"Carrie," Danny called, attempting even here, hopelessly, to establish some ground of mutual understanding. "I need to talk to you. I'll call you tomorrow morning? Will you be there?"

She had been placed in too painful a situation; he could hardly blame her now as, retreating, she said with a twitched smile of civility, "Sure, Danny. Tomorrow any time."

"Carrie, I'm sorry," he called after her.

Eyes adjusted to the hall light, Danny stepped back blindly into a room pitched in near-perfect darkness. His hands again were very shaky as he undid his pants, which dropped with a clang of coins to the floor. He steered his way across the room with his feet and, touched with a weirdness that sat as mildly on his skin as moonlight, bumped his toes in soft collision with the body of that Asian woman, a near stranger, who lay half-sleeping on his floor, on his bedding, in his sweat clothes.

. . .

Performing one unappealing task he'd been putting off for days in order to put off for a few more minutes another that was still less appealing, Danny bounded up two steps at a time to the Professor's office. He'd not seen Umeda in nearly a week. Nervousness had turned his body fluttery. It was already two o'clock and he'd not yet called Carrie. He'd promised to call in the morning. He was only making things worse for himself by not calling.

Minowada-san—who'd cut her hair, whose cuteness instantly struck him—looked up from her desk. "Is the Professor here?" Danny asked her in Japanese.

Miss Minowada's dark eyes dilated. Her look was queer—Danny grasped that immediately—and even before she spoke he realized that something was hugely wrong.

"He is gone for"—she struggled for the word—"for the funeral."

"Who is . . ." Danny paused, too, in search of some word that would carry a finality less brutal than *dead*. This search was important—it was important that he get things right—though none of this was quite real. "Who is it that has died?" he asked. The moment's abruptness was what made everything so odd. Danny was still gathering his breath from having run up the steps, two at a time. And yet his body, so sensitively tuned, had already begun to adapt: the skin up and down his ribs prickling with cool horror.

Simultaneously, at the mathematical top of his mind, he was struck by wonder at the role this woman with the attractive new haircut had come to play in his life. He had once envisioned her—implausibly, no doubt—as a potential girl friend, but it was as though fate itself had deputized her to serve as Danny's own personal harbinger of death: John Lennon, the assassination attempt on Reagan, and now this. Danny's mind widened to the astronomical odds involved—the elaborate backdrops that had to be fabricated, the thousands of miles crossed, the intricate concatenations engineered, before the two of them could be placed here in the Professor's office, Danny standing and Minowada-san at her desk, in the roles assigned to them. "It is the Professor's baby," Miss Minowada said.

The horrifying and the rational became one as Danny perceived that only for the next moment would both of the babies he'd seen on the night of the Professor's party be alive for him. After that, one of the twin babies would be dead forever. "Is it the boy or the girl?" Danny asked in Japanese.

Minowada-san dropped her eyes as if in shame. In English she delivered the sentence: "It is the boy."

Little Naohiko-chan, Danny was now told, had been found dead one morning. The girl, Komako, was fine.

"It is better the girl should die," Minowada-san said, and this too horrified Danny. Perhaps she meant only that the Professor, as a typical Japanese man, valued a son above a daughter, but Minowada-san's remark seemed a betrayal of something even larger than her sex. And what a thought, what a concealed sentiment, for the baby girl to live with . . .

"The Professor," Danny said in English, "he is very upset?"

"Oh yes, very upset," Minowada-san replied, though it was hard to envision what this meant. Did that strange, brilliant, intense, restrained man actually weep, as any father might? Did he cling to his wife for comfort?

And for Danny himself—What was the proper response to a death so poignant and yet so peripheral? How was he supposed to feel? he wondered, as, outside again, he drifted on his bicycle toward the river. He'd seen the child only once—recalled it less by its red face within its blue pajamas than by the rising, dank warmth issuing from its fierce little body.

How in this impenetrable country did one acknowledge the death of an infant? Danny rode over to the florist's near Carrie's where he'd bought the flowers the morning after their first night together. The same spooky old woman emerged, a look of recognition on her face despite all the months since Danny's last call.

"Flowers," Danny said in Japanese. "I need flowers." And here his scanty Japanese failed him. He did not know the word for funeral, and felt uneasy with *shinu*, the irregular verb for *die*. He had learned a number of euphemistic constructions, similar to *pass away*, but could recall none as he stood there in a sort of luxuriant contoured valley, pots and pots of opening blossoms—yellow, red, orange, purple, white —mounting at his feet. The old woman appeared to have lost more hair since Danny had last seen her. Years ago, Mrs. Nebbin, Bump's wife, had lost her hair in what turned out to be useless radiation therapy. "A little boy. . . has become dead. . . my professor's child," Danny said in Japanese, speaking in clumsy fragments that attempted no connectives. "I need flowers . . . What do you think would be good?"

The woman's unshaken smiling face suggested that Danny's speech had been unintelligible. She extended her hands, palm out, to encompass the range of flowers available to him.

"My professor's child," Danny said, making another attempt, even as the thriving vegetation at his feet filled him with a mind-jamming dread. Was he about to commit some social clumsiness? "The child is now dead. Flowers, should I give them to the Professor?" Danny asked while starting to back out of the shop. He felt overcome—the bright organic pigments, the sweet warring perfumes, and also that subterranean odor of rot, like turf under too much water, the same smell as outside the shop, sunny rot, Kyoto under the spring sky. As he backed away she came forward, bald scalp gleaming, and that mouth of hers fixed grimly, for he'd made himself understood at last. "A dead child," the old woman said in Japanese, moving closer, tracking him.

It was an eerie confrontation, worse in its way than the conversation with Minowada-san. At the grasping approach of this woman with the metallic mouth and emergent scalp Danny's confusion leapt into a suppressed panic, an irrepressible need to flee. "Later, I come back later," he said in Japanese, and repeated this in English as he retreated out the door. "A dead child," the woman cried, still approaching—as Danny, quickly bowing, hands fumbling at the door, fled into the crowded street.

Fearful, dreading Carrie's anger, Danny was nonetheless not much relieved to meet instead what seemed like genuine amiability. He had prepared all sorts of explanations—honest, self-castigatory, heartfelt—but she didn't want to hear them as they sat over dinner in Mr. Happy, a place whose menu described itself in English as a "Western-style whole family restaurant." Actually the claim was not all that unreasonable. One found here all the familiar ersatz trappings of a franchise restaurant in the States, the fake brick walls, the synthetic tabletops meant to resemble wood, the black Naugahyde booths, the Muzak, even a cowboys-and-Indians mural; save that there were no other Occidentals in the place, Danny and Carrie could really have been at home. "They must have had American help," Carrie said. "The Japanese are fantastic imitators, but I don't think they could have come up with anything quite this horrible themselves." Danny searched her long laugh for forced gaiety, but found none.

Clinging as he was to the notion of her hidden anger and jealousy, it took him some time to suspect that it was relief she actually was feeling. She had won a full pardon, at last, in finding him in bed with another woman—something his insincere shows of forgiveness had never provided. She'd been freed. Still, in her reluctance to hear his story there was perhaps a touch of jealousy after all. "Carrie, just listen to the whole thing once, okay?"

"You don't have to explain yourself to me."

"I don't *have* to, I want to," he snapped, but added softly, "please listen. Anyway, as I said, her name was Judy Ishida. I met her on the corner of Imadegawa and Higashiōji, when she asked me the way to Ginkaku-ji. She's from Oregon. Her father's Japanese. Her mother's Chinese." Danny paused. How much of the story to go into? Carrie's objections nipped at him: What *was* he hoping to accomplish in setting this out? Yet it was pleasant to be talking of Judy to anyone, to feel the memory rouse in narration; for early this morning, alone on the floor where they'd so recently made love, Danny had failed to revive any aspect of her, to know again the woozy feel of her bulky body under his hands. The failure had badly depressed him, as it again exposed—awful, such moments of revelation—time's omnivorous, desolating march, the heartless speed with which the past is buried. "Anyway, it's funny, but that first day I really hoped we'd run into you. I even took her to Texas. I guess I wanted to make you jealous. She spent the night that night, but I didn't touch her or anything."

"Danny, it really doesn't matter."

"Anyway." Danny glared at the little paper American flag that had flown atop his greasy fried chicken. It had come to a bloody end in a little pool of ketchup. "Anyway, I took her the next day to Byōdō-in, and to the zoo, and Nanzen-ji, and the laundromat—"

"Sounds exciting."

"—and then back to my place, where this time we"—why was there no word for the act which was neither boastfully vulgar nor prudishly oblique?—"did go to bed, and then you came over."

"Perfect timing." Carrie sipped from her coffee cup.

"And I would have called you yesterday, as I said I would, but Judy left later than I thought, and then I found out—Carrie, this is really terrible—then I found out that Professor Umeda's little twin boy died a couple of days ago. You remember him. You saw him at the party."

"Oh, that really *is* terrible. Course I remember him. You remember I held him for a moment." Her face had shifted in all those fractional ways the eye could never isolate but which taken in conjunction made clear that she felt the horror. Carrie could be truly compassionate. He could forgive her nearly everything—her complaining, her idleness, her dishonesty—for that. "Oh God, that's really awful."

"Yes it is. It really upset me. Or, I don't know, I was upset because I wasn't more upset. You know."

"Umeda must be devastated."

"Yes, I guess so. I don't know, I haven't seen him."

"How did he die?"

"Crib death. No one understands it."

A pause ensued which, lengthening, tacitly became a commemoration for the dead. How long should such a break extend?—for extended too far, it inevitably smacked of self-congratulation. Or so, in the confusion of how much Danny actually was and should be feeling, it now appeared. He recalled a statement of Greg's—*Even a little self-hatred makes things a lot more complicated*—and said, in a somewhat brutal shift that was largely a lashing at himself, "Sure about no dessert? Some genuine imitation apple pie?"

"Maybe some more coffee."

"Anyway, that's how you happened to come over and find me in bed with somebody else."

"You don't need to apologize."

"*Please* quit telling me that. *Must* we be so cool and groovy and adult about things? If I don't explain, where does that leave us?"

"How do you mean?" Carrie asked.

"I mean where does that *leave* us?" Danny repeated. "What about us, Carrie?"

"What *about* us?"

"We seem to be talking in circles," Danny accused her. Oh, this was absurd. They were both such incompetents, they couldn't even manage to stage a decent argument.

"Danny," Carrie said, "you seem to be trying to make me into some kind of bitch, when what I'm saying is I'm willing to forget all about it."

While hers seemed an offer of genuine forgiveness, it contained, nonetheless, its own ugliness: a cynicism that said, *We've both been lying to each other.* This was a cynicism Danny could not live with. Not forgiveness, not a balancing of transgressions, but to feel that Carrie understood the line of events that had led to this point—that was what he wanted. And to believe she understood he'd been as honest all along as he knew how.

"Look," Carrie said, "I know I haven't exactly been an angel to you, but I think you've been blaming me for all sorts of things I'm not responsible for. Things happening literally thousands of miles away, Danny, in Michigan."

This was doubtless true, to some extent, but the perceptive look in Carrie's eyes, suggesting the possibility that she had a better understanding of what was going on inside him than he himself did, made Danny nervous, and a little resentful. "And I suppose you don't take it out on me when a whole week goes by without somebody in your family sending you another goddamned Care package."

"I'm sure I do. What I'm saying is that's all in the past. We should forget all about it."

"I'm not sure I want to," Danny said.

"Which means?"

Carrie was growing impatient. It was in response to this reediness of hers that he presented what seemed at last (though accompanied by a subtle, disconcerting sensation that he was merely slipping down a predetermined route) the sort of climacteric from which irrevocable and possibly disastrous consequences might ensue. "Which means," he said, "I'd like maybe to have us cool things off for a while."

Carrie nodded. "And what about the trip?"

"I don't think I'm going," Danny said.

"You're going by yourself? To Hiroshima?"

"Yes," Danny said firmly. Then, "I think so."

"You know, Danny," Carrie began, placing her coffee cup in its puddled saucer, leaning forward, fixing her shrewd small blue eyes upon him. Here was clearly a remark she'd long prepared, and although much of the night still lay before them Danny saw that this was intended as a kind of farewell address—one that would sting a bit. It occurred to him that he, too, should have prepared some farewell remark, but he simply hadn't perceived until now that this might be where they were headed. What did it say about Carrie that *she* had understood this? "I don't know why you feel compelled to push everything into a crisis. There's really no need. Maybe Greg gets into all these crises because he honestly can't help it, he's just too weak. But you're not. You have a choice."

"The whole question of choice is exactly—" Danny started, but she rode right over him.

"You have a choice, and you shouldn't play this follow-the-leader game of his too far. And another thing. He's pleased. You know, he's really pleased as punch, when things go wrong for you."

"She said," Danny continued, hoping this would sting a little, just as Carrie in the original telling had hoped it would sting, "that you're pleased as punch when my life starts falling apart."

The expected denial did not come. "Well I don't know. I mean, God, I'm sure there's a great deal of truth to that. She's very sharp, Danny, much sharper than you've been wanting to credit."

"For God's sake, Greg, we're not talking about whether Carrie—"

"But what I don't know, what I really can't tell you, is how much of my being pleased is something really despicable and how much is just a kind of perverse, but not blameworthy, not, not—" Greg was launched in all his finicky exposition; pleased as punch at the moment, certainly. "Not contemptible, camaraderie. I mean it's nice to feel you're not the only one dropping into an abyss."

"Are you dropping into an abyss?"

In the lustrous matrix of the Kamo River the neon signs of Kyoto's downtown circulated with all the uncluttered and unhurried beauty of Euclid's plane geometry. Circles and squares, rhomboids and ellipses: that language so much more fine and cleanly than words could ever be. Danny tried to sharpen the focus of his eyes. While they had both consumed enough drink—again, again—to be gloriously drunk, the glory had not come. They were unequal to the river's excellences and Danny observed with contempt the sloppiness of his feet on the cobbled causeway.

"Of course the word's a joke," Greg said. "The concept's a joke. The whole thing's a joke. But of course you don't quite see that."

Greg was trying to sting him back. Irritation was running on both sides tonight. "What don't I see?" asked Danny.

"I mean this solitary trip to Hiroshima. Holy Jesus what a cliché. I don't mean you shouldn't go. But I say to myself, Jesus, how does he manage to avoid seeing what a cliché he's living—young Daniel Ott, Earnest Pilgrim, taking a one-year leave from Corporate America to figure out the meaning of life, now heading off for a brief inspection of the City of the Dead."

"But it isn't—"

"I suppose that's why I envy you," Greg said—surprisingly. "It's so odd to be feeling *envy*. I mean I knew, way back when, I think I can pride myself on a precocious sense of decline, I really can, I *knew* something ghastly was coming. But *envy*? Wide-eyed Danny, don't you even see that every damn move I make I'm aware of the cliché I'm living in? Harvard Lampoon army brat, so full of promise, who won't settle down, who wanders all over God's green earth drinking and doping too much and having what he likes to think of as brilliant, cryptic conversations, all tossed to the wind? Shit, it's endless, this conversation about clichés is a cliché."

"But it isn't," Danny insisted. "We had this conversation once before, don't you remember? We were crossing that bridge there?" Before them stood the Shijō Bridge, its traffic, stopped for an incoming train, brake lights on, lying outstretched in a red and white purring slumber. "We'd been drinking a lot, and I said something like, *You know isn't it funny how to everybody else we look just like two drunks*, and you said something like, *That's hardly a surprising mistake*." Danny only now realized that this was a distinction he'd tried and failed to make the last time around and, further, that in struggling to articulate the point he'd lost the link to Greg's last remark.

"To answer your question . . ." Greg began.

"What question?"

"Abysses. You asked whether we're dropping into an abyss. Now it does seem abundantly clear that a sense of making progress has recently, or fairly recently anyway, quietly withdrawn itself. It's so strange, these things just going away and you don't know why, you don't even know they've left at first. You say the same things, you say, *We are hurtling into the future at an unbelievable velocity* or you say, *Dinosaurs weren't designed just to enrich the imaginations of children but were actual creatures that dominated this very earth*"—Greg stamped his foot—"*for millions of years*, but suddenly the phrases are no longer calling up anything. And there you are—but where is there? What's the next step when one day it comes to you how you haven't had an interesting thought in months?" Deepening his voice in a melodramatic impersonation of himself, Greg repeated, "And there you are—but where is *there*?" and laughed heartily.

"I just had an interesting thought, and just this month, too, just this week in fact," Danny said. "I figured out what I want in life."

"And what's that? I can tell already this is going to cheer me up."

"This is going to sound like a meaningless riddle, a stupid paradox, but it isn't really." On the threshold of disclosure Danny was again met with a sense, as they stumbled over the dark causeway, of their egregious physical and mental clumsiness, and of how difficult, how nearly impossible, to convey this point adequately. "Well, first I read this article, correcting the English for a friend of Dr. Kobayashi's, about some lab experiment. They offered the rats a choice of water bottles, some of which were laced with alcohol. The alcohol doesn't really matter, it's irrelevant to my point, but it's a nice coincidence. Anyway, some of the rats naturally gravitated to a strong alcohol mixture, some to a weak one, and some to plain water. Hard stuff, beer drinkers, and teetotalers, you might say. They were trying to isolate genetic affinities with alcoholism, but that doesn't really matter. The point"—the sentence had already opened unfaithfully, for four or five valid points radiated off at least; meanwhile the river's silken geometry permuted itself again and again; Danny pushed on: "the point is that the animals drank where they wanted. They just *knew* what they wanted, and they went for it. Just as simple as that." This thought hung suspended; then, blessedly, a refining linkage, the happy ladder to a new geometric plane, presented itself: "It's customary to say that animals don't have free will, only rational humans can have free will, but there's another way of looking at it, where you say that for human beings things get too complicated to make any pure decisions. But rats *know* where they want to drink. A dog *knows* whether or not he wants to lie in the sun." Tremulous, as delicately linked as two lines of light on the river's ebony skin, the next extension shimmered into words. "What I want, Greg, is to know what I want."

The sentence had come out disappointingly rather than boldly simplistic, and Danny hastened to amplify: "What I need is someone to conduct an experiment on me that will prove whether I prefer orange lights to blue lights, scotch to cocoa, apples to oranges. I don't know."

"No, Danny, that's *excellent*, I like that," Greg reassured him, nudging them toward the old roles of teacher and student, philosopher and disciple. Even now, ridiculously, Danny warmed to the instructor's praise.

"That relates somehow," Greg began, "that somehow . . ." The sibilants emerged just a trifle raggedly. Clumsiness. All the nice distinctions were a lie, they were stumbling at each other in the dark. "—relates to what I was saying about clichés. And kind of contradicts what I think about animals. I told you that? How sad, how *horrifying*, to think that *any*one goes around more benighted—"

"Yes, you did. And I told my mother. Last fall, as we were walking through the Tokyo Zoo. And she said, 'Your friend Greg sounds very brilliant.' "

But why was this recollection, meant to be affectionate and tributary, instead so immensely sad?

It is difficult, perhaps impossible, to say whether one is ever capable of greatly surprising oneself, or if after committing even the most vile irregularity there isn't some part of oneself that acknowledges the act as something foreseen all along—Danny reasoned—and which says, *It was to rise and do this that I have remained dormant for so long*. But in any case he'd never manifested such quiet, cerebral, grisly satisfaction in seeing his body and mind malfunction.

This appetite could now be shown to have existed all along: the sweaty elementary school boy's disappointment in seeing the level of his fever fall and his bedridden days coming to an end, or the martyred book-weighted law student's pleasure in having another groaningly large assignment placed upon his back, or the bitter satisfaction in being the desolated lover with a stigma of love burned into the flesh of his left hand. Yet this appetite apparently was far larger than Danny had ever surmised. He'd had bad periods before, of course, weeks and months of them over the years, but he'd always wanted out. This cool, calibrating self that traced fresh difficulties with a dispassion which imperfectly masked gratification—here was something new. This was someone who took in everything and cheerfully announced, *Danny is waking up sweating in the nights* or *His mind has turned too jumpy to appreciate the quiet claims of a bamboo grove* or *Just as in his freshman year, Danny has become quite particular as to where he will leave his fingerprints.*

Wasn't there some disappointment, then, in receiving a bit of really good news, a letter from Huck, Meadows saying that Jack Jacobusse would be spending June and July in the London office, August vacationing in Morocco, and if Danny would be willing to share his Park Avenue apartment with another summer associate he could have it for a quite reasonable five hundred dollars a month? Good news of this sort threatened the subtle, perverse pleasure Danny was feeling as it gradually transpired that Carrie and Greg would be making the Hokkaidō trip without him. A central balance was shifting, Danny was losing that fulcral role he'd held onto so desperately, and yet over the tumult of his qualms and jealousies an inner voice said simply, *Let them go.*

Let them all go. Let Mom marry a shoe repair man, if that's what she really wanted, *and Dad take up with a stripper.* Go ahead: *Let the whole thing collapse.* Even as Danny admired the way they were written, he dreaded those regular letters from Mom. You *did* have to admire them—the way she filled her pages with all sorts of local news and familiar chitchat (she was showing him that the world was intact over there, nothing had really changed), but spoke as well with such directness of Bump, of the coalescing features of her new life (she was showing him that this, too, would have to be confronted, it was reality). He scanned those letters; he couldn't bear to read them word for word.

Meanwhile, there was proud satisfaction in knowing that for all his difficulties his work for the Professor remained excellent. Danny wrote clear, concise memos on recondite, sprawling international law cases, read and discussed Hobbes and Locke, Hans Kelsen and John Austin and Blackstone and H. L. A. Hart. Politely, inevitably, the two of them would argue, and Danny took pride in keeping his end up, while the Professor displayed an ill-concealed exasperation at Danny's mutinous attempts to assert uncertainty. "It is a well-established tenet of international law . . ." the Professor might begin, and Danny couldn't let that go unchallenged. If the Professor, who had borne so enormous a load of sorrow (for what could be a more bizarre and haunting tragedy than the death of a twin child?), could carry on as before, surely Danny could maintain a hard, scholarly competence.

And there was a kind of brutal satisfaction in the realization that, deluded all along, he'd not yet begun to confront the enormity of Hiroshima, or of those stored explosives—in America, in Russia, in China and France and India—prepared at any time to enlarge that blast exponentially. Danny read John Hersey's *Hiroshima*, and a novel called *Black Rain*, and a book called *Hiroshima Diary* by a doctor who'd treated and been treated for radiation sickness. The Professor was helpful here, though something creepy was at work in his quiet dispassion as he steered Danny toward little-known books and pamphlets and test results, toward diaries, photographs, drawings. Still, the Professor's was probably as logical a way to proceed as any, here where one was dealing, after all, with the unimaginable insanity of world destruction. Instinctively retreating from the vastness, Danny's mind clung to isolated images—the light-seeking radiation burning upon a woman's flesh the flowers of her patterned kimono, or a man plucking a victim from the river only to feel the skin of the other's hand slide off entire, like a glove . . . Danny's culpability lay not in failing to assimilate—he saw now—but in believing that he had successfully done so, and then assigning a special but peripheral place to what was the largest event in history, from which time itself should perhaps be reoriginated: *in this, the thirty-sixth year after the blast, I made my way to the city of our era's birth.*

Coming to full flower, spring discharged what was perhaps an exclusively Oriental pollen. In any event, Danny suffered his worst hay fever in years. Lying in bed, sinuses half dammed, he could choose only between breathing painfully through his dry, swollen mouth or effortfully through his wheezing nose. The medicine he bought provided little relief. Itches burrowed like tiny sand fleas into his face. Worst, most frustrating of all, was the subcutaneous tickle in the roof of his mouth, which a fingernail couldn't seem to get at. Only slightly more effective was to attack it with the blunt pressure or stroke of the tongue. As the cherry leaves emerged from the falling blossoms the weather turned damp and warm. Spring was moving, soddenly, suddenly, into summer.

"You not only sound awful, you look terrible, too," Carrie kidded him. She herself, in cutoffs that exposed most of her thighs (still a bit tan from the Trinidadian sun, and rimmed halfway up, where she quit shaving her legs, with those short downy golden hairs that stood out perpendicularly), was looking very good indeed. Her teasing contained lingering affection and, perhaps, a hint of renewed availability; she seemed sincere, anyway, whenever she asked him to reconsider making the Hokkaidō trip. But Carrie, too, was a temptation he took satisfaction in forgoing. Logistically this was easy because he had no phone. He felt little desire to call her, though late at night he would often begin hoping she might again unexpectedly appear. Appear in her short cutoffs with a bottle of liquor, asking him out, inviting herself in.

His schedule had once more been wrenched awry, largely because he couldn't sleep at night, or remain asleep, but this didn't explain why the hours had become so ductile, narrowing and widening by turns. In leaving Carrie he had removed from his schedule what for months had consumed the largest share of his time, but the expected vacuum hadn't resulted. His days were usually full, as minimal errands expanded to consume the shrunken hours. To manage to eat three meals, take a bath, shave, maybe read a newspaper—here were the makings of a full day. And yet waking with an internal thump in the night, body sweating out the beer he'd swallowed to help himself across sleep's shifting edge, Danny would find the minutes dragging with a ponderousness not known since he'd been a schoolboy imprisoned by a tyrannical classroom clock, or had sat beside Mom on a wooden pew, toward which an incomprehensible minister lobbed threats and censure. Danny seemed to sleep best now in the late morning, once it had definitely become time to rise, as though his body needed to know that it was transgressing before it would fully let go. Whether he actually was sleeping more or less these days was hard to say, given the way he tossed about at night, but in any event he was often still in bed at eleven in the morning.

Greg woke him one morning at noon. "Are you sleeping or merely napping?" Greg asked him.

"Neither. I'm just getting up," Danny said.

"I like the empty beer bottles. So homey." Greg was wearing shorts and a T-shirt. The day was quite warm, apparently. The room brimmed with light. "I came to ask you to reconsider. You should come with us tomorrow morning."

Danny shifted under the blanket. He'd awoken with an erection. There'd been a dream about going—it now appeared—to the laundromat with Greg's friend Noriko. "When are you leaving?"

"Tomorrow morning."

"I meant how long are you going to be gone?"

"It looks like almost three weeks. I'm starving. Come on. I'll talk you into it over lunch."

"I'm tired."

"Come on, I rode all the way over here."

"Throw me that shirt on the chair. And the pants on the floor," Danny said. He slipped into both while still in bed, and leaving his shirttails out he stood. In the mirror on the wall his hair, which was growing long, leapt up in tangled clumps. "I look just like a scarecrow, don't I? Where's my brush?"

"Come on, don't touch a thing, it's perfect."

The street blazed with light. The sky was a burnished blue, vast and weightless and just a little cool. Greg had shaved off his beard recently, and shed some of the weight he'd gained over the winter. In his T-shirt and shorts he looked much as he had the second time Danny had seen him, jogging along the Kamo River. Around the corner from Danny's house four little girls were playing on straw mats spread out in a parking lot. The last few days had been as hot as summer, but today was purely spring. "Where you been?" Greg asked. "Nobody's seen you."

"Who's nobody?"

"Everybody. *Me, myself, and I, he said solipsistically*. Look at those girls. They're studying hard. Have to begin early in this country, huh?"

The girls were playing school. One, the littlest, wearing a massive snowy diaper, was staring with a fine simulation of plunged concentration into an unillustrated book. Glancing down into it Danny caught an upside-down inkling of the density of its kanji characters and was struck poignantly by the realization that the little girl would be reading these before he was. Danny was everywhere reminded of how little Japanese he'd learned. The very city itself, lying under the kanji *dai*—大 —of Mount Daimon, continuously reminded him of his ignorance.

They headed, at Danny's insistence, toward a Western-style coffee shop, Big Time, rather than to a Japanese restaurant, because Danny wanted an egg salad sandwich. It was the closest thing he was going to get to breakfast food.

"But the sandwiches are so *small*."

"We'll each get two," Danny said.

Greg, ordering for both of them, was soon exuding satisfaction once more, pleased at so confounding the waitress by asking for five egg salad sandwiches that she'd fetched another waitress for confirmation. "You must come along," he said. "You can fight with Carrie all the way. I'll mediate."

"We don't fight. We never fought. We squabbled."

"Come along and help keep Peter in line. I'm afraid he really *is* an unspeakable jerk."

"You don't make it sound too tempting." Although Danny believed himself closed to persuasion, he nonetheless wanted Greg to attempt it. There were claims of friendship Greg might invoke, chiefly the enormous fact that in not so many weeks Danny would be leaving Japan while Greg himself, though he still talked vaguely of departure, would in all likelihood be staying on. But Greg did not invoke them.

Greg said, "I liked what you said the other night about those dipso rats. You thought I was too drunk to drink it in, so to speak, but I wasn't. Come along on the trip and we'll devote our whole conversation to animals. We will develop a Comprehensive Theory of Animals. Or perhaps that's overly ambitious. Maybe something along the lines of Our Friend the Raccoon."

Danny laughed.

"I'm quite serious."

"I wasn't laughing at that. I realized suddenly that while you were talking about animals I was staring at the tooth marks on your forehead."

"Okay, okay," Greg said, "ridicule my intellectual ambitions. Snub your best of pals. Ruin his travel plans." He held up his hand, palm out, like a policeman halting traffic. "Don't. Don't worry about me. Remain unswayable."

Yet in Danny's own mind, as Greg paid the bill and they shuffled back out into the afternoon sun, he was suddenly not at all unswayable. He felt prepared, in another unexpected reversal, to abandon everything toward which he'd been building so painstakingly these past few weeks. Was this cowardice?—or friendship calling? A false self?—a true one? All Danny wanted was to learn what it was he actually wanted . . . Back in the room, having resumed the positions from which they'd started, Danny on the bedding, Greg in the doorway, Greg said, "And another thing. It occurs to me that I may long ago have burdened you with an unwanted gift. Inconsiderate on my part, and for which now I would like to make some sort of amends."

Curiosity that pricked all his faculties alert prompted Danny to sit up. Here was something rare, something indeed Danny had seen but once before and in the same positions then as now: Greg seemed genuinely embarrassed. "What are you talking about?" Danny asked, though in truth he knew—and now knew the real reason Greg had biked over today.

"The joint. The dope I gave you. It occurred to me that you don't like it anyway, and of course there's always the danger of your getting caught, whereas I need it desperately if I'm ever going to tolerate three weeks of this Peter character. So I thought perhaps some mutually advantageous exchange—"

"I smoked it."

"Oh no, you didn't. You don't even like dope. When did you smoke it?"

"Last week," Danny said.

"You smoked *all* of it? I mean that's extremely powerful stuff, to say the least. There isn't a roach around?"

"All of it. At a couple of sittings."

A pause ensued. "Well, how was it?"

Greg knew where Danny had hidden it—in a gap between two tatami mats. What in the world was Danny going to do now if Greg were to stoop in search of it? "Great," Danny said.

Yet Greg seemed rooted in the doorway, a ghastly, malign smile pasted on his face. "Isn't it amazing stuff?"

"Mm-hm. Definitely."

"I mean I thought that was some of the best pot I ever had in my life. Didn't you think so?"

"I don't know. I'm not very experienced with drugs."

"No. No, and you're not a very good liar," Greg said, still smiling. "You know, Dan, I may have pulled some shit maneuvers on you this year, including the business with Plumfield's wastebasket, but I've never lied the way you are now. Well," he said. "Anyway. I'm about to commit a rudeness." And quietly snapped the door shut behind him.

. . .

Down the hall from Danny in his freshman year at U. of M. lived a bizarre kid from Grand Rapids named Winston Waits with whom Danny shared a single bond—they'd both been accepted at Harvard. Win had chosen U. of M. in order to remain in proximity to his psychologist, a fact almost boastfully divulged. He was the first specimen, and hence uncategorizable, of a type Danny'd later learned to recognize and disparage—one of an outstretched intellectual community that, armed with a panoply of scientific-sounding terms, could be almost exoneratingly articulate as to why they behaved so badly. At the time, Win had frightened and fascinated Danny. It was only years later, running into him in Harvard Square (for Win, too, had felt Harvard's eventual pull, homing there for business school), that Danny successfully identified Win as the voluble fool he was. Nonetheless, over the passage of years, Win Waits' reason for turning down Harvard looked sounder than Danny's own—that a former schoolmate and distant friend had committed suicide by defenestration from William James Tower, home of B. F. Skinner's behaviorist pigeons.

One of the things Win's doctor had asked him to do, midway through freshman year, was to formulate a list of the big changes and events in his life since entering college. On hearing this, skeptical Danny, himself always addicted to list making, had for the first time wondered whether this doctor might be offering something useful. And now, years later and ten days after Carrie and Greg had left Kyoto together, Danny recalled crazy Win Waits (who had seemed less crazy, more pathetic, that afternoon in Harvard Square as he'd explained how he wanted to go into the family business, which happened to be insect extermination: "I'm big on *tradition*, America needs *tradition*") and began a list outlining his own year in Japan. "One: Mom and Dad got divorced." With Carrie and Greg gone, Danny now felt alone, as he had on his arrival in Japan. It was remarkable how large a part the two of them still played in his Kyoto life. Without them, Danny inhabited a world where Professor Umeda—to whose house he would be going later this afternoon—was the only large proximate figure.

"Two: Penny's getting married to a doctor. Three: Mom's marrying Douglas Nebbin." The writing of *Douglas* rather than *Bump* was an act of deference toward Mom, faint defiance toward Dad, whom Danny would be seeing in just a few weeks. Summer had come. Seated in just undershirt and undershorts, Danny felt damp at his armpits and crotch. He seemed to be doing better, for the most part, since Carrie and Greg had left, though he still carried on, often to ridiculous extremes, little half-humorous games of mock criminality, as with all the precautions about fingerprints, or the need almost daily to locate a new hiding place for the joint Greg had given him. (He'd finally settled, quite wittily, on placing it—leviathan joint—in Hobbes' *Leviathan*.) And he'd accomplished very little. The turns in the weather made him sleepy.

Increasingly he dreaded Greg and Carrie's return and he had lately contrived to leave earlier for Hiroshima than he'd told them; they would arrive home to find him gone. "Four: contracted syphilis." Yet here the list began to look not only useless but laughably lugubrious. Self-pity and wild inaccuracy simply bayed from within its terseness. To narrate truthfully his dealings with Carrie he would have to unravel all the claims Greg had placed on him, all the unseen ties Japan had placed upon him from the start, would have to, merely to draw a rudimentary portrait, go all the way back to the sharply recollected image of himself dozing on the plane with his sleepy passport photo looking up from the seat beside him. "Five:" Danny wrote, but the mendacity of the whole enterprise overcame him and the number sat blank until he realized it was time to dress for the Professor's. He'd not been to Umeda's house since the disastrous party at Christmas. The Professor had invited him this afternoon to meet Harvard's Professor Horne, whom Danny knew by anecdotes only, which included Horne's delivery of a lecture while wearing a Groucho Marx mask and Horne's taking the Professor to the infamous all-you-can-eat steak house. Danny put on a shirt from the cleaners and a tie (the first he'd worn since the Professor's party). His face was stubbly. Last night at the bath he'd forgotten to shave.

Although Danny was forewarned by an absolutely gargantuan pair of scuffed brogues in the Professor's entryway, Stanley Horne turned out to be bigger than expected—a couple of inches taller than Danny, a plump sandy-haired man who, sweating heavily, rose from one of the chairs in the Professor's Western-style room to shake Danny's hand. "You look familiar," he said.

"I've been meaning to take one of your classes," Danny said, which was true. A scheduling conflict had kept Danny from Horne's class in international civil procedure. Danny greeted Mrs. Umeda in Japanese and answered her deep bow. She asked him in Japanese whether he would like something to drink.

"Won't you have some whiskey?" Professor Horne said. "I bring Masahiro here some whiskey"—this was the first time Danny had ever heard anyone refer to Professor Umeda by his first name—"and then find I'm the only one drinking it." A big bottle of Jack Daniels sat on the table before him.

"Whiskey, please, thank you," Danny said in Japanese to Mrs. Umeda.

"Anyway, to finish that long story about Harris," Horne said to the Professor, "him and the other fella both show up in Brussels with the wrong set of figures. Line by line, everything exactly wrong in exactly the same way." Professor Horne rumbled with extended laughter, rattling his glass as he did so; Professor Umeda smiled politely.

In a place where large legends flourished, Horne was something of an outsize legend at the law school. He was inhumanly impervious to all disasters and adversity, legend had it: he got away with everything. Not much liked but universally respected, he was reputed to be an absolute master at goading selected students, not with the old-fashioned autocratic bullying Harvard was notorious for, but through much cleverer and more devious machinations.

Arriving at Harvard with the expectation of hearing an old-fashioned patrician English at the lectern, Danny had soon discovered that atrocious grammar and a clogged, cliché-strewn prose were the rule. All those fine points he'd picked up along the way (at home, where Mom and Dad took a smug pleasure in deploring the grammar on television; in his own reading; at U. of M., where fortunately he'd had fine composition classes), all the nice distinctions between "continual" and "continuous," "enormousness" and "enormity," "disinterested" and "uninterested," the proper use of "presently" and "hopefully" and "transpire"—these were time and again unwittingly trashed by his lecturers. Yet Stanley Horne, or so the story went, took lassitude a step further by deliberately adopting all sorts of outrageous mispronunciations, solecisms, slang, and jargon. This "him and the other fella" talk was apparently typical. Perhaps especially perverse in a scholar specializing in international law was his Anglicization of foreign terms as to render them unidentifiable to all parties, American and foreign alike. One of his students (a story too idiosyncratically perfect to be wholly apocryphal) had sat through an entire lecture, during which he'd taken copious notes, wondering who or what "Billy Dukes" was, only later identifying this as Horne's rendition of *billet doux.* Horne got away with these, as perhaps with everything else, because he was, in a viciously competitive institution which granted the term grudgingly, a brilliant man, one of a mere handful of students in the law school's history to graduate *summa.* He had clerked for Justice Harlan and he'd once, so the story went, called Justice Douglas "addled" to his face.

"What brings you to Japan?" Danny asked him.

"It comes by way of a stopover. I'm on the way to Hong Kong. There's this shipping conference I'm supposed to give a paper at. I do hope the food's better than the last time. Last time I was in Hong Kong, I couldn't find a Chinese restaurant." He produced another rumble of laughter and drained his drink. Faint, in some corner of the house, a baby, the Professor's solitary daughter, was wailing. "I vowed no more of these overseas conferences after the last one in Bombay, where my shoes were stolen. I can't imagine what possible use they were to the thief. There can't be an Indian in Bombay who could use them, you see. I wear a size thirteen, triple E." Horne lifted for examination his sock-shod foot. A tiny hole in the toe revealed the crinkled gray edge of a Band-Aid. "Perhaps they were taken merely as a curio. In any case, my hosts were most gracious, absolutely insisting that a new pair be made for me. Well you know, I'd always secretly hankered after a pair of custom-made shoes." And there it was: setback transformed into triumph for Stanley G. Horne, Thomas Jefferson Professor of Harvard Law School. "Although to be fair, that was hardly the most disastrous conference I attended. That honor would probably go to one in Lima"—he pronounced this as one would the bean—"where the hotel ceiling fell on me."

"How terrible," Professor Umeda interjected.

"I must in fairness point out that my hosts at the conference, who were extremely gracious people, had emphatically advised me *against* that particular hotel. I remember thinking, as I lay there among the rubble, that here were the makings of a very interesting tort suit, with all sorts of marvelous transnational angles, but unfortunately I was absolutely uninjured."

Mrs. Umeda appeared in the doorway with a tray, bowing her head, apologizing for her rudeness in interrupting their conversation to bring them something to eat—indeed conveying her profound regret that the food could not enter on its own impetus. "Ahh, here it is," Horne announced. "Professor, I'm afraid I've put out both you and lovely Michiko"—this was the first time Danny had heard her name pronounced as well—"and it was so kind of the two of you to indulge me in this little dish I've heard so much about.

"As I understand it," Horne said to Danny, "and Michiko, you must correct me if I'm wrong"—which she was immensely unlikely to do, even if she had known English—"little fish or eels, about the size of worms, are put into a steaming broth, into which *bean* cakes are added. Now as the little buggers start to boil, they naturally head toward the comparatively cool *bean* cake. They burrow into the *bean* cake, see, and expire there, imparting what I'm told is a most unique flavor to the *bean* cake. Certainly a most ingenious dish, and one I've longed for years to try."

Mrs. Umeda placed on the table before each of them a bowl of pale broth containing two large steam-misted rectangles of tofu. It was a dish Danny not only had never tried, but had never heard of, in all his months in Japan. Couldn't Professor Umeda see that Horne relished this moment simply for its blend of the exotic and the somewhat disgusting? That he doubtless placed such instances into a collection of international culinary anecdotes? *In Lagos I was once served chocolate-covered aphids* or *It is the texture of the goat's eye the Turks prize so.* And this relish for the indigenously revolting was what had prompted Horne to take the prim Japanese professor, Masahiro Umeda, to the all-you-can-eat steak restaurant in Newton. How Horne must have savored the occasion when it turned out they were on hand to witness a house record being broken—seventeen steaks consumed by someone sitting at the table right beside them!

"I suppose I'm lucky to be heading to this conference at all," Horne said, bisecting one of his bean cakes with a chopstick, "and not to have ended up cooked to a teeny-weeny cinder inside Griswold Hall. You hear about our little fire, either of you?"

Behind his glasses Professor Umeda looked—a peculiar expression Horne seemed to provoke in him—both alert and blank. "I don't think so," Danny said.

"Oh, isn't it just like a self-important place like ours to figure everybody's got their ears turned to the slightest ripples on its waters? We had a little blaze, recently. A student of mine, apparently somewhat miffed at the grade I'd given him, tried to set fire to my office. Unfortunately, he mistook my office for Len Zutto's. You remember Zutto, Professor?"

"Oh yes," Professor Umeda said. "I am grateful if you would give to him my regards."

"I had him for Secured Transactions," Danny said. Poor Zutto, a stooped balding man whose only law-school legend was that he had no stomach, no intestinal system at all, his entire cancerous and ulcerated digestive tract having been removed piecemeal in a string of operations. He'd been one of Danny's favorite professors.

"I don't know *how* the kid managed to get the offices confused. The names are clearly marked. I guess it's no wonder he choked on the exam. Actually, it was a fine exam content-wise, but the kid misbudgeted his time. Never even answered the last question. Poor Len lost all sorts of irreplaceable papers."

"Oh God, that's awful," Danny said, restoring to the table his short whiskey glass, which he'd instinctively been resting in the heel of his hand lest he leave fingerprints.

"And of course the whole thing's done nothing for his health."

"The young man must have been *insane*," Professor Umeda declared.

"Well he definitely's got some screws loose. They got him up to Maclean's now." Horne tore hungrily into his second bean cake. "To make it all the more awkward, it's a black kid. From Memphis. Quite bright, and a real vocalizer. He and I used to have a real go in class discussions."

"Perhaps twenty years ago, perhaps twenty-three, there was an arsonist in Kyoto," Professor Umeda said, "a student of Zen religion, who razed Kinkakuji, what you call the Golden Pavilion, one of the most famous temples in Japan."

"Well, in this case, I don't think the loss was quite that large, though Zutto may disagree with me there." Horne laughed and then, his broad sandy face turning somber, homiletically continued, "The kid got the wrong guy. Sometimes there simply is no justice."

Conversation drifted to various other Harvard professors, a mix of news and light gossip in which it was tacitly conveyed that Danny was not to participate. After each name arose, Professor Umeda would say, "I am grateful if you would give to him my regards," and Horne, "Of course, Masahiro," and "Sure, Masahiro," and "You are remembered with great affection." Horne, crunching on an ice cube, then turned to Danny and said, "Masahiro tells me you are quite brilliant." In Horne's mouth *Masahiro* became *Mass Hero*.

"Actually I'm afraid I'm not as useful as I should be. It's a pity I don't speak better Japanese."

"Yes, he is very helpful," Professor Umeda said. "He is very strong, in his opinions. We have very strong discussion. We were talking recently about the work of Hans Kelsen. Donny does not have such great regard for his work. Perhaps you share this opinion?" Umeda, like his secretary Miss Minowada, had trouble with a flat *a* sound, and *Danny* often became *Donny*.

"Well, I tell you, that's theory, and I'm not a theoretician, I'm afraid," Horne said. "No, something much more pedestrian than that, I'm a lowly legal technician. I leave that whole theory bag in the able hands of my colleagues. Men like you, Mass Hero."

"But perhaps you share Donny's conviction that the theories of Kelsen do not reflect the actual law in society?"

"I'm sure that Don here," Horne replied, bending Professor Umeda's mispronunciation into a stranger's name, "isn't wholly off base. You must give my compliments to Michiko, who was wonderfully accommodating about meeting my little culinary whim."

Professor Umeda, still canted toward his guest, nodded confusedly at this conversational shift. This was the first time Danny had ever seen Professor Umeda appear less than formidable and the sight inspired within Danny something he wouldn't have guessed was there—a very tender solicitude toward this peculiar, humorless, tight-skinned man. "But surely you are deliberately overstating your case," Danny said to Professor Horne, who swung gradually toward Danny a broad face whose brows were lifted, mild curiosity in its small pale blue eyes. "You would surely agree that you can't really understand any field of law without some notion of the policy or theory behind it," Danny said.

"Yesss," Professor Horne replied. It was a technique Danny had often seen employed at the law school, an acquiescence so colorlessly vouchsafed as to suggest that nothing really had yet been expressed; that the speaker must, if he would avoid simplistic platitude, continue more boldly—or recklessly.

"I mean property law, criminal law, tax, even your own civil procedure, these are all based on notions of what men are, of what rights they have, of what rights government has."

"Yesss. Oh yes."

"In your own field," Danny continued, "how does one make sense of the shifting attitudes toward sovereign immunity without talking about theory?"

The question was met only by a disconcerting stare, a short but weighted pause expressing both the indecorum of Danny's attempt to lead this hot Kyoto afternoon toward a full-scale academic controversy and the heavy reluctance with which Stanley Horne now was entering the dispute. "Hans Kel-sen," he chanted. "Now what does Hans Kelsen tell you about your absolute right to sue the government?"

"As Professor Umeda already pointed out, I'm not in sympathy with Kelsen."

"Nothing. Not one blessed thing. To his credit, he doesn't attempt to." Horne, now sitting forward, was brandishing his empty glass with pontifical gravity; Danny, while attempting to resist it, felt himself somewhat overborne. "He merely attempts to tell you what the law *is*, which means he comes out merely useless but not incorrect. Or no more incorrect than most. Of course he could have gone the other way. Every ten years or so, some earnest aca-demic comes along with a theory for deriving an *ought* from an *is*, and he gets kicked around for ten years until the next one surfaces.

"Meanwhile"—Horne had settled back in his chair—"the law muddles on, my friend, routinely doing the impossible, as it must: determining culpability, imprisoning people, assigning a dollar value to a lost limb, a blinded eye."

"And does so, however fumblingly," Danny broke in, "on the basis of developing theories about rights." It surely *was* indecorous to be forcing this exchange, yet Professor Umeda himself had initiated the discussion (though now looking on in unhappy alarm at the adversarial way Danny was confronting his superior), and Danny felt that far more than a point of legal scholarship stood to be vindicated.

"You talk about *developments* . . ." Horne reposed still more sedately in his chair. This, and the bemusement in his voice, maddeningly suggested that the discussion only claimed him in part. "Gimme one. Gimme one little development, one teeny-weeny basic tenet we can all agree to."

"You wouldn't be prepared to admit"—Danny began stiffly; his voice tended to lift and turn brittle when challenged in the classroom—"that a society, say, that denies black people suffrage is fundamentally inequitable compared to one that does?"

"Oh *I* would. *I* most passionately would. *But who am I?* Look around, travel a bit, you soon see universal suffrage hardly's the rule. Suffrage itself's hardly the rule.

"Now I tell you, Don. I'm playing devil's advocate on you, which may not be fair outside the classroom, and may not be gracious to our gracious host. And of course you must know some theory, you're going to make sense of things. But for all the world's fun-da-mental in-equities," Horne huffed, blowing Danny's slightly pompous phrase into absurdity, "I've never seen the theory yet could tell me what the fair compensation is for an amputated arm, a poked-out eye. My friend, true justice requires true knowledge of man's nature, and who can plumb the human heart?"

No use denying it: Horne was magnificent. Masterful—that sanctimonious and conclusive aplomb with which, veering into a sudden moral folksiness, he could deliver one of his little rhetorical homilies.

Yet Professor Stanley Horne was not quite finished. He had reserved one final observation. "I leave that task to larger minds than my own," he pronounced, rubbing his broad jaw in such a way as to convey the unmistakable impression that, in fact, there were none.

"Who can plumb . . . the human heart?" Danny chanted over and over as he pedaled home, deepening and fattening his voice into a risible orotundity which Professor Horne had escaped. "I leave that . . . to *larger* minds than my own. My friend, my young friend, my wee little friend, I leave that . . . to larger *minds* than my own." Danny locked his bicycle. "Who can plumb the human *heart*?" he was whispering as he discovered that the door to his room stood ajar. Imposing no fingerprints, somehow coolly prepared for this, he kicked the door open with the toe of his shoe. There on the bedding, hairy in just gym shorts and a T-shirt, lay Greg, eyes upon him. "You've taken to wearing ties in my absence," Greg said. "I think that's *nice*."

"What in hell are you doing here?"

"Catching twenty winks. Waiting for you. Planning a homicide—that girl played 'Tie a Yellow Ribbon' three times a while ago. Absolutely unbidden, there came into my mind a really vicious, thoroughly unpleasant play on words: 'Tie a Yellow Woman to the Old Oak Tree.' String the girl up. Please, step right in," Greg said. "Treat the place as your own."

Danny closed the door behind him. "You're supposed to be in Hokkaidō."

"So hey we got back early. I mean I must say I thought I'd get a warmer welcome. You don't seem overjoyed to see me."

"I'm overjoyed." In truth, part of him was greatly cheered by the sight of Greg. "Just overjoyed. How was your trip?"

"Not as awful as it should've been. A certain Ottian presence was clearly missing from the outset. Very pretty. Very exhausting. *Humorous.*"

"Where's Carrie?"

"Home I guess. She wants to see you."

"You hungry? I've just been eating worms in bean cake at Professor Umeda's. I've got to get something to get the taste out."

"I'm never not hungry." Greg rose from the bed. His face was suntanned.

Repelled by the thought of any sort of Japanese food, Danny insisted on their riding over to McDonald's. They took their quarter pounders and french fries and banana shakes down to the river. The two of them sat on a stone bench, Greg talking about his trip and Danny trying to appear attentive while not actually listening. This was a defensive move. For weeks now, not at first consciously, he had been accumulating a nervous, charged tension, a rebellious self-resentment, designed to culminate in his trip to Hiroshima; he had nurtured this unease with a sort of husbandry, observing with satisfaction the birth and rebirth of so many exacting quirks. All of this was threatened by Greg's reappearance, the lure of old loyalties and compatriot laughter. "Now this is really brilliant. You must listen very carefully," Greg was saying. "There I am, there is the waterfall going ppsshh, ppsshh, there behind me is the Buddha, and it occurs to me that if we have free will, granted now for the sake of argument, then a failure to *like* most things—Brussels sprouts, say, or spiders, or bean cakes with worms—is a kind of sin, or at least is unworthy of us, as human beings."

"That's nothing. I recently figured out what the worst fate in the world is, the very worst one. You want to hear it?"

"It'll happen to me probably." Greg laughed. "I hope to God this isn't some kind of prophecy."

Before explaining what the worst fate in the world was, Danny took the opportunity to say, "You're always suggesting that I don't look ugliness in the face but you know I figured out the worst fate in the world and you never did. The very worst fate in the world," Danny said, "is to have been very sick, is to have been near death, and to wake up in the dark and realize with this tremendous relief that you're alive. You don't know where you are at first but you realize you're in a tight place. Then you realize you're in a coffin. *Then* you realize they thought you died and they buried you alive. And what do you do then, after you've pounded and screamed and no one comes and you realize you're just going to have to wait and die right there a second time? What do you do? You have to leave some sort of message, don't you? You have to pray that somehow they'll find you and realize that the worst injustice in the world has befallen you. Do you twist your body into strange, painful contortions to show them? No, you need something more conclusive," Danny continued hesitantly, for his smugness was beginning to be tinged with fear. He'd been delivering this little black scenario with a self-satisfied detachment, but now some of the horror he'd felt when the image first came to him, lying half-awake one night this past week, reasserted itself. "What you do, what you have to do, Greg, is knock one of your teeth out and scratch a message into the wood."

"Sounds a little like my forehead," Greg said and laughed again. But then he said, redeemingly, "No, I really like that. That's really excellent." They sat in silence a while, Greg tossing cold bits of french fries to a gathering ring of pigeons. Then Greg said, "You know, Carrie and I slept together a few times on this trip."

Danny's instantaneous reply arrived with a rare sense of perfection, a certainty that his answer could not be bettered: "I thought that had begun long ago."

Greg's face, open and congenial, did not alter: he missed the connection altogether. "That's what you said to me, after you got back from Korea," disappointed Danny explained. "When I first told you I'd slept with her. Don't you remember?"

"I guess so. And anyway, I do love to be quoted," Greg added, blithely pocketing the moment's triumph as his own. "Anyway, I feel silly reporting in to you like this, like you're my big brother, or dorm father, but I just wanted to avoid any misunderstanding, like when you accused her of sleeping with me after she gave you the clap."

Disappointed the moment before, Danny now felt really offended. It was not merely the insensitive inaccuracy (for Greg knew it was syphilis rather than gonorrhea she'd given him); rather, what got under Danny's skin was that quiet, so-casual assumption of shared experience, mutual familiarity with all the untanned, covert regions of Carrie's body. "I just didn't want you pissed at me again," Greg went on, uprooting another bunch of fries from his bag. "Not that there's anything to be pissed about, I mean you and she'd gone separate ways, and anyway she and I are done. It was just for the trip, it turned out. You know, I think she's hung on you still. She's a lot more attached to you than I realized."

"Will you do me a favor, Greg?"

"Sure."

"Don't tell her you saw me today," Danny said. "Tell her I'd already left."

Greg ripped a french fry in half, tossed one piece to the birds, put the other in his mouth, and laughed. "The fries aren't meant to be symbolic. Honest. Just another case of life imitating very bad art." What was he talking about? "Sure. I won't tell her, though she really wants to see you. She's real crazy about you, Dan."

"I'll see her when I get back."

Still later, after Danny'd been cajoled over to the Texas and John Coltrane's "Ballads" was again playing over the loudspeakers, Greg said, "I think Carrie's been put in an awkward position because she doesn't really have any girl friends here," and Danny was struck anew by the sudden queer parity Greg had established. He was now an expert, in regards to Carrie. Greg and Guy Huesing—the two of them could have quite a little chat some day.

But when, Danny wanted to know, when had it become clear to her—*before* or *during* the trip—that she was going to sleep with Greg?

Curiosity burned him. He wanted in, Danny wanted in on every prurient detail. He felt betrayed by the both of them and yet, oddly, not the least bit hostile. So long as Greg didn't talk too much.

And later still, once they'd finished their beer, things turned dangerous, suddenly Greg with real friendliness was proposing: "If you want, I'll go with you to Hiroshima. I'd like to see it. I've never been there."

"No. I mean if it's okay, I think I'd rather go alone," Danny said. "It's just that I'd always envisioned it as sort of a solitary trip."

Danny knew this was the right decision and yet, alone at last, lying on the floor of his room and staring at the paper bags of folded clothing standing against the opposite wall, he felt that the trip was misconceived, that something had already been spoiled. He should have left days ago . . .

And while he lay uneasily there his body was abruptly jolted, as every misgiving within him coalesced around one specific fear—which, it now was clear, was something that had been troubling him from the moment he'd discovered Greg in his room. Danny sprang to the bookcase. He pulled out Hobbes' *Leviathan*. The joint was not there.

But the joint was there, tucked into the table of contents. Though he couldn't be certain, Danny could be almost certain that he hadn't placed it there. No, he'd slipped it right into the middle of the book. Someone searching this neat little room, if he knew what he was looking for, would not need much time to find a hidden cigarette. And it was like Greg, in one of one-upsmanship's subtly downplayed maneuvers, not to remove it, but simply to move it. With shaking hands Danny tucked the fat joint back into the center of the *Leviathan* and—caught, found out—placed the book, as perhaps he'd been planning all along, in his knapsack, for the trip tomorrow.

Seated at last in the dining car of the bullet train to Hiroshima, a high-speed travel movie playing on the other side of the windows, Danny ordered eggs and cocoa. It was just a few hours after dawn, most of the mist having cleared only to reveal clouds, fog, smog, smoke, for it was going to be a gray day. With intentional slowness Danny ate his eggs, drank his oversweet cocoa, then ordered—though the dining car was filling up and the waitresses probably did not appreciate his lingering—a cup of coffee. He watched roll by an unpardonably ugly terrain: serried, sullied, bracketed and wired, its bleached sights obscured but not softened by the grime in the air, only expunged now and then, swallowed entirely, when the train howled into a tunnel. Out there the day was probably hot, for even at dawn his shirt had clung to his back, but here in the train's dining car, bulleting along at over a hundred miles an hour, the circling air was refrigerated.

Osaka, Kobe, on toward Okayama, and then Hiroshima, now less than two hours distant. The world's fastest trains. Rocketing by platform after platform of crowds assembled (from the viewer's perspective) for a moment's glance. The blur of stations at a hundred miles an hour, an instant's impression of waiting patrols of students in quasi-military uniforms, outposts of a country whose Constitution renounced militarism forever, but a mentality that waited, steadily as a machine waits, for the slipping change, the quiet go-ahead amendment, the liberating spill of money. Money was packed into this train, nearly all of whose passengers were businessmen in suits and ties, off on business errands. Except for the waitresses, there was hardly a woman on board.

Danny paid his check, returned to his assigned seat (which fortunately but perhaps not accidentally was located beside an unassigned one; the train clerks seemed—or was this crazy?—to keep the gaijin segregated), and drew from his backpack *Leviathan*. He carried the book into one of the Western-style bathrooms and slid the lock's metal bolt into place and sat down fully clothed on the toilet.

If it came to that, he could hardly pretend to having failed to see or to understand the large, wordless No Smoking sign that depicted a cigarette laterally slashed by a thick red line. Would an alarm go off? *You're trying to get caught*, a voice within offered. *You're trying to get thrown out of the country*. The neighbors, all of Mom's friends in Heather Hills, were going to have a gossip's field day when he was arrested. Hobbes still unopened, Danny lit an experimental match and held it up over his head, recalling as he did so a sculpture that had stood in the lobby of his high school, a bearded man in a toga holding up a lantern, gone to search the wide world over for a wise man. Or a virtuous man? And what was his name? It was a famous Greek myth.

No alarm sounded, though it was plenty loud already in here, where one actually felt, as one didn't in the dining car, the distance being traveled and all the strength required, the fuel incendiarized, to move so many megatons of steel.

And what about cameras? Wasn't it possible in this watchful land of such ingenious gadgetry, such proud miniaturization, that there were hidden cameras monitoring these bathrooms? He could dismiss this fear as preposterous, paranoia gone amok, but he dropped his pants anyway, to sit for all such hidden eyes in a less suspect pose. More reasonably he asked—*What about ways the train conductors have for opening locked doors?* "They hafta be able to get in," Danny said aloud. For if a man were to have a heart attack in here, behind the bolted door, there was doubtless a means of removing the corpse. Danny plucked the joint from *Leviathan*, lit one end, placed the other to his lips and sucked in deeply, resting his other hand on the lock as reinforcement against the train conductor's passkey.

He inhaled a second time, painfully as the smoke elbowed down his throat and into his lungs. The joint was gradually burning itself up while he held the smoke inside him. There was an answer here (intricate but theoretically obtainable, to be arrived at collaboratively by a physicist and a physiologist) as to the single most efficient way of smoking a joint by oneself. How deeply did one inhale, how long hold in the smoke as the cigarette dwindled? Danny drew in a third time, recalling Greg's boast that here was the finest dope in the world, and lifted his head as he did so—the motion of the train assimilating this motion. His lungs had opened far wider than he could ever have anticipated and pinched suddenly by edginess he licked his thumb and forefinger and squeezed the cigarette. An ember tore squarely into the ball of his thumb. He lifted the joint and held it close, staring it right in its worm-sized face: it was out.

But the rumbling shudder of the train had worked on him: its musical infiltrations claiming the nerves and bones of his body. He sat for a while, letting the land and the time puddle away, then re-collected himself with a jerk. He was not focusing; it was the dope—and having recognized the symptoms, and the cause, he discerned the hopeful promise of regained control. And yet, drawing his pants back over his white hips, he unfocused again, then, refocusing, realized he'd unfocused.

It was on leaving the bathroom, his feathery hands rechecking his fly, that he realized, or admitted, or readmitted, how dishonest he'd been with Greg when explaining his motives for avoiding dope. (This admission was an acknowledgment of dishonesties tissued thick with years, freeing and beckoning him toward things blocked all of that time (and Greg was waiting patiently there (but this was getting quickly off the point))) . . . It was true, as he'd said, that he was extremely, amazingly susceptible: it made his hands shake, it thickened his tongue till he could scarcely speak, it edged the edges of his vision toward mild hallucinations. But it did not, as he'd said, merely bore him, or make him sleepy, or depress him. For chiefly it was this immense reverberative network of nerves, this sense of stifled shocked voices on every side. *Careful*. He stood outside the bathroom, a sea of black-haired heads before him, all waiting to lift and study him as he walked past—and then began a cautious stroll back to his seat.

Someone, a man (Japanese), was sitting in the seat beside his, which was his definitely for there on the floor was the backpack. But seats on this train were assigned, and no one had been sitting here; at none of the stops had somebody gotten on and sat here. He could not, Danny could not, ask the man to let him by. No way, no way was he going to seat himself beside this highly suspect stranger.

Danny swung around in the swaying aisle of the train and he was heading now for the nonsmoking car, car number one, the only one whose seats were not reserved. He paced down the cars' long corridors, pushed each door open with the printless heel of his hand, crossed the metal coupling, entered another car, another, then realized in leg-locking horror that he'd left the joint and the book in the bathroom. But he hadn't. *Leviathan* right here, clutched fiercely in his own right hand. *You're trying to get caught*, that voice repeated. "Shut up." He was standing before the dining car, and he went in.

In the back of the car a hilarity-sharing party of businessmen sat in cirrus clouds of blue cigarette smoke, that poisonous atmosphere Japanese males seemed naturally to gravitate toward when seeking companionship and relaxation. The dining car was full. A waitress told him in Japanese to wait a moment. Keeping his head down, for Danny felt sure his face must record the transformation, his pupils now be the size of saucers, he excused himself and went again into a Western-style bathroom that might or might not have been the same one as before. He couldn't tell.

As he sat this time, eyes closed, a clean hateful image of himself was projected, almost as though he *were* being photographed: a pale, red-haired gaijin absurdly seated fully clothed on a toilet on the bullet train, sucking like a child the thumb he'd burnt on the forbidden cigarette. In response to this, in defiant answer to all his rude observers, Danny drew the joint from the book, his hands shaking less now, and took another remunerative hit, and a second. Pure sunny inspiration told him that when he was apprehended by the police he would pretend to speak no English. In schoolboy French he would field their questions, until at last they brought to interrogate him someone who knew French, whereupon he would switch to German, and if need be to Spanish—until he was straight again, until they released him, until they conceded he'd outwitted them all.

He slipped the joint back into *Leviathan* and went a third time to the dining car, which was no longer full, and ordered coffee. Outside, the hills still loomed grayly through a mist of smoke and dirt and fog. A city rolled by and Danny was struck initially by how many aerials there were—hundreds and hundreds really, prodding the sky any which way—then by a subtler apprehension of the whole electrical network, the telephone poles and power lines, the huge humming ugly infra-system that usually dissolves from one's sight, and finally by a freshened perception of the ugliness of this whole Japanese countryside. There, right before his eyes, a steam shovel was tucking into another hillside. "It's like New Jersey, south of Manhattan," Greg had prophesied of this terrain west of Kobe. But more accurately what this was was a hideous parody of all those old *sumie* landscapes he'd seen with Carrie in the museums. A delicate mist-hung mountain landscape opening to unveil, faintly, in the distance—what? A corrugated shed, a power line, a smokestack, a derrick, a traffic-congested street, a larger-than-man-sized replica of a bowling pin . . .

Here it was, spread out before him, the absolute refutation of that pervasive Japanese conviction—which he'd so much wanted all year long to believe with them—that all things could be assimilated into their remarkable land while leaving its soul intact. All year long, despite the evidence, the loudspeakers at Ryōan-ji shouting *This is a sacred garden preserved for quiet meditation*, all of Greg's nasty jokes. To believe in that Japanese pride which continually said, *The commercialism is only superficial, no people on earth love nature and beauty as we do*. But that was merely to comfort themselves, lies, the whole packed country was dishonest, for a people who truly loved nature would never have permitted this. Danny felt pleased to find these observations coming so clearly, to feel the warmth of the coffee cup in his hands. If only the train would quit plunging through tunnels! Each time the same, a sudden *ka-shurrrr*, and there was his sickly reflection slapped against the window, floating on the blackness. And each time, each time a high protestive whining that seemed to come only partly from the train, partly wrung from the mountain itself.

Inside his chest, attuned to the motions of the train, but detached from them as well, really, lay a cool thudding and with his just-a-moment-ago clearheadedness he tried to articulate precisely what it was like; this thudding was very peculiar. And victoriously he perceived that it was just as though someone were packing snow into channels or tubes inside his chest, but with another moment, another rotating breath, the analogy seemed extravagantly absurd. He drained the coffee cup to its near-bottom, where the sugar grains gritted a moment on the tongue before sliding into dark disappearance. "A man can't be blamed for his susceptibilities," Danny muttered, with mock dignity; then remembered, with a giggle, Nagaoka-san's apology for his susceptibility to alcohol: *I am easily drunken.*

He was coming to Hiroshima at the wrong time; the trip had become a cliché; he had failed to prepare properly. He was going to be seized by the police, who were not going to listen cooperatively to his French, his German, his rusty Spanish, but were going to demand, unmistakably and peremptorily, that he produce his alien registration card, which he had forgotten. Which he hadn't forgotten, though, for it was tucked into his backpack. Which was lying on the floor beside a suspicious Japanese man who was not sitting in his assigned seat. Any movement was—Danny perceived this constantly, through all his thinking's fluctuations—perilous, and yet he didn't like the thought of his backpack lying unattended. He gathered up *Leviathan*, paid his bill, and headed toward his seat down the long mobile run of swaying corridors, each numbered significantly, like the enchanted numbers of a fairy tale.

Eyes lowered, head lowered, Danny had gone some distance before he grasped that he'd somehow gotten turned around and was walking away from rather than toward his seat. The realization stabbed him; for a moment he actually wanted to cry. To cry at the immovable notion that in all this head-humming weirdness he was not, as it seemed, touching on variant conjectural lines, equally valid for all their unconventionality, but that he was simply *wrong*, had chosen a direction that simply would not do because it was *wrong*. He went into another Western-style bathroom, this one definitely different from before's, and sat a minute or two with his head in his hands. The thrumming of the train was all-embracing here and it held him whole a while. Then, on shaky legs, limping, his red-haired head above the field neatly laid out as a farmer's field of Japanese heads, he hazarded the long passage to his seat. The man who'd invaded the seat beside his had vanished. The backpack was still there. Danny collapsed into his seat and pressed his cheek against the vibrating window. A man's voice ripped over the loudspeakers, speaking Japanese—they were approaching Hiroshima. Then a softer, mending female voice, speaking an English pastel-tinted with a Japanese accent, told him the same thing—they would be in Hiroshima in two minutes.

Danny zipped his book inside his pack, efficiently, though his hands were trembling, and stationed himself in the aisle before the nearest door. He watched an abutting concrete platform lead up, crowds of people, the bilingual sign in red—just like those for Kobe and Okayama—saying Hiroshima. This definitely was not what he had expected. He had expected, even here at the station perhaps, some reference to the blast, but instead everything shone newly, warmheartedly. The train halted and—and steeled by the sudden, consummate certainty with which he knew this to be true, he stepped out into the strangest city in the world.

The Peace Museum—he wanted the Peace Museum, and he had a map of the city in his pack that would direct him there. But he didn't want to open the pack again. He wandered across the ringing floor of Hiroshima Station and out at last into the steamy street where in the concrete glare a pocket of policemen stood. "*Pardonnez-moi, je ne parle pas anglais*," Danny rehearsed, then the same in Japanese: "*Suimasen ga, eigo wa dekimasen*."

He needed to take a taxi if he wasn't going to consult his map, although he could ask directions. The difficulty at this point was that he could be walking away from the Museum rather than toward it, which meant the thing to do if he wasn't heading there now was to *stop*. Danny halted. Heavens, the day was so hot. He could turn around, begin walking the way he'd come, but there was no reason for believing it more likely the Museum lay that way than this. This way than that. Not even the slightest reason for favoring one direction over any other. He had halted before a sidewalk fruit stand and its proprietor, another severely hunched old woman, came forward with a high indeterminate greeting. Apparently his pausing had been taken for interest. She, too, had a mouthful of metal teeth.

She was a little scary, with her eyes pinned upon him this way, and as a talisman to ward her off Danny picked up a bag of what seemed to be oranges and extended a thousand yen. Her eyes, like her breathy unintelligible call of thanks as she laid the change into his palm, was a prod demanding action, and not to act suspiciously was to head in the same way he'd been going. He had been given a direction, then, and strode purposefully along until out of her sight.

The fruit was not oranges but something Danny'd had before, *hassaku*, a cross between an orange and a grapefruit whose bitter membranes are not eaten. Danny dropped the peelings into a trash bin and broke the cloudy globe into halves. Though too warm, the fruit was nicely sour. Cleansing. Each segment was strewn with seeds. Nearby there was little except concrete about, but Danny waited, seeds under his tongue until he was able to spit them into a sheltering clump of bushes.

A potential source of help, one of Greg's *bozos*—black leather jacket in all this heat, and a cigarette affixed to his lower lip—materialized in the haze. Sure enough, all disdain vanished at Danny's approach. The boy, for he was a boy, turned nervously solicitous, giving his directions as though a great matter hung in the balance. And on parting, the boy faintly, quickly—a purely Oriental reflex, a deference which for all his studied disaffection he would never unlearn—bowed, and Danny bowed more deeply in return.

He'd been heading the right way, then. Neatly, almost surreptitiously, Danny scattered the pips here and there where the soil invited. Danny Orangeseed. Silly. He crossed a river in this city of five rivers, perhaps—no, surely—one of those into which the bombed inhabitants had fled to escape the flames. He was feeling better, more like his usual self, though it was hard to say, the day was already so hot. Beneath his pack the back of his shirt was soaked through. In Kyoto he had studied the Hiroshima map and though he couldn't consciously call it to mind it was guiding him. He was being guided. For a long time honking traffic went by, went on building the heat. A building appeared on his right—somehow clearly the Museum. Which meant the hypocenter could not be far away.

Large green spaces—so rare in Japan, such an honoring tribute—opened on his right. Children playing, screaming. A metal-skinned balloon—the silver sunny shiver of aluminum foil—drifting overhead. Danny spit more pips into a clump of bushes and as he did so he was unexpectedly faced with another fiendishly laborious hypothetical task. Could he, if forced to it, retrieve his steps to the fruit stand to recover each and every seed he'd spit out? Stooping, combing the ground on hands and knees, could he find them all, each pip, among the fallen leaves and branches, tin cans and newspapers and pink plastic chopsticks? The absurdity of this chore in no way diminished its burden (for somehow surely it *did* matter, and the mind itself (which after all had conceived it) knew that the task spoke of the near-impossibility of undoing any action (of passing cleanly, tracklessly, from place to place)). A rivulet of sweat plummeted from his left armpit down his ribs to lap against the elastic band of his undershorts.

And here it was in English etched in a black memorial stone: the Hiroshima Memorial Peace Museum. Not until he'd come to Japan had he understood what a daily comfort this was—to read signs, to make one's way by a known alphabet. Greg was crazy. Limping, he mounted a flight of stairs. Admission was nothing: fifty yen. He paid and made his way in. The Museum was dark and air-conditioned. Headphones, too, were available in English, but Danny decided against them.

Heat had chased the visitors away, the Museum was not too crowded. Here were photographs of the city, before and after. Danny read, he studied everything, he drifted. Here was a book, whose pages had been reduced to ash by a blast two miles distant. Here were lock and key, heat-fused into one. Here were roof tiles bent, as in a kiln, a kiln in which people jerkily danced, for a moment; photographs of burn victims, human skin become a swollen black carapace; and his eyes continued to read, his mind to study, as his own failure welled up: he was not taking this in, he was not beginning to take this all in. Here was a mutated fingernail, black and half-an-inch thick; here, maybe some teeth. Here, in glass cases to which people came with heads wound in headphones were more photographs of radiation sickness, here a poor horse, hide strewn with keloids. Here a little girl, whose blackened back had turned bumpy and blistered like the skin of an alligator. And Danny felt at last a welcome sour nausea stir; he was going to be truly sick. In this cool tomb of a museum his body had begun shaking and he was about to vomit.

He scurried to a bathroom in the back of the Museum, beyond stands selling books and photographs he would have to examine, and plunged his head over the open bowl. The rising subsided. He was not going to vomit. He sat fully clothed on the toilet a few moments, head in his hands, and forgetting where he was seemed to hear the bone-vibrating rumble of the train, then realized he was still more stoned than he'd realized. A second push of nausea squeezed his stomach and again he lowered his head over the open bowl of river water. As he did so, his mind went black a moment, as if swallowed up, and *It's like drowning* a voice said, recollecting the notion that your life passes before you as your lungs fill with water and your body subsides into the sea. But in fact what he now recalled had little, nothing to do with his life: how a boy at Greyfield, plump Bradford Beggs, repulsive even there among that encircling group of elbowing, acned boys, how he used to shake pepper on a deviled egg until the whole thing was lightly ash-skinned, and then would eat it with a grin of aplomb, somehow magically managing never to sneeze. Again Danny wasn't going to vomit. He sat once more on the toilet, as the image of Beggs—that plump, small-eyed, little-pig-face face—faded.

Yet there was a connection he saw, he saw in an ascendancy of the rational mind: Beggs' failure to sneeze back then; his own to vomit now. No one else was in the bathroom. He drew *Leviathan* from his pack and, secure in the knowledge that he was totally mad, no one had ever been crazier, lit the joint, now a stump of itself, took two hits, and buried it, still faintly burning, in *Leviathan*. He pressed down hard, then opened the book once more: the page was faintly charred, the joint was out.

Feeling better now for this attempt to purge himself, less self-dissatisfied as the nausea safely diffused throughout his limbs, Danny returned to the entrance of the Museum. Here again was Hiroshima before the blast; here was the razed city afterwards, with the battered globe, like a ruined skull, of the Industrial Hall—now become the Peace Dome—still standing. He had attained that condition he had been seeking: faintly sick, a little numb, but the mind continuously ingesting new data, the horror still unfolding in his head. He studied again the radiation victims, the fingernail, the blistered stone Buddhas, the granite steps onto which the shadow of a seated man, a chemical visible ghost, had actually been burned by the force of the blast. Then the condition shifted, or his mind became full, and he needed to leave—quickly to leave.

Limping he clumped back out into the gray steaming afternoon. Danny was sweating again and his head was still buzzing. He was limping because of a stone in his shoe. There'd been a tiny little pebble in his shoe all morning; there had been the same tiny pebble in his shoe (if memory was trustworthy) for days now, a little local ache that never quite reached consciousness and any attempt at remedy. Ahead of him on the right loomed, as in the photographs, the Peace Dome, left to stand just as the blast had left it; nearer, also recognizable from photographs, and toward which Danny now hobbled, stood the ugly covered-wagon-shaped monument that marked as best could be computed ground zero. Children in uniforms were scampering through the haze. A dove, one of the Hiroshima peace doves—no, it was just a pigeon—whirred up on the right. The light, and his own sweat, stung his eyes as he made his way. *History begins right here* a voice within dutifully instructed, but the words were meaningless. Here again waited only failure. He had no further demons to invoke, to make him other than what he knew he was: a tiny ridiculous figure with a backpack under a gray sky.

It was time to leave.

Hurrying now, body lubricated by sweat, he retreated across the river, past the clumps of shrubbery where he'd spat the *hassaku* seeds, down past the fruit stand. The woman who'd sold them to him was gone. And all the while he went on drawing up a mental report; he saw that he'd been assembling notes for a memo to Professor Umeda—that expert on the blast, on the deaths, the illnesses, all the legal cases, all the legal responsibilities of war. Compensation for the victims under Article Seventeen of the Constitution. The rules of war, of surrender, of civilian bombings, of atomic bombs, according to the tenets of international law.

He bought a ticket to Miyajima, less than an hour away. Island of the Vermilion Gate in the Timeless Inland Sea—so his brochure had said. And one of Japan's "Scenic Trio," though how these had been selected was doubtless one of those mysteries he would never unravel. He would spend the night there. He found his train, took a seat, settled his head for a while against the glass. He saw that a bit of a breeze had started up; the sky's heavy haze seemed to be breaking. His head was still swarming. He consulted his watch—he would be there in forty-five minutes. Again it seemed he might be sick. It was going to be awful, too embarrassing for words, if he vomited on this train. Once, now so long ago, Penny had vomited on herself, on him, as they sat wedged in the back seat of a convertible on Woodward Avenue waiting for the light to change, on their way home from a Fourth of July celebration in Greektown where (so inexperienced with alcohol) they'd both drunk too much. So long ago, that would have been 1974, his junior year, and his own proper Penny had vomited a purple winey clinging warm stinking mess over their hips. Poor sweet Penny, the most embarrassed he'd ever seen her, as she'd begged him, and he'd agreed, to say it was he, not she, who'd been sick. Solid chivalrous trooper, he'd lied to the Cogswells, who'd never had a serious complaint about him before that, and to Mom and Dad. Oh, he'd loved Penny for asking that of him.

At the next stop he ought to get out if there was really a chance of vomiting—but when the train lurched to a halt he remained motionless. He closed his eyes, letting the push-and-pull of the reviving train lull him. He would be well, would be himself again soon . . .

He awoke with a start, as if he'd been kicked. He didn't for a moment have any idea where he was. Layers had to be peeled away before he understood that he was on the train to Miyajima, consulted his watch, reconsulted his watch, suspected, then determined with near-certainty that he'd dozed through his stop.

The train was braking to another halt. Hastily, his heart in his mouth, he gathered up his pack and in broken Japanese asked of the man beside him, sleepy himself, "Miyajima—that way?" and pointed behind him.

"Miyajima?" the man asked loudly. "*Miyajima?*" Danny's question awoke the train car.

Mortifyingly, they began on every side to call out, again and again, that Miyajima lay behind, that he'd missed his stop, that he was going the wrong way. The train braked and Danny plunged through the opening doors, pack in hand, their voices at his back. And wanting to get clear, free of them and of this tiny horrible station, he bustled his ticket to the fare-adjustment window (though perhaps the smart thing to do was simply to wait for a train going in the other direction), handed the man a thousand yen, received a handful of change, and stepped out openly into the street. He did not know where he was.

In his hurry he had even missed the name of this town. A little community somewhere south of Hiroshima, he supposed, though the advertisements in the shop windows—for Seiko watches, for Panasonic tape, for Coca-Cola, for Lady Borden's Ice Cream, for Fuji film, for Campbell's soup—were just the ones you saw in Kyoto. A smoky thirst burned his throat. He needed a drink, some coffee, he needed to eat, to vomit, needed to think, to sit, to shit, he needed a place to lie down. He bought a can of Coke and carried it across another bridge over a cement-lined canal. The whole time carrying, as on a platter, the platter of his shoulders, his crazy head from place to place to place. Danny sipped from his Coke. Immediately he felt better, much better. And looking up through the gray, breaking sky, he glimpsed through a gap in the clouds a wan sliver of moon and this vision seemed to promise some useful, some most lovely, linkage. *What was it?* But what the vision recalled, he saw with plummeting resignation, was merely another such moment. Months ago, his first weeks in Japan, his birthday. He'd caught a glimpse of the moon over Daimon-ji that day, near the outset of this bizarre year, and had felt an equal closeness, a similar momentary promise.

This hint of a beckoning infinite regress, of moments of yearning tied not to any real object or goal but only to other such moments, wearied him and he took a seat on a park bench that stood suspended over a vast mud puddle. He folded his feet under him to keep them dry and drank deeply from the can. Across the river stood a hunched old woman, walking a dog, the woman who'd sold him the *hassaku*, the woman who'd sold him the flowers the day after he slept with Carrie.

But the woman who'd sold him the fruit was in Hiroshima, the balding woman who'd sold him the flowers was in Kyoto, and even now he was not thinking clearly. From where he sat, he could see her, could see her reflection in the canal, and could see his own in the puddle below him. His own face, looking up weary and skeptical.

He had crumpled up and thrown away the mental memo he'd been preparing for the Professor. Somewhere in the last hour he had finally declared to himself that the Professor's whole noble endeavor was irredeemable nonsense. Danny *was* thinking clearly as, his tired face looking up at him, he saw without doubt what he had always seen: the Professor's field was a sham, there was no such thing as international law, no such thing as human rights. Professor Horne had been onto the truth, or closer to it. Theory meant nothing. And it didn't matter a bit—was completely irrelevant—whether we'd chosen our lot in life or not. With nations, as with people, one was either dominating, dominated, or threatened with domination. It was clear there was only force on the one side, luck and cleverness on the other; bullies on the one side, potential victims on the other, scrambling frenziedly for shelter.

Bullies with sticks to root out your eyes, with knives and bombs that rained from the sky, bullies with boots who kicked you in the head as you lay helpless on the playground. Right here was the meaning (he'd seen this long ago) behind the Professor's laughter at that story about how those salmon which the Russians had used to stock their rivers had swum to Japanese waters to spawn. Cosmic justice—or at least the hope that the clever boy must ultimately vanquish the lumbering oversized bully. Danny recalled how Greg had rushed in to the aid of the man being kicked on the playground and, in shame at the way he himself had instinctively hung back, he lifted his gaze from his own face in the puddle to the woman across the canal who (mysteriously, for she walked with such painful slowness) who was (he looked both ways as far as the eye could reach) who was nowhere to be seen.

4

WITH DAD ON SAIPAN

*

*

Mia cara Carrie, dear darlingest girl, Danny composes, *who would have thought during exam period in Cambridge last May that almost exactly one year later I'd find myself playing tennis on Saipan, while my crazy father drinks whiskey sours and watches on the sidelines? Yet here I am . . .* Danny no longer needs full concentration on this match. The letter assembles in his head as his feet plant themselves, his knees dip, his body lunges, plunges into the ball. The sun is enormous overhead, one-third of the sky has been blasted open to make room for it, and under its steady, exacting press his limbs glide on a pure lubrication of sweat and sunscreen lotion. Now in this, the third set, he knows he's playing the best tennis of his life.

The first set had gone badly, almost a rout. Danny went down six games to two, with even those two scant wins hard-fought, seesaw struggles. This big, big-eared kid from Indiana on the other side of the net, with his cropped military haircut (the island is dotted with American military), is what at Greyfield, where Danny last played on a tennis team, they'd called a *cruncher*. He really can pound hell out of the ball. That first set was painful, getting thrashed under this blowtorch of a sun, and all the while Dad behind a rakish pair of sunglasses looking on from his high, shaded line-judge's chair. At the end of it, Danny'd wanted to quit. The soldier, too, had wanted to quit.

"You want to call it a *day*," Dad repeated incredulously. "Two young guys like you, you should be just getting started! Cameron . . ." Somehow Dad had caught the kid's last name; Danny hadn't. "Now are you telling me that after all your basic training you can't play two meager sets of tennis?"

"I can go another." The kid's ears were bright red. He bobbed nervously.

"And what say you, Danny?"

"I can go another."

If (no; *when* was the proper opening note) . . . *When, Carrie, you come visit in August we'll go to all the Japanese restaurants and make extremely informed comparisons.* From Saipan Danny will be heading straight to New York, and in just a few weeks Carrie, too, will have left Japan. In August she'll come stay with him in Jacobusse's elevated Park Avenue apartment with its carpets and china in glass cabinets and sofas and framed prints and windows commanding the city. Danny's body hums with the awareness that it is love for her, in part, that guides the ball so unerringly. So suffusing is this love that it brims over to color the way he draws on his shirt in the morning, looking from a balcony of Saipan's Eagle Hotel down on the endless Pacific, or the way he drives in their rented Granada (not easy to find a Ford, but Dad had persisted) through a flaming tropical dusk, or tears with a very sharp knife into another steak. He had thought that he and Carrie had severed irrevocably, that enough nastiness and resentment had accumulated to render any reconciliation impossible; yet when he returned in such sorry shape from Hiroshima she swept away all supposed obstacles, taking him in with a simplicity equal to his own simple need to be held. "Shh, shh, darling, darling, darling," she sighed, as his breath stumbled toward something he'd threatened all year to do: he broke into tears. The *rightness* of her embrace, the consolations of her murmured reassurances, had been a needed boon, a rare blessing. Love for her was what had brought that second set, perhaps the toughest he'd ever played, into reach. Each of those fourteen games had proved a battle, each point had to be scraped off the scorching pavement. But in that second set Cameron's serve began to soften, the heat getting to him. And Danny at last had beaten him, eight games to six, and returned proudly to Dad's high midcourt throne.

"Now you guys are beginning to warm *up*. I'd say you two are building toward a real slam-bang finish. The excitement is almost insupportable."

"I think I've had enough, Dad. I think we've both had enough."

"Cameron, you're not tired. Are you tired?"

"Pretty tired, sir."

"Cameron, when I was a soldier we had to carry fifty-pound packs for fifty miles. You ever carry a fifty-pound pack for fifty miles?"

"No, sir."

"Cameron, you too tired to go another set?"

"I can go another."

"And what say you, Danny?"

Dad was having a great time. He was playing a game, one elevated far above that being enacted out on this blazing tennis court, and as happened so often with these games of Dad's there seemed no possible way for Danny to win. To refuse to play a third set was to lose; to play and lose the match was of course to lose; and to play and win the final set, the match, was merely to accomplish Dad's true bidding. One's only refuge was an ironic look that said *I'm wise to you*, that said, falsely but spiritedly, *You are not manipulating me*. Danny grinned and paused, maintaining in that suspensive instant a slight ascendancy. Then: "I can go another."

Yet the last word turned out to be Dad's (Danny had forgotten what a talent, at once charming and infuriating, this man had for prodding others), calling out, as the two players trotted back onto the court, in a hoarse whisper ostensibly meant for Danny but which Cameron could not fail to hear—"Come on now, Dan, you've got him on the run."

You've got him on the run. Truthfully, Danny does. Up three games to one now, and about to break serve once more. Love, anger, relief at having left Japan behind (after a nine-month sojourn which, distilled through a few days' distance on Saipan, has become a success, a bold and enormously successful experiment), and also the lift and wonder in coming to this remote tropical island and miraculously finding that the street signs (green fluorescent tabs with dotted white lettering) are the very same as those in Danny's Heather Hills—all of these emotions are trueing his game now. He can slice the ball low, knowing it must skim with a whisper over the tape, can blast the ball hard, knowing it must fall within the baseline. Cameron serving at love-thirty tosses the ball skyward as Danny shifts his racket but doesn't draw his calves into their deepest poised tensity, for he knows the serve will not go in. He knows this, and he is right: the ball caroms off the racket, both long and wide, all of its fierceness needlessly spent. Cameron tosses again in the heat, but the controlling angles, the airborne mesh of muscle and geometry, are subtly wrong; and refusing or unable to adapt to his failure, Cameron double-faults into the net. Big-boned Cameron is melting out here. Danny retrieves the first ball, Cameron the second, and they shuffle into new positions. The heat has pounded everybody else off the courts. The breeze, which makes a papery sound in the palm trees, has died and Danny can hear with honed clarity the delicious clatter of ice cubes in Dad's drink. Cameron's badly tossed first serve slaps the tape. The second comes in soft, grown plump, and Danny's flattened, punched forehand powers it low and hard into Cameron's backhand. As hoped, as expected, Cameron's rummaging return lob is shallow and Danny moves in. For a moment the ball is swallowed whole by the sun, then reappears loose in the air and just where Danny knew it would be, dropping toward a rendezvous with his clenched racket. *Hard,* with that rare pleasure of feeling all one's power subordinated to one's will, Danny smashes it far *harder* than is necessary to secure the point. The ball bounces where it should and whizzes on to strike the wire fence with a satisfying clank, like that of a key nudging a heavy bolt. It's four games to one, Cameron on the run, as they switch sides.

When he tosses the ball skyward Danny knows—and what privileged, sublime knowledge this is!—that he has never played better. How sweet and fine to feel your body risen through its fatigue to come down *hard* on the ball like this. His first serve catches the outside corner of the service box, a near-ace; Cameron's short return offers a put-away volley into the emptied right half of the court. Danny, fifteen-love. How satisfying this sense of points accruing, of the server's dancelike alternating footwork behind the baseline. How satisfying again and again to hit the ball hard and so low your eye tells you it probably won't clear the net—but the ball each time just does. What experience in the world offers greater pleasure than this sense of being guided from within by something that has sharper vision than your own vision? Grunting as he comes down on the serve, riding a forty-to-fifteen lead, Danny forgoes the percentage shot and slams the ball flat out, putting everything he has behind it. He catches the same outside corner with which he began the game, but this time the ball, carrying some additional bounding refinement of desire, passes to the fence untainted by any opposing racket: a clean ace.

Not wanting to beat too badly this coworker, this kid who has struggled so manfully out here, Danny in the next game instinctively eases up. He has this kid beaten and it makes no difference, it is only proper that, as happens, Cameron should hold serve.

Again and for the last time they switch sides in the baking heat. A low military jet roars by, blocking the sun for one blinked instant. Far out to sea there sits a distant freighter, so slow it seems rooted, yet moving as steadily as the tortoise in the fable to some destination that may lie halfway round the world. Yesterday, touring the island with Dad in their Granada, the two of them inspected caves and pillboxes constructed by Japanese soldiers for the defense of the island. Hunching, Danny crawled into a pillbox that overlooked the ocean and peered out just as those Japanese soldiers day after day must have done. Only a few miles away lay the heat-hazed flatness of Tinian, from which the *Enola Gay* took off to bomb Hiroshima.

So close, only a few miles across a thin strait, and Danny had longed to cross that calm stretch of sea (though aware there was little chance of getting Dad to make such a trip). Now, serving at five games to two, Danny knows he must bear down to atone for the laxity of his last game. He hears again his father's glass being set down, feels his watching father leaning forward in his chair. *Carrie, I've been so stupid*, he writes, tosses the ball up and comes crashing down upon it. It's as if Cameron, too, realizes that Danny must play this last game at apical strength, for in four quick clean-angled points, neat as Euclidean geometry, Danny has the game, the set, the match.

With a scissoring fine-footed leap, and a heart full of gratitude, Danny hurdles the net to shake the kid's dripping hand. "You just wore me out," Cameron says.

"I was lucky," Danny says, which he knows isn't true, but adds what is: "You're a better player than I am."

Dad comes forward holding his glass and sunglasses in one hand, two hotel towels in the other, and says gruffly, as if the length of their battle had inconvenienced him, "Christ, I thought you guys'd never finish," then convivially adds, in what he knows is an ingratiating stylistic reversal, "Cameron, can I buy you a beer? Or even a couple of beers?"

"Yes, yes, thanks kindly," Cameron says, accepting the towel with the same jerky nodding Danny noticed before. He is surprisingly awkward off the court.

The three of them, then, with Dad, the shortest, in the middle, cross the terrace and troop in all their sweatiness into the hotel's nearly empty, air-conditioned bar. They settle at a table, Dad on one side,

Danny and Cameron on the other. In this frigid haven Danny feels the sweat drying patchily on his overheated body. Despite the many applications of sunscreen, his skin tightens here and there with the beginnings of a burn. "Cameron," Dad says, "what'll you have?"

"I guess a Budweiser."

"What about a Heineken? They've got Heineken."

"Bud's fine. They all taste the same to me."

Dad asks the waiter, an unhappy-looking man wearing a name tag that says Tom Foon, for two Heinekens and a Budweiser. When Mr. Foon returns and moves to pour the first Heineken into the beautifully frosted glass, Dad peremptorily says, "No. No, I'll do that," and waves Mr. Foon away. With fixed concentration, Dad pours some Heineken into one glass, some Budweiser, which has arrived in a can, into another. "Now taste them, Cameron. Tell me they taste the same."

Big-eared Cameron, sweat-drenched, sips from each with a dutiful look of seriousness. He has perhaps picked up in the military this manner which manages to suggest both a straight-faced ductility, a bottomless patience for the irrational whims of his superiors, and also, redeemingly, a submerged, abeyant grin. "This one's better," he declares, pointing to the Heineken glass.

"But is it *much* better?" Dad always loves to drive a point home.

"This one's *much* better," Cameron answers him.

"Well, you've just learned something," Dad says and in one of those winning gestures at which he's so adept he extends the Heineken to Cameron and takes the Budweiser for himself.

"Oh I'll drink the Bud, I don't mind," Cameron says. "I ordered it."

"No way, you deserve the best. You worked like a *dog* out there."

"Well, thank you, sir," Cameron says, jerkily nodding again, and while raising his head he raises with it the glass of Heineken. His large Adam's apple throbs once and he sets down a nearly empty glass.

"I think you're going to need another. Now what'll it be, Cameron?" Dad's question is a challenge.

"A Heineken," Cameron replies.

"Three Heinekens," Dad calls over his shoulder to dour Mr. Foon, who is peering out the window at the placid ocean. "Cameron, you know you'll never meet another one like me."

"No, sir."

"I thought your motto was *Buy American,*" Danny says.

"Cars. American *cars,*" Dad says, but does not turn to look at Danny. His attention is fixed on Cameron. "Cameron, what kind of car does your Daddy drive?"

"He doesn't drive a car so much, he drives a Dodge pickup."

"Where did you learn to play tennis like that?"

Cameron clears his throat. "There's a country club up at Red Rock, that's not far from Gloria, I used to caddy. There's a tennis pro there name of Rick Ross gave me pointers."

"*Who?*"

"Rick Ross. He almost played Davis Cup."

"Rick Ross of Red Rock . . . Never heard of him," Dad announces with pleased finality.

"Well, far and away he's the best around Gloria, but maybe that ain't saying so much." The kid laughs in his own pleased way and, this time ignoring the glass, lifts the bottle to his lips. He is taking satisfaction—happily complementary to Dad's needling—in the smallness and the destitution of his Indiana hometown.

"How old are you, Cameron?"

"Twenty, sir."

"You joined the service right out of high school?"

"No, sir. I went up to Bloomington a year and tried to make the tennis team. But when I didn't, I joined right up."

"How do you like Saipan?"

"'Snot bad. No complaints so far."

"How long you been stationed here, Cameron?"

"Oh I'm not here," Cameron says, "I'm on Guam. A whole passel of us just come up for the weekend."

"This your first time on Saipan?"

"Yes, sir."

"This is my second time," Dad remarks significantly, and waits until Cameron, who is a little slow to play these conversational volleys, asks, "When were you here last?"

"I was here on June 15, 1944. Does that date mean anything to you?"

"I think it was the day we invaded, sir."

"Saipan was supposed to fall in a couple of *days.* It took a couple of *weeks.* Thirty-five hundred American boys were killed here." Dad is enjoying this chance to impersonate the grizzled old soldier who remembers, down to the last bloody detail, every gruesome campaign of his career. Actually these facts come to him so readily through a visit earlier in the day to the Saipan Museum. Furthermore, it's almost certain that he wasn't on the island on D-Day—June 15th—when the Marines landed; it seems the army arrived a few days later. Though his memory can be pretty good, Dad's recollections of the War seem all a blur. "It was my third beach landing. You know, you ought to pray you never have to do a beach landing. That's pure hell is what that is. You're so scared it'll make you shit your pants."

This kid, Cameron, emits a grunt of laughter. But his face the very next instant wears a deferential gravity when Dad admonishes, "No, I mean that literally. It's not just a vulgarism. You're so goddamned scared out there, you'll shit your pants. You ever think you want to see combat?"

The kid bobs uneasily, sensing some imminent rebuke. "Sort of," he says, "I mean if we had to."

"*Don't*. Don't ever think you do. Because you don't."

"No, I imagine not," Cameron says, nods, and lifts the bottle to his lips.

Danny feels himself being shouldered sideways out of this conversation and experiences less resentment than a perhaps unreasonable sense of want: he suddenly yearns for admittance to this fraternity. Not to have gone to law school, but to be stationed right here on Saipan.

Danny doesn't like the way Dad is needling the kid, although Cameron himself is transparently pleased to be here. Cameron likes Dad and he's enjoying this game. He returns the bottle, empty, to the tabletop and, forgoing the napkin, wipes his lips on his wrist sweatband. "Mm," he grunts. "Mm, mmm."

"Three more Heinekens," Dad calls out, though his second is, like Danny's, barely touched. Apparently they are going to lounge in this bar and get drunk before dinner.

"You two on vacation?" Cameron asks them, head bobbing.

"Actually, we're ships passing in the night, my son and I. Danny's returning from a year in Japan, and I'm embarking on a trip around the world."

"What were you doing in Japan?" Cameron asks, unwittingly snubbing Dad by latching onto the wrong half of his remark. Dad has been telling everyone on Saipan that he's on his way around the world—and nowhere has he received the response he's obviously seeking.

"I spent a year studying law with a Japanese professor," Danny tells Cameron. "Now I'm going back to law school in the States." Their eyes meet, avert. They are more awkward talking together, the two of them, than Cameron is with Dad, where the comic roles of martinet and subordinate are clear. Cameron's meditative mulling nods create a likeable but somewhat dimwitted impression: he seems, like someone silently moving his lips while reading, in a continuous visible process of assimilation. "Where you studying law?" Cameron asks him.

"In Boston."

Unhappy Mr. Foon brings the new bottles of beer. "Danny's up at Harvard," Dad says. "He's on his way to being a big-time Wall Street lawyer."

This comment is a complex mix, as are so many of Dad's remarks these past few days. The reference to Wall Street serves partly as boast and partly as declaration of a bond with Cameron—the two outsiders looking in at the Ivy League lawyer. This complexity in all dealings with Dad, the way most observations seem to pull two ways at once, depresses Danny, who had hoped that a year's absence would have smoothed away these old, petty tensions. In the last two days he has come to see that the only way he could ever free himself from his father would be at last to grow indifferent, and Danny knows he will never, must never, do that.

The tensions remain, but something new has entered in just the same. Danny feels, as he did with Mom in Tokyo, that clarifying sense of dual focus—of both playing the son, in all the patterns and rites established over a lifetime, and with detached fascination observing himself in the son's role.

"Is it rough there?" Cameron asks Danny. "I hear it's real rough."

"The work's not so bad," Danny says.

Cameron nods, assimilatingly: *I met this guy from Harvard Law School who says it's not so rough.*

"All the way around the world," Dad muses. "Do you like to travel, Cameron?"

"That's part of the main reason I joined the Marines."

"All my life . . ." Dad begins, and Danny knows the continuation almost word for word. "I've wanted to make the big circle, to go one time around our big blue beautiful globe. And then one day last winter I said *I'm going to go*, and that was that."

The melodrama of this speech pains Danny; he does not want to be forced to confront how pathetic is this enactment of his father's dream (this pilgrimage that will take him to a number of bars and lobbies and hotel rooms, nearly interchangeable with these on Saipan, in which he will shower and shave and eat overpriced meals and drink scotch and find all his nationalistic generalizations confirmed, while saying to himself *Now I am in New Delhi* or *So this is Barcelona*), and yet conversely, vengefully, Danny longs to tell Dad what a sham, a close-minded burrowing, this look at the world is.

"That was that," Dad repeats.

Cameron gets up abruptly after his third beer—apologizing, shaking hands, bobbing throughout—and shuffles to the door, his lanky body hulking a moment over abstracted Mr. Foon at the cash register, who is still gazing out the window.

"You didn't have to mention *Har*vard," Danny says, burring his voice over the name in order to convert the rebuke into a form of joke.

"It's nothing to be ashamed of."

"And I'm not ashamed. I just didn't feel like clobbering him over the head with it. Es*pec*ially *af*ter"—Danny says, again seeking the refuge of humor—"I'd already clobbered him out there on the court."

"Clobbering? I just corrected a misapprehension. Harvard is not *in* Boston, by the way. What you told him was in fact wholly inaccurate." The excitement of channeling this supposed error to its most telling, its most absurd expression, has brought Dad forward in his chair: "I merely corrected a lie you'd told."

The conversation's ostensible humor has abruptly turned genuine: Danny has to laugh. "It's a good thing you set him straight," he says.

"Least I could do," Dad replies. "The least I could do."

Danny drains his beer. "I better go up and shower. You wanna come up?"

"I think I'll sit right here a while," Dad says. "Then I'll go crap out a while."

This expression *crap out*, a substitute for *take five*, is a favorite of Dad's, and one Danny hasn't heard in over a year.

Danny leaves Dad in the bar, then. As he steps from the room he half turns to catch a glimpse of Dad, who has swung round to peer thoughtfully—like Mr. Foon—at the sea. Danny goes up and showers, spreads cooling Solarcaine over his sunburnt hands, legs, neck and face, and lies down—a delectable sensation—between fresh sheets. He listens, but hears nothing from Dad's room. Danny had dutifully suggested they might share a room (this trip must be costing Dad a fortune), but he'd felt relieved when Dad booked two adjoining rooms instead. They needed space and privacy; they were at each other too much to be living that close. Danny sleeps, wakes—the transition each time made seamlessly, shuttered in utter darkness—dresses, combs his still-wet hair, and steps over to Dad's room. No answer, but the door is open.

Dad is singing in the bathroom. It's a favorite song of his:

And if . . . you ask . . . her why the hell she wore it . . .
She wore it for a soldier who is far . . . far away.

Danny stretches out on one of the beds, hands laced behind his head, bilaterally symmetrical as viewed from the light fixture on the ceiling, and feels himself tipping again toward sleep.

"That was really something out there," Dad announces. He has come from the bathroom naked, a towel slung over his shoulder. He has just showered, too, and runs the towel briskly through his curly silver hair. Mom always used to be kidding Dad that he watched his weight the way a woman did; he's pretty wiry, even now. The hair at his crotch is still dark, Danny notices. "You really hung in there tough."

"Actually, it was the best I ever played," Danny confesses.

"I don't doubt it."

Danny is glad he thought to wear a tie, for again this evening Dad is fussy with his appearance (though everyone else on the island, sensibly, goes around day and night in shorts and T-shirts). Dad puts on tan slacks, a white shirt, a blue madras jacket, blue and tan tie. It is good, gratifying, to see how favorably time has treated this man who says into the mirror now as he brushes his hair, "You had your fill of steak, champ?"

"I think I could manage another."

"Beats a sharp stick in the eye I'll bet."

"Handily," Danny says.

Yet seated at last with a menu before him in the hotel restaurant, which for all its gouging prices and mediocre food has a fine view of the ocean—still vibrantly enclosing the ruddy treasure of the day's last sunlight—it is not steak Danny craves but Japanese fish and rice. To fulfill Dad's role, however— the man who has ransomed his son from a year's captivity in a land where steak was not to be had—Danny orders sirloin, medium rare, and a vodka and tonic. "I was thinking about one of the guys you mentioned . . ." Dad begins, after the drinks arrive.

"What guys?"

"Your friends in Kyoto. The one whose mother sent him cookies."

Actually Danny has mentioned only one such guy—Greg—of whom he has spoken at some length. His friends somehow don't impinge on Dad's thoughts, Danny sees again, and sees how different this is from Mom, whose interest often outlasted his own, so that years after a fight or mere drifting had distanced him from someone, she would be apt to say, "What ever happened to Billy Balchan?" or "Does Wally Howell still play the cornet?" Dad was much better with his girl friends and had in fact been quite attached to Penny, for whom he composed that little jingle, boisterously sung whenever she appeared at the house: "Penny, she's not a bad Penny, but she turns up all the time." Yet it wasn't merely Danny's friends or activities that failed to impinge. Having Dad here before him in his snazzy madras sportscoat—this man who so loves parties—recalls to Danny all those futile efforts to replenish his father's store of party-chat wisdom. Dad had amassed over the years a little store of miscellanea that he was forever trotting out on social occasions (the Apollo flight that got five inches to the gallon, the etymologies of maudlin and tawdry, the carpenter ant's ability to sprout wings for a single mating flight), and to which Danny unsuccessfully sought to add enriching nuggets (the pyramid-building Mayas' inexplicable failure to invent the wheel, Cantor's concept of larger and smaller infinities, the need to install a new bathtub in the White House to accommodate the three-hundred-pound Taft). Much of the frustration was that it never became clear exactly how or under what criteria Dad fixed on the particular minutiae he did.

"You mean Greg. And cake, not cookies."

"I'm reminded of this guy in the crazy army we used to call the Polish Peacock. Billy Dumbrowski. A Hamtramck kid in fact. Always combing his hair and worrying about how he looked, didn't matter one iota if he was thousands of miles from the nearest woman and people were shooting at him day and night. There the rest of us'd be, spattered with mud, our feet green with jungle rot, and there he'd be, the Polack Peacock, combing his gorgeous locks. Looking like a million bucks." There is a pause. Outside, the sea has lost the treasure it hoarded so closely; night has driven all veins of sunlight from its depths, and what light there is—silver strings from ships, streetlights, pulsing washes of neon—is surface light only. "Billy Dumbrowski . . . Why did I bring him up?" Dad asks. Bewilderment has added years to his face.

"Something about my friend Greg. His Mom sending him a cake."

"That's it," Dad says, and looks like himself once more. "Gorgeous Billy Dumbrowski's poor mother in Hamtramck sent him fried egg sandwiches in the mail. Billy's favorite, you understand. Now can you imagine what those sandwiches would have looked like, after being shipped around the South Seas for a while? The poor woman had no concept of where her son really was, what kind of a war he was fighting. *Absolutely no concept*. You want my roll?"

Danny, ravenous, has already eaten his own as well as all the crackers in the dish. "Sure, thanks, if you don't."

"Poor Dumbrowski was gorgeous, but none too swift upstairs. Dumb—just as his name implies. In fact we used to call him that as a nickname: What the Name Implies. Later shortened to just What the Name. He used to open bottles with his teeth and of course one day—crack—there goes What the Name's million-dollar grin. I think that kind of dispirited him. His whole appearance went downhill after that.

"But what was extraordinary about Billy, I've never seen anything like it, was the way he could talk about women. Danny, you've never seen anything like it. The man was a poet, a true poet, the only one I've ever met, on the subject. He would talk for *hours*. Men would *listen* for hours. I mean that literally. He would drag out these hoary, you can take the word as a pun, these hoary old stories of his, and you'd listen as though it were the very first time you'd heard it. He'd have you drooling. He would go on and on about some whorehouse in Malaysia or someplace, you know the arrangement, the story surely goes back to Roman times, where a woman would be lowered in a basket—"

"Yes, yes I know it," Danny says. This is Ann Arbor fraternity house talk, the dateless guys sitting around together on a Saturday night, and he doesn't want to hear Dad go into this.

"—so you wouldn't have to do anything. Just lie back and get yourself a fuck."

The sound of *fuck* on his father's lips—which for all Dad's love of the salty and off-color was rarely employed—disturbs Danny; for years Mom somehow managed to curb Dad's profanity (a losing campaign from about the time Danny himself began occasionally to swear), and in impassioned moments Dad still sometimes instinctively calls someone not a *bastard* or a *cocksucker* but a *yo-yo* or a *dumbbell*. Yet this story seems to be, perhaps, a call for confidences, and "I got syphilis while I was in Japan," Danny confesses.

"Did you?" Dad's pride is unmistakable, and impels Danny to add bluntly, "Carrie gave it to me." He has told Dad all about Carrie, too. Danny winces at the thought of how *furious* she would be if she knew he had mentioned this.

"Oh geez, that stinks. What did you do?"

"Went to a clinic," Danny answers, deliberately misinterpreting Dad's question. What did you do about *her* is what Dad is asking. "It was very inexpensive. The Japanese health care system is really remarkable."

Disappointingly, there is very little in this restaurant to suggest that the two of them have landed in the South Seas. But for a big potted cactus in one corner, a fan-shaped weedy object on the wall that might be a grass skirt, and a few other superficial touches, one might almost be sitting in a seaside restaurant on Cape Cod.

The dinners arrive, and Danny's medium rare steak is as thoroughly broiled as Dad's well-done one. "We'll correct *that*," Dad says, with that ugly eagerness of his when he's about to summon somebody for coming up short.

"But Dad, this is the way I want it."

"You ordered it medium rare."

"And I've changed my mind. This is the way I want it," Danny repeats.

"Danny, we're paying an arm and a leg, the least they can do is cook it the way you ask. Waiter," Dad calls.

"Dad, if you go ahead and complain," Danny says levelly, "I'm getting up and walking right the fuck out of here."

A crackling, ionized pause ensues, during which they glare at each other across the tabletop; then Dad says reflectively, "I don't know where you get your obstinacy, your mother is such an even-tempered woman," and Danny says, which turns out to be just the thing, for Dad laughs boisterously and they are allied once more, "I get it from you, Pop."

They are allied and yet, as made evident by this reference to Mom (not often referred to these past few days), they are farther apart than they have ever been. For it has always been primarily through her—as she mediated, mended, clarified, reminded, glozed and extenuated, as she concocted justifications and proposed compromises and tendered proxy apologies—that they have communicated and cohabited. These past few days Danny has felt her absence each time it became apparent there was some additional detail about his stay in Japan—concerning his room, his work, his trips, his plans—about which Dad knew nothing. In the old days, Mom would have passed all of this on, reiterating as necessary to ensure that most of it finally penetrated.

"You know," Dad says, "I still can't believe I'm being dumped for Bump Nebbin. I fully understand that I am incorrigible, and that any woman, even your mother, must eventually lose patience with me, but *Bump Nebbin*! It seems a little like jumping out of the frying pan into the deep freeze, doesn't it honestly?"

It's not clear whether Dad recalls having already presented this little joke by mail. "I don't know. I guess so," Danny says.

"One of the things that always kills me about Bump is the way he handles his poker losses. We'll finish up a typical session and there I'll be, maybe fifty to the good, and maybe Sam Mercellino's up thirty bucks, and Al Adams's even, and that leaves Bump. *How'd you do tonight, Bump?* somebody asks him, and he says, *Oh, not too bad. Down ten dollars.* And there I am, looking at the fifty bucks in my hand. Needless to say, I never had the heart to correct him. *Oh not so bad*," Dad mimics with some skill, catching the low gassy singsong of that neighbor, Mom's fiancé, who was always dropping steaks off his barbecue. "*Down ten dollars.*"

Dad goes on, "I just can't understand how she would consider *marrying* him. I told her that. I probably shouldn't have, and I regretted it afterwards, but I did tell her that. I said, *Alice, are you really going to marry that man?* Matrimony to *Bump*? I don't mean to be uncharitable, Danny, I'm quite fond of Bump, but you know his limitations. I ask you, Is this a man who's going to *excite* her? Or make her laugh? Or protect her, for God's sake?"

This theme of *protection* was a familiar one of Dad's, who had been waiting steadily over the years to shield his family from the Indians, the Vandals, the Pirates. And though the Pirates never came, it was an appealingly romantic notion, and something far more than merely appealing: for the man truly was prepared (through all their misunderstandings and fights Danny had known this, had been comforted by it, from childhood on) to lay down his life for his wife or his child.

"Well as I understand it," Danny says, "old Douglas Nebbin has got plenty salted away, and isn't money the only protection one needs these days?"

Dad ponders this a moment, then asks, "Why do you call him *Douglas*?"

"That's his name," Danny says.

"Everybody calls him Bump."

"Everybody doesn't. Anyway, I didn't mean anything by it."

"Hell, the hell you didn't. Look I don't object," Dad says, "obviously you can call the man whatever you like, he's going to be your stepfather"—pause—"but don't say you didn't mean anything by it." Dad bites fiercely down on a carrot stick.

And of course Dad's right and Danny has trapped himself once more, for he did mean something by it: that it should be accepted now, on faith, that anyone Mom would choose to marry doesn't merit a belittling nickname. Unwilling to retract his initial claim of not having *meant anything*, however, Danny says quietly, "The man's name is Douglas Nebbin. You were the one who insisted on being so literal not so long ago. About the location of Harvard University."

They eat in silence. A third round of drinks arrives. Danny's dry steak is effortfully chewed and swallowed. Six Japanese businessmen are shown to a neighboring table where with a great deal of shifting and fussing, as enormous issues of modesty and social standing are tentatively settled upon, they seat themselves and order some sake. Within minutes of the sake's arrival, they are enclosed in a red-faced, smoky, laughing ring of intimacy. At another table nearby sits a young Japanese couple (most of the guests in this hotel are Japanese honeymooners) wearing matching powder blue shorts and pink and blue tops. "The desk clerk was telling me," Dad says, "that from a hotel's point of view the Japanese are the best tourists in the world. They're neat, they spend piles of money, and they stay together and don't wander off the beaten track." This is precisely the type of observation from Dad, ostensibly impartial or even commendatory but actually deprecatory, that will usually infuriate Danny, but this time it does not—in large part because the neatness and the spending are indisputable, and the huddling tour-bus mentality is something he himself has grown to scorn.

"You know I'd really like to go to Tinian to see where the *Enola Gay* took off. It would sort of balance my trip to Hiroshima. We could fly there—it takes twenty-five minutes—or take a boat."

"We could." This means *no*.

"That's another thing you've got to do when you get to Japan," Danny says—a barbed joke, for of course Dad isn't going to Japan. "Visit Hiroshima."

"I think I'd rather go to hell first," Dad says.

"Oh it's a little hellish. But you know"—and this argument seems unassailable—"especially in your case you ought to go. I mean it had such a di*rect* effect on your life. There you were, out here in these crazy islands, waiting for orders to invade Japan. I would just think you'd want to see it now from the other side."

"Would you? Well I wouldn't, thanks."

"You know it's much more horrifying than you might think."

"All the more reason to give it a miss." Eyes on his plate, Dad is trimming the fat from his steak. Keeping his weight down. "I've seen quite enough things in my life that horrified me, thanks, and I plan to spend the rest of my life trying to forget them." Dad salts his trimmed steak. "You're not going to drag your vacationing father into a discussion about nuclear *war*, are you Danny?"

"But you know you don't really know, no one does, how awful it was. Maybe you think you do, but you don't."

"Well I'm sure I don't," Dad answers. "And I daresay you don't either."

"*That's what I'm saying*," Danny counters, his voice involuntarily lifting. He can never enter any impassioned argument without hating himself—his boyish shrillness—just a little. Danny sees, for one shrugged-off instant, what a pain he's being, and has always been—

perceives just what an undeserved misfortune, a lifelong calamity, it was for Dad to have been given, as his only child, the son now sitting before him. Danny continues in a lower voice, "You know, I spent weeks before I went, reading everything I could about it, in the hope that I would be able to get some tiny, vague—"

"Just tell me this," Dad interrupts, leaning forward; his voice, his face, everything bespeaks his conviction that he has plumbed to the nub of the matter. "Do you suppose if the Japs had had the bomb, and we didn't, they wouldn't have dropped it on us?"

"Oh for God's sake, that's not the point. The question isn't *who* did it, but the fact that ever since, day after day, we've all been living with the prospect—"

"Just tell me," Dad repeats, "would they have dropped it on us?"

"I guess so," Danny says. "Sure."

"You guess so, do you? Well let me clear something up for you," Dad says. "Let me reassure you on one point. You can safely bet your sweet Occidental ass they'd have dropped it. They probably wouldn't have hit a second-rate city the way we did, I mean they'da hit New York if they could."

"We chose Hiroshima partly for its density of population," Danny says.

"Did you know they had enough anthrax stored in Manchuria to kill every human being on this earth?" Dad says, with volume enough for the party of Japanese businessmen to overhear if they chose. "Danny, these people committed atrocities, systematically, and we've been whitewashing history ever since. Look, we're friends with the Japs now, which is good, I'm all in favor of friendship, but that's no reason to start whitewashing history, to forget how these people committed atrocities, just like the Nazis. In the case of the Nazis, the Jews to their credit haven't let us forget."

"I don't think it's fair to bring in the Nazis. I mean that's a different scale—"

"Did you know, did you know, Danny, they conducted starvation experiments? Very Nazi-scientific they were. They took these poor bastards, prisoners of war, brought them just as close to death as possible, then would see if they could bring them back."

"Yes, I read about that." Lights from within the restaurant have misted the window in gold, but Danny can still make out the black shapes of boats bobbing at the shallow edge of the ocean.

"The prisoners, they were mostly Aussies I think," Dad goes on, as if he doesn't believe Danny has actually read about it, "outwitted them by catching and eating rats. Raw. How's that sound for dinner, huh? Or did you know they beheaded American prisoners after Japan surrendered, because they simply couldn't bear to set the poor bastards free?"

"Yes, I read that, too. Dad, I've read all sorts of books about the War."

"*But you weren't there,*" Dad pronounces in triumph. "They beat the hell out of prisoners, Danny. They beat the living Jesus right out of them. Sweet kids just like that Cameron you played today. Good Midwestern farmboys like that. You know the popular thing to say is, *They were wrong and we were wrong, that's what happens in war,* but that's just not so. They were a hundred times worse to their prisoners than we were."

"Surrender is a much more shameful thing for them. I mean look at Suicide Cliff out there. You saw what they did. They have a long tradition—"

"Oh *shit*, Danny, deodorized *shit*. Leave that to the sociologists, all the intricate whys and wherefores. Just make sure you don't lose sight of the basics. All I am saying"—Dad proclaims, and this is a role he has been savoring these past few days, the self-righteous crusader for the literal, the unsparing truth—"is that we shouldn't pretend, in order to be *nice*, that we were as bad as they were. When we weren't."

"And all I'm saying," Danny replies, "is that you might want to see things from the other side. Might actually want to go see for yourself."

"Danny, Danny you're so goddamn cocksure about what people ought to do. Well, you stay so goddamn cocksure, you're never going to understand *any*body. Or *any*thing."

Here is another *never* from Dad, and it hits Danny painfully. Dad seems always unaware of what harrowing effects the word can carry when delivered from father to son. To be told, as a high school student, when you still believe anything's within your grasp if only you will strive for it, *You'll never play cards as well as I do, you haven't the card sense* or *You'll never be a wrestler, Danny, you're not aggressive enough. . . .* This was instruction of a sort that tore at your heart.

"You can have no idea how strange it is," Dad goes on, more gently, "just to be here. To come back after all these years, after your wife has left you for a friend of yours, and to come here where you literally fought for your life, deliberately to the very place where you took shrapnel in your leg, and to find this . . ." Dad waves his hands. "You have no idea," Dad says in a strange voice—hushed, husky, wondering—and Danny all at once can believe these words are true. "You haven't a clue how very *strange* it is. To remember stumbling around in the mud with a gash on your leg that's become infected, and you're sure you're developing gangrene and they're going to have to cut your leg off at the crotch. To have your wife of more than thirty years leave you. To be on your way around the world for the first time, and right at the outset find you maybe just can't face the trip. You don't know if you can face the trip you've been waiting your whole damn life to make, and you can't sleep, and you're guzzling away like some pathetic wino in the hope of catching a mere hour of unbroken rest, before you wake up again with your head buzzing and ticking away like some goddamn *bomb*." In the silence that stretches before them—enormous—their glances lock and Danny instantly knows the combat between them is over. A clot of self-reproach, of sadness, of hot, swallowed love, burns in his throat, as if he is about to cry. It's over.

"You're jet-lagged," Danny says, and clears his throat. "The whole first week I was in Japan, I kept waking up at all hours of the night."

"I probably am," Dad says.

Their plates are taken away. Dad orders brandy, says to Danny, "Any dessert, kid?" and Danny orders brandy also. From earliest childhood it was at the dining room table that most family tensions erupted and from those earliest days Danny learned that the best way out was with a bright flow of words, a display of the gifted child's precocity which parents and son alike gloried in. Inspired, Danny now catalogues some of the crazy things he ate in Japan—oranges broiled on the top of a gas heater, raw squid, fish eggs wrapped in sake-marinated seaweed, raw egg over rice-and-seaweed for breakfast, pizza served with a maraschino cherry—and the old trick works again, the dinner finishes with a gold wash of laughter, a warm accompanying gold-brown wash of chugged brandy. In the lobby, Danny says, "We need some air," and leads a strangely compliant Dad out into the enveloping, fragranced darkness.

On the lawn, just a few steps, faintly wobbly for the liquor orbiting through the bloodstream, and the hotel stands well behind them. Danny's head floats back on its neck, taking in the stars. The dinner, the argument, are at once hugely diminished. Ursa Major, Ursa Minor (with Polaris so low in the sky—irrefutable evidence of how close they are to the Equator), Cassiopeia, Draco the Dragon, and low on the horizon but visible, nonetheless, that winter hunter, Orion. There, in all their dynastic endurance: bright and precise as they should be, no longer needing to be supplemented by the imagination, as he'd always had to supplement them in Japan. There they are. At the round edges of Danny's hearing the Pacific Ocean is tumbling gently, endlessly. In the darkness big-throated flowers are slipping their scents into the air and Danny inhales broadly. That the stars would burn with this brightness and the blackness between them be this glossy and profound so elates him that he feels a starlike flickering in his fingertips and knows at once, incontrovertibly, that the comely and the good are ascendant in the end.

"I gotta piss. Let's go back in," Dad says.

"I do too. We can piss out here."

"Mustn't deface the hotel grounds," Dad mumbles, and Danny follows him, laggingly, back across the lobby and into the elevator.

"What time you want to get up tomorrow?" Danny asks his father as the car climbs. The door opens and they step into the red-carpeted corridor.

"Any time you get up, just knock on my door," Dad says. "You'll probably want to sleep in. You played like a tiger."

The two of them scrabble for their keys. "Thanks for dinner, Dad," Danny says, hoping once again to catch his father's eye, but Dad keeps his head down as he turns the lock and steps inside. From within the room, a muffled voice of pain calls, just as the door clicks behind, "Goodnight, Danny."

Repeated inquiries in the hotel lobby, telephone calls by the desk clerk, poor directions, and a drive in their Granada that culminates in a cul-de-sac of dilapidated warehouses asleep in the brilliant morning sun, a return to the lobby for new directions—all of these resolve, dissolve into a lean brown hand yanking at a starter cord. The engine catches.

The boat vibrates away from a wooden post slimed with adhesive marine life. "You don't watch out, you're going to burn to a crisp," Dad says.

Two six-packs of beer sit beneath a Mexican straw hat beside the boat's owner, a gray-haired and sun-browned man of indeterminate Asiatic origins who has introduced himself as Mr. Ken. Danny'd liked the way Dad had held out firmly, refusing to take another screwing from the people at the hotel, who had tried so hard to steer them first toward a two-hundred-dollar-a-day boat for divers and then toward some glass-bottomed sightseeing cruise. This old wreck will do fine, it's all the boat they need, though Mr. Ken is tirelessly apologetic. "You come back nex' year," he says, "I have very big boat. Very fine boat. You come back nex' year."

Strung loosely across an enormous sky, the few heavy-looking cumulus clouds enhance rather than detract from a blue that holds the whole of the sea in its rondure. The sea flares and crackles with light as the sea creates and re-creates by the thousands miniature fleeting replicas of itself—fierce, flashing fire-dots, painful to the eye. "Mr. Ken, you don't have any kind of cooler, keep these things cold?" Dad asks.

"Nex' year," Mr. Ken chants.

"Jesus," Dad says, yanking open the day's first beer, "in this heat we'll have to drink fast."

"How did you sleep?" Danny asks him.

"Just fine."

The answer comes back a little too quickly. Dad's face is obscured behind the same pair of sunglasses he wore all day yesterday, but it seems he did not sleep well, and, further, that he resents this inquiry and regrets having confessed last night to sleeplessness. "It took me a week to get over my jet lag when I first arrived in Japan," Danny repeats. These vague difficulties Dad is having seem so out of place on this tropical island—among the tennis courts and sailboats and discotheques and tattoo parlors and bougainvillea and flame trees, the flawless blue of the afternoons, the star-encrusted night skies—that Danny must keep reminding himself of their existence. Momentary marvels keep beguiling Danny into rapture. Bats flapping over a pond that has turned the most delicate hue imaginable in the dusk light, a milky peach-tinted flesh color; a small green lizard on the rusted side of a stranded tank, pausing to inflate into a globe its surprisingly pink throat; a fish breaking the sea's skin just long enough to catch one splash of sun on its mailed flank—what gloom in the world can stand up to sights like these? "Can I have a sip?" Danny asks, extending his sunburnt hand.

"You can have your own, you know." Here is another family joke, a timeless tug-of-war in which Dad was always expressing feigned (for the most part) resentment at Mom's and Danny's frequent requests for sips or bites.

"I don't want a whole one. I need a clear head for my snorkeling." This deliberately exaggerated confession of vulnerability, son to father, produces the desired mollification and Dad hands the cool can, its shell slippery with condensation, to Danny, who takes one long, frothy sip. The beer is hard and wonderful, a blend of liquid and gas, metal and salt, a fiery coldness that uncakes his dry throat and aches sweetly in the top of his chest.

Danny massages sunscreen onto his neck. For protection he is wearing a baseball cap borrowed from Mr. Ken and long pants over the tennis shorts which Dad bought him for yesterday's match and which today will serve as a swimsuit. Danny starts to ask Dad about how the people in his office reacted to his finally taking so extended a vacation but swallows the words instead, not wanting to hear anything more about the Japanese carmakers who have shaken that complacent pride in Ford which has anchored Dad's life for as long as Danny can remember. This swallowing down of questions has become a common practice these past few days, especially questions about Mom, who is forever on Danny's lips. Danny senses that things would be going much better for Dad if only the two of them were constantly talking—but given the span of forbidden topics, what is there to say? How to cheer up this man in the straw boater and the dark glasses, when the bluest sea in the world, the brightest sky above the world, do not do so?

"You know that couple we saw in the lobby, you said were Japanese?" Dad says. "He had such curly hair."

It was amazing how many Japanese honeymooners there were. One saw them everywhere: lying by the pool with Sony Walkmans clamped over their ears, riding rented bicycles down Beach Road, strolling hand in hand on Suicide Cliff, standing in the hotel lobby, the new wives watching the new husbands drop American quarters into the slot machines. "He'd had a permanent," Danny offers eagerly. "They're really popular over there. In fact, probably more popular with men than with women."

The weary shake of Dad's head indicates that he has not absorbed this as Danny'd intended—a surprising and charming bit of local color—but only as one more absurdity springing from that illogical, fathomless land of his competitors. "That's crazy." Dad here on Saipan seems to be taking sanctuary in the notion of other people's craziness. When they'd driven to Suicide Cliff and Danny, reading from the brochure, explained how, faced with American victory, the Japanese families had lined up by age, older children pushing their younger siblings, parents pushing the older children, Dad had said simply, *Pure craziness*. And when, driving down a narrow dirt road, they'd been met by a farmer brandishing a rifle, *Maybe it's because of drugs*, Danny said, *I hear they grow a lot of drugs here*, but Dad answered, *Oh no, he's just some sort of crazy man.*

Danny, rubbing sunscreen on the backs of his hands, says now, "You know Penny Cogswell got married."

"Yes," Dad says, "yes, I guess I did hear that."

"To a doctor from Southfield. You remember how you used to sing when you saw her?" Danny lifts his voice in the old tune: "Penny, Penny, she's not a bad penny, but she turns up all the time."

Yet this, too, is the wrong, or not the right, recollection to offer, for the familiar jingle seems only to make Dad more pensive—though under the hat and glasses it's hard to tell. "Well, they'll be rich anyway," Danny adds.

"So will you, Danny."

"I suppose." But why do these four words of Dad's (which seem to contain neither boasting nor envy, but to be merely a flat statement of likelihood) not seem liberating? Why, instead, do they sit with such sour heaviness in the ocean air?

Dad yanks open another can of beer. The two of them sit in silence while brown Mr. Ken guides them around the island toward the spot where, he has assured Dad, who pressed him on this, there is no danger of sharks, and where, he has assured Danny, who on this point pressed him likewise, the scenery is "most beautiful." Perhaps a hundred yards off a few palm trees bask along the beach, their fronded crowns a honeyed mass of sunlight. "I haven't swum in over a year," Danny says. "I hope I'm all right."

"Hell, you hadn't played tennis in over a year either."

"Here," Mr. Ken says. "This place is most safe. Most beautiful."

"You sure about sharks? I don't want my boy eaten by any sharks."

"No shark. Not here, never. We're inside the reef." He points to a distant line of white-caps. "See the others?" he says, pointing to two other boats not far away. "They dive here. Dive, scuba dive, every day. No shark, you have my guarantee," he says happily, his wrinkled face creased to the sun. "My guarantee," he repeats, though it is hard to envision how, given the nature of the danger, this guarantee might ever be redeemed. Not scared before, Danny finds these denials unnerving.

"This okay with you, kid?"

Below them, particolored fish are flitting and angling over bright blooms that lie under some ten or fifteen feet of water. "Sure, looks great," Danny says, though a bubble of fear has affixed itself to his stomach.

"Frog feet," Mr. Ken says, drawing from a plastic trash bag a pair of black flippers. They are surprisingly heavy. It has been years, perhaps not since Boy Scout days, since Danny last wore flippers. As he slips his bare feet into them, a squeaking run of chilliness, for all the day's heat, scrapes up his spine—a primordial distaste, that human revulsion from the reptilian in itself. The first pair, to Mr. Ken's surprise, are too large. "I have small feet for my height," Danny explains.

"There is no worry," Mr. Ken says. "Many feet, I have many, many feet."

"Yes . . ."

The second pair make a snug fit. Danny removes his shirt and jeans.

"Jesus you're thin. What did they do to you over there? You look like one of those bastards they conducted the starvation experiments on. If I were a shark, I wouldn't give you a second look."

Danny answers, "I've shed everything but the muscle, Pop, the brains and the muscle. You saw me out there on the court, just like a tiger. Your totally non-chicken-shit son whomped him. Nailed his butt. Gave him a trouncing. Shellacked him. Wiped up the court with him." Nervousness has provided Danny's speech with a slick quickness; Dad laughs appreciatively. Danny brandishes his pale burnt arms in the air, stroking at imaginary tennis balls, and continues with neat rapidity: "Drubbed him. Squelched him. Beat the pants off the sucker. KO'd the bastard."

"I think he nearly whipped the pants off *you*," Dad says. "Where would you have been without that flukey net shot?"

"Deliberate, every shot deliberate. That was just to make things more exciting," Danny says, and winks; and Dad laughs again. Danny begins smearing a film of sunscreen onto his chest and back and shoulders.

"If I were you, I'd just leave my shirt on," Dad says. "That's a big sun up there."

"I suppose." Danny somehow doesn't want to swim in his shirt; no, he wants to be stripped down when he enters the sea. "If it's really great, you got to promise you'll come in, too."

"I think I'll just sit right here. The sun feels good."

"Goggles," says Mr. Ken.

Again the unwelcome resiliency of rubber, this time to the face. "Breathe in, through the nose," Mr. Ken instructs, as Danny recalls, from way back at Scout camp, the point of this. He breathes in and vacuum suction alone holds the mask on his face. "It's a good fit," Danny calls a little loudly, as though with this glimpse of them through glass he has been transported some physical distance. "Do I look like a frog?" he calls to them. "I feel just like a frog."

"The frogs'll take you for one of their own."

"Mouth," says Mr. Ken, offering a dripping snorkel, fresh from a rinse in the sea. Danny fits the snorkel against his teeth, breathes in and out. He plucks it from his mouth and says to Dad in sham amazement. "Hey, I think that water's *salty*."

"Ah, very salty," Mr. Ken says. "Snorkel okay? Okay, put it in the goggles."

Danny slides the snorkel's tube into the elastic slit on the side of the goggles.

"Good. Now spit. Spit in the goggles."

This instruction, too, calls Danny back to camp, but this time he cannot make sense of it. "Mm?"

"Spit. Spit in the goggles," Mr. Ken repeats, then holds out his hand. Danny passes over the goggles and Mr. Ken, hacking from the depths of his throat, produces a yolky clot on the inside glass. With his fingertips he smears the mucus over the entire lens, then swishes the goggles in the sea. "To keep clear," he says.

"Yes," Danny says. "Now I remember." Mr. Ken has fit a portable aluminum ladder over the side of the boat. Danny first puts his T-shirt back on, then reinserts the mouthpiece and slips the strap of the goggles over the bulge of the back of his head. "Go in slow," Mr. Ken advises. "Go in backward."

Danny with his hands on the ladder turns and lifts his right leg to wave a flipper at Dad in a slapstick farewell. He descends two steps of the ladder, dangles one leg off the end, and waits a moment for that neat, voluminous click with which the waiting shark severs lower from upper leg. Go in slow, Mr. Ken had advised, but Danny does not. With a push on the ladder he drops straight down.

Rising bubbles blind him—deafen him, popping in his ears. Then his plummeting body halts, poises just as though he is standing on solid ground, and his eyes take in a miraculous sight. Fish—some of them big ones, over a foot long, and all sorts of enviable colors, oranges, purples, icy green-blues—are wiggling away from the invasion of himself. The floor of the sea, which lies further down than he'd thought, is a garden, shells and coral and big bright filamental blooms, motioning voluptuously up at him. His standing body levitates by degrees toward the surface. As his head breaks free he swallows salt water, not air, chokes, removes the snorkel, laughs, chokes again, refits the snorkel against his teeth, and plunges once more. He swims toward a richly pigmented purple-and-white-striped school of fish which, at his approach, disperses in an orderly unpanicky way, so that by the time he reaches where they'd gathered they have shimmered off equally to every side. Already his lungs are giving out. He surfaces and this time remembers first to exhale—a hard kick of air that sends water jetting from the top of the snorkel to rain upon the crown of his head.

Dad is calling to him, and Danny removes the mouthpiece and cries, "What?"

"What's the point of a snorkel, if you don't stay on the surface?" Dad is laughing at this.

"I know, I know," Danny calls. "It's just too much fun to dive." He fits the snorkel back into his mouth and floats a moment. Nervousness rather than exertion has him breathing in these rapid jerky pants which, amplified by the surrounding water, make such a desperate sound as they scrape through the snorkel. He is made aware, too, of his own heart beating within his chest, his chest beating within the larger fluid of the bay, and this tickling awareness of his own physicality so excites him he must immediately move. Again snorkeling improperly, for he knows he is supposed to leave his hands at his side and propel himself solely with his feet, he strokes and kicks across the surface, takes a deep breath, and plunges.

The sea is shallow enough here that the angling sun perfuses cleanly to the coral and sand bottom, on which lie shells and stones, and also stray human cast-offs (cans, a bit of rope) which the sea's gentle ministrations are rendering into organic forms once more. Oh this light is splendid! Glittering like knives, like the blades of saws as it quarries down toward the sand's jeweled litter. Danny pushes toward the bottom but with maybe five feet remaining his ears cry out in pain and his lungs start burning. He rises and breaks the surface's porous crust of prisms, spouts like a whale, waves, and plunges once more.

He enjoys in these first seconds after a deep inhalation, as all his clamoring capillaries are freshened by a wash of oxygenated blood, a sense of satiety so capacious it seems he can stay under forever. Slowly, for he has all the time in the world, his legs propel him down toward a waving fine-tressed anemone. It is remarkable how quickly his body adapts to its palmate feet, which already have become a fine-tuned further extremity, allowing him with the most subtle of motions to veer and shift and sweep. He studies the way the angling, dulcified light, like sugar grains falling though a child's glass of lemonade, sifts down to touch the bottom, the way the boat's cavernous shadow shifts and sways. Already he has begun to feel at home, as though he were a frequent swimmer here, or somewhere quite similar, surrounded by like depths, like distances.

And yet his thudding heart keeps marking time throughout; his lungs begin to ache. Only by an act of willpower does he quell their demands, stroking on into the sheer slanting shadow of the boat, tasting its serial coolness along the length of his entering body. He feels his lungs burn hotter still and thrashes to the surface to spout once more.

"Mr. Ken says you mustn't touch anything. A lot of things are poisonous."

Danny, treading water, extracts the mouthpiece and says, "I know, I'm not."

"You're supposed to swim along the surface, where we can watch you."

"I will," Danny says, "I will." But he cannot yet bear simply to float there. Exhilaration, beauty, *love* call on him to range and scout, to slide down through thermal striations to a relative coolness where his ears thud and he can watch at his approach the tinier fish dart into coral coverts, the bigger fish, too large to hide, flutter and fan into the marine-misted distance. Down below, out of range, lie a couple of starfish whose shapes suggest—lovely, lovely—that symbol for bigness under which he lived this past year, the ideographic *dai* on the face of Mt. Daimon. Twenty, thirty times he dives, investigates, ascends, and sends a gout of water into the sky. At last content to pause, he lies on his stomach, the whole of the sea pillowed beneath him, and breathes steadily, confidently through the protruding snorkel. His big heart is thumping. In the sunny water, but invisible in the shaded, little golden motes are seen floating, just like the sun-charged particles one notices, when the light's right, afloat on the circulating air of a room. As though the sea were dusty. As though this reef, with all its coral-walled chambers and poisonous intrigues, were a mansion, a sunken palace.

"Danny," Dad is calling. "Mr. Ken says you're tired. He says you better rest a while."

"Not good to swim too long," Mr. Ken affirms, as he pulls Danny up into the boat. Dad hands him a towel and an open can of beer. Danny sits, folds the towel over his shoulders, drinks deeply from the beer.

"Mr. Ken, you need a beer," Dad says.

"No, no, no beer for me."

"You don't like beer?"

Big mirth seizes Mr. Ken's small face, creasing still further those sun-rucked, amiable features. "Oh yes, beer very much. But you see, I am quickly a drunken man. So I do not drink when I am working."

"Hell, that's no problem. Absolutely no problem. Drunk or sober, we'll get the boat back to harbor somehow. I guaran*tee* it." Dad extends a can to Mr. Ken, whose wrinkled face and hands hesitate, tempted, enchanted, before it. "Go ahead, go ahead," Dad urges, and Mr. Ken clasps the beer.

"Dad, you ought to go in," Danny pants. "It's beautiful."

"I'm enjoying sitting right here."

"You can take my flippers and everything. You really can't imagine how pretty it is."

"I'm enjoying sitting right here. And this is very pretty too. I can see the fish and the palm trees."

"You have to take one *look*," Danny insists and—unwittingly—they have returned to the language of dinner last night, when Danny had been urging his father toward Hiroshima. But the blazing sun unfocuses the momentary contention, burns it off. They sit in a comfortable silence. Danny refuses, Mr. Ken accepts a second beer. "We go new place," Mr. Ken says. "There is airplane. You can see airplane," he cries excitedly.

"An airplane?" Danny says. "Underwater?"

"Old war airplane underwater," Mr. Ken says, his sweating face ashine in excitement. After two unsuccessful pulls, followed by a grunted exclamation which presumably is an expletive in whatever is his true mother tongue, Mr. Ken manages to start the engine. The boat chugs forward.

"Nex' year, you come nex' year, I have very big boat," he repeats. He is red-faced and happy; the beer has already worked on him. "You come nex' year, Mr. Ottu?" he asks.

"Maybe. Maybe I come back."

"You come back with friends. *Many* friends," Mr. Ken presses, "for it is very big boat I buy."

"He calls you Mr. Auto," Danny murmurs. "It's very appropriate."

Dad grins at him, grins at Mr. Ken, who chants, "Tour boat. Sightsee. Scuba. Banquet. Everything."

A mass of cumulus blots the sun as the boat swings out. Danny begins to worry that, like Mr. Ken's tour boat, this warplane will prove illusory. But not many minutes pass—just long enough to apply a new coat of sunscreen—before Mr. Ken points and cries delightedly, "There. There she is."

Unbelievably enough, there she—it—lies, a cool brown rusted wreck submerged in deeper water than Danny'd hoped: beyond the capacities of his raw lungs and sensitive, popping ears. The plane is buried deep enough that the sun touches it languidly with a creepy, crepuscular light. This flying contraption is far more bat than bird now.

"Dive in?" Mr. Ken says. "Have a look?"

"It's too deep. I can't get down that far."

"Have a look from the water? Have a look? Have a look?"

Somehow Mr. Ken's unintended parroting of Danny's own entreaties with Dad a few minutes before creates an irony which compels Danny, who feels fear gathering in his stomach again, to climb down from the boat into this deeper water. With his hands on the ladder he asks, "You're sure the water's safe here?"

"Very safe," Mr. Ken says. "They dive every day. Scuba dive."

"Do we have your guaran*tee*?" asks Dad.

"Oh yes, I guarantee."

Danny inserts the spicy snorkel against his teeth, takes a last look through the goggles at Dad and Mr. Ken, both lolling with sun and drink, and drops over the side of the boat. In the momentary flash of blinding bubbles he waits again for the bone-crushing jaws of the cruising shark. His vision clears. Glimpsed from within the boundaries of the sea, the aircraft is a fabulous barnacled apparition, something (Mr. Ken was right) he shouldn't have missed. But it's an eerie, ghostly one as well: one can almost feel a presence rising through the cold, conductive depths. He recalls Dad last night saying, "You have no idea how *strange* it is," and comes up for air

"Is it an American plane or a Japanese?" he shouts, bobbing in the light.

"What?" Dad calls.

"Ask Mr. Ken. Is it an American or a Japanese plane?"

"Japanese," Dad calls. "One of theirs."

Danny dives again and immediately beings to write, *Hey, listen, mon, this very nice place, mon. Plenty girls on the beach, sunken airplane too. Crazy.* The rusted aircraft is missing limbs—a tail, a wing. Danny swims deeper, narrowing the distance, allowing the plane's coldness to touch him once more as, focusing through the lens of his goggles, he snaps a mental photograph, then kicks up for air. "I wonder if he parachuted out," Danny pants. "Do you think he's still in there?" There is no reply, and Danny dives once more.

Dear Grego, he begins, more satisfactorily, *You remember the time you came asking for the dope back. Of course you were right that I lied. But after you left, I felt terrible and I ran out looking for you. I meant to tell you tbat.* Indeed he'd meant on returning from Hiroshima to explain not only what he'd done with the joint, but the whole insane trip. Somehow he'd not been able to. It was all so overwhelming—Kyoto, too—all of those last days were so *confusing*, as, panicky about leaving Japan, he'd turned panicky about everyone else's future besides. Danny had watched a conservative, almost parental side to himself emerge, eagerly stocked with prudent advice: Greg was to go to law school, to abandon dissolution, to make something of his life. The interlude was over, the real world called and could no longer be put off! While aware of how ludicrous his role had become, this advice simply had to be given. And had been given at length.

Greg to his credit had not mocked him but had met the questions seriously, a little nervous himself as he offered in reassurance, "I don't think I'll be here more than a couple more months." No, no doubt about it—Greg was scared.

And Carrie . . . how Danny had longed to set her house in order, send her off to business school! March the two of them off, pens clipped to their shirt pockets!

Carrie, though, he didn't worry about so much, and Carrie he would be seeing later this summer. But the mere sight of Greg those final few days triggered such awful forebodings that there was no pleasure left at all, only a furious and jittery impatience, at hearing the familiar phrases unroll—"the pursuit of fecklessness," "the central paradox," "hyperbolic accuracy"—or at listening to Greg somberly deliver another of his only-half-joking crazy boasts: "I think I've made some really important progress these past few months in learning to appreciate the kiwi fruit." It was true that Greg had handled the surprise of Danny's farewell gift with a characteristic winning grace; when he opened the little box of business cards that said only Grego Blaising, and below that International Raconteur, he said, "Good Lord how *thoughtful*. I've been meaning to have these made up for ages." But Danny had felt hurt when Greg changed his mind and did not accompany Carrie to see him off at the airport. Greg merely grinned, extended his hand, said, "I'm afraid I'm pretty much dog-shit at any kind of good-byes. . . ."

Danny spouts once more, removes the snorkel, and says, "I've seen enough of this place, can we go back, back to the other one a little while?"

Crimson-faced Mr. Ken helps him aboard. "Sure, Danny," Dad

says, and hands him a can of beer. "Whatever you want. Mr. Ken, take us back to the other place."

"No, no, no." Alcohol has made Mr. Ken endearingly strong-willed. "New place. Very beautiful."

"Is it shallow?" Danny asks, running a towel through his hair. "I want it shallow."

"Very shallow. Very beautiful." Mr. Ken starts up the engine, whose mild roar satisfies the need for conversation. Theirs is the only boat visible on the sea. After a while Danny asks his father, "What place in your round-the-world voyage are you most looking forward to?"

"Oh, I'm looking forward to them all," Dad says.

"But there must be *one* place you're most excited about."

"All of them," Dad says. "I have an open mind." And a few minutes later, surprisingly, for this might be sentimental and he is rarely sentimental, he says, "It's a shame your mother and I didn't make a trip like this. We had the money. And now we never will." Dad offers this statement with a tranquil assertiveness that actually amplifies the sadness, the mortal cruelty of another *never*. Danny longs to correct, to soften the remark. But the remark is accurate, and just, and in truth leaves little room for amelioration. Danny's thoughts drift from his sad father to his sad friend, and *Grego*, he writes, *Because I am hard on myself, work myself hard, I didn't see at first that your drive comes from a different source from mine. Also, because your boasting, your arrogance hides it. I mean that maybe you have so much self-hatred, which there's no reason for.*

Carrie, too, had seen this, though her phrase was *He's so unhappy with himself.* They'd been discussing Greg while lying naked on that high bed, the day of Danny's return from Hiroshima, having made love after so long an interval. She had taken him back so simply. He had to forgive her everything for that. Amazing how uncomplicated it all was, it all could be. What in the world had they squabbled over so frequently? This was where he needed to be, he knew, on a bed in the Sunshine Mansion in the late afternoon with the warmth of her genitals radiating against his thigh (just as the sun is flashing on his bare leg now), and he'd asked her the question he'd often wanted to ask: "Last fall, why did you choose me? You knew we both were after you."

"I don't know why. I liked you. And Greg seemed so intense."

"Thanks a lot." And Danny'd laughed. "Makes me sound so exciting. Old watered-down Danny."

"You were the one who threw me out of bed," Carrie'd said, and while this interpretation was hardly a rational appraisal of what had happened in those disastrous self-pitying weeks after Carrie's return from America, it flattered him and he felt grateful to her. "Bad-intense, not good-intense," she went on. "I mean, you know after I first slept with him in Hokkaidō, about six the next morning, I'm still asleep when he announces in this solemn voice, *The less said about coyotes today, the better.*"

"Coyotes?"

"Just nonsense. One of his little jokes. But that's how he *is*. You wake up at six in the morning, your back's aching from sleeping all night on some hard floor, and he's trying to be madly charming. He's so unhappy with himself. He's sitting on a tack, every minute."

Mr. Ken cuts the engine and the boat after a moment's shudder attunes to the restless, restful bob and drop of the sea. "Very good place," he says, "very safe. Very beautiful."

They are back in sunny, shallow water. "I'll just take a couple of dives," Danny apologizes, for he worries that Dad's not enjoying the boat trip. "Then we can go back and have lunch."

"Take as long as you want," Dad says with a complaisance that at bottom seems mere boozy listlessness. "I'm perfectly content to sit right here."

Danny fits the rubber mask over his face, slides back into the black frog feet—again with that prehistoric repugnance—and slips over the edge of the boat. His body rises to the surface, he waves, takes a deep breath and dives.

The water here is a few feet shallower than where they'd first anchored. Ears popping, he can almost reach the very bottom. Perhaps six or seven or eight feet above it, he swims along levelly, inspecting its strew of marine life. He catches a glimpse of a black-and-white-striped shellfish as it scuttles for cover. It seems to be the same creature that the Japanese call *kuruma ebi*—automobile shrimp—and which Danny has often seen cruising in the tanks of sushi shops. He'd love to show one to Dad. A little packed urban community down here. A beautiful shell, orange whorls and ivory orifice, catches his eye and, ignoring the press on his ears, he kicks down toward it. His fingers touch it, slip; his lungs have begun to blaze; panicky and yet overridingly acquisitive, he reaches again, seizes the shell, and, triumphant, kicks with his prize toward that larger blue dome floating above the sea's blue dome. He surfaces, spouts, gasps, chokes, laughs, and says, "Dad, I brought you something," bearing the shell before him as he flutter-kicks to the edge of the boat. Dad reaches down and takes the shell.

"There's all kinds of stuff down there," Danny says. "Wait a moment."

"Mr. Ken says don't touch."

"I'm ex*treme*ly careful."

Danny regathers his breath, waves, and plunges once more. This desire to excavate from the sea all sorts of cheering souvenirs for Dad wires his body with an electric purpose. He is going to bring Dad riches; he is going to draw him out from under the cloud that has settled over him. Sad, all these sad old men. Prematurely old Umeda, with his dead son and the burdens of the world on his shoulders. Waiting steadily for new and larger wars, for Russia to invade Poland, for the entire Mideast to go up in one great petrochemical blast. Danny has escaped. That's how it feels. He has managed to slip out of his old world into a strange new one, for a year, and now will be returning safely home. Law school and the law firms remain intact, the dollar remains healthy. Solidarity reigns in Poland, the largest bombs still go undropped, Carrie will be staying with him in a Park Avenue apartment. It will all work out. One jeweled blink, a silver glint in the muck, draws Danny down to the sea's tighter mesh, where shadows congregate and his head thuds and creatures scatter like so many brooms, leaving plumes of sediment behind them. Among softly erect ocher and umber seaweeds his fingers locate the light source—the ring from a flip-top can—and prise it from the sediment that has all but buried it forever. The ascent must be painfully slow; never rise faster than your own bubbles, he recalls from Scouts. As he thrashes toward the loose, overarching theater of light where the old boat bobs and the distant palm trees thresh, a memory lifts like a bubble within him gently to break in his head: he recalls looking down from the airplane, bound for Japan nearly a year ago, and seeing the Pacific swimming dreamily below. Again he sits in that elevated humming place, his passport photo on the seat beside, smiling hopefully up at him.

* * *

"Was that your boy I saw yesterday on the tennis court?"

The voice is a woman's, and toward its unexpected promising femininity he turns his face, eyebrows uplifted engagingly. She is sitting a short ways down the rail of the bar. She is not so young as instantly he'd begun to hope, though younger than he himself, and a good-looking woman besides. She exhales sideways a neat cloud of cigarette smoke. Though it is dusk and the day has begun to cool, the air-conditioners are still going full blast and the smoke-cloud is chopped up by the circulating air.

"Sure was. It was quite a match. You're a tennis player?"

"More a tennis watcher. I do so think it's such a lovely game." Hers is the spare, hard, slightly soured prettiness he associates with women smokers. She is thin and honey-haired and, obviously, though for reasons not wholly isolable, wealthy. But what is she doing here? The hand that might wear a wedding ring lies buried at her side. "You know he's quite a nice-looking boy."

"It was quite a battle. It went three sets. But my kid finally won."

"Oh how nice. I thought so. I thought so." She has that way of distending her vowels, whereby *so* becomes *sa-o-u*; in his mind this is an East Coast woman's affectation, though plenty of women in his own Detroit, spurning their flat Midwestern accents, talk that way. You can hear those voices languidly appealing to each other across the sun deck at Riverfield, the country club he has belonged to for nearly twenty years, or at the juice bar at the Orchard, the health club he joined this past December. "You kna-o-u, I was so afraid that other boy was going to collapse in the heat. He was so frightfully *pale*."

Her misconception is so improbable that for a moment as he studies her face, the blueness of its eyes evident even here in the dusk-shadowed bar, he does not fully grasp it; then he replies, "The red-head, the pale one, that's my kid. Danny."

"How *extraordinary*," she says with such conviction he is made unaccountably a little uneasy.

"Everyone says the kid looks remarkably like his mother. She's back in Michigan, though," he adds, pleased with this fluid turn in the conversation. "So I guess you'll have to take the resemblance on faith. Where are you from?"

"Baltimore, I suppose. I don't know *why* I was so sure the other boy, the one with the crew-cut, was yours." She raps deliberatively on the bottom of her pack of Benson & Hedges with one hand, nudging loose a long-filtered cigarette which she plucks with the other, while he fishes a lighter from a pocket of his peach-colored blazer. He scoots over to the stool beside hers in time to light the cigarette without even a moment's delay. "*I* know," she exclaims, emitting another cloud of smoke. "Because I saw you pat that other boy, the tan one, on the fanny."

He laughs loudly at this, for the solemnity of her declaration is so absurd, as is the sound of *fanny*. She too is faintly absurd, with her grave musings and all her gracious and stilted talk, but it's an absurdity which only enhances the desire that nerve by nerve has already begun to ramify inside him. Another tropical night is falling and out of the sleepless hash of these difficult last few days a sharpened conviction arises, that this woman undressed and flat on her back is exactly what he needs. "Maybe I did. I don't remember."

"How long have you been in the Marianas?"

"Saipan? Just a couple of days. I'm on my way around the world."

"How energetic of you . . ."

"I was here once before, in '44, when we took the island, but we weren't drinking good scotch like this in those days." He chuckles. "God no, we'd drink anything we could get our hands on—fermented petroleum flavored with gunpowder and old rifle butts."

"Yes . . ."

Her face hovers toward sociable concern; she does not seem completely to understand he's joking. "How long have you been on the island?" he asks her.

"Well, we've been over a week I suppose. One does so lose track of time out here, doesn't one?"

This *we* all but closes in his face the door of that sought-after bedroom, but he carries on in the pared hope that the unnamed party is not the husband he knows it is, or is some husband whose presence can be hospitably ignored. Yet his presence having been broached, this man begins to arise unstoppably in her conversation—a busy man, a successful man, an artistic and taoutally clever man—until almost as a logical culmination he appears in the flesh. He is disappointingly tall and good-looking, and partakes of some of his wife's laughable weighty dolor. Introductions having been exchanged, hands shaken, lugubriously he announces to his wife, "I finally reached Jamie. Not a word yet, not a single word."

"Well, I'm terribly sorry, Alec," she says, turning toward him with a pretty look of concern. She's good at this game and he likes her for it. "I don't mean to be drawing you into our little family problem like this. I mean that's hardly proper etiquette, is it? But we're saou concerned about our Jamie. He's a junior at Vanderbilt, and the world's sweetest boy."

"Fran*cine*."

"My husband thinks I spoil the boy. Perhaps I do," she confesses with satisfaction. "Well now, Jamie has a roommate who has been taking advantage of him horribly all year long, simply horribly, and who has recently gone certifiably *mad* don't you know, stealing every single thing Jamie owned before disappearing completely. Not just the money, I suppose I could understand that, but all of Jamie's shirts, even though the two boys are not at all the same size, and even Jamie's underwear."

"His underwear too?" he asks her and she nods vigorously. Eyebrows lifted, he glances from the woman to her husband for some corroboration that their sweet Jamie is a faggot, but nothing is forthcoming either way.

"His shoes," she goes on, "even though they don't wear the same size. His umbrella." She shakes her head with weary melancholy and turns to her husband. "But I just learned from Alec here the most extraordinary thing. You know those two boys we saw playing tennis yesterday? Well *his* boy isn't the one with the crew-cut, his is that extremely nice-looking red-haired boy. Danny."

"But that's what I assumed."

"Did you?" she marvels. "I don't know how you do it. Truly I do not. But Alec," she resumes, "you must join us for dinner. You and Danny please."

"I'd like that, we'd both like that, but I have to make some calls. Maybe another night." He drains his drink and after a last relay of pleasantries shakes hands with both of them. Hers sits lightly in his as in vain he scouts her fine eyes for some slick hint of mischief. "I hope your boy gets his umbrella back," he calls from the door, suddenly resentful of the way he's been chased from this bar. He considers leaving the hotel for another bar, but the thought of the street out there with all its discos and rusted cars and Japanese signs and porn shops, its noise and confusing choices, amplifies the buzzing in his head he's had to endure almost continuously these last few days and he decides instead to retreat up to his room, where there's a bottle of duty-free scotch.

He listens at Danny's door. Earlier the kid had been playing a language tape on his cassette recorder. He raps lightly, just hard enough that if the kid were awake he would probably hear it, and if asleep not be disturbed. Poor sunburnt Danny—returning from all his snorkeling only to play two more sets of tennis against a kid from California who, though no better than the kid from Indiana he played yesterday, ripped him up pretty badly. Too tired: Danny had just been too tired.

Receiving no answer, he goes to his own room and pours himself a scotch and tepid water. There is ice in the room's little refrigerator, but though he usually drinks his scotch on the rocks he does not do so now because of the problems his teeth are giving him. Danny keeps reassuring him that what he's suffering is jet lag, but he knows jet lag alone could never do this. His head is buzzing and pounding and every one of his teeth hurts, just as though all the fillings in his head had been burrowed out and new ones put in. In the last year he's seen two men in his immediate office, neither one yet sixty, go through the humiliation and agony and expense of having dentures installed. And then having to listen to how *natural* they look. It cheers him to know that Danny's teeth have always been properly cared for, unlike his own, unlike those of nearly all the men and women of his own generation. Danny, for whom the Depression is a bore and a joke, can't see what a blessing this simple fact is. But that's all right: he shouldn't have to. And this sense of progress, one generation to the next, offers its bit of heartening compensation. Another generation it'll be a pill, or a shot, and never worry about cavities again.

Danny's angry now, or may still be angry, about being pushed into the match today. 6-2, 6-3. And all the while the kid's face and arms and legs turning redder and redder, the knowledge that the sunscreen wasn't working and the court's misery was really only beginning. How the kid glared—let the old man have it!—after the first set. Glared viciously, those eyes of his so clearly saying, *Damn you, damn you.*

But then for a while in that second set it looked as though Danny was actually going to do the impossible again and come from behind to squeeze out a victory. Having gone down 3-0, he scraped his way back to even, before—too tired—letting the last three games slip quickly away. He wishes Danny weren't angry and that the kid could see how it does the heart so much good to return here and in a kind of dream watch your son play tennis where people were trying to kill you, where friends of yours were killed. On the very same island where you came the closest you ever did to dying, the shrapnel lodged to this day in the calf of your left leg. "It does the heart good," he says aloud and pours himself another drink.

Danny talks to himself, too—out there on the tennis court mumbling to himself, or sitting in the boat with a towel draped over his narrow shoulders. Alice was forever citing this as another way the boy was supposed to be so much like him, but somehow the observation never quite penetrated. Until now—isn't that funny. He carries his drink out onto the balcony, wondering whether it's true, or whether this is just another failure to observe his son closely, that Danny lost weight during his year in Japan. And the boy even seems to be talking a little differently, weird new mannerisms, though it was hard to tell. Danny has turned so prickly, too, though this comes partly from his own failure to explain things well. All of Danny's prudish disapproval showing at that story of Dumbrowski's. *Lie back and get yourself a fuck.* Yet that story was, if properly told, only innocent and comic and endearing.

But how was Danny going to begin to grasp that crazy Billy What the Name Implies Dumbrowski, the Polack Peacock, was just a kid, maybe younger even than Danny, somebody who dearly loved himself, the simple kick of being alive, with all those hours spent grooming with a little comb and mirror while everyone else had begun to sink into the surrounding muck, the hopelessness, and whose own slow sinking, teeth shattered by a beer bottle cap, feet green with jungle rot, skin dyed yellow with Atabrine, was all the more poignant for his being so sweetly stupid and so fervent? Out in a place where they had to put hot pepper on the antimalaria pills, because otherwise the men would only pretend to swallow them, where a couple of men in the division actually shot themselves for a ticket out, dumb Dumbrowski held to that vision: an angel of a woman dropping down from above, on a mission of mercy, love, and long-sought peace.

Down there on the right, next to the playground on which a couple of dark cars are parked, that blush of pink neon must be the Comfort Rose Health Parlor. He noticed it earlier today. All of that so grim. Slot-mouthed women. In Hawaii, before heading out for the real islands, the men used to line up for hours in front of the little shacks, bring a book to read, write a letter home, while you waited.

Doubtless it seemed an exaggeration to Danny, but they *had* listened for hours as gorgeous Dumbrowski related his minute by minute, scrap by scrap accounts—Polish girls, Jewesses, Italians, Canadian girls from Windsor, lunch-counter girls and telephone operators, whores and housewives, they all succumbed, under the bushes beside the railroad tracks, spread-eagled on the hoods of cars, in the balconies of movie theaters, in greasy toolsheds, in bathrooms, in phone booths, and in king-size beds with silk sheets and goosedown pillows. An occasional inconsistency in Billy's stories wasn't merely ignored, it was genuinely untroubling. For Billy was their expert and there was no gainsaying his experience and good looks, and the letters, the pictures, the packages he received from women back home. Gravely, respectfully, the men would bring him their questions: who would be more passionate in bed, Lana Turner or Rosalind Russell? What would Russian women be like? Did Roosevelt have any sort of sex life? And gravely, respectfully, he would answer them.

And dumb Billy Dumbrowski, true to a code that would only seem screwy now, that great Don Juan, that despoiler of dozens and dozens of women, used to boast that he'd never done anything more than kiss his fiancée, Lanie Duggar. Even now the name is fixed in the memory, when so much has been forgotten, for she'd become a kind of virgin queen for all of them—the purest, prettiest girl in the world (as the photographs testified), for whose protection all stood chivalrously ready to die.

Lanie Duggar: there was a special pride attached to her, for she was a Detroit girl. And long afterwards in Detroit, Dumbrowski now many years dead, he'd actually tried to look her up, puzzling through the Duggars in the phone book one night in a drugstore on Woodward and McNichols while knowing all the while it was a futile gesture, for by now, with her new last name, she would have steered her painfully untouched body into the daily thump-thump of marriage and kids. Still, he'd wanted her. Really *wanted*. He was a stranger desiring another stranger across an immense and hostile city and the idea of looking her up had come as an illumination: he was in need of a vision, a woman dropping down from above.

To recall that earlier version of himself paging through the Duggars in the Detroit phone book as he stands on a balcony of Saipan's Eagle Hotel (despite the name, Japanese-owned, he'd discovered—the sneaking bastards), stands with a drink in his hand while the stars are emerging and in the distance people are playing tennis under a blaze of silver light—all of this is to evoke a character who's nobody he honestly knows, someone far more distant than his own son asleep in the next room. A cool breeze, that provided by the air-conditioner, ruffles the hair at the back of his neck. He'd left the sliding door partly open; but he can let that go for now. He sips again from his drink. You can't really grasp it, no, just as you can't really believe this is the very same island. Simply to be here at all—to have become what you are, or to have been what you were—is so strange, but that isn't really the word. It's *strange* that it isn't more strange in the way one would think it would be strange—but hell that isn't right either. It is less painful, given his aching teeth, to take the drink in occasional deep gulps rather than steady smaller sips, and he downs nearly half the glass.

Against the bewildering entire strangeness of his standing here he deliberately channels his mind backward along a single line, a quivering thread of physical desire, beginning with that blonde downstairs, her name already forgotten, who had said with such self-congratulation, "*I* know, because I saw you pat his fanny," as he'd looked down her blouse for a glimpse of drooping tit. It was perhaps unfortunate, but bored-sounding women had always provoked him—he took their languor as a challenge. Oh, he'd have her talking quite a different way. Gasping in his ear. *Please*. And she could make him feel better, they all would make him feel better.

He feels them—women—all around him. All the Japanese honeymooners, one can't help thinking about it, the goings-on in all these many rooms. Kids, those inept and jubilant couplings, tonight, night after night, new couples, new couples. It wasn't the absurdity of longing deeply for someone you'd never met that made it so difficult to picture that brown-haired man combing the drugstore phone book, perhaps, but, perhaps, the calling up of all those whole lost neighborhoods of confusion and shame and guilt now behind him. He has settled those questions somewhere along the line, but he used to wonder why it was so hard for him to sit home at night, when all the other men on the street seemed to manage it so easily. Why *was* he so restless? Was he right, was it true that he simply burned more intensely than they did? He had worried about himself; he truly had.

Danny was a worrier, too. That had been such a funny thing when he'd started up with Penny, for he'd approached her with the same solemn worried intensity he'd applied to his studies or his tennis. *I'm not to be laughed at*, the kid always seemed to be saying. And even now the kid was still applying to college, with his language tapes and all his talk about the older partners in the firm who liked him. Cute as hell sometimes: the kid proudly announcing that he can use chopsticks with either hand. Passing the kid's room on the way down to the bar he'd opened the door and found Danny lying sunburnt on the bed, the tape playing some crazy birdlike patter that must have been Japanese. Still applying to college, still preparing for entrance examinations that would never come. The kid will find that out, eventually. All the exams are over. But the boy never could understand that he'd beaten the system—that he was in clover. *Kid*, he'd wanted to say back then when the boy was still in high school, *wipe that harried look off your face, you've got your hands on the tits of a sixteen-year-old girl. Hey boy, that's the opportunity of a lifetime.* Oh the kid could drive you crazy. Saying today, in that cheerful fact-finding sort of way he has, "Now where exactly on this island were you hit by that hand grenade?" No concept in his foolish head. No concept of what was involved. The notes of a song, that simple little jingle, float into his mind: *Penny, Penny, she's not a bad penny* . . . He'd sung that for Penny, what, a thousand times? And each time elicited from her, freshly, that smile and identical girlish blush and the dropping of her eyes; hard to believe she was now old enough to be getting married.

A chain of disembodied laughter—drawn-out, silverly feminine—flutters up out of the night to firm his spine as he stands here, recalling various women. He draws forth another name: Maggie Fairwood. About her, sadly, he has lost almost everything, face and scent and voice, but with fierce loyalty he holds on to that name, for Maggie had been so heartbreakingly good for him, saying, *Jesus, honey, I don't know how any woman resists you*, saying, *You really give it a whirl, honey, you really give it a whirl.* Nearly forty, and a divorcée to boot, Maggie had seemed so old to him. (Which was funny, for now she really was—

seventy, probably, or even dead by now.) And *so* tantalizingly scandalous. He couldn't have been more than twenty-nine at the time, for that's when he switched to Ford, and he'd met Maggie while they were both at Curbett's. He'd hated everything about that job, until one night this blonde buxom divorcée actually led him with a breathtaking smoothness back to her place, out of his clothes and into bed. The truly beautiful thing about Maggie was that she just hadn't given a shit. That had been liberating, that had finally eased his aches in a permanent way. *She* really had been a woman dropping down from above, though back then he'd not understood all that. After working late one night at Curbett's they even did it in the supply room, standing up, all proprieties shattered, then slipped, gulping the air of pure freedom, to the floor in sweet leveling laughter. *You really go the distance, honey*, she'd said. *You really go the distance.*

Yet poor Maggie, as became increasingly clear, was nursing her own inner aches. There was something (it has escaped him, he has buried it) something dreadful in her life about which she talked only rarely, only after they'd made love. . . . Some core sadness even more intimate than their climbing into bed together. It was a dead brother, he is tempted now to say, but that wasn't it exactly. *Brain damage*, he thinks, her brother had had brain damage. This isn't it either, though, but it's closer and his mind swings out, away from the memory. No, he doesn't want to bring this back.

He turns into the room and pours himself another blow to the heart and sits down on the bed. What he needs to do is to stay awake a few more hours, build a solid fatigue that will last all night but no longer, wake in the morning with a clear, cleared head. He takes a deep swallow from his drink. Cooler in here, the air-conditioner roaring, but it's still no good. The walls bind him too closely. And it's no good out on the street, either. He's tried that and it just gives him the shakes. He rises from the bed and shuffles out onto the balcony, where again he feels better, just the needed mix of openness and enclosure. Branches of light stretch and shatter, stretch and shatter between the sea's dark little community of boats. It is strange, this sense of fitting into things and places only with difficulty, requiring so many little adjustments—the shifting of a leg, the cocking of his head—to get things balanced.

Yet he's encouraged by this sense that he's now channeling his thoughts in a kind of purging. He needs to clear his brain. It is useful to remember, as he hasn't in months, in years perhaps, Maggie Fairwood undressed on the storeroom floor, the panting, those big rapturous poppings in the bloodstream. All that endless fussing with girdles, which all the women wore, and seamed nylons snapped into little eyelets on their plump pungent thighs. Or the little drugstore at Woodward and McNichols (he'd gone there seeking peace, he recalls now, from a bar next door where he'd seen a broken-down old woman, an alcoholic, thrown out for pissing on her barstool; she'd found some old lecher who would buy her drinks as she stroked his leg, and she didn't dare get up to go to the bathroom for fear of losing him), the drugstore where he began sifting through a Detroit phone book that would by now have turned yellow, if any were still to be found. Or Billy Dumbrowski combing and recombing his hair. These are images that, stirred up by his flying all the way out here, must again be let out of the mind. Or little Al Zwick playing "She Wore a Yellow Ribbon" or "Danny Boy" on the harmonica as a tropical night fell. Zwick died, too; not spectacularly like Dumbrowski, whose gorgeous head, the story went, was severed by a sword in the Philippines, but of minor wounds, improperly treated, that no man should have died from. Careless treatment, shortages of medical supplies. Zwick died in a hospital bed. "A toast," he says aloud and lifts his drink, but at the sound of one of the dark cars starting up in the playground forgets to sip. Kids. Parking.

According to Alice, it was years and years after he returned from the War before he stopped having combat nightmares. He'd grown to view this as another piece of her storymaking, an exaggeration shaped by a grateful desire to pay tribute to her husband with the two Purple Hearts. But he sees now, and this is a staggering realization, sees now that she was right, that *he* has been the one altering and forgetting the past. It was all true. He remembers it now. He used to wake up all the time, in a bath of sweat, having dreamed that he was out here again, thick in the heat and the blood and the rot and the waiting and the fear. That exact fear has come back, that cold sweat leaking out of the palms of his hands, and it's impossible to believe he could ever have forgotten it.

No, Alice was right. She used to tell him, and the word always made him so nervous, it sounded so unmanly, that he was very sensitive. *You were just a boy, Alec,* she would say, bless her. Poor girl, with her miscarriages and the fights they used to have because she finally wanted to adopt and he couldn't bear the thought of going through all the screaming bother for a kid who wasn't your own. Hard to believe she'd carried Danny the full nine months, and brought back this red-faced creature with a big umbilicus in its belly. A father, someone who'd been to war, who'd seen all sorts of things, but he'd never known that about babies—how the umbilicus took weeks to fall out, turning black in the meantime, poking out from their navels like an old cigar butt. He hadn't understood at first, it took some time to sink in, that this little visitor had come as a houseguest for, oh what the hell, the next twenty years or so. He hadn't understood anything. He had buried so much it took him years to make even the simplest connections. Years had to pass just to see one day what should have been obvious—that Danny was indirectly named for warmhearted Al Zwick, who played "Danny Boy" so hauntingly on his harmonica. *Is Danny still asleep?* he wonders. He knows he shouldn't have pushed Danny into the match this afternoon, and to balance this additional small guilt he must now shift his weight from one leg to another and take a medium-sized sip from his drink.

He is feeling better, though. These last few days have been tearing at him, fear in the stomach like a swallowed razor blade. Could it really be, he's repeatedly had to ask himself, that this whole round-the-world voyage he'd always dreamed of making is actually a dreadful, a catastrophic mistake? That he has begun it too late? Or at the wrong time? That he will now have to go back home in shame?

Hong Kong, Singapore, Bombay, Cairo . . . How long is he going to last unless things ease up? He can't go on this way—simply cannot. Because it's killing him. He'd never expected coming back to be so hard. It had all seemed so distant, everything so long dead. . . . Yet as he lingers on this balcony in his peach-colored blazer he senses that merely by standing here something useful is indeed being accomplished. He is clearing his thoughts. He is preparing for sleep.

Tonight he will sleep better. This hope, like the first truly cooling breeze in a steamy tropical nightfall, freshens him just as, minutes before, he'd been freshened by that string of girlish laughter floating out of the tropical night. Women in the darkness. Bless them all. "Another toast," he says aloud and drinks. He should wake the kid for dinner. He recalls how pale and thin Danny had looked in the boat this morning. And how touchingly much like a small boy again, with such obliging eyes as he brought forth from the ocean floor, one at a time, his small treasures—a seashell, a bit of tin can, a blue starfish wrapped tight around a stone. Those eyes saying, *Here. Here. Here. These are for you.*

A NOTE ON THE TYPE

The text of this book was set in a digitized version of Bembo, a well-known monotype face. Named for Pietro Bembo, the celebrated Renaissance writer and humanist scholar who was made a cardinal and served as secretary to Pope Leo X, the original cutting of Bembo was made by Francesco Griffo of Bologna only a few years after Columbus discovered America.

Sturdy, well balanced, and finely proportioned, Bembo is a face of rare beauty, extremely legible in all of its sizes.

Composed by Maryland Composition Company, Inc.
Baltimore, Maryland
Printed and bound by Fairfield Graphics,
Fairfield, Pennsylvania
Designed by Mark Argetsinger